Also by Sam Barone

Dawn of Empire

Empire Rising

Quest For Honour
(Published outside the United States as
Conflict of Empires)

Eskkar & Trella – The Beginning

Battle For Empire

Coming Soon – Summer 2013

Clash of Empires

ISBN: 0985162627
ISBN 13: 9780985162627

Eskkar Enterprises

Please feel free to contact the
author with suggestions and comments

www.sambarone.com

SAM BARONE

BATTLE
FOR
EMPIRE

The Land Between The Rivers

A Alur Meriki Passage from Elam
B Battle at the Stream
C Alur Meriki Camp
D Ur Nammu Camp
E Jkarian Pass
F Dellen Pass
G Orodes Passage

H Chaiyanar's Supply Beach
I Zanbil Resupply Depot
J Sushan (Susa) - War Palace
K Elam's main Palace at Anshan
L Sargon's Ride to Zanbil
M Arattta Camp

Prologue

3103 BC, the Palace in the city of Akkad, in the Land Between the Rivers . . .

"Tell me a story, Grandmother."

The childish words caught Trella by surprise. She rose from her seat at the window to find Escander standing a few steps behind her. The words and intonation might be those of a little boy, but the youth facing her had already entered his manhood.

"And who let you into my rooms unannounced?" She frowned at him and shook her head, annoyed only at herself for not hearing his approach.

"You did, Grandmother, else your guards would have stopped me." His voice now held all the confidence of a young man. "So you must still want to see your favorite grandson."

"I'll speak to the guards about their carelessness later. No doubt they've been sleeping at their post again."

Escander smiled at her jest.

The hard-eyed and well-trained bodyguards from the Hawk Clan remained ever alert outside Lady Trella's quarters. They had a very short list of those allowed entry to her chambers unannounced. King Sargon, her eldest son, as well as her two other children, Zakita and Melkorak. Escander's name came next.

After that, except for a handful of trusted servants and close companions who had served Trella through the years, everyone else, including her other grandchildren, had to seek an audience or wait for approval to enter Trella's wing of the Palace. Even now, the King's Mother had many enemies, and not all of them dwelt outside the royal residence.

Her frown faded. Trella held out her arms and let Escander embrace his grandmother, her forehead resting easily on his shoulder. His body felt warm and reassuring, strong and full of life against her.

Trella remembered how often she'd held the boy as a child. He needed her touch then, even more than her own children. *Tell me a story, Grandmother.* Escander was always pleading and cajoling her while growing up, using the same words and plaintive voice she'd found difficult to refuse.

Escander occupied a special place in her affections. Sargon had carried his son Escander to Trella when he was little more than two years old, the boy sobbing, his face buried in his father's shoulder. The poor child had just learned of his mother's death, and Sargon, his own grief scarcely under control, handed the frightened and bewildered boy to Trella.

"Please care for him, Mother." Sargon touched the boy's cheek and brushed away a tear. "He means so much . . . there's no one else I trust with him." Sargon, too, had tears in his eyes. He'd loved only two women in his life, and both had died in childbirth.

From that day, Trella raised Escander as her own child, though she never let the boy forget the memory of his real mother, a good woman who cared deeply for both Sargon and their son.

Trella brought her thoughts back to the present. She separated herself from her grandson's embrace. "And what brings you to me now? It's after midday. I know you returned to the Palace last night. Were you too busy to visit your grandmother?"

Almost a month ago, Escander had ridden north, traveling with his uncle Melkorak to inspect the border villages and their garrisons. They had returned to Akkad yesterday.

"The night was late when we arrived, Grandmother, and I didn't want to disturb you. I planned to come this morning, but Father summoned me. We spoke for some time. He said . . . "

Escander met her eyes. "He's sending me to the steppes, to visit our allies and learn from them. But before I leave, he wanted me to speak with you . . . to ask for your help."

Trella studied her grandson carefully. Midway into his fifteenth season, Escander appeared taller than she remembered, more man than the boy who'd ridden out with his uncle only a month ago. Escander's shoulders had grown broader, his arms thick with muscle, much like his grandfather, Eskkar.

The young man's light brown hair would have swirled around his gray eyes but an unadorned strip of black leather kept his long hair away from his face and off his neck. A broad forehead gave his face a rugged look. His keen wits and quick tongue nearly matched her own.

It was his mouth that intrigued Trella the most. Escander had the same mouth and jutting chin as his grandfather. When Escander smiled, Trella saw the stamp of her husband's face on the boy, Eskkar's blood flowing through their grandson's veins.

The youth had indeed grown into a man, Trella reminded herself. Already he knew the ways of power, and the many secrets of Akkad's rulers. Now the time had come for Escander to prove not only his manhood, but his readiness to take the crown of Akkad someday.

For that to happen, he needed to travel to the steppes, to earn the respect of their allies and learn the grim ways of warfare, where lessons came only through battle and at the risk of his life. Sargon's firstborn son had died there. Now Escander would follow the same path, and possibly meet the same tragic end.

"Do you approve of what you see, Grandmother?" He smiled.

Again Trella saw Eskkar's features reflected in her grandson's face. This time a pang of loneliness swept through her. "Don't question your elders."

She'd been gazing at him for some time. "You come to see me with no warning, asking silly questions."

"My father said there were many things I should know before I leave." Escander met her eyes, his expression serious.

"And what could an old woman tell you that the King could not?"

"You're not so old, Grandmother." Escander reached out and touched her cheek. "You've scarcely changed since I was a child."

"Which, as I recall," Trella said, unable to conceal a smile, "wasn't that many years ago."

She pushed his hand away. In one more year, she would reach her sixtieth season, and her hair had long since turned to gray. Nevertheless, she thanked the gods that her wits remained sharp, even if her body had thickened somewhat with age and the burden of birthing three children.

At least she still stood upright, and retained some of the grace that had marked her girlhood. And men yet looked at her with favor, and while she might smile back, she had never taken a lover.

"I don't think your father sent you here to talk about your childhood." Trella linked her arm within Escander's and guided him to the wide table that butted against the window overlooking the garden below. Two chairs, each with a thick russet cushion, added a touch of luxury to the otherwise spare furnishings. "Now, tell me exactly what King Sargon said."

"That you should tell me about my grandfather, that it would help me in the north." Escander settled into the chair beside her. "And about Father's own journey there. All about it. The good and the bad."

"Oh, Sargon said that, did he?" Trella leaned back in her chair. "Is my son now afraid to speak to his son? Perhaps I should talk with him, not you."

Escander reached across the table and took her hand. "Be serious, Grandmother. Everyone knows there are secrets only you know and understand, about the dangers in the steppes, and what happened to my half-brother there. Father knows, but he can't . . . won't talk about it."

"It's too painful for him." Trella squeezed Escander's hand for a moment.

Her thoughts went back to those days of danger, of pain, and of sorrow. And of happiness. Those feelings, too, had faded away, replaced with a sense of serenity as she drew closer to her end of days.

She raised her eyes, looking over the boy's shoulder and beyond the window, at the green and brown hilltop less than half a mile away. Lately Trella spent more and more of her time staring at the sight. Her husband Eskkar was buried there, near the crest of the hill. The unmarked grave dove deep into the earth.

Obeying Eskkar's final wishes, Trella had washed and dressed the King's body in his warrior's garb by herself. Then she placed the great sword on his breast and folded his hands around it. No gold or jewelry adorned the body, only his favorite cloak with the Hawk Clan emblem draped over the burial shroud.

For many years, two elderly women lived nearby, watching the site for Trella, lest any foolish grave robbers seek to loot the grave. But by now no one showed any interest in the spot, its location almost forgotten.

"Tell me a story, Grandmother." Escander still held her hand.

He'd followed her gaze, and knew where her thoughts had taken her. Once again she heard the child speaking, but the earnest eyes that met her own looked anything but childlike.

"You've heard all the stories, Escander. There's nothing more to tell."

"I've heard all the tales of the mighty Eskkar and his brave son Sargon, who fought together to save Akkad. Now it's time for me to learn the truth, so that I will know what dangers to expect. The secrets only you and Father know."

"The truth," Trella mused, "after all these years, the truth is hard to remember . . . even harder to tell."

"No one speaks of the time when my father went to the north. Is the truth so difficult to reveal? Is that why he asks you to do it?"

"The good and the bad, that's what he asked?"

"The good and the bad," the young man repeated, his voice serious. "Tell me the truth, not a story, Grandmother."

"It would take hours, even days, to tell you everything." Trella leaned back in her chair. "When are you leaving?"

"My father the King agrees that it might take some time for you to instruct me. He said the Hawk Clan could enjoy a few more days guzzling wine and chasing women before my journey begins."

"My son becomes even more presumptuous as he grows older."

"Everyone knows, Grandmother, that you're the only one he listens to. At least, since my mother died."

"If only that were true." Trella's eyes softened the words. Sargon did still come to her for advice and counsel, and when he didn't seek her out, she had other ways of getting her ideas and thoughts into his mind.

Power, she reminded herself, comes in many ways, and Trella still retained much of the authority that had once been hers alone. "Everything? He said to tell you everything?"

"Yes, everything." The boy settled back in his chair and made himself comfortable, now that he saw her acquiesce.

She gazed into his gray eyes, and realized that the boy she'd raised from a child had truly gone, replaced by the calm young man with the emanation of strength before her. Eskkar, she remembered, had much the same aura, a powerful presence that men deferred to almost without thinking. "You know what your journey to the steppes means, Escander? What it really means?"

"It means that I will be king someday, if I pass the test, and if one of my half-brothers or sisters doesn't have me killed first. Or I'm being sent to my death, like my older brother before me."

Trella nodded in understanding. After Sargon's first wife died, he took a second wife, Escander's mother. Two years after Escander's birth, she also died attempting to give life to a still-born daughter.

In his grief, Sargon had taken to his bed chamber a long string of willing women, who produced a multitude of sons and daughters. Trella had tried to restrain Sargon's passion, warning him about what might happen in the future, but in this, her son had refused her advice.

Now every one of those sons and daughters, encouraged and guided by their scheming mothers, could make some claim to the throne. The danger that Trella had foreseen had come to fruition. The only suitable heir to the Kingdom of Akkad stood in the way of his jealous kindred, each of them eager to rule. The thrust of a knife or a drop of poison hung over his head. Escander did indeed have many enemies.

"You must always beware of your siblings," she said. "But I will keep watch over the most troublesome."

Escander shrugged, in just that certain way Eskkar used to do. For a moment, Trella almost lost control of her emotions. She'd loved Escander's grandfather since their first night, and now as her life drew to a close, her heart went out to this boy.

"Whatever happens here will happen." Escander dismissed any concerns with a shrug. "I know the ways of the Palace and its intrigues. But what I will face in the northern lands is still hidden. That's why I must hear the truth now, and not from the steppes barbarians. Besides, if I ever do come to rule, I'll need to look every man in the eye and read their thoughts, the way only you can, Grandmother."

They both knew what this journey to the steppes meant. Trella had often wanted to warn Escander, to tell him what he needed to know and what dangers lurked in his path, but it remained her son's place to tell him these secrets. The Palace intrigue, she knew, unraveled nearly every hidden thought and desire.

Escander would be on his way before anyone learned of his departure, but tongues would whisper about his destination, and the plotting would begin. Even so, she felt satisfied that at last King Sargon had grasped what had to be done, even if he couldn't do it himself.

She stood up and went to the door and called out to a servant. "Ask En-hedu to join me."

Trella waited by the door until En-hedu arrived from her rooms down the corridor, then the two women whispered together for a few moments. Trella returned to the table and settled herself comfortably in the chair. "En-hedu will watch the door, to make sure no one hears our talk."

"What if En-hedu listens?"

"En-hedu doesn't have to listen, she knows the truth. She was there for much of it." Trella poured water for herself, and a half cup for her grandson. She gestured to the pitcher of wine, but the boy shook his head. Trella had spoken to him often about the dangers of too much wine, and at least he had learned that lesson well.

"Where should I begin?"

"Start with when you first met King Eskkar."

"No, you've heard those stories before. And even if they seem like tales to impress children, what you've heard is mostly true. Your grandfather was indeed a great man."

She took a sip from her cup. "Your story, what concerns you, began long after the building of Akkad's great wall, the wall that saved us from the barbarians." Trella closed her eyes for a moment, to count the time. "Twenty-seven years ago, when Sargon was a year younger than you, that's when your story begins."

"So long ago," Escander said in surprise. "How can it matter now?"

"The very young and the very foolish," Trella said firmly, "think that everything starts with them, and that only their days are important. But to rule wisely, a king has to think many years into the future, and must always remember the failures of the past. Eskkar learned that lesson well.

A good leader plans for six months ahead; a great leader plans six years into the future. The events from long ago can affect you today, Escander, but if you're not interested, you can leave and let an old woman return to her rest."

"No, no, I'll keep silent, I swear it. Not another word."

"When you have questions, good questions, ask them," Trella said. "Otherwise, how can you learn anything? Do you want to plod along like your half-brothers?"

"You know the answer to that, Grandmother. That's why you've favored me all these years, though you tried hard not to show it."

"Let me see, then." Trella drummed her fingers on the table. "In that time, the lands under Akkad's control stretched ever further south, ever closer to those of Sumeria. As the Sumerian cities expanded their influence northward, the border disputes began. The age of mighty cities had arrived, and it was inevitable that Akkad would clash with the growing power of Sumeria. In those days, the southern cities grew even faster than Akkad, since they had the trade on the Great Sea as well as the Two Rivers."

"Then came the war with Sumer," Escander said. "That's when my grandfather proved once and for all his greatness as a leader. His tactics in that war are still talked about among the soldiers."

Trella shook her head. "The only thing good about that war was that the actual fighting ended quickly. Eskkar gambled his life and the existence of Akkad in one battle, and only his skill as a leader saved them both."

"The cities of Sumeria still defer to our leadership." Escander's tone implied that it would always be so. "We can take care of the Sumerians if need be."

"Ah, the arrogance of youth, who thinks that what is, will always be. I hoped you would know better. Yes, they still respect our power. Just as they wait for Akkad to make the slightest mistake, so they can attempt to overthrow our rule once again."

Trella had spent most of her life in that struggle, determined to ensure that the city of Akkad never made that mistake, never lost its power. Still, it remained a natural conflict of interests that would likely never end.

He nodded, accepting her rebuke. "I take nothing for granted, Grandmother. I lay down each night to sleep wondering if I will awake in the morning."

"A wise thought to keep in your head." Trella let her mind return to the past. "Where was I? Oh, yes. After the Sumerian War, we overcame other minor battles and skirmishes, raids and marauders, good crop years and bad. Despite all these difficulties, the city grew greater and stronger each day. Akkad spread to both sides of the Tigris, and Eskkar built this palace for us on the west bank."

She paused for a moment, remembering those happy days. "But after many years of peace, we were caught by surprise when the new threat of war came from the east. Eskkar looked to his son to assist him. But Sargon, your father, had grown into a rebellious and lazy young man. A great disappointment to us both. He sorely tried your grandfather's temper, which Eskkar could never quite control."

"I've heard that King Eskkar could bellow and roar like a lion, though never at you, Grandmother." Escander squeezed her hand again. "But my father, a disappointment? I've never heard anything about that."

"Few remember those days," Trella said, "and even fewer want to speak about them. So while Akkad basked in prosperity, a new war loomed. Meanwhile, your father, the heir to the kingdom, wasted his time drinking, gambling, and whoring with friends as shiftless as himself, despite our strictest commands. That's when a stranger arrived from Sumeria, and brought with him the first stirrings of the Great War to come."

"Ah, the mysterious stranger, whose name no one knows."

Trella smiled. "In truth, at that time no one in Akkad knew his name or face, save Eskkar."

"But now . . . after so many years? Why is his name kept secret?"

"Because if he still lives, he might yet be of help to Akkad in the future. The bond between him and Eskkar proved stronger than time or distance. And even if he has passed beyond the veil, he will have whispered his secrets to his heirs, and his sons may yet honor the bond that exists between our families. So to this day, only Sargon and I know his name. Now I will share that secret with you. The man's name was Bracca, and he was a companion of Eskkar's during much of his youthful wanderings. They shared so many dangers that each owed the other his life."

"I've never heard that name. And after this Bracca came, King Eskkar went north once again, to the barbarian lands, to seek allies."

"No, that's not the way it happened. You must learn patience. Always you want to jump ahead in the story, just as you did as a child. At that time, Eskkar's focus remained on Akkad's old enemy, the barbarian clan from the steppes, the Alur Meriki." She shifted in her chair. "Even in the steppes you will find enemies."

"Enemies? But I've offended no one outside the Palace, let alone in the north."

"Eskkar had many enemies throughout the land, even among the clans of the steppes, and some of them may still be alive. Those who've died may have passed their hatred of your grandfather to their children. Blood feuds can span generations. Your name will bring danger from many sides, and you will have few friends to stand by you. That is why the test worries your father so much."

"But if I survive . . . if I return?"

"You will survive. I see Eskkar's spirit in you, and that gives me hope. He always managed to outwit his foes."

"He had you to help him, Grandmother. And the luck of the gods. I've heard those stories, how he often gambled his life in some desperate battle, trusting to chance to see him through. But my luck remains to be tested."

"Don't believe all those tales about your grandfather's luck, Child. Eskkar succeeded because he always managed to anticipate and outwit his enemies. Every one of his foes underestimated both his courage and his wits. Now, try to keep silent for a few moments."

"Yes, Grandmother."

"Where was I? Oh, yes, the stranger came to our house – we still lived in the Compound across the river then – to speak to Eskkar. The Great War had already begun, though Eskkar and I didn't realize we were at war. By the time we found out what had happened, it was nearly too late. Our enemy had already plotted our downfall, and sent the first of his minions into our midst, to spy on Akkad and its allies."

"But everyone said how strong and powerful Akkad was."

"You said you wanted to hear the truth, all the secrets. Now pay attention, and listen to the truth about your father, Sargon. And learn about the cunning of the Great King of the Elamite Empire. What you hear might just save your life."

She sighed. "I remember the night it all started, the night the stranger arrived to see your grandfather and brought with him the news, both good and bad, of what was to come."

1
=

3130 BC, the Palace of King Shirudukh of Elam, in the City of Anshan . . .

General Jedidia shifted his weight once again, the hard stone of the bench growing more uncomfortable with each passing moment. Despite the pleasant surroundings, he much preferred the back of a horse and galloping over rough terrain, rather than the unyielding seat beneath him.

Tall and dark, Jedidia appeared as fierce as any of his hardened soldiers. Black hair half concealed a wide brow, and his hook nose jutted arrogantly from beneath deep set brown eyes. A thick beard covered his chin and reached well onto his muscular chest. A fighting man, Jedidia had earned the respect of the men he commanded. He had little interest in any other accolades.

The narrow waiting area, just outside the main garden of King Shirudukh's Palace, offered its own collection of flowers and shrubs, but Jedidia no longer noticed either their beauty or pleasing fragrance.

Instead he sensed the hint of danger that always lurked within the walls of the Palace. Not all the men summoned before King Shirudukh survived the invitation. A man of violent and unpredictable moods, the King had little patience for any who displeased him, let alone dared disobey him. Those unfortunates often departed missing a finger or two, or even a hand.

Jedidia grimaced at the thought. In battle, he'd faced death often enough, and with less concern. But this intolerable waiting galled him. The unexpected summons could mean anything. Whatever the reason, Jedidia felt in his bones something important in the wind. Whether a death sentence or a promotion remained to be seen.

A small serving table, provided by King Shirudukh's servants, offered fat dates, red grapes, and slices of golden melon, neatly arranged and surrounded by fresh flowers.

Nevertheless, the tempting morsels lay untouched. Neither General Jedidia, nor the other two occupants of the small courtyard, Grand Commander Chaiyanar, or Lord Modran, felt any desire to eat before meeting with their sovereign. Only a fool ate, or drank for that matter, before an audience with King Shirudukh. A slight belch or worse, a loud fart, might be interpreted by the King as a sign of disrespect.

Each of the three generals occupied a bench of his own. Across from Jedidia slouched the short and slightly rotund Grand Commander Chaiyanar, eyes closed, his head lolling back against the wall. Soft, Jedidia thought, soft but cunning. On the bench beside Chaiyanar's, Lord Modran, handsome and vain, stretched out his lean frame, legs askew. No hint of softness in Modran, Jedidia knew. The man could fight or ride with anyone.

As usual, Jedidia felt uneasy in their presence. His blunt words and common upbringing contrasted against their more polished tones, and he lacked their skills in dealing with the King. Both men looked down on Jedidia, dismissing him as a simple soldier who had risen from the ranks.

And they were right. When Jedidia was ten years old, his father had sold him to the King's soldiers. After a brutal upbringing among the soldiers, Jedidia had fought his way to the rank of general in less than fifteen years.

For the next ten years, Jedidia had killed the King's enemies, as the Empire of the Elamites continued its remorseless expansion. Now, approaching his thirty-sixth season, Jedidia preferred nothing more than a hard fight and the opportunity to bring the terror and horrors of war down upon his enemy's head.

After exchanging a few forced pleasantries on their arrival, none of the generals had spoken for some time. Each of them resented and distrusted the other two, a natural enough situation when vying for the King's favor, and the subsequent increase in power that flowed to his current favorite. Who, Jedidia mused, would occupy the most favored place after today?

Summoned by their King to appear at midmorning, they entered the Palace only to learn from Shirudukh's chamberlain that the King found himself delayed by important matters of state, and would the three generals excuse the slight delay. Jedidia's teeth had clenched at the chamberlain's hint of a smile. They might be generals in command of thousands, but here in the Palace, they awaited their summons like any supplicant.

From where he sat, Jedidia could hear the important matters himself. At least three women's voices on the other side of the wall, all of them chattering, laughing, or moaning with pleasure, no doubt faked for their master's gratification. Meanwhile, the King's most senior commanders continued to wait, as the ruler of the Elamite Empire indulged his desires, his pleasure likely enhanced by his awareness of the anxiety of those waiting to see him.

None of the generals complained, of course. If anyone expressed the slightest sign of impatience or anger, the other two would be certain to repeat it to the King. Even a hint of disloyalty could be fatal. The less said, the better.

General Jedidia glanced again at his rivals. He despised the soft Chaiyanar and scorned the arrogant Modran. Both men held similar feelings about Jedidia. The three had hated each other for years, as they clawed their way to the top of Elam's armies.

Only fear of the King's power kept them from each other's throats. As a smiling Shirudukh often reminded them, they were the three legs of the stool that supported his power. Jedidia had always bristled at that humiliating image, though he forced a smile to his face.

Shirudukh understood the ways of power. He kept his generals and their armies at a distance, maintaining only a small but loyal force in the capital city of Anshan for his personal protection. All the traders and merchants operated under his rule and those of his advisors.

The knowledge needed to govern a large empire rested only in Shirudukh's hands. Any senior commander who showed the slightest interest in such matters soon disappeared.

The sun climbed higher and higher, and Jedidia saw that midday had come and gone, yet Shirudukh kept them waiting. The heat grew more oppressive, and Jedidia felt the sweat under his arms.

Even so, the pitchers of water that rested on the table remained untouched. No one dared be away taking a piss should the summons come. Nor, once the meeting began, would any of them ask for permission to leave. The King tolerated no slights either to his authority or his presence. Even his generals were expected to hold their water until Shirudukh dismissed them.

At last the gate to the inner garden creaked open, and a servant appeared, bowing low before the chafing generals. "The King is ready to see you, My Lords."

With a breath of relief, Jedidia rose, stretching his shoulders. Chaiyanar, closest to the gate and moving faster than the others, fell into place behind the servant. Modran managed to step in front of Jedidia, forcing him to bring up the rear.

Their guide hurried them out of the courtyard, nodding to the four soldiers guarding the entrance, and into the Palace's main garden. The ever-vigilant guards took a few moments to insure that the visitors remained unarmed, despite the fact that the three men had already surrendered their weapons when they arrived at the Palace.

Inside, small trees along the inner walls provided shade, and their pink blossoms added to the scented air. Pots filled with white and yellow jasmine bloomed, interspersed with shrubs speckled with glistening crimson berries. A wide buff-colored linen cloth, stretched over four supporting poles, provided shade for the King, who rested on a raised divan covered with pillows.

A young boy, no more than eleven or twelve, wielded a large fan to provide a breeze for the Empire's ruler. But even the blossoming flowers could not compete with the strong, almost rank perfume from the King's three slave girls, all of them naked, who lounged at Shirudukh's feet.

One of the girls, still flushed from her recent exertions, rested her breast again Shirudukh's leg, as she ran her fingers along his inner thigh. After a quick glance at the visitors, the slaves returned their adoring eyes to the King, each one eager to be the next to satisfy his slightest desire.

The peaceful setting contrasted with the presence of the King's guards, tough and brutal soldiers who obeyed only King Shirudukh. They stood with their backs to the walls, their eyes fastened on the visitors. Jedidia counted eight of them, and knew another twenty waited just beyond the garden, ready to respond to any threat against the King.

"Ah, Grand Commander Chaiyanar, Lord Modran, General Jedidia, it is good to see my victorious generals again." Tall and broad, King Shirudukh possessed a booming voice that filled the garden. Long brown hair, carefully arranged, reached to his shoulders. A long nose protruded over a wide mouth and thick lips.

Aside from a linen wrap tossed carelessly over his genitals, Shirudukh's chest and legs were bare. Chaiyanar, who had taken position directly in front of the divan, bowed first, a deep gesture that nearly brought him to his knees. "My King, the honor for my victory belongs to you."

Lord Modran bowed just as low, and perforce Jedidia followed his example. It would not do to show the slightest disrespect.

"Our enemies fled at the mention of your name, my King," Lord Modran's deep voice added emphasis to his simpering utterance.

"Our soldiers knew they would be victorious in your service, my King," Jedidia said, hating the fawning words even as he uttered them. "They were eager to humble your enemies."

Shirudukh waved away their flattery. "You have all fought well, and now the Empire of Elam stretches from one end of our land to the other."

With that, Jedidia agreed. Since the fall of the last three Kassite outposts in the east, all of King Shirudukh's enemies had been vanquished or destroyed. From the Indus to the western mountains, every city and village bowed to the King of the Elamites, and paid tribute.

"But your losses were heavy." Shirudukh voice turned grave. "And the cost to my treasury was high. Nor will we find much gold or anything of value in the lands of the Kassites." He frowned at his generals, as if the near total destruction of the enemy's cities and villages were a failure on their part.

"The wealth will return, in time," Lord Modran said.

"Perhaps. But even so, we must find a new source of gold and slaves, as well as a way to expand the Elam Empire."

Jedidia's eyes widened in surprise. Expand the Empire? Were there new lands to conquer?

King Shirudukh noticed Jedidia's expression. "Yes, General Jedidia, it is never too early to begin planning for our next conquest. But this time we will wage war not against a handful of cities, but against a rich and fertile countryside. The Land Between the Rivers, across the Zagros Mountains, awaits us."

Grand Commander Chaiyanar recovered first. "My King, I have heard of this land, but it is hundreds of miles away, across the mountains." Chaiyanar couldn't keep the doubt from his voice. "How will we fight such a war, so far from our cities?"

Jedidia had his own misgivings. He knew something, of course, about The Land Between the Rivers. Traders ventured there often enough, but the long and dangerous journey made only the most valuable goods worth the risk. He, too, wondered how it would be possible to fight battles so far from home, and on the other side of the rugged Zagros Mountains.

"It can be done," King Shirudukh said. "The land there is fertile. Its fields and herds will produce more than enough to feed our soldiers while they march and fight. And the cities quarrel constantly with each other. We will take advantage of that distrust, and their cities will fall before us."

"How many men will you send against them, my King?" Jedidia's soldiers were exhausted, their ranks thinned by the long fight against the Kassite forts and villages. He needed time to regroup and rearm. Chaiyanar and Modran had lost even more soldiers than Jedidia.

"Ah, a good question. The answer is simple. We will send all of our armies across the mountains at the same time, leaving only enough men to maintain our garrisons."

Chaiyanar, quicker with his sums than the others, spoke first. "If we take all our soldiers, my King, that would be more than thirty thousand men."

Shirudukh leaned back against the divan, and one of the slave girls rose hastily and rearranged the thick pillows. "We will send more men than that. This campaign must be swift and absolute. I intend to conquer the entire region within two to three months. And to accomplish that, we will have to prepare an army of almost fifty thousand men. The cities in The Land Between the Rivers will either submit when they see the size of our forces outside their gates, or they will be crushed, quickly and savagely, at whatever the cost. Even if all their cities join together to resist us, they cannot field more than fifteen or twenty thousand men."

"My King, it will take many months to raise and train so many," Lord Modran protested. "And how will we supply them?"

Shirudukh frowned at Modran's question. "There will be time. You will have two years to recruit and equip new men. During that time, you will stockpile whatever supplies and weapons you need, and prepare for the invasion. Then, just before the end of the harvest, we will invade."

Jedidia considered the time span. The main harvest still lay months away. So Shirudukh's plan meant at least two years. More than enough time to levy and discipline new men, while gathering the many materials needed to wage war.

"My men will be ready, my King, to march at your command." For once, Jedidia had managed to speak first.

"And after your victory, Great King, who will rule these new lands?" Chaiyanar couldn't keep the anticipation from his voice. "The city of Sumer is reputed to be the wealthiest in those foreign lands."

Shirudukh nodded approval at Chaiyanar's eagerness. "The city of Sumer is indeed a ripe plum, as is Isin. But Akkad is the jewel of the Land Between the Rivers. It is surrounded by fertile land and filled with much wealth. One of you, perhaps two, will rule those cities in my name. And at least one will return to hold the lands of Elam."

Jedidia saw Lord Modran open his mouth, then close it. Jedidia, too, resisted the urge to ask who would get what. Whomever their ruler named today would mean nothing. The King would play the three of them against each other for the next two years, until he made his final decision.

King Shirudukh rose, and one of the slave girls gathered his linen garment and fastened it around his waist. "Come. Let me show you our next conquest." He strode across the garden to a small table, waving the nearby guards away.

Jedidia and the others moved to the other side and faced the King. Glancing down, Jedidia saw a map spread over the surface, the four corners held down with small chunks of marble.

"This is the Land Between the Rivers." Shirudukh pointed out the two mighty rivers, the Tigris and Euphrates, and the main cities of Akkad, Isin, and Sumer. Then, step by step, the King outlined his plan of attack.

"There is yet much to learn, of course, and many more details will be needed. But I have already dispatched the first of my spies across the mountains, to gather information, and to smooth the way for our armies. When all is ready, we will work out the details of command, the soldiers needed, and the supply routes. At the start of the campaign, I will move my Palace to the city of Sushan, to be closer to the Great Sea. But until then," Shirudukh's voice hardened, "you will tell no one."

The King stared at each man in turn, a grim look that warned them not to discuss the invasion with anyone. "With the conquest of The Land Between the Rivers, the size of our Empire will nearly double. These new lands and cities will provide great wealth to the empire. And I intend to take that prize."

Jedidia nodded. New battles to be fought, new territory to conquer, and new spoils to gather. The prospect was indeed exciting. With any luck, Jedidia's own wealth would triple.

"And who rules the strongest of these cities now, my King?" Lord Modran, always cautious, wanted to know the worst.

"Akkad is the most powerful city in the Land Between the Rivers," Shirudukh said. "It is ruled by a northern barbarian, who seized power fifteen years ago. He is said to be dull of wit, and his wife and others rule in his name. Sumer, near the Great Sea, is weak, with only a small army. Isin is warlike, but the smallest of the three cities. Sumer was defeated by Akkad not long ago, and now frets under Akkad's growing power and influence. Isin, too, has no use for Akkad. Our invasion will give both of them the chance to turn on and destroy their rival."

Jedidia had heard of Akkad's ruler, a common fighting man named Eskkar. Traders claimed he seldom uttered more than a few words, and that one of Eskkar's wives talked in his place. Against such a weak ruler, if Shirudukh could turn Isin or some of the other cities against Akkad, victory would be assured. No single city, especially with its forces depleted by war with its neighbors, could resist the might of the Elamites.

"And now, my faithful generals, you may leave and return to your duties," Shirudukh said, his interest already reverting to his slave girls. "Just make sure your men are ready when I summon you."

Jedidia bowed low once again, as did the others, and they slipped out of the garden. Already planning ahead, he wondered how he could turn this opportunity to his advantage. In war, battles sometimes went wrong, and either Chaiyanar or Modran could meet with some mishap that would offer Jedidia the chance to rise above his fellow generals.

Even more intriguing would be the chance for Jedidia to destroy one or both of them. That would give him more satisfaction than all the gold in Akkad.

As General Jedidia left the palace grounds, he knew Chaiyanar and Modran would be thinking the same thoughts. Conquering the Land Between the Rivers would provide each one of them an opportunity to get rid of a rival, or at least weaken his standing with the King.

No doubt Shirudukh had already considered all these possibilities, as always playing his generals against each other, and in so doing, maintaining his own power. As long as they distrusted and contended with each other, none of them had the opportunity to strive for the kingship.

Still, the next two years, Jedidia decided, would present many chances to increase his personal authority. He would add thousands of skilled fighting men to his forces. And when his rivals marched into battle, anything could befall them. With luck, Jedidia would return from the invasion and destruction of the Land Between the Rivers with even greater triumph and power.

2

The summer of 3130 BC, the City of Akkad . . .

King Eskkar stood at the Workroom window, staring down at the garden courtyard below. The deepening shadows within the Compound's walls told him the sun had already set. The two willow trees that shaded the house's private well had spread their branches, and threatened to intertwine. For the last few years the gardener had to trim the topmost branches and boughs, to keep them within the walls.

As always, living things struggled into existence, grew strong and hearty for a time, then succumbed either to their enemies, fate, or in this case, the gardener's saw. Men were much the same. They strove for mighty endeavors that often came to naught, despite all their efforts.

Now, much like the trees that struggled against the gardener's blade, Eskkar planned a new and dangerous endeavor, but one necessary if the City of Akkad were to continue growing. Once again he would be risking his life against a hardened and steadfast enemy.

In three days the campaign long planned in secret would begin. Without fanfare, Eskkar and a small contingent of soldiers would ride out of the city, heading northwest. Fewer than a handful knew what he intended, though many had participated in the preparations.

The myriad and diverse rumors, carefully fed by Trella's network of agents and spies, had already run their course. Another wearisome training mission, everyone said, as they nodded their heads knowingly. But only Eskkar and a few others knew that barbarian horsemen were once again on the move toward the Land Between the Rivers.

The barbarian horde, known as the Alur Meriki, traveled in a long migration cycle. This time they returned, after many years, to the northern lands, moving across the foothills of the Zagros Mountains on their journey to the west. Aware of Akkad's strength and long reach, the Alur Meriki would seek to avoid any direct conflict.

Nevertheless, there would be numerous raids on Eskkar's northern border. The barbarian honor code would accept nothing less. And so more than a few villages and countless homesteads would be destroyed, farms and crops burned, people and livestock killed.

Eskkar had decided the time for barbarian raids had ended. For the last two years, he and Trella had planned for the day when the barbarians returned to the fringes of Akkad's lands. Many of the people no longer remembered the daring raid that brought the Alur Meriki within Akkad's walls during the war with Sumer, but Eskkar had never forgotten. In that battle, the barbarian horsemen had discarded their warrior code and attempted to sneak into the city by treachery.

This time Eskkar intended to crush the Alur Meriki once and for all, and put an end to their depredations. The fact that Eskkar had been born into that same clan, had lived as one of them until his fourteenth season, mattered not at all.

Three quick knocks sounded on the open door. Eskkar turned away from the window, to see Annok-sur, his wife's closest friend and companion, standing in the doorway. Her presence surprised him. She had left the Compound well before dusk, to return to her home a few steps down the lane. Something important must have brought her back.

"What is it?"

Before Annok-sur entered, she turned and spoke to the guard at the landing. Then she closed the door.

"Lord, I need to speak with you about . . . something has come up."

Her demeanor told him as much as her words. Tall and sturdily built, Annok-sur's long hair contained more gray than brown, though she was only a few years older than Eskkar. As leader of Akkad's network of spies, she held more power than anyone else in Akkad, except for Trella and Eskkar.

Her husband, Bantor, was one of Eskkar's top commanders and Captain of the city's Guard. Despite her responsibilities, Annok-sur seldom let her thoughts or emotions show in her face or manner. Now she seemed hesitant, almost agitated. He waved her toward the table, and she accepted his offer to sit.

Eskkar sat as well, but not across from her. Somehow facing his friends over the width of the wide table always seemed so formal. Besides, he wanted to see her in the fading light. Over the years, Annok-sur and her husband Bantor had grown into part of Eskkar and Trella's family. "Something that can't wait until tomorrow? Should I send for Trella?"

Trella had gone to visit Hathor the Egyptian, Eskkar's second in command, and his wife, who had just delivered her third son. Their dwelling, too, was but a short distance away, though in the opposite direction from Annok-sur's.

"No, I'm glad that she's not here. Otherwise, I would have to ask her to leave the room. I gave my word that I would speak to you, and you alone."

Eskkar furrowed his brow. Trella had been at his side and involved in every decision for almost fifteen years, and no one stood closer to Trella than Annok-sur. For her to go against that confidence surely meant something serious had arisen.

"A man called at my house just after dusk. He gave no name, just insisted that he had to speak with me. The guards refused to pass him in, but he persisted. He wore a hooded cloak that kept his face in the shadows. He told the guards he had something urgent to tell me, and that they should give me that message."

Annok-sur took a deep breath. "Naturally, I came. The man surrendered his sword and knife, and we spoke in the courtyard. He declined to enter the house. He made sure no one could overhear our words, and he kept his face in the shadow of his hood."

"How did you know he didn't mean to attack you?" Annok-sur had almost as many enemies in Akkad as Eskkar and Trella.

"No, I sensed that was not his purpose. But I kept both guards close by, just far enough away so they could not hear the man's softly spoken words."

"What did he want?"

"That's what surprised me. He wanted me to bring him to you, in secret. He wants to talk to you. No one, he insisted, must know his name or his face, or even that he visited with the king."

"You said no, of course."

"Yes, but he expected that. He asked me to give you a message. He had a presence about him, a force of will that I found hard to deny. He was very . . . persuasive. He said you would see him when you heard the message."

"This stranger seems very sure of himself," Eskkar said. "What did you tell him?"

"I refused to carry a message to you without knowing his name. He thought for a moment, then gave me one that he said you would understand, and the message. The name he gave is Master Guide Tarrata."

By now, Eskkar's curiosity had taken control. Tarrata was not an uncommon name, and Eskkar had known several over the years. None that he could recall held any claim on his time.

He shrugged. "What was the message?"

"He said," she paused again, as if to make sure she had the words right, "that he was the man who left you the five silver coins buried beneath the bloody rock along the southern road that leads to Orak."

"Ahhh." Eskkar leaned back in surprise as the memory swept aside the years. Orak was the old name for Akkad. Trella and he had changed the city's name soon after they defeated and drove off the barbarians more than fifteen years ago.

Without thinking, he touched the scar on his leg, the wound that had nearly killed him when it became infected. Eskkar had been almost delirious when he limped into Orak for the first time. Now he remembered the name Tarrata well enough. Not just a guide, though. A caravan master as well. Tarrata had died in the same fight against bandits that had left Eskkar with the wounded leg.

"Describe the stranger."

"It was hard to see much beneath the cloak, but he was smaller than I am by a good three fingers."

Annok-sur leaned forward. "A black beard covered his chin, and his nose had been broken, I could see that. A faded scar stretched down his right cheek. His complexion seemed dark, and he might have been born in Sumeria. I couldn't place his accent, but he could have come from the south."

It had to be Bracca, the only close friend Eskkar had ever had. He had never told anyone about the coins, and even if someone had gotten the story from Bracca himself, Tarrata's name likely wouldn't have come up.

"Bring him here. Give him back his weapons and bring him here."

"Lord, are you sure? At least let me hold his weapons."

"No, I can take care of myself if need be. Make sure that we are not disturbed. Find Trella, tell her everything, but ask her to wait downstairs until I summon her."

"Do you know who he is?"

"Yes."

"And you trust him?"

He shrugged again. "After a fashion."

Annok-sur waited a moment, until she realized Eskkar didn't intend to say any more. "Be careful, Eskkar." She extended her hand and brushed his arm. "You take too many foolish chances."

Her concern touched him. Over the years, Annok-sur had become like a sister to him. Her devotion to Trella was beyond question. "I'll take care."

After she departed, Eskkar returned to the window. The ground below now held only darkness. The moon hadn't risen yet, so the sky displayed the vast spread of stars, like sparkling silver sand flung high across the heavens.

As the years passed, he spent more time studying the night sky, and often spoke with reputed wise men who claimed to know the secrets hidden from ordinary men's eyes. Still, Eskkar guessed that they knew little more than the old shepherd whose wisdom first gave the stars meaning to a young and wandering barbarian outcast.

His thoughts returned to Bracca. Over the years, Eskkar had wondered often enough what had happened to the wily, smooth-talking Sumerian who lived as much by his wits as by his sword. The two of them had met by chance and nearly came to a death fight. Instead, they became companions.

For almost five years they fought and drank and whored together through good fortune and bad. Both had escaped death more times than Eskkar could call to mind. He remembered his disappointment when Bracca went south with the merchant Aram-Kitchu.

Eskkar pushed the old memories aside. Whatever evil tidings brought Bracca to the Compound in secret like this meant something truly important had occurred. Otherwise he could just have given his name to the guards at the gate, and been assured an entrance.

Eskkar went to the wall behind the table. The great sword hung there, not the original he carried defending Akkad against the barbarians, but a finer one that Trella had ordered made for him two years ago. Beside it hung another sword, a shorter blade much like those used by his soldiers. As finely cast as his long sword, its blade was both wider and a bit longer than the usual short sword the city's guards and soldiers used. Eskkar carried the smaller one when he moved about Akkad. Its bronze edges were honed so sharp they would cut through bone.

Pulling the shorter blade from its scabbard, he tossed it on the table. A hanging pouch held sharpening stones, and Eskkar removed one and dropped it beside the sword. Bracca was, after all, Bracca. A devious, dangerous man, he was as liable to do anything for gold as anyone else.

Almost twenty years had passed since they parted, and that length of time can change a man, even make him forget old loyalties. Once they had been friends, each trusting the other in the face of death, but now?

Eskkar didn't intend to take any chances. He stepped out of the room onto the landing, and gave the guard there a series of orders. The man raised his eyebrows at the unusual instructions, but nodded understanding, before he dashed down the stairs to do the King's bidding. Then Eskkar summoned one of the servants, and bade her bring candles and refreshments.

Eskkar waited on the landing, gazing down into the house's Great Room. The thick outer door, still open to take advantage of the evening breeze, led to the main courtyard. It didn't take long before he heard voices approaching. Then Annok-sur, accompanied by two guards, escorted a man wearing a long cloak into the house. The garment's hood hid the visitor's face.

The stranger glanced around, and lifted his eyes upward toward the stairs. He appeared surprised to see the King there.

Looking down, Eskkar glimpsed the familiar scar. Despite the years, he recognized Bracca. "Come on up."

The man glanced around the Great Room a second time, and started for the stairs. He ascended slowly, and just before he reached the landing, Eskkar turned and stepped inside. The servant was spreading the pitchers of wine, ale, and water on the table. A large platter of dates, nuts, figs, as well as the sweet cakes made of flour, dates, raisins, and butter rested in the center.

As ordered, she had lit four of their thickest candles, a huge extravagance, but one that almost banished the night. Eskkar wanted plenty of light while he studied the features of his visitor.

"Close the door," Eskkar said to serving girl, as she scurried from the room after darting a curious glance at the hooded stranger. Eskkar moved behind the table and sat, the sword close to his right hand.

Bracca entered the workroom and glanced around, noticing the two doors. One led to Eskkar and Trella's bedroom and the other to the Map Room.

"We're alone up here, Bracca," Eskkar said. "And I've ordered the guards to remain downstairs. So you can speak without worrying about anyone overhearing your words."

Bracca took one last look around the room. Another table across the room, a handful of chairs, stools, and a bench. Two chests, covered with brightly colored blankets, completed the simple furnishings.

"Nothing very fancy. Not what I expected for the King of Akkad. Still, you've done very well for yourself, Eskkar." He pushed the cloak back away from his face. "Better than I ever thought you could do."

"It serves me well enough." Eskkar saw more than a sprinkle of silver in the man's once black-as-night hair, though Bracca was about the same age as Eskkar, both in their mid-forties. Eskkar's hair still retained the dark brown color of his youth, except where his temples had started to gray. Old age, the curse of every man, approached. Already he could feel the first hint of it in his bones. "I was lucky a few times, Bracca."

Bracca moved to the table and slipped into the chair opposite his host. "Nice sword." He gestured toward the weapon. "Mind if I try it?"

"Only if you want your hand cut off," Eskkar said pleasantly. "There's wine and ale, food if you're hungry."

"A cup of ale would be good," Bracca said. He selected the ale pitcher, filled his cup halfway, then paused to examine the cup. "Nice carving on these, but I doubt if you picked them out yourself. You never had an eye for such things."

He raised the cup up in a gesture of thanks. "Well, to an old friend, and to King Eskkar of Akkad. You've done very well indeed." He took a few swallows, then sighed. "Good brew. Don't get anything near as good in the east."

Eskkar watched his old friend's movements. Shorter than most men, and quick as a cat in the old days, Bracca still appeared to carry plenty of hard muscle on his frame, though the loose fitting tunic concealed most of his strength. Even so, the man's arms looked as strong as ever. Many a dead man had underestimated Bracca's toughness and quickness with sword or knife.

"You look fit and as ready for a fight as ever." Bracca had observed the movement of Eskkar's eyes. "Though it seems strange not to see that long sword sticking up from your shoulder. We surprised a lot of enemies in our wanderings. We were both quicker than we looked. I never understood how you could draw that blade so fast."

The two companions had always presented an odd contrast. Bracca, short, dark, and quick, had provided the perfect compliment to Eskkar's height, powerful frame, and long arms. And just as in the old days, the man seemed to read Eskkar's thoughts. He would have to take care not to reveal too much. "So you've been to the Indus. Are you still working for Aram-Kitchu?"

"Ah, well, there's a long story. Yes and no, I suppose. Aram-Kitchu is dead. Not long after we forded the Indus, he took a bandit's arrow in the back and died soon after. Half the caravan died that day, too. Before he passed on, Aram asked me to continue the venture and return the wealth to his family. One thing led to another, and by the time I reached Sumer, almost a year had passed, and I had become Aram-Kitchu."

Eskkar smiled, as much at Bracca's story telling skills as at the story. "That seems convenient."

Bracca laughed, the familiar quick burst that always came easily to the man. "Yes, I suppose it was. But as I was carrying a fat bag of gold, his widow accepted me into her household. Since she didn't enjoy the prospect of finding a new husband, soon she and I were wed. We decided I should take on Aram-Kitchu's name. It seemed easier that way to keep the trading ventures going."

"So you became wealthy and respectable at the same time?"

"As respectable as Aram-Kitchu or any greedy trader could ever be. He'd also taken three wives in the land of the Indus, so now I've a good-sized family there, too. In fact, I own two large estates in that land, along with a few hundred slaves and servants."

"I'm glad to hear you've plenty of gold." Eskkar poured himself a small cup of ale and laced it with water. "I gave orders to double the guard on the coin storeroom as soon as I learned it was you."

Bracca laughed again. "We did steal quite a few purses, didn't we? Still, I'm glad to see you survived your wounds and found those coins. Enough of us died to earn them, as I recall. But all in the past, that. Now you're the mighty King Eskkar, revered by his people and ruler of the greatest city in the west."

"You missed a few good fights," Eskkar said. "I could have used your help once or twice."

"If I'd stayed, then I'd be the King of Akkad, and you'd be working for me training horse fighters." Bracca smiled at the idea. "But as it is, I've come to save your worthless life once again."

"Who wants to kill me this time?"

"Not you in particular. It's just that the ruler of the Elamites wants to conquer Akkad and add it to his empire. He hungers for the caravans full of tribute he'll expect delivered each year."

"Elamites?" Eskkar frowned. "Who are the Elamites?"

Bracca shook his head in feigned disappointment. "You see what I mean? You don't even know your peril. A vast army marches toward you, and you've never heard of them."

"Enlighten me, then, friend Bracca."

"The Elamites are a warrior race far to the east. For twenty years, they have fought and conquered every city and nation in the land of the Indus. Now their eye has turned toward the west. Already they are planning their first steps toward the Land Between the Rivers. In two years, perhaps a little more, they will be here, knocking at your gates."

"Ah, then at least I can sleep well tonight."

"Sleep lightly, my old friend. The Elamites are a dangerous enemy, and they have a long reach. They prefer to kill their enemies' leaders well before their armies arrive. Well before they invade, they target those wise and strong enough to resist them. Poison, assassins, treachery, betrayal, the Elamites are masters of all of these. The weak and foolish they leave alive and in power. Until they're ready to crush them."

"And how is it, friend Bracca, that you know so much about these Elamites?"

"Oh, did I forget to mention that I am in their pay? Very well paid, I might add. I gather knowledge for them, especially from the Land Between the Rivers. The more they know about Akkad and its allies, the easier it will be to conquer the city. When the time comes, I'll be one of those dispatching assassins to eliminate any who still stand in their way."

"And that would be me?"

"Well, not only you." Bracca took another sip from his cup. "In Akkad I suppose Trella would be their first target. Her reputation is well known. In Isin, it would be King Naxos. Of course, it might be easier to turn him against Akkad. The Elamites always try to sow distrust among those they are preparing to attack. A good tactic, that."

He shrugged. "Their plans will be decided when they are ready to move against you."

King Naxos of Isin ruled his city state with a strong hand, but every powerful man posed a potential threat to Akkad's rule. Which was why Annok-sur kept so many spies in Isin.

"What of your own cities to the south, Bracca? Is Sumer and the rest of Sumeria to be spared this invasion?"

"Alas, no." Bracca's voice held a hint of sadness. "The southern cities must also be brought under Elamite rule. Only the entire wealth of the Land Between the Rivers would be enough to justify the war and satisfy King Shirudukh."

Eskkar had never heard of this King Shirudukh. "And that would be bad for your trading ventures." Eskkar grunted in disgust.

If any of this were true, he should probably kill Bracca tonight. Eskkar had only to raise his voice, and the four guards now waiting on the lower landing would burst into the room, swords in hand.

The idea tempted Eskkar. After all, many years had passed, and he owed the man nothing. A day or two in the torture pit would make Bracca reveal everything he knew. Besides, a spy was always a danger, and someone as clever as Bracca would make the best and most dangerous spy of all.

"So why are you telling me all this, Bracca? Especially since you'll be one of those plotting against me."

"Ah, I have my reasons." Bracca leaned back in his chair and made himself more comfortable. "For one, you saved my life, and more than once. For another, I never felt good about leaving you here. I was certain you were going to die, but I suppose I should have stayed with you to the end. It's what you and your foolish barbarian code of honor would have done, if our situations were reversed. But Aram-Kitchu was leaving, and I had only a moment to choose. It was five years before I learned you were alive. Still, if you had died like you were supposed to, my only regret would be leaving behind those five silver coins."

Eskkar remembered the sadness that had come over him when he awoke from his fever and delirium to discover that Bracca had indeed gone. "We did save each other's life a few times. But things worked out well enough."

"Yes, and I'm glad for you. But I wouldn't have come upriver and risked getting my throat cut just for that. There's something else I should have told you, wanted to tell you long ago. Do you remember the fight at Marcala?"

Eskkar thought for a moment, but the name evoked no memory. "Marcala? No, not really. Where was it?"

"The gold mine in Sumeria. We rescued the slave from the mine for his mother, and stole the Village Elder's gold."

"I remember . . . the time the madness came over you. You killed the slave master, the one twice your size. I really thought he would take you down."

"Dargo, his name was. Yes, the battle rage was upon me that night." Bracca scratched at his chin. "Not important now. But that fight . . . I should have died that day. I'd brought death down upon us all. There was no reason for you to stay and fight beside me. That's why I told you to go, expected you to go. You shouldn't have stayed."

"Perhaps I was foolish." Eskkar drummed his fingers on the table, his hand almost brushing the hilt of the sword. "But what does it matter now? I'm sure you didn't come all the way to Akkad just to thank me for saving your miserable life on one particular day."

"Well, of all the fights we were in together, that's the one I can't forget. So, yes, I did come to warn you because of what you did that day. I don't expect you to understand why." Bracca paused to take another sip of ale. "That, and maybe because I don't like the idea of the Elamites just marching in and crushing the cities of Sumeria. I was born there, you know. And I've seen what they do to a conquered city. Even worse than what you did to Larsa."

Eskkar grunted. In the Sumerian War, he had reduced the city of Larsa to a pile of rubble. Even today, no one lived there. That single act of retribution and terror still gave pause to anyone thinking about attacking Akkad. "Whatever your reasons, I thank you for the warning. But why the secrecy?"

"Because even among my own men, the Elamites have other spies who watch my doings. They trust me, I'm sure of that, but they take no chances with anyone not born into their ruling clan. Tonight, I had to wait until all the others were busy with their own pleasures before I could slip away. As it is, I must return to my inn soon enough. My vessel's cargo is sold, and tomorrow we take ship for Sumer."

"I'm sorry you have to go." Eskkar meant the words. Despite Bracca's gloomy forewarning, Eskkar sensed that his old friend would have liked to spend some time talking about the past, like old comrades who have fought side by side. Eskkar would have, too.

Bracca nodded. "It can't be helped. But before I go, I'd like to speak with your wife, Trella."

Eskkar's frown returned. "So you can learn more about her, if you need to send assassins?" His fingers reached out and caressed the sword's hilt.

"Always the suspicious barbarian." Bracca shook his head. "No, so that she can hear my words herself. As I said, I've learned much about her. Some men say she rules Akkad as much as you."

Or with even greater authority than the King, according to more than a few of those rumors. Esskar studied his visitor. Well, why not? She would want to know what had been discussed. Besides, she was already the most guarded person in Akkad. And after tonight, that protection would increase.

Esskar rose, picking up the sword as he stood. Bracca's eyes widened when Esskar lifted the blade, but Bracca made no move and showed no fear. Esskar turned his back to the table and replaced the blade into its scabbard, still hanging on the wall. "I'll summon her." Walking around the table, Esskar went to the door, pulled it open, and stepped onto the landing.

Four Hawk Clan guards, one of whom carried a strung bow in his hand, looked up anxiously from the lower landing when he appeared. With his left hand, Esskar gave the signal that all was well, though none of the guards bothered to relax. In the chamber below, Trella sat on a bench, her head almost touching that of Annok-sur. Both raised their eyes to Esskar.

"Trella, will you please join us."

Without waiting, Esskar returned to the table and again took his seat. Bracca hadn't moved, and he still held his ale cup in both hands.

A moment later, one of the guards pushed the half-open door aside, glanced inside the chamber, then stepped back to allow Trella to enter. She swept into the room, moving with purpose until she reached the end of the table. As if by chance, she took the one place at the table where her body would not block the light from any of the candles. She, too, wanted to observe their visitor's face.

"Yes, Husband?"

"This is my old friend and companion, Bracca." Esskar kept his eyes on his guest, to see what reactions Trella's presence evoked. "We rode together for several years. Bracca has come to warn us of a new danger."

"Then he is doubly welcome to our home." She gazed down at Bracca, smiled, and inclined her head in a slight bow.

Whatever Bracca had heard, whatever he'd expected, Trella's appearance and manner caught him off guard. His mouth opened slightly as he gazed up at Esskar's wife.

Trella, now just thirty years old, wore an unadorned linen dress that barely brushed the floor, though one that showed her figure to its best advantage. Eskkar noticed that it was not the every-day garment she'd worn when she departed to visit Hathor's household. After hearing Annok-sur's words, Trella had changed into something finer, to reflect the important status of Eskkar's guest.

As she spoke, Trella held her head high, and her shoulders back. Her feet were bare, and her only jewelry was the single filet of silver that kept her thick black hair away from her face. Not only was Trella's face devoid of the fashionable oils or copper paints to color her eyes or cheeks, but her face showed no hint of ever having used the artifices that most women of wealth employed. The bright candles sent glimmers of light shining in the lustrous hair that brushed her shoulders.

Under the influence of her smile, Bracca slowly rose to his feet, the chair scraping awkwardly as he stood and returned her bow. Trella's eyes held his own, and it took a moment before Bracca remembered to break the silence.

"My thanks to the Queen of Akkad for her hospitality."

To Eskkar's ears, Bracca's voice sounded a trifle unsure, though he doubted anyone else would have noticed. Eskkar held back the smile at Bracca's reaction to Trella's presence. He'd seen the effect before.

Trella, of course, noticed everything. Her eyes now studied Bracca, his face, hands, even the man's clothes and the manner in which he wore them.

"For such a close companion of my husband my name is Trella. Please call me that. And if there is anything that you want or need, you have only to ask. Now please, sit." She selected the pitcher of ale, and refilled the guest's cup.

Bracca sank back into the chair, then had to move it back to the table. "Thank you, Queen . . . Trella. Lady Trella."

"Eskkar recounted several stories about your travels, and how you brought him safely to Orak." She handed him the cup, and gracefully took her own seat at the table.

"Did he, now? Well, Eskkar was never very good at telling stories. Sometimes days would go by, and all he ever did was grunt."

Trella laughed, her white teeth flashing in the candlelight. The melodious sound filled the room. "He took some persuading. I explained that I needed to know his thoughts and deeds . . . all those things that helped him survive so many battles. The more I learned about him, the more I could help him. He told me your wits were as quick as your sword."

Bracca glanced at Eskkar. "And what else did you tell her of me?"

Eskkar laughed. "Nothing good. Only that you kept getting us into trouble and then I had to save both our skins." He paused a moment, remembering Bracca's earlier words. "Nothing about Marcala."

"Marcala?" Trella inclined her head. "I believe there's a gold mine near the village of Marcala, in the western part of Sumeria."

"You are well informed, Trella," Bracca said. His composure had returned. "But the Marcala mine produces little these days. It is said that you are also from Sumeria."

"Many things are said about me," Trella answered. "Most of them are untrue. But Eskkar said that you've come to warn us of some new danger?"

Neither Eskkar or Trella ever volunteered any information about their past. The less said about Eskkar's days as a wandering rogue and bandit the better. Nor did Trella want any more known about her early life, and the fact that she came to Akkad as a slave.

"Ah, yes, the Elamites. I was telling Eskkar that they plan to move against this land, once they have finished consolidating their conquests east of the Indus."

Bracca repeated what he'd told Eskkar before she arrived.

"Why would they want to invade our land? I've heard that the lands of the Indus are vast and fertile, full of many different peoples."

"Indeed they are, Lady Trella. But the constant fighting has drained every city of its wealth. Meanwhile they have a large army eager for war and glory, with leaders that demand ever more loot. And each conquest only serves to whet their appetite for the next. If the Elamites wish to survive, they must add to their empire, and so they now have cast their eyes to the west."

"The Sumerians sent over twenty thousand men against us in the war against Sumer," Eskkar remarked.

"I know, and you defeated them at Isin. The Elamites will field two or three times that number. And these men are well trained and well supplied, not like much of the rabble Sumer sent against you. I know all about that effort. I delivered many of the weapons that King Shulgi used to arm his men against you."

"The fight at Isin was no hillside brawl," Eskkar said, annoyed in spite of himself at his friend's knowledge.

Bracca raised his palms. "I meant no offense, Eskkar. I know how hard you and your men fought to win that victory. But this coming fight will be different. This time the men you will face are battle-tested veterans, conquerors of many cities. Already the first few spies are in Akkad, Sumer, and Isin. They will lie in wait, until the time comes to strike. I know. I helped put them in place. Soon more will come."

"If you know so much about these spies," Eskkar said, "perhaps you can tell me their names?"

The moment he finished asking the question, Eskkar regretted it. If Bracca were going to reveal their names, he would already have done so. A quick glance at his wife confirmed it. Trella had not asked the obvious question, because she knew what Bracca's answer would be.

"Well, that's something I cannot tell you." Bracca sent his eyes from husband to wife. "If I did, suspicion would fall on me, and I can't have that. Besides, the Elamites would only find others to serve them, and you would be no better off."

Eskkar frowned. His thoughts returned to the idea of the torturers, and their ability to extract information. Trella, meanwhile, began asking questions about the Elamites, their customs, the way they lived, how they were ruled. Soon she'd drawn Bracca into giving more than just brief answers. Eskkar listened, but kept his attention on Bracca. The man had always been devious, capable of anything. Yet the more Eskkar saw and heard, the more he felt the man could be trusted, at least in part. For some reason, Bracca wanted to help.

Bracca's answers grew shorter, and at last he lapsed into silence.

"Your warning is well delivered, then," Trella said, "and again you have our thanks. We will be on our guard. Will it be possible for you to provide us with more information when you next visit Akkad?"

"It is unlikely that I will visit your city again anytime soon. I do, however, journey to Sumer at least once a year, sometimes more often."

"We have friends in Sumer," Trella said. "If you wish, you could send a message to Eskkar through one of those."

"Perhaps. Though most of your agents in that city are known to . . . the Elamites. Perhaps, if it could be managed safely, I will consider it."

Trella caught Bracca's slight pause, and understood its meaning. Bracca knew the names of her spies in Sumer. Which also meant that at least one or two of them were in his pay as well as hers.

"I think it could be arranged." Trella kept her face as neutral as her voice. "Such a man would have no dealings with any others. He would wait only for you to contact him."

Bracca considered her words, weighing the risks. He would be placing himself in danger. "How soon can you give me your man's name?"

"I can tell you his name now." Trella chose a name from those she and Annok-sur had selected. "It is Steratakis, a trader from the city of Lagash. It will be a few months before he is established and in place. He will make himself known to you."

"I make no promises, but I will see what can be done." Bracca drained his ale cup and stood. "I must return to my inn. We depart for Sumer at first light."

He turned to Eskkar. "I said before that you had done well. Now I see that you've done far better than that. Just watch your back."

"Are you sure you don't want to stay and join us?" Eskkar rose as well. "You were always handy in a fight."

Bracca shook his head with a hint of sadness. "Not this time, friend Eskkar. This time, you're on your own. But I see you have a better companion to help you." He faced Trella. "Keep him safe, and watch for your own safety."

Bracca drew his cloak close, and lifted the hood up over his head. "I'd better leave." He bowed a farewell to Trella.

Eskkar stepped around the table, and placed his hand on Bracca's shoulder. "Before you go, I want to thank you for seeing me safe to Orak. Without you delivering me to the healers, I would never have met Trella. And now I have to thank you again for warning us."

Bracca, half way to the door, halted. "It's nothing that you wouldn't have done for me, if you had the chance."

Eskkar laughed. "Don't be so sure. But you can consider your debt at Marcala paid."

"Well, then I'll sleep better tonight."

"I'll see that Annok-sur passes him through the gate." Trella moved beside their visitor.

Her voice told Eskkar that she wanted a moment alone with Bracca. Eskkar stayed behind as the two of them stepped out onto the landing, and he heard their footsteps on the treads. A murmur of voices floated to him, then silence.

Eskkar went to the table and poured himself another ale. He rarely drank more than a single cup, but tonight was no ordinary night.

He raised the cup to his lips, then hesitated. For a brief moment, Bracca had been alone in the room, while Eskkar went to summon Trella. More than enough time to slip a bit of poison into his cup.

"Damn the gods." Eskkar poured the contents of the cup back into the pitcher. The ale, the wine, even the water, would all have to be discarded, just to be safe. He didn't think Bracca had done any such thing, but the man had warned Eskkar of the very possibility. And it was just the sort of devious thing that Bracca would do.

Eskkar muttered an oath at the evil gods who bedeviled him. Once again, events outside his control were trying to take over his fate. Soon new enemies would be coming for him, eager to strike him down and take by force what he and Trella had labored so long to build. And this time they would move in secret.

Poison, a knife in the back, an arrow from a rooftop, any of a handful of ways to kill a man. And starting tomorrow, Eskkar would have to guard against them all.

He blew out three of the candles, returned to the window and stared down into the garden once again. The watch fire in the courtyard provided enough light to see the leaves on the trees, the branches swaying gently in the night breeze. Bracca had spoken the truth. Eskkar had never admitted it to himself, but Bracca should have stayed at Eskkar's side, either to nurse him back to health or see to his burial.

Eskkar's only friend had broken the sacred code of the warrior, something Eskkar had never done. No doubt the failure to stand by his friend and brother in arms had gnawed at Bracca over the years.

In a way, that proved the man's worth. A lesser man would have soon shrugged off any concerns. Add to that whatever guilt Bracca felt over the fight at Marcala, and the result had brought Bracca to Eskkar's house, to pay his debt to the man he once called his friend.

"What are you thinking, Husband?" Trella closed the door to the Work Room and moved to his side.

"That we've enjoyed many years of peace. That all the problems we've faced since the war with Sumer now seem insignificant. Now threats of war and invasion will change our lives once again."

"Yes, but thanks to your friend, at least we are forewarned. With that knowledge, we can do much to prepare." She laid a hand on his shoulder. "You were glad to see your friend. You tried to mask your feelings, you both tried, but the friendship was there. Bracca felt it, too."

"Well, I suppose. But one thing hasn't changed. Wherever Bracca goes, trouble follows."

"Even so, I'm thankful that he came. Will this change your plans for the Alur Meriki?"

Eskkar considered that for a moment. "No, Bracca's warning only makes the conflict with them even more important. One enemy will be bad enough. The sooner the barbarians are dealt with, the better."

He placed his arm around her shoulder and drew her close. "And now I will have to worry about you every time I leave the city."

"Do not fear for me, Eskkar. Annok-sur and I will take extra precautions. And King Shirudukh of the Elamites may find that Akkad is not as easily taken as the cities of the Indus. He may even find that he is not as safe on his throne as he thinks."

Eskkar kissed the top of her head. "Then starting tomorrow, we will begin preparing Akkad for war."

"Yes, and just like last time, no one must know what we are doing."

"Bracca's spies will soon know what we are up to. He said Elamite spies are already here. He could have named them."

"No, not without putting himself at risk. And we may need his help in the future for more important tasks. I will think about that tonight." Trella leaned her head on his shoulder. "Tomorrow Annok-sur and I will consider what to do. Perhaps we can find a way to take care of the Elamite spies in our city."

In spite of the grim prospect that faced them, Eskkar managed a smile. From tonight on, Trella would turn all her thoughts and efforts into meeting this new threat. Whatever might come from those plans, Eskkar had no doubt that Trella and Annok-sur would teach the king of the Elamites a thing or two about terror.

3

Three days later, in the first light of dawn, Eskkar led a column of horsemen out of Akkad and headed north. The spring morning air still held a chill, but that would soon fade as the sun rose higher. Once again, the long sword jutted up over Eskkar's right shoulder, and it hung as easily as in his younger days.

The smooth-gaited stallion between his legs felt natural, too, the result of many days working with the animal over the last two years. Eskkar always remembered one of his father's sayings – when you ride to war, better to leave behind your sword than your best horse.

Two summers ago, Eskkar had selected the stallion from a string of animals brought down from the mountain country. A group of twenty animals arrived at the cavalry barracks just north of Akkad, and by chance Eskkar happened to be there that day.

Like every person born on the steppes, fresh horses always aroused his interest. He had joined the other horse trainers and handlers as they drifted over to examine the new stock.

Destined to be ridden by the senior commanders, all of the horses represented fine breeding, tall, powerful, and sleek. Except for one, which appeared stunted compared to the others. This bay looked blunt and coarse, with a shaggy coat and a sad little tail that scarcely reached its hocks.

The four horse trainers inspecting the animals gave the odd-looking bay the briefest glance before moving on. Eskkar agreed. The bay didn't belong with this group of fine horseflesh, and he wondered if perhaps an animal had fallen ill or gotten injured, and some clever trader had foisted off an inferior beast on Akkad's buyer.

Trailing behind the trainers, Eskkar stopped in front of the rejected animal. The horse, which appeared too sleepy to pay any attention to those examining it, lifted its head high and eyed him with an expression of superiority out of place with its lowly status. Man and horse stood sizing each other up, and neither showed the slightest intention of lowering their gaze first.

"What do you think of him, My Lord?"

The voice at Eskkar's side belonged to the horse master who had delivered the animals. Eskkar turned to face the man, who had the dark features and short stature that often marked those born in the southern lands of Sumeria. Since almost all the men who worked Akkad's horses came from the northern lands, the Sumerian seemed as out of place as the bay.

Nevertheless, Eskkar knew that many fine horses came from Sumeria, though they tended to be small and fast, more suited to the desert than the mountains. Eskkar recalled seeing the Sumerian once before, and even managed to remember his name, Dimuzi.

"An odd horse to bring to Akkad's barracks, Dimuzi. My commanders need strong warhorses. This one looks more suited to pull a cart than carry a fighter."

The Sumerian refused to acknowledge the rebuke. "There is more to A-tuku than you might think, My Lord."

Eskkar had spent many years in Sumeria riding with his old companion Bracca, and had learned most of the dialects spoken in the southern lands. A-tuku was the Sumerian word for "strength."

Dimuzi unfastened the horse from the holding rail, and turned the animal around. "Look at these hind legs, My Lord. What do you see?"

And Eskkar had looked. A casual glance turned into a studied examination. Muscles bulged in its hindquarters, which, now that he saw the horse from the side, appeared oversized. Eskkar ran his hand down the horse's flank. Hard as bronze.

Interested now, Eskkar inspected every aspect of the animal. He saw a wide chest concealed under the shaggy brown coat that turned black down the legs. Deep hooves that would not wear under heavy riding joined to thick fetlocks that indicated the animal would not go lame easily. Forearms and shoulders showed plenty of power, and the wider than usual nostrils would provide plenty of air for the animal's lungs.

"He might make a good mount." Eskkar reached out and rubbed the horse's neck, moving slowly so as not to upset the animal. At the touch, A-tuku turned to stare at him, as one equal to another.

"What would My Lord think if I said that A-tuku can run faster and longer than most of these other animals? He hates to be bested in a race, and he never gives ground. A-tuku is not aggressive, but every horse that has challenged him has regretted it."

Eskkar knew that Sumerians could never resist bargaining, always pointing out the best features of whatever they happened to be selling. "Is there nothing wrong with him, Dimuzi?"

The man lowered his eyes. "He needs much work, My Lord, and patience. So far only I have been able to work with him. But in his heart, A-tuku is as brave as any horse I have ever seen. For the right rider, he might make a fine warhorse."

Eskkar doubted that. While Dimuzi spoke, Eskkar had circled the animal, and now he stroked A-tuku's forehead. The proud horse's large eyes held his gaze for a moment, then reached out to nuzzle Eskkar's cheek. The simple gesture ended Eskkar's doubts.

"Bring him to my stable, Dimuzi." Eskkar patted the horse's neck one last time. "And I think you'd better plan on staying with him. At least until he proves himself one way or the other."

The Sumerian and Eskkar had worked with A-tuku since that day. Dimuzi's words had proven true. The horse could run, all day if necessary, and it would not quit as long as another horse challenged it. From the first, Eskkar knew he would have to earn the horse's trust. Soon he spent almost every morning working with Dimuzi and A-tuku, teaching the horse the skills needed by a warhorse.

Despite being a hand's width smaller than Eskkar's other horses, A-tuku carried his master's weight as easily as any. Eskkar quickly grasped that he possessed a unique animal, and soon a bond formed between horse and rider as close as any Eskkar had ever known. Together they had raced against every horse in Hathor's cavalry, and fought against them, too, in the mock battles so necessary to train horse and rider in the art of war.

A-tuku's careless gait had proven faster than even Dimuzi had expected. While a handful of powerful warhorses in Eskkar's stable had won races when carrying his weight, in any long run they had all been overtaken by smaller and lighter riders.

Dimuzi claimed that A-tuku had never been beaten when he carried the diminutive Sumerian. And that had proven true. But more impressive was the fact that A-tuku seldom lost even when Eskkar rode him. Eskkar's eyes still gleamed with pride whenever he swung onto his new warhorse's back.

Now the cares and worries of Akkad lessened with each of A-tuku's long strides, as Eskkar left behind the petty problems of a growing and often chaotic City. Even the prospect of a hard fight couldn't dispel the satisfaction he felt at abandoning the cares and endless disputes of the city. He sensed that A-tuku felt much the same, glad to be away from the usual training grounds and out riding free on the open grasslands.

Eighty of Eskkar's best riders rode with him, twenty of them Hawk Clan, the elite force whose bravery had marked them above their companions. Formed as a band of brothers after Eskkar's first battle as leader of Akkad, every Hawk Clan fighter had pledged his loyalty to Eskkar and to his comrades in arms. Hawk Clan warriors not only acted as bodyguards to Eskkar and Trella, but they also insured and enforced the King's power in Akkad.

For this expedition, no new recruits or untested fighters accompanied Eskkar. Every highly trained rider in the troop had fought in at least one action. All of them knew how to fight on horseback. Whether sword, lance, or bow, these men had mastered them all.

The troop of horsemen traveled light, each carrying only his weapons and a water skin. In the preceding days before Eskkar's departure, Trella's clerks and supply people had labored efficiently to ensure that grain for the horses and provisions for the men awaited at each stopping point.

Without worrying about their next meal or what the hunt might bring, the riders covered the miles at a steady gait, pushing their mounts just hard enough to challenge the muscles of both man and beast. Once past the farmlands and irrigation channels that surrounded Akkad on all sides, Eskkar enjoyed the green and lush countryside. The occasional farm or herds of cattle and sheep only made the ride more pleasant.

Eskkar and his men reached the first resupply point, thirty-six miles from Akkad, late in the afternoon, and found it manned by six guards and as many pack men. Food and water waited, with two spare horses in case any of the animals had gone lame. As always, Trella's planning left little to chance. When Eskkar told his wife that he and eighty men wanted to cover almost two hundred miles in less than five days, Trella made sure that everything needed would be available along the route.

Three cooking fires already burned, sending crooked trails of smoke into the sky. The mouth-watering aroma of burning mutton floated over the campsite.

Eskkar slid to the ground with a grunt of satisfaction and lifted his long arms to the sky in a welcome stretch. Despite all his recent training, many months had passed since he'd spent an entire day on the back of a horse, let alone a long ride that finished with the prospect of sleeping on the hard ground.

Nevertheless, Eskkar knew he would sleep well tonight. He filled his lungs with the clean air of the countryside, so different from the thick city-smells of Akkad.

All around him, hungry men swung down from their mounts and stripped off their horse blankets. All the riders saw to their horses' needs first, then rushed to join the lines already forming beside each fire pit.

Drakis, one of Eskkar's senior commanders, stood near the largest cooking fire. Eskkar handed A-tuku's halter over to one of the camp's liverymen. The horse had learned to accept the ministrations of others, though it still proved restive if anyone other than Eskkar or Dimuzi attempted to ride it. Satisfied that his horse would be well cared for, Eskkar turned to find Drakis jogging over to greet his commander.

Short, with a wide chest and thick arms, Drakis had a coarse black beard that climbed up his cheeks almost to his eyes, but failed to cover a scar from a Sumerian arrow that had nearly torn his eye out. Even before that battle, he'd proven his courage in the fight against the Egyptian invaders who had once seized Akkad.

"Must you look so happy, Captain?" Drakis clasped his arms around Eskkar and gave him a powerful hug. "I've been riding for three days, and every bone in my body aches."

Only Eskkar's most senior commanders, or those who had known him in the old days when he was Orak's Captain of the Guard, dared to call him 'Captain.' Still, Eskkar preferred that title to the formal 'Lord Eskkar,' as he was known in Akkad or even worse, 'King Eskkar.'

Such a subservient address, unique to the dirt eaters, always rankled something in his head. A warrior should not need to preen himself before his men, especially while on campaign.

"Serves you right," Eskkar said, when Drakis released him. "You should spend more time on your horse." Eskkar found a fresh patch of grass and spread his cloak, to mark it as his sleeping place. "Tomorrow night will be even worse, after another long day's ride."

Drakis swore at the outlook. "I had to waste two days taking the hill trail and swinging around Akkad."

A city dweller most of his life, Drakis spent the least amount of time of any of Akkad's commanders on the back of a horse. He had ridden in from one of the southern training camps, detouring around the city so that no one would know of his whereabouts.

"Another ten or twenty days riding, and you'll toughen up." Eskkar laughed at the look of dismay on his commander's face.

"You enjoy riding and camping out too much, Captain," Drakis said. "If this fight wasn't against the Alur Meriki, we would have insisted you stay in the city."

Eskkar ignored Drakis's comment. No one had tried to dissuade him from this campaign, not even Trella. Every one of Akkad's commanders knew his experience fighting the barbarian Alur Meriki Clan would be needed in this encounter. They also were aware that Eskkar had a personal score to settle.

Born and raised in the Clan, Eskkar's entire family had died one night in a blood feud, murdered on orders of the clan's Sarum, or king. Only fourteen years old, Eskkar killed his first man that night, stabbing him in the back with a knife. Nevertheless, the stroke came a moment too late to save the life of Eskkar's younger brother.

In almost the same instant, and with her dying breath, Eskkar's mother had cried out for him to run from the Clan and save himself. With his family dead around him, Eskkar had no other choice but to flee.

Luck and his father's fastest horse had helped him escape the same fate as his kin. Even as he ran for his life, Eskkar swore to avenge his family's murder. For the next fourteen years, he had endured the lonely life of an outcast, hunted by his own people yet never accepted and always distrusted by the dirt eaters he was forced to live among.

Eventually he arrived in Orak, where he spent three years as a soldier and handler of horses. A slow spiral of apathy ensued, and Eskkar indulged his fondness for ale to hold back the gloom that filled his dreary days.

Then a stroke of chance and the threat of a barbarian invasion by the Alur Meriki had made him Captain of the Guard in Orak, and the gift of a slave girl named Trella had upended his existence. Trella's keen wits turned Eskkar's life around, and in time placed the power of Orak in his hands, soon renamed the City of Akkad.

And in saving the City from destruction by the barbarian warriors, Eskkar had extracted the first payment of his blood debt. Now he intended to take the full measure to avenge his family's murder at the hands of his former clansmen. At the same time, he would end the Alur Meriki's never-ending depredations against Akkad and its people once and for all.

"By the gods, I haven't been this hungry in months." Eskkar heard his stomach growling with anticipation for a haunch of burnt meat. The cooks had already started handing out the thick slices of mutton.

"Well, there's plenty of food, and ale, too" Drakis said. "Not like the last time we rode out to fight the barbarians. After we've eaten, I'll fill you in on what the men are thinking."

Later, Eskkar's belly stuffed with food and the raw ale favored by the soldiers, he stretched out on the ground with his hands behind his head and let himself relax. "How are the men?"

Drakis tossed the last of the bone he'd been gnawing into the fire, dragged the back of his hand across his mouth, then wiped his fingers on his tunic. "Good. All the subcommanders now know that you're coming. We'll pick up the rest of the horsemen as we travel north. By the time we reach Aratta, our entire force will be assembled there."

Drakis glanced around. All the men were too busy eating and talking among themselves to pay any attention to their commanders. Nevertheless, Drakis lowered his voice almost to a whisper, and his broad white teeth flashed a wide grin in the fire's light. "They'll be surprised to learn where we're going."

The soldiers believed they were on another training march, destined for the tiny village of Aratta, almost two hundred miles northwest of Akkad. Aratta bordered the unclaimed lands, and the village lay just a hundred miles from the base of the Zagros Mountains. When Eskkar and his men arrived at Aratta, talk of a training mission would vanish.

"If we make good time," Eskkar said, "we'll reach Aratta in five, six days at the most."

"And have time to rest there for a day or two," Drakis agreed. "Then the hard march begins."

For months, troops of men and horses, companies of bowmen, spearmen, and slingers, had trained in the cool and hilly horse country, so different from the level countryside surrounding Akkad and stretching south almost all the way to Sumeria.

To maintain the secrecy of this campaign, Eskkar had relied on his subcommanders to prepare the men, and without his usual close inspection of their progress. Now those leaders of ten, twenty, and fifty would be judged by their peers for each and every failure.

"I hope they're ready." Eskkar knew just how much depended on the men and their preparations. "We're going to need every man."

Drakis's laugh held little mirth. "Oh, they are ready. Whether we have enough soldiers to do the job, that's another matter. I still think you should have brought the whole army."

Eskkar grunted. That argument among his senior commanders had gone on for nearly a year. But he had overruled every objection. Too many men away from the city would weaken its defenses, and worse, jeopardize the plan's secrecy. No, if he could not defeat the Alur Meriki with almost a thousand picked men, another few hundred wouldn't make a difference. At any rate, he didn't intend to go over those arguments yet again.

"Get some sleep, Drakis. Starting tomorrow, we'll be doing some real riding."

Drakis groaned.

Smiling at his friend's discomfort Eskkar wrapped himself in his cloak, rolled over onto his side, closed his eyes, and promptly fell asleep. Throughout the camp, one by one, the men of his troop did the same, covering themselves with their horse blankets and drifting quickly to sleep despite the cold earth.

Drakis gazed at the relaxed figure of his friend and commander, and shook his head. The man could sleep soundly on a pile of rocks. With a sigh, Drakis nodded to the guards, kicked dirt over the fire, and tried to get himself comfortable on the hard ground. Eskkar had spoken the truth. Drakis knew he would really be stiff by the end of tomorrow's ride.

In the morning, Eskkar climbed on A-tuku and again led the men north. They hadn't covered much ground before a gentle rain fell from an overcast sky. The wind coming down from the north drove the moisture into their faces as they rode. By midmorning, the drizzle stopped, the sun pushed the clouds aside, and the riders made better time. Still, the wet ground slowed their pace, and most of the sun had descended below the horizon before they reached the next resting place.

Two more days passed in much the same way. As they rode north, the land gradually changed to more hilly terrain, and the thick grass of the south gave way to sparser clumps of vegetation. At the village of Morphoza they joined up with Hathor and two hundred of his horsemen.

Originally from the far off land of Egypt, Hathor commanded Akkad's cavalry. As tall as Eskkar, Hathor possessed the lean body of an experienced horseman. His bald head and darker complexion made him appear even more ferocious than he was.

He had fought against Eskkar in the battle to retake the City, and been captured before he could kill himself. Only Trella's intervention had kept Hathor from Akkad's torturers and saved his life. Every other Egyptian renegade had died that night.

Over the years, Hathor had become one of Eskkar's closest friends. The two men shared many traits. Both were outcasts living in a strange land, and both had found a new home in Akkad. Now they fought together to preserve their adopted city.

The next day, Muta, Hathor's second in command and another two hundred and thirty riders from the training campground of Ramparna linked up with them. With the men that accompanied Eskkar, Hathor's force of mounted horsemen now numbered just over five hundred.

When Eskkar and the cavalry rode into camp at Aratta, he found the remainder of his soldiers waiting. Two hundred archers, carrying the longer and more powerful war bows, had arrived the day before, commanded by Mitrac, Akkad's master bowman. Two hundred spearmen, led by Alexar, and a hundred slingers, under Shappa's command, had reached the gathering place eight days earlier.

Another hundred or so supply men guarded the supplies, extra weapons, and spare horses. Not counting those, just over a thousand fighting men stood ready, though almost none of them knew what enemy they might soon be facing.

In the center of the camp, a large square of linen stretched between four tall posts hammered into the ground. Soldiers and commanders watched in silence as Eskkar dismounted beside the makeshift awning, large enough to shelter ten or twelve men from the sun. The trodden down grass felt soft beneath his feet, especially after so many days of riding.

A glance up at the sun told him that mid-afternoon had just passed, so plenty of daylight remained. Eskkar used it to inspect the men, to see for himself if they were ready to fight, and to search their faces for any signs of fear or doubt.

Eskkar strolled through the ranks, talking to the men and especially their commanders, the leaders of ten and twenty who directed much of the actual fighting. Once any battle started, it fell to these subcommanders to provide the leadership and maintain discipline in the face of the enemy. Their decisions in the heat of battle might mean the difference between victory or defeat.

What Eskkar saw and heard reassured him. The men looked fit and ready to fight. His presence in these unclaimed lands dispelled the last rumors about a training mission. Only a fool could believe the King of Akkad would journey so far north, and with so many veteran soldiers, without a real enemy in mind. Nevertheless, the prospect of a fight only whetted the men's good spirits.

The sun still remained above the horizon when Eskkar and his leaders gathered outside the shelter to eat. The cooks had slaughtered ten cattle that had been turning on spits since morning. After each man received a

thick slice of beef, the cooks tossed all the scraps and handfuls of vegetables into the cooking pot. A cup of stew would complete the soldiers'
hearty meal.

Eskkar chewed away at the tough morsels as eagerly as any of his
men. Unlike his soldiers, he knew it might be a long time before any of
them feasted this well again.

A fine rain began to fall, so Eskkar moved beneath the linen awning.
One by one, his commanders finished their supper and joined him. Drakis
came in last, after making sure the Hawk Clan guards had formed a perim-
eter around the shelter, far enough away to ensure that none of the curious
soldiers listened to their leaders' conversation.

Hathor unfolded the linen map on the grass, stitched with colored
threads to show its features, that he'd brought with him from Akkad. Made
by Trella's craftswomen, the map identified landmarks, watering places,
and possible camp sites.

All the terrain from Aratta to the Zagros Mountains, and the particular
gorge that was their destination, could be identified easily enough. The
map itself was but a copy of the master layout that rested in the Map Room
back in Akkad.

Eskkar and the others took their places around it. He gazed at the faces
of his commanders. Only his most senior men, Hathor, Alexar, Drakis, and
Mitrac, knew the true target of the campaign. The rest of Eskkar's commanders present, Muta, Daro, Shappa, and Draelin, did not. Or at least,
Eskkar hoped they still didn't know.

Back in Akkad, only Trella and a handful of others knew the soldiers'
destination. Trella had gone to great lengths to keep their purpose secret.
The fewer who knew the truth, the better. Even so, all these men had their
wits about them, and any of them might have figured out their real enemy.

"It's time to tell all of you who we're going to fight," Eskkar began.
"You can forget the rumors and wild guesses. We've assembled this force
to march against the Alur Meriki."

Broad smiles greeted his words from those who knew or had guessed
right, while a gasp of surprise escaped from those who'd guessed wrong.

"For almost two years, Trella and Annok-sur's agents have collected
information about the Alur Meriki Clan, and the route of their migration.
Ten months ago, we learned that the barbarians had started their return

from the northeast, hugging the foothills of the mountains. The Clan had traveled nearly to the Indus before they swung north, and some of our spies claimed the barbarians had been pushed back by those dwelling in that distant land."

And that had made more sense as soon Bracca delivered his warning about the Elamites. Of course they would be eager to get rid of a large, hostile force on their northern frontier.

"Now the Alur Meriki are moving back toward these lands," Eskkar continued. "They're not foolish enough to ride through Akkad's country-side, so they'll stay close to the mountains. Far enough away to think they're safe from our soldiers, but close enough to raid our outlying settlements. But this time we have a surprise for them. We're going to cut across their route and force them to fight, at a time and place of our choosing."

He glanced around the circle of faces. Shappa and Draelin had their mouths open. Even Muta and Daro appeared concerned. Eskkar turned toward the youngest commander. Always start with the most junior of your men, Trella had advised. Let them offer their thoughts before the words of the more senior men tended to discourage such discourse.

"Well, Shappa, what do you think?"

When only in his fifteenth season, Shappa had led the newly formed troop of slingers against the Sumerian cavalry. He and his men, most even younger than himself, had managed to hold off a superior force long enough for Eskkar to charge to victory.

Now in his early twenties, Shappa's slim build had changed little in those years, except that he cut his hair short to make himself appear older. Freckles and scars from the pox were sprinkled equally across his cheeks.

"How many fighters do they have?"

"Trella's people estimate that Thutmose-sin, their clan leader, has between twelve hundred and fifteen hundred fighters available. When he includes the young boys and old men, Thutmose-sin can add another three or four hundred to that."

Eskkar ignored the small signs of surprise that came from the men. The Alur Meriki were still considered to be the fiercest fighters in the land.

Shappa's eyes widened. "How many men will we have to face them?"

"Only those here at Aratta," Eskkar replied. "It was necessary to assemble this force in secret. The Alur Meriki have their own spies, and of late they've gotten into the habit of dealing with traders and others who can supply weapons and goods as well as information. That's why this 'training mission' was scarcely mentioned. Except for those here, and a few back in Akkad, none are aware of the real plan."

Eskkar turned to Daro, who had commanded the river archers during the battle against Sumer. "And what do you think of all this?"

"So we'll be outnumbered?" Daro kept his voice confident, though he had only twenty-four seasons. Long brown hair reached nearly to his shoulders. Tall and with the deep chest and muscled arms needed to work the long bow, Daro had married Ismenne, the Map Maker, the woman whose skill had created the map that now rested at her husband's feet.

"Oh, yes," Eskkar said. "But to make up for that, we've picked a place for the battle that will be to our advantage. When the fighting begins, the Alur Meriki, their horses and herds, will be short of water, and weary from their climb into the foothills. The battleground we've chosen is at a small stream that flows out of the mountains. It had no name, but Hathor calls it Khenmet, the water that springs from the rock."

He reached out and tapped the spot on the map with his finger. "If they want that water, they will have to come against us, or die of thirst. Meanwhile we'll have plenty of food and water."

"And that will make up for being outnumbered?" This time Daro let a hint of skepticism slip into his voice.

The smile left Eskkar's face. Daro, too, knew how fierce their opponents were.

"It will have to," Eskkar replied. "I want them to fight. If they thought they were at a complete disadvantage, they might retreat, or slip into the mountains. I want to make certain they give battle." He turned to Alexar. "Has any word of our real plan spread through the ranks?"

"Not yet." Alexar, only a few years younger than Eskkar, had risen to command all of Akkad's infantry. He, too, possessed the deep chest and powerful arms of a bowman.

Alexar and the first troop had marched into Aratta more than thirty days ago, and he had made most of the preparations for the campaign, collecting the food and supplies needed. "I've been talking to the men every day. Most of them still think it's just another damned training march.

They're sick of the hard training, and they've been cursing us all for the last ten days." He chuckled. "I can't wait to see their faces in the morning."

Eskkar joined in the laughter that followed. "Good. Then we'll spend one last day tomorrow training together for the encounter, then move out at dawn the day after. Once we start north, we'll be committed to fighting the barbarians. Our plan," Eskkar tapped again on the map, "is to use water to defeat the Alur Meriki."

Eskkar hunched himself a little closer to the map. "At the battleground, the Khenmet flows directly out of the mountain, near the crest of the trail the Alur Meriki are using. It only flows on the surface for a few hundred paces before disappearing underground. It's fordable even for the barbarians' wagons, and it's the only watering place within three or four days march. We will get to the stream first, and hold it against them."

He drew his knife and used it to point out the landmarks, while every one of his commanders leaned forward to follow his movements. First their starting point at Aratta, then the trail they would follow along the base of the mountains, and finally the location of the stream. All in all, they would have to traverse almost one hundred and fifty miles, most of it over rough ground and uphill.

"With their wagons and herds," Eskkar went on, "barbarians can't move too fast. If they decide to turn around and go back, it will take them at least another four or five days to return to the last stream. By then more than half their people and most of their horses and herds will be dying from thirst. Their only other choice is to attack us, and drive us away from the stream."

The discussion started, with those who'd been unaware of the plan asking most of the questions. Eskkar's other commanders joined in, as each explained how their forces would be used, and how they would work in conjunction with the rest of the soldiers.

Outside, the shadows lengthened, making it hard to see the map. Eskkar called out to the guards, and they brought two torches, which they shoved into the earth. Questions were asked about tactics and the use of the infantry and cavalry. Dusk fell, and now the flickering torches provided the only light.

After a while, Eskkar leaned back, only half hearing their words. He knew the battle plan. He, Trella, and Hathor had gone over it often enough back in Akkad. Now his concern focused on his commanders.

They would be the ones that would make the plan succeed. Eskkar studied their faces. No one showed any trace of fear or doubt. Each of these men, some as mere boys, had followed Eskkar into battle against vastly greater odds before. They all trusted him, his judgment, and battle skills. They knew he would not risk their lives on some foolish expedition. And their belief in his luck gave them confidence.

The torches burned themselves out, and still his commanders talked, argued, and explained. The shadows beneath the shelter grew deeper, until none could see the map before them. When the last question had been asked and answered, the moon had risen well into the sky.

"Get some sleep." Eskkar stepped from beneath the linen and drew in a deep breath of the fresh night air. Like the others, he would sleep under the stars tonight, rain or mist not withstanding.

No leader worth his salt would take advantage of a shelter while his men had only the hard ground for their rest and their horse blankets to keep off the wet. Eskkar watched his commanders, yawning now, as they moved off to check on their men one last time before bedding down for the night.

Hathor lingered behind. "Well, we're committed now. Will it be as close a fight as I think?"

"Yes, it will. No Alur Meriki warrior will refuse to face a smaller force, no matter what position we hold. That's one of the reasons I didn't bring more men. We must make this encounter a challenge to Thutmose-sin, one he dare not avoid."

The name of the great chief of the Alur Meriki, Thutmose-sin, had struck terror and fear into the hearts of his enemies for many years. He would not let a force of dirt eaters defy the Clan. Such a challenge could not be ignored.

Eskkar clasped Hathor's shoulder. They had fought together once before against overpowering numbers, and that had strengthened the bond between them. Eskkar counted the Egyptian among his closest friends, just as Trella considered Hathor's wife, Cnari, one of hers.

"You and your men will be well tested, Hathor. These fighters are not like any we faced at Isin. They will not break easily, nor will they turn and run. We will have to kill them all."

"My men are ready, Captain." He placed his hand over Eskkar's. "We will not let you down."

"I hope so. Otherwise our wives will never forgive us for getting ourselves killed."

4

Two days after Eskkar's departure, Trella climbed the stairs and entered Eskkar's Workroom, the frown on her face deepening when she realized she had kept her guests waiting. She'd asked them to join her at midmorning, and the sun's rays showed that time had come and gone. The two women awaiting her made no comment, of course. Both knew Trella rarely arrived late for any meeting, especially one she had called herself.

Annok-sur occupied the same chair that Bracca had used a few nights before. Tall and spare, she had almost twice as many seasons as Trella. Despite the age difference, the two had forged a strong friendship. Annok-sur guided the large number of agents who collected information not only within Akkad's walls, but throughout the land.

She also made sure that trouble-makers, or those that might present a threat to Eskkar and Trella's rule, left the city. Not all of those who departed did so voluntarily. Those too stubborn or stupid to accept Annok-sur's suggestions to move on found themselves, in the darkest hour of the night, floating face down in the Tigris.

Rumors whispered about bodies found miles downstream from Akkad, many bearing signs of being tortured. Troublemakers who chaffed under Eskkar's rule soon learned to keep their discontent to themselves. The people of Akkad might respect Eskkar, and revere Lady Trella, but they feared Annok-sur, whose network of spies and informers blanketed the City.

Beside Annok-sur sat a much older woman. Uvela believed she had
nearly sixty seasons, though she could not be certain of her age. Unkempt
gray hair cascaded over her shoulders and reached nearly to her waist. A
worn and faded brown dress served her well enough, and helped her blend
into Akkad's poorest districts.

No beauty even in her youth, Uvela's face now displayed the lines and
creases that came from spending her days in the sun. She had survived
many years of hard physical labor. She'd seen two of her children die from
hunger, and another daughter, Shubure, raped and sold into slavery. Nevertheless, at an age that few women ever reached, Uvela remained both
alert and spry, and her sharp eyes missed nothing. She could still put in a
full day's physical labor if called for.

While yet a slave, Trella had met Shubure, Uvela's daughter. Trella
had befriended the girl, and that act of kindness had saved Shubure's
life. Soon afterwards, mother and daughter became the first of many
women Trella relied on to gather information useful to the future rulers
of Akkad.

Even now, Uvela remained the most important of Trella's eyes and
ears within the city of Akkad. Uvela possessed an incredible memory for
faces. She spent her days at the docks, watching people come and go into
the city. Whenever Trella and Annok-sur wanted someone found, information gathered, or someone watched, they turned to Uvela.

Trella closed the door and took her seat across the table, her back to
the wall where Eskkar kept his swords. With the Hawk Clan guards at the
foot of the stairs, no one could overhear their conversation. "I'm sorry to
keep you waiting. There was a . . . problem with Sargon."

She didn't need to say more. Trella's oldest son, Sargon, had entered
into his fourteenth season a few months ago. At that age most sons were
well prepared to work beside their fathers or carry on whatever trade they
had mastered.

Sargon, however, had grown openly rebellious of his mother's wishes,
and even Eskkar's admonishments had little effect on the boy. Sargon preferred the company of his companions to working beside the soldiers and
planners who had built and defended Akkad. Nevertheless, he remained
a favorite of those living in the city, and most inhabitants took a tolerant
attitude toward the heir's youthful wild streak.

Annok-sur and Uvela held a different outlook, as did most of those working or living within the Compound. They understood that Sargon's indifference and lack of diligence promised trouble as he grew older, which did not bode well for the City's future.

"It's of no matter, Trella," Annok-sur said, clearing the air. Whatever new trouble Sargon had gotten himself into didn't concern them, at least for this meeting. "We've been talking about Uvela's new great-granddaughter."

That brought a smile to Trella's face. Uvela lived with her daughter and her extended family.

Composed now, Trella shifted to face Uvela. Despite the steady influx of newcomers to Akkad, Uvela knew more people within the City's walls than anyone. Now that knowledge would be put to use.

"We have need of your skills once again," Trella said. "And this time it may be even more vital to Akkad than ever before."

For more than ten years, Annok-sur and Uvela had helped Trella plan for the continued growth of Akkad, and their influence helped create the policies and laws that guided the city's growth. Their most important function, however, was to insure that Eskkar and Trella's grip on the city remained unassailable. To accomplish that, Annok-sur and Uvela maintained and controlled the large numbers of spies, mostly women, who moved quietly about the city.

In a world ruled by men, women were considered of little use other than to provide comfort to their husbands or masters, work hard from dawn to dusk, and produce children. In consequence, men spoke freely in front of their women. Since Trella had done so much to protect the safety of women, they were grateful enough to help her whenever they could, even if it meant spying on their husbands.

The network of agents also extended far beyond Akkad's walls. Every village in the Land Between the Rivers had at least one of Trella's agents, watching and listening for threats against Eskkar's House. Spies also reported on activity in Sumeria. The southern cities of Sumer, Isin, Uruk, Lagash, and Nippur all contained elements hostile to Akkad and remained a constant peril to its dominance.

Anyone who might threaten that authority was noted, observed, and in some cases, eliminated. Women, it turned out, had proved especially adept at adding a drop or two of poison to a man's ale.

Trella understood well the uses of power and terror, and she used both of them to keep agitators and troublemakers under control. Thieves, pickpockets, even murderers had little to fear from Trella's informants. But threats to her husband, her family, or her city would never be tolerated.

"I asked you here, Uvela" Trella began, "because a new enemy has arisen that threatens not only Akkad, but all of us and our children. Eskkar has learned that a mighty empire exists to the east, and this enemy plans to invade our Land Between the Rivers. Based on the little that Annok-sur and I could discover in the last few days, the Elamites, that is their name, intend to conquer or destroy Akkad, and subject her and all the other cities in these lands to their rule. The Elamites will demand tribute, gold, and slaves in large quantities to feed their growing empire."

Trella paused a moment to let her words sink in. The pleasant expression on Uvela's face vanished, replaced by shock and surprise.

"When these Elamites capture a new city, many of its leading families are killed outright," Trella continued, "especially those that resisted or might threaten their rule. For those families permitted to live, hostages are taken back to the land of the Indus. In this way, the Elamites intend to ensure that Akkad and the other cities they capture will remain docile under their rule. Of course many of their soldiers are stationed in each city to enforce the Elamites' rule. They kill or torture any who fail to obey, often along with their families."

Uvela took only a moment to comprehend the danger. "When will this happen?"

"As far as we know, not this year, and probably not the next," Trella said. "But within two years, the Elamite army will be on the march to our lands. Akkad will likely be their first destination. If they can capture this place, the other cities will either be destroyed in turn, or forced to submit to their rule."

"How did Eskkar learn of this?" Uvela's calm expression had returned. "How certain is he that they will come?"

"I cannot tell you how we learned of this. That is a secret that must be kept. In fact, it must even be kept secret that we know of this at all. But Eskkar and I believe that this warning is true."

"Well, if we have a year or two to prepare," Uvela said, "then there is much you and Eskkar can do to ready Akkad's forces."

"Our soldiers may not be enough," Trella said. "The Elamites have many thousands of trained soldiers, far more than can be raised in this land. Akkad's walls and defenders may not be enough to withstand their greater numbers."

She told Uvela about the Elamites' habit of striking early, and of their practice of infiltrating the cities of their victims.

"It is likely . . . no, it is almost certain, that there are already one or two Elamite spies living within Akkad, and probably Sumer and Isin as well. These are the closest cities to the eastern borders. And it is also likely that Eskkar and I are first on their list for assassination. Annok-sur's role in the city is well known, and she would likely be another target for assassins. The Elamites prefer to strike down those who they think will be most dangerous to them long before their armies appear outside the city's walls."

"Then these spies will have to be found," Uvela said. "We can start by looking at anyone who recently arrived in Akkad."

"Yes, we must do that," Trella agreed. "But many of their spies may have been living here for years. They might not even be from the land of Elam. Any Akkadian might now be in their pay. Not to mention that every merchant, trader, boat captain, anyone who travels to the east and south, may be willing to sell information. Even loose talk may help the Elamites learn of our strengths and weaknesses. And once an Akkadian takes their gold, he may be unable to stop spying for them."

"There are many Akkadian traders doing business with the eastern lands, perhaps fifty or sixty," Uvela said. "If we add in their caravan masters, ship captains, guides, overseers . . . we may be talking about hundreds of people, perhaps more. For a handful of gold, any one of them might become a paid informer."

Trella and Annok-sur had come to the same conclusion. The problem seemed insurmountable.

"What does it matter what information these spies pass to their masters." Uvela shifted in her chair. "Even I can estimate the number of soldiers in Akkad's army, how they are organized, where they are stationed. I suppose that information could be just as easily obtained about Isin and Sumer and the other cities. During the Sumer War, we had a good grasp of our enemies' forces, as they did of ours."

"That's true enough." Trella brushed a few strands of hair away from her face. "But I think there are several problems that need to be addressed. First, we need to gather as much information about our enemy as we can. That must be done as quietly as possible. Annok-sur and I are meeting with Yavtar tomorrow. He knows some traders who may assist us."

Yavtar, once a river trader and now one of the wealthiest men in Akkad, had twice fought at Eskkar's side. Yavtar had also developed the fighting boats used during the Sumerian war, and knew much about the trading routes that extended to the far eastern lands.

"Meanwhile," Trella went on, "we don't want to let the Elamites know that we are aware of their intentions. In this conflict, they already have the advantage of knowing more about us than we do about them. That must change."

"And then," Annok-sur said, speaking for the first time, "we will need to expand the protection around our most important leaders. Trella and Eskkar, of course. Also Bantor and the other commanders. That will include the Noble Families and a few others."

Nine families now comprised the Council that advised Eskkar and Trella. Their advice and influence were important parts of the strength of the City.

"Can we trust the Noble Families?" Uvela's oldest daughter had suffered under one of the ruling families before Eskkar came to power. "Some of them may be willing to take gold from these Elamites."

"We must trust them, to a certain extent," Trella said. "We have to in any case, since they will learn sooner or later about the threat."

"Most are loyal to Eskkar." Uvela paused for a moment, as if considering each of the Families. "But what if the Elamites offered to make the head of any Noble Family the next ruler of Akkad, in return for his support and help? That kind of offer can tempt almost anyone, including any of the younger and wilder sons of the Nobles."

And Sargon could be counted among that number. Trella put the painful thought aside.

"That will have to discussed." Trella smiled at Uvela's quick grasp of the situation. "But right now I am more concerned with finding a way to turn our enemy's strength into a weakness. Eskkar and Bantor will prepare our soldiers for battle, of course. As we gather knowledge of the Elamites, we will also prepare for the invasion. When it comes, we must try to guide the war so that our soldiers are victorious."

"How will we do that?" Uvela's voice sounded dubious.

"Eskkar gave me the idea years ago," Trella said, "when we fought the Alur Meriki at the walls. We will make our strengths seem like our weakest points, and at the same time we will ensure that our weaknesses appear much worse than they are."

"After all," Annok-sur said, "it will still take months for information, or perhaps I should say misinformation, to make its way back to the Elamites. This war will not be like the war against Sumer. In that conflict, news could travel from Akkad to Sumer in a matter of days. By the time the Elamites discover they have been misled, it will be too late."

"If we can guide the course of the war in our favor," Trella said, "we may help bring victory to our men." She glanced at each of the women. "What we discuss here must never leave this room. Right now, only Eskkar and Bantor know what we know."

Uvela nodded in understanding.

"Then we are agreed." Trella leaned back in her chair. "Tomorrow we will make lists of those traders and merchants who deal with the eastern trade. We want to know everything about them, especially if any seem to be in possession of extra gold, or whose sons are quarreling with their fathers or brothers."

"That will be a long list." Uvela shifted in her chair. "What will we do when we discover who they are? Kill them?"

"No, not yet." Trella's voice took on a hard tone that few ever heard. "I want to use them. But first you must find them for us, Uvela. Once we know who they are, we will observe them and discover who else is in their pay. Only when we are sure of ourselves will we get rid of them."

"Meanwhile," Annok-sur placed her hand on Uvela's shoulder, "you will start your most trusted informers searching for any foreigners who have moved into Akkad in the last year or two. Strangers and newcomers must also be found and watched. In the coming months, we must learn much not only about our enemy, but what his plans are."

"All this may take longer than a few months," Uvela said.

"Yes, but we have time." Trella took a deep breath. The war had indeed begun. "Just not any to waste. We have much to do, and it must start with you. Find them for us, Uvela. Find them all. After that, we will watch them, and then we will decide their fate."

5

Four days had passed since Eskkar and the soldiers broke camp at Aratta. The Akkadian force had marched hard every day, moving deeper into the foothills of the Zagros Mountains. A little before noon, under a gray, cloudy sky, Eskkar rode at the head of the column, trailed by his ten Hawk Clan bodyguards. Hathor, Eskkar's cavalry commander, usually led the way, but the Egyptian horse master had ridden on ahead to check on the forward scouts, and Eskkar had taken the lead position.

As he reached the crest of a higher than usual hill, Eskkar held up his hand. His guards, riding in a column of twos, halted, grateful for the rest whatever the reason. The remainder of the force continued up the slope.

An eagle's view lay before Eskkar, and his eyes swept the countryside around him. To his left rose the base of the mountains, an impassable wall of gray and red-hued rock that towered like a giant over the tiny figures of men. The higher peaks carried caps of snow, most of which would not melt even by the end of summer.

To his right, the empty southern lands lay bare, except for the long tendrils of rock and earth that stretched into the horizon, gradually diminishing in size. He gazed out over a vast panorama of rugged country. This high up in the foothills, Eskkar guessed he could see eight or ten miles.

He recognized the landmarks. The army had traveled as far north as possible. Now the men of Akkad would follow the foothills eastward, until they reached the tiny stream called Khenmet. That destination, though, still lay almost fifty miles east of them.

From this spot forward, the army would be crossing over a long series of ridges and steep hills that extended downward from the Zagros Mountains, like the spread fingers on a man's hand. Between each finger of rock lay mostly bare land, sprinkled with wild grass that disappeared with the next climb. Marching across these spurs, both man and beast would be put to the test by the earth gods.

Satisfied that no danger appeared close by, Eskkar twisted on his horse to study his soldiers. The first half of the column was comprised of spearmen, archers, and slingers, all marching in dogged silence as they fought the hilly slope. Behind them rode the double column of horsemen who brought up the rear.

Every man wore the linen tunic Trella's supply clerks had issued. Sand colored, the thick cloth provided warmth while leaving the arms unencumbered and lower legs bare. A wide leather belt that could be laced tight to support the weight of a sword and knife circled each soldier's waist, and sturdy brown sandals protected their feet. Though they had marched a long way, the men displayed little signs of weariness. Months of strenuous training now proved its worth.

The formation showed the importance Eskkar assigned to those who fought on foot. In the event of an ambush by barbarians, the horsemen would charge forward in response. If the enemy attacked from the rear, Muta could wheel his horsemen around in time to face any assault, while archers and slingers provided additional support. On either flank, outriders guarded the twisting line of men and horses.

Since leaving Aratta, each day's journey had challenged every man in the army, and pushed both men and horses to their limit. Still, the march had proceeded smoothly, though slower than Eskkar expected. By his calculation, they were at least half a day behind schedule. So far they'd seen no sign of the enemy.

Today the weather gods had seen fit to bless their journey. Except for a brief rain that slowed them down two days ago, Eskkar's army had made good progress. Now cool winds blew down the slopes, and the flinty snow-capped mountains wreathed in dirty-white clouds threatened to ignore the pale green signs of spring and send one last storm upon them. Tonight the men would huddle close together for warmth, wrapped in their blankets.

The terrain they'd traversed slowed the soldiers' progress. Under those conditions, the four hundred men on foot kept to a pace almost as well as their mounted companions, often forced to dismount and lead their horses. At the end of each day's march, every soldier, mounted or walking, dropped wearily to the ground. Legs and feet suffered the most, but many complained about sore backs from carrying the equipment and supplies Eskkar and the other commanders insisted on.

Despite the best efforts of his men, Eskkar fretted at the time lost on the march. And from this point forward, the ground would be even more inhospitable.

A shout turned his head back toward the east. Two horsemen, scouts ranging ahead of the main force, had raced over the top of the next hill. From the riders' rapid pace, Eskkar decided the chance of good news to be slim. As they drew closer, Eskkar recognized Hathor.

The tall Egyptian must have something of importance to relate, otherwise he would have stayed with the lead scouts. At last the cavalry commander arrived, his big warhorse breathing hard from the steep climb up to where Eskkar waited.

"I think we've been spotted." Hathor guided his horse alongside Eskkar's, so the two men faced each other, their knees almost touching. "We saw at least twenty barbarians, moving to the south, less than two miles away. They saw us at the same time, so there was no use trying to hide. We turned back at once, and I'm sure they're following our tracks."

Hathor and ten riders would be no match for twenty barbarian warriors, not in open country.

"Damn the luck." If Eskkar's main force had made better time, say covered another fifteen or twenty miles, being observed by the enemy wouldn't have mattered. The army would be close enough to the stream to reach it ahead of any Alur Meriki force.

Now the situation could be reversed, with the Akkadians caught short of the stream and needing water. Eskkar noticed Hathor's grim jaw. His horse commander had come to the same conclusions.

"What will the barbarian scouts do?"

Eskkar frowned. "I'm not sure. It depends . . . it depends on too many things. How many men they have, what their orders are, how good their leader is, how large a force they think we might have."

Hathor glanced down the hill, where the last of the horsemen still slipped and stumbled on their way to the top of the crest. "How much faster can we move the men?"

"Not fast enough, not if we want them to be able to lift a sword when they get there." Eskkar took a deep breath and swore. "We need to get to the Khenmet first. I'll take a hundred men and ride hard for the stream. That should be enough to hold it. Then you . . ."

"No, I'll do it, Captain." Hathor used Eskkar's old title, the one he preferred. "You can't leave the men behind. They'll start thinking the worst the moment you're out of sight."

Eskkar's grip on the halter tightened. A-tuku lifted its head in response, and Eskkar patted the animal's neck to steady it. The two commanders didn't have time to argue, and besides, he knew Hathor spoke the truth. "All right, you go. Take two companies and get to the stream as fast as you can. Hold it until we get there."

"I'll take Draelin's men with me."

Those two companies, almost every man a veteran of the Isin War, numbered one hundred riders. Not enough to drive off any sizeable force, but even if Eskkar sent all his cavalry, it wouldn't be enough to withstand the full might of the barbarians. If he sent any more, he'd be splitting his force, always a dangerous tactic in enemy territory.

"I'll be waiting at the stream." Hathor turned his horse around, touched his heels to his mount, and started down the hill, shouting orders to his subcommanders as he went.

"Leave Muta with me," Eskkar called out as the Egyptian rode off. Hathor waved one hand in acknowledgement. If an Alur Meriki horde suddenly appeared galloping over some hilltop, Eskkar wanted at least one senior cavalry commander with him.

Muttering an oath at his bad luck, Eskkar took one deep breath, filling his lungs, then bellowed out the names of his senior commanders. "Drakis! Alexar!"

When they joined him, Eskkar repeated Hathor's grim news. "We'll have to make better time. I don't want Hathor and his men surrounded at the stream and overrun before we can get there."

Drakis shook his head in disgust. "I'll tell the men. But we won't get there before late tomorrow, if the ground stays as bad as this."

"We can leave some gear behind," Alexar said. "Maybe some of the food and spare arrows."

"No, not after carrying it this far," Eskkar said. "We're going to need all those supplies even more. Just get the men to pick up the pace."

Drakis nodded and turned his horse around. "I'll warn the men what's at stake. Let's just hope Hathor doesn't run into trouble."

Eskkar grunted. The war gods and the Alur Meriki made that hope a faint one. The barbarians would find Hathor's men soon enough. Eskkar just hoped that the Egyptian didn't find himself facing the full might of the Clan's warriors.

⸺⸙⸺

Chief Bekka, leader of the Wolf Clan, frowned at the warrior who had galloped to his side. Approaching his twenty-eighth season, Bekka's stocky frame sat lightly on his brown and white warhorse. "A force of dirt eaters? Here? This far north?"

"Yes, Chief Bekka." The scout, a brawny man named Unegen and a leader of twenty, kept his reply formal. "I counted eleven of them. They saw us, and did not run, at least not at first. Only when we moved toward them did they turn away toward the west, riding at a canter."

Bekka didn't like the sound of that. Until this moment, he'd considered scouting these bare hills a waste of time. As the youngest of the Alur Meriki clan leaders, Bekka often drew the worst assignments, such as scouting ahead through empty hills and checking anything of interest along the route. And while that assignment often proved fruitful, this barren terrain promised nothing but rocks and hills.

He'd been about to return to the main caravan. Enough daylight remained to ensure that, if he and his men rode hard, they would reach the wagons of the Alur Meriki in time for Bekka to have a late supper with his wives and children. "Perhaps they were other steppes warriors. Even the accursed Ur Nammu occasionally ride this far east."

Unegen shrugged. "Perhaps it is as you say. They weren't close enough to be sure, but they all wore the same clothing and did not look like warriors."

He guessed that Unegen had wanted to add, 'to me, at least.' Bekka grunted at the subtle criticism. All the same Unegen was one of his best scouts, and an Alur Meriki horseman who couldn't tell the difference between a dirt eater and a steppes rider at any distance didn't deserve to be called a warrior.

Dirt eaters all tended to dress the same, unlike warriors who liked bright colors and wore whatever clothing they preferred, mixed with the occasional animal skin. Dangling feathers ornamented bow and lance tips, and leather strips slung across shoulders held knives and food pouches.

"Your men are following them?"

"Ten men," Unegen said. "I brought the rest back with me."

Bekka opened his mouth, then closed it again. Unegen had taken the right course of action. If there were a large force of horsemen operating in this land, it could only mean trouble. Bekka considered his options. His clan numbered just over eighty, but they were scattered over the countryside, mostly to the south, hunting game and searching for anything of value along the caravan's route.

Bekka had already scouted those lands when Unegen caught up with him. Like everyone else, Bekka assumed any danger to the Alur Meriki would come from the south, not their line of march to the west. Now that assumption would be tested.

A force of horsemen this far north had to be a war party of some kind. The steep hills and endless boulders of these foothills held no dirt eaters or places to grow food, not even enough grass to support sheep or goats for any length of time. These barren lands were meant to be crossed as quickly as possible. The only reason for anyone to be up here was to get water at the stream that flowed from the mountains.

Supper with his family would have to wait. "I'll gather my men and head southwest. We may be able to cut them off. You return to your scouts, and see what else they have discovered. As soon as you learn anything, send riders to find me. I don't want to waste time looking for you."

Unegen nodded. "And the caravan? Should we dispatch riders to tell them what we've found?"

The great caravan of the Alur Meriki moved slowly toward them, still a few days travel from here at their creeping pace. Bekka considered sending word to the caravan. However, he didn't know anything for certain. And only a fool of a clan leader would waste Thutmose-sin's time over a single sighting of so small a force, especially one that had turned away at first sight of Unegen's scouting party.

"No, not yet. Not for a handful of riders. If there is any danger, we have more than enough time. I'll collect as many men as I can and follow you."

Unegen shrugged again. "I'll return to my men." He'd done his duty, and he had his orders. If trouble arose, Chief Bekka would deal with it. Unegen turned his horse around and rode back toward the west. Somehow he felt certain he would get little rest tonight.

At midmorning the next day, Hathor and his two companies reached the crest of one more hill and halted for a brief rest. He felt as weary as any of his men. Not that he cared about that. The exhausted horses, however, needed rest and water. Man and beast had emptied the last of the water skins at dawn, and neither would get much rest, let alone anything to drink, until they reached the Khenmet.

"Commander!" A man raised his arm and pointed to a somewhat higher hilltop a little to the south and about half a mile away.

Hathor's eyes followed the direction, and he saw them, a line of horsemen coming into view. By the time the last rider appeared on the crest, Hathor had the count. Fourteen barbarians, sitting stolidly on their horses, staring down at the intruders.

Hathor's men saw them, too, and now they chattered among themselves, and the ragged line they presented brought a growl to his lips. "Shut your mouths! And form up, instead of gaping. Do you want these barbarians to think you're a bunch of sheep?"

A few grinning heads lowered in embarrassment. While the Akkadians settled down, Hathor made up his mind. That number of barbarians presented no threat to his hundred fighters, and there was no reason to suppose the enemy would waste a large force of riders in these desolate hills.

But somewhere behind them, more barbarians would be gathering. Nevertheless, it would take time, and Hathor might as well push on. The stream, if he remembered right, couldn't be more than twenty or so miles ahead, a good half-day's ride.

The distance no longer mattered. He had to reach it before dark. The new moon had moved into the sky only two days ago. It would rise late, and the slight light it would shed meant no horse could travel safely after dark, not in this rocky land.

Hathor turned to his subcommanders. "Get the men moving. We've still a long way to go."

He put heels to his horse and led the Akkadian cavalry down the hill. He refused to look at the Alur Meriki warriors, though he knew his men would be glancing up at them every few steps. Hathor understood what thoughts raced through his soldiers' minds. They were moving deeper and deeper into the heart of enemy territory, riding straight into danger. And that was exactly how it felt to him, too.

———

On the opposite hilltop, Bekka watched the dirt eaters, his lips moving slowly as he counted the strangers. Unegen, who sat beside him, had sharp eyes indeed. Not another clan of steppes warriors, but dirt eaters. Nonetheless, these strangers knew how to handle their mounts, unlike most of the dirt eaters the warriors encountered. It didn't take long before Bekka had a good idea of who the unknown horsemen were, and where they might be headed.

"Where are they going, Chief Bekka? Are they lost?"

A stupid question, but Unegen was young, less than twenty-two seasons, with much to learn. Bekka softened his reply. "They're heading for the water that flows from the mountains."

Unegen digested that for a moment. "Why go there? Why don't they run from us?"

Bekka ignored the first question. "They don't run from us because they're from Akkad, and they've been taught how to fight by the demon Eskkar, curse him." He spat on the ground to appease the gods for speaking the traitor's name. Bekka's horse jerked its head at the rider's sudden movement.

Bekka faced his subcommander. "Take two men and ride to the caravan as quick as you can. Find Thutmose-sin and tell him everything that we've seen, that we first found eleven, then one hundred dirt eaters. Say that they're heading for the water, and that I will raise as many men as I can to stop them from reaching it."

Without waiting for Unegen to reply, Bekka started giving orders to the rest of his men. In moments the Alur Meriki horsemen disappeared from the hilltop. Once out of sight, they broke into groups of twos and threes, and rode off in different directions. The Alur Meriki had more than one war party scouting these lands, though most of them were too far south to help Bekka. Something tightened in his stomach. He had a feeling that he was going to need every man he could gather.

⸺◦⸺

Hathor and his men pushed their way east, up and down the seemingly endless succession of hills. They rode with care, bows strung, swords loose in their scabbards. Although he could see nothing that smacked of danger, Hathor felt the eyes of the Alur Meriki watching his progress.

His own scouts, six riders spread out along the line of movement, rode with even greater caution, arrows nocked and bows at the ready. At the crest of any hill, they might encounter a hidden band of barbarians ready to cut them down.

The rest of the cavalry rode together, four abreast, with the five pack animals under careful guard in the middle of the column. So far the pack horses hadn't slowed him down, and Hathor didn't dare abandon them. Those animals, and the supplies they bore, might mean the difference between defeat or victory.

The sun moved higher in the sky, passed its highest point, and began to descend. No Alur Meriki had yet challenged their passage, but Hathor knew that time approached. As soon as the barbarians gathered enough warriors, they would harass his movements, even if they lacked enough men to stop him. When they thought they had enough, they would attack in earnest.

The Akkadians kept moving, the men dismounting to lead the horses up the steepest part of the trail. By now his riders were too tired even to swear at their misfortune. The sun kept moving, too, falling toward the horizon.

A shout from his rear guard snapped Hathor's head around. A band of twenty or so warriors, perhaps the same one he'd seen earlier, was traversing another hill to the Akkadian right. They'd come from the south, and now moved in the same direction as Hathor. The barbarians had fresher horses, and their riders didn't carry the burden of the extra food and weapons.

Whatever the reason, they were making better time across these hills, and at this rate they would reach the stream before him.

Up ahead, Hathor watched his scouts disappear over the top of the next hill. A few moments later, one of them reappeared, waving his arms. Hathor kicked his horse into a canter, and rode up the hill to join him.

"The stream's not much farther, Commander. I think I recognize the landmarks you described." He pointed to a pair of almost identical boulders, tall and slim, that pointed like angled fingers toward the mountain peaks. Each stone stood four or five times the height of a man.

Hathor halted his men while he studied the landscape. Mountain crags towered to his left, while fingers of rock extended from their base, as if to lend support to the vast weight of stone soaring above them. He, too, remembered that two large boulders marked the trail, with the stream less than a mile ahead.

Of course all the rocks looked much the same, and it had been over a year since he'd ridden these hills. Still, he agreed with the scout, it couldn't be much farther. If it were, they weren't going to make it before dusk.

"Two more hills," Hathor said. "Call the rest of the scouts back, except for two. We might as well all arrive together."

No sense in having a few men picked off by the barbarians, or even having his scouts chased back to the main force.

Draelin rode up to join his commander. Hathor had given him responsibility for the rear guard.

"Any sign of the barbarians?" Draelin's face showed that mixture of nervousness and excitement that often accompanied men riding into battle.

"No, but they're probably all around us by now," Hathor said. "The Khenmet isn't far ahead. Tell the men we just need to push over one or two more hills, and we'll be there. Tell them to ready their weapons, and make sure they stay close together."

Draelin laughed. "They'll be glad enough. They're sick of riding and walking."

Hathor's second in command turned his horse and rode back to the rear. As the word spread through the ranks, men prepared themselves and their horses. They loosened their packs, so they could be discarded at a moment's notice. The short rest would have to do.

Hathor waited until Draelin gave the signal that he was ready. "Move out!" The Egyptian's voice easily carried the length of the column.

They rode down the slope, enjoyed a brief respite of almost flat ground for a few hundred paces, then another gradual ascent up the next hill. Once again Hathor found the two scouts waiting at the crest, and when Hathor reached it, he understood why.

A line of barbarian warriors stretched across the top of the next hill. As the rest of Hathor's men reached the top, he took a count of the enemy.

"Between forty and forty-five," Hathor commented, as Draelin reached his side.

"There could be five hundred waiting for us behind the hill."

Hathor shook his head. "If there are, we're finished, whether we go forward or back. So it doesn't matter. They're between us and the stream. We've no choice now but to attack." He stretched himself upright and took one last look around. The hills behind them remained bare of life. For this battle, at least, only the barbarians in front of him mattered.

Nevertheless, Hathor didn't like what he saw. He and his men would be attacking uphill, always a disadvantage. That, too, no longer mattered. His men needed the Khenmet's water.

"Form the men in two lines, sixty in front and forty behind the center. That way they won't be able to charge downhill and just ride through us. You take the left flank, and I'll take the right. If we can envelop them, so much the better. As soon as you're ready, we'll go. Tell the men to shoot as soon as they're in range, but not before."

"Yes, Commander."

With a shout of excitement, Draelin wheeled his horse around and trotted off, calling out orders as he went. Hathor called up his leaders of ten and twenty, and gave them the necessary orders. "Remember, watch for any sudden shifts of their line. Wherever they try to break through, shift your men to take them from the flank."

Each of his commanders would pass his words to the men, so that every man knew what was expected of him. It took only moments, as these

Akkadians had trained and practiced maneuvers such as this hundreds of times. When Hathor felt satisfied that every one understood the order of battle, he moved to his own position just to the right of center and waited until Draelin situated himself in a similar position on the left.

The column of fours broke in two parts, then separated again, forming a front line of sixty riders, with the second line of forty about thirty paces behind the first. Each man settled into position a pace apart from his neighbor. As Hathor inspected his men one last time, he saw no signs of fear or confusion, only riders loosening swords in their scabbards, testing their bows, and fitting arrows to bowstrings.

Almost all of these men had fought a mounted battle before, and at Isin they attacked an enemy four or five times greater in size. These Akkadians knew what to look forward to. The Alur Meriki, Eskkar claimed, did not expect to confront men who could ride and shoot at the same time. Now that idea would be tested.

Hathor glanced down the line to where Draelin sat astride his horse, bow in hand, waiting the command to attack. Hathor saw the excitement on their faces and reflected in their movements, but still not a trace of fear. All the men were ready. Hathor drew his sword, raised it up, then swung it forward. "Move out!"

Draelin's shout echoed his commander's. The two lines surged forward and down the hill, moving at an easy canter and maintaining a good line. Nevertheless, the animals sensed the tension of their riders. Horses whinnied in excitement and tried to surge ahead, while the ground shook from their hooves as they went down the hill.

As soon as the horsemen reached the middle of the flat expanse, the men would kick their horses into a fast canter. The Akkadians wouldn't be in range of the barbarian bows until they reached the foot of the next hill. Then the order to gallop the horses as fast as possible would be given.

Hathor tightened his grip on the sword as the front line reached the bottom of the hill and increased their speed across the open space.

—⟨⟨⟨◊⟩⟩⟩—

From the opposite hilltop, Bekka sat on his horse and watched the Akkadians make their preparations. They wasted no time, showed no confusion, and he detected no signs of fear in any of the riders facing him. Every rider carried a short, curved bow, much like those his own warriors carried, and Bekka guessed these intruders knew how to use them. They handled their bows and horses almost as well as his own men.

Never before had Alur Meriki horsemen faced dirt eaters who knew how to use a bow from horseback. Their calm preparations proved that they had faith in themselves and their weapons. Their leader didn't even bother to urge his men to the attack.

The more Bekka observed, the less he liked the prospect of this battle. In each previous encounter with Akkadian soldiers, every warrior who had faced Akkad's dreaded longbow archers soon learned to respect the power of those weapons. If these dirt eaters had mastered the same skills with the smaller bows . . .

Kushi, a leader of twenty who had joined Bekka earlier in the day, moved his horse beside that of his chief. One of Bekka's cousins, Kushi had taken charge of Unegen's men in his absence and was now Bekka's second in command. Together they watched the dirt eaters form two battle lines. "They'll flank us."

Kushi, too, understood the size of the line and what it meant. The mass of horsemen in the center would slow down any charge trying to cut through the Akkadians, which was exactly what Bekka had intended to do, tear through them and regroup on the far side. Now he knew that wouldn't work. His warriors would break through the first line, he felt certain of that, but those that survived would be riding into forty more enemy arrows shot at close range.

Long before his Alur Meriki fighters, those that survived the first encounter, could hack their way through the second line, the weight of dirt eaters on their flanks would be on them, putting arrows in their backs. If the enemy knew their business, Bekka's warriors would be enveloped and cut to pieces. He could lose every man.

Bekka took one final look behind him. For most of the day, warriors in two and threes had ridden to join him. Many of these he had dispatched as soon as they arrived, ordering them to scour the countryside until they located the two main war parties still many miles to the south.

By now a large force of warriors would be galloping over empty lands toward this place from many directions, but none had arrived yet. He'd hoped to convince the enemy horsemen that he had reserves behind the hill, perhaps even make them hold off their attack and send out some scouts, but the Akkadian commander hadn't wasted a single moment worrying about that.

Instead, the Akkadians would soon be pouring arrows into his flanks. Bekka's men might hold the center, might even inflict heavy casualties on the men charging up the hill, but whatever advantage he got during that first exchange, he would pay twice over for it when the dirt eaters reached the crest and wheeled their horses into his flanks and rear. Then it would be the Alur Meriki under the gauntlet as they were driven down the slope, while bowmen shot arrows at them from every direction.

Even if Bekka could win this fight, or manage to slow down the attackers, most of his men would be dead. Across the hilltop, Bekka watched a tall rider on the left flank draw his sword. For a moment, he wondered if it might be the traitor Eskkar. Not that it mattered. As the weapon swung down, the Akkadians gave a shout and the line began its descent.

"Damn them." Bekka just did not have enough warriors, and he didn't intend to waste the lives of his kinsmen fighting against a trained force more than twice the size of his. "Get the men out of here. We'll form up on the other side of the stream."

If Kushi were unhappy with the order, he didn't show it. "Yes, Chief." He rode off, shouting orders as he went, and no doubt giving thanks to the gods that he wasn't in command.

Bekka took one last look at the Akkadians. "Damn you to the pits, Eskkar." Then he turned his horse around and started down the slope. Some of the men protested, and few launched arrows at the approaching horsemen, but most seemed glad enough to avoid this fight. The Alur Meriki had no qualms about turning away from a fight against superior numbers. A war leader was expected to win fights, not waste the lives of his warriors.

Nevertheless, by the time Bekka splashed across the stream, he had started worrying about how news of this retreat would be received in Thutmose-sin's tent. The punishment for cowardice in front of an enemy was death.

6

The halting horn's deep bellow signaled the end of another day's traveling. With sighs of relief, the women and old men driving the Alur Meriki wagons eased them to a stop, each one turning this way and that, searching for the best place to set up camp. But though the day's journey had ended, much still remained to be done before anyone could take their ease. Everyone, women, girls, younger boys, and slaves who'd walked beside their family's wagons all day, now readied the night camp for their kin.

The youngest wandered off to gather wood and dung chips for the fires, while others pitched sleeping tents beside the wagons. The herds of sheep, cattle, goats and pigs also needed to be settled down for the night. That task fell to the older girls and young maidens not yet women.

With long switches, they guided the weary animals to their final foraging of the day, letting them search out the occasional clump of grass before settling down to their own respite. As during the day's march, the food animals stayed north of the wagons.

On the south side, warriors and older boys saw to the horse herds. Every fighter in the Clan possessed at least two or three horses. No young man dared approach a maiden's father seeking to take a wife without a satisfactory number of horses to prove his status and worth. The most successful men boasted even larger herds, eight or ten, more if the warrior had a slave or two to tend them.

The day's journeying had ended, and everyone in the caravan looked forward to a night of rest. The gradual climb up the slopes of the foothills had wearied the long line of travelers, hindering the caravan's already slow pace. Still, everyone knew that in another four or five days, the Clan would start its descent into the grasslands that bordered the northern steppes.

Thutmose-sin, the Great Chief of the Alur Meriki Clan, rode up to the two wagons that contained his wives, children, and possessions just as the final blast of the horn sounded. He'd spent the day riding to the south, examining the land and making sure that his warriors attended to their duties. Thutmose-sin, too, looked forward to a peaceful evening with his kin.

Tall and broad, Thutmose-sin had more than forty-five seasons. Nevertheless, he yet possessed much of the strength of his youth. Spending most of each day on the back of a horse ensured a man stayed fit. Thutmose-sin seldom let a day go by without taking time to practice with at least one of his weapons.

Doing so kept him proficient with sword, lance, bow, and knife. No leader of the vast Alur Meriki Clan dared appear weak. A challenge to his rule could arise at any time, and Thutmose-sin kept himself prepared.

As he slid from his horse, Thutmose-sin heard the rolling beat of hooves, mixed with the shouts and curses of those forced to scatter as a rider galloped his way toward the Sarum's wagons. Thutmose-sin's guards, all of them kinsmen to some degree, moved forward, should they be needed. But the arriving horseman dragged his mount to stop before the guards could intercept him.

The rider's horse, covered with dried lather and foaming at the mouth, had to spay its legs wide to keep upright. The rider slid down from his exhausted mount, and glanced around, until his recognized his Sarum. The copper medallion that glistened on Thutmose-sin's chest identified him to all as the Great Clan's leader.

Thutmose-sin recognized the dust-covered warrior. Unegen, one of Bekka's leader of twenty. Thutmose-sin made it his business to know as many of his commanders and leaders of twenty as possible. This one had already been marked down as one who might be destined for more responsibility.

A slave ran forward, carrying a water skin, and handed it to Unegen. By the time he handed it back, Unegen had gulped down half a skin of water and poured the rest over his face and chest. Like his horse, sweat and dirt covered most of his body.

Thutmose-sin felt his peaceful evening slipping away. No one rode a valuable horse as hard as Unegen had unless he carried important news. And such news seldom boded well.

"Great Chief," Unegen began, "I am . . ."

"I know who you are." Thutmose-sin voice remained calm. After all the years of fighting with other steppe clans, dirt eaters, and trouble makers within his own clan, not much remained that could rattle the battle-hardened leader of the Alur Meriki. "Did Bekka send you?"

"Yes, Sarum. He ordered me to bring you this news. We were riding to the west and we encountered eleven dirt eaters on horseback. They turned back when they saw us, and we followed. They rode hard, and by the time we caught up with them, the eleven had turned into a hundred, all of them carrying bows. They moved toward us, and we gave ground. Bekka ordered me to report to you, and to say that he thought the dirt eaters were heading for the stream."

Strange riders of any kind in these empty foothills likely meant trouble. "These dirt eaters, they showed no fear at encountering our warriors?"

"No, Sarum. They moved with purpose and with great speed. They rode . . ."

"Hold your words, Unegen. I want to summon the clan leaders. We might as well all hear your news at the same time."

Thutmose-sin turned to his guards. "Find Altanar and Bar'rack. Tell them to come at once." By now those two clan leaders had returned to their wagons somewhere in the caravan. The only other clan chief, Urgo, had camped a hundred paces away. Thutmose-sin would fetch Urgo himself. Three more clan leaders were out scouting and raiding with their men to the south and southwest, picking up slaves, livestock, or anything else of value to the Clan.

Unegen, Urgo and Thutmose-sin already sat on the mostly bare ground just beside the Sarum's wagon when Bar'rack and Altanar arrived. The five men formed a close circle, their feet almost touching. Chioti, Thutmose-sin's first wife, made sure that each man had a cup of water at his hand before bowing low and leaving them to their business. She would make a circuit of the wagon, to make sure that no one loitered close enough to hear what the men said, or disturbed the gathering.

More than a little nervous at being the center of such a gathering, Une-gen repeated what he had told Thutmose-sin. "These dirt eaters showed no fear of us, and they rode their horses well." He reconsidered his words. "I mean, they rode well enough for dirt eaters. And they carried bows. Not the long bows used from the city's walls, but ones such as we use."

Thutmose-sin smiled. No warrior would ever admit that a dirt eater could ride as well as the clumsiest member of the Alur Meriki.

"And Bekka believed these riders were heading for the stream?"

"Yes, Sarum. Where else could they be going?"

Only a young warrior in his first council meeting would dare to point out something to his Sarum.

"If they rode hard," Altanar said, "they might have reached it by now."

A year older than Thutmose-sin, Altanar led his own clan with both wisdom and strength. He had taken an arrow in his shoulder fighting at Orak's walls and nearly died. Since that battle, Altanar had stood beside Thutmose-sin and, as much as any friend could, helped him rule the Great Clan.

"These riders," Thutmose-sin picked at a clump of the sparse grass before him, "they must be from Akkad."

"Who else would have so many horsemen?" Bar'rack's words carried conviction. "Akkad has grown bold if they would challenge us in these hills, so far from their walls."

Bar'rack, the youngest of the clan leaders, had led the Antelope Clan for the last six years. Twelve years ago, Bar'rack's brother had been slain by the outcast Eskkar and his soldiers just before the siege of the village began.

Bar'rack had sworn the Shan Kar, the blood oath to kill the slayer of his kin. He, too, had taken an arrow in his arm at the siege of Orak. Since then he nursed a deep hatred of Eskkar and all dirt eaters.

"They cannot hold the stream with a handful of riders, especially if they are not carrying the long bows." Altanar, like the other clan leaders, retained a healthy respect for the skill of the Akkadian archers. "Our warriors will sweep them aside, if Bekka and his men have not already done so."

"Perhaps they intend to ride into the mountains," Bar'rack said. "They might know trails through the foothills. Wherever they go, we'll hunt them down."

"There are no trails through the hills for so many men, no paths that go anywhere," Urgo said, joining the discussion for the first time. "Besides, they know we would track them down and kill them within days."

Every eye went to the oldest man in the circle. Urgo, another cousin of Thutmose-sin, carried nearly ten more seasons than his leader. Many considered him the wisest of all the warriors, and his advice helped govern the Clan.

Urgo also planned and mapped out the routes chosen by the Alur Meriki in their migrations, making sure they traveled efficiently and that the Clan always journeyed over routes with plenty of forage and water. His sharp wits could recall better than any of his fellow warriors every trail, path, stream, and river that the Clan had traversed in the last thirty years.

Last year, Urgo's horse had slipped on some rocks, throwing its master. The fall broke one of Urgo's legs. He also hurt his back. The injuries had almost killed him, and now pain accompanied Urgo's every move, forcing him to stay close to his wagon. He could only ride a horse with difficulty, and for brief periods.

"What do you think, Chief Urgo?" Thutmose-sin used Urgo's full title, to make sure the others listened to his words.

"The outcast Eskkar still rules in Akkad, and he is no fool. He would not waste horses or men so far to the north without some purpose. If he has decided to come forth from his walls and challenge us, the best place for such a challenge would be the stream. If he has enough men to hold it against us, even for a few days, many of our horses, herds, and women and children will die."

All of them understood the need for water. The large number of horses and livestock, as well as the people of the Alur Meriki, depended on reaching the stream within the next few days.

"How can he challenge us with only a hundred or so fighters?" Bar'rack shook his head. "We've seen no sign of men or horses from the south. Our riders would have warned us if such a force approached."

"He would not challenge us with so few," Urgo agreed. "If he plans to do so, then he will bring many more men than a hundred."

Thutmose-sin turned to Unegen, sitting in silence between Altanar and Urgo. "What direction did these riders come from?"

"They came from the west, riding along the base of the foothills. We were hunting, and did not expect to see an armed party approaching from that direction. The land there is almost empty of game, and there is not enough water and grass to sustain even a small herd of horses."

"If Eskkar amassed a large force of horsemen far to the west," Urgo said, "and he was cunning enough to know when and by what route our caravan travelled, he could move his soldiers toward us without being seen by our scouts."

"Well, we'll know soon enough," Altanar said. "We should send more warriors to the stream."

Urgo shook his head. "It may be too late for such a move. Our water stocks are already low, and the caravan will be out of water in two days, three at most. We expected to be at the stream by then. If we find the Akkadians there, and cannot drive them away from the water, we will lose many animals."

He glanced around the circle, taking his time before speaking. "I think we should turn the caravan around. If we push hard, it is only four days back to the last watering place, perhaps less. And much of the traveling is downhill. If it turns out there is no danger, we will have lost but a few days."

Only a man with Chief Urgo's wisdom and experience could speak about turning back in the face of a few dirt eaters. Anyone else would have been branded a coward for uttering such despicable words.

Thutmose-sin considered Urgo's suggestion. The caravan had turned back before in the face of some unexpected obstacle, but not for many years, and never because of a threat from mere dirt eaters.

"Many will die if we turn back," Altanar said. "We have no water to spare."

The Alur Meriki women's duties included laying in stocks of water to supply each wagon with enough to reach the next watering hole. And they had done so. But no wagon wanted to burden itself with extra water weight when there was no need.

The women knew when the caravan expected to reach the stream. Most would have stored a little extra for their families, but not enough for the horses or herd animals. Hundreds, perhaps many more, would die of thirst. No one had considered the possibility that they might be prevented from reaching the water.

"We have time yet before we make such a decision," Thutmose-sin spoke quickly before an argument started. "Besides, by now, Bekka may have dealt with the problem."

He turned toward Unegen. "Return to your clan chief. Tell Chief Bekka to search out the route to the west, and see if there are any more dirt eaters approaching. When you have learned what you can, return here." He gazed at each of the other clan leaders. "Is there anything else to say?"

No one answered. The silence, of course, only meant that no one wanted to challenge Thutmose-sin's decision, not necessarily that they approved of it. He stood, ending the meeting. "Meanwhile, Altanar and Bar'rack will gather our forces and move toward the stream, just in case they are needed."

The others rose with their Sarum, bowed, and departed. Only Urgo, climbing slowly to his feet, lingered behind.

Thutmose-sin met his gaze. "You are troubled by this, old friend?"

"Yes, Cousin. These dirt eaters, Akkadians as they now call themselves, have grown strong. Twice before we have fought against them, and both times we've taken heavy losses. During these years, their numbers have grown, and now they deem themselves rulers of this land."

Urgo did not have to add 'as we once did.' The burden of those defeats weighed heavily on the leader of the Alur Meriki. Thutmose-sin had an even more personal reason to hate Eskkar and the dirt eaters of Akkad – the whorl-shaped scar on Thutmose-sin's forehead had come from the pommel of Eskkar's sword.

Thutmose-sin had been within a single sword stroke of killing the outcast leader of Akkad's forces. Instead, Thutmose-sin's sword had shattered on his foe's blade, and Eskkar recovered enough to strike back, hard enough to render Thutmose-sin unconscious.

"They do not rule these lands yet," Thutmose-sin replied.

"Still, there is no denying their power and fighting skills any longer." Urgo shook his head in dismay at the idea. "The traitor Eskkar is no fool, to send a hundred armed and mounted fighters to their death. Even he cannot afford to waste so many men. I still say you should turn the caravan around while you deal with this threat."

"And if the purpose of these strangers is to split our warriors away from the wagons, then what?" Thutmose-sin shook his head. "We might be risking more if we turn back."

"Perhaps it is as you say."

Urgo did not sound convinced. Thutmose-sin clasped his hand on the older man's shoulder. "A handful of warriors should not make our people turn in fear, old friend." He smiled at his cousin. "Tomorrow we will know more about what lies ahead. Then we will decide."

Urgo's stared into the eyes of his sarum. "Let us hope the decision is not already made for us."

7

athor slid down from his horse, patted the animal's neck, and stepped into the stream. The clear water, fresh from the mountains, chilled his feet, and he stood in it only long enough to quench his thirst, scooping handful after handful to his mouth. Around him, all the men and horses gulped the cold water, cleansing their dry mouths, tossing it over their faces and chests, and filling their bellies. Some in their exuberance splashed water on one another. The refreshing water tasted even sweeter after driving the barbarians out of their path.

The horses attended to, Hathor's riders guided their animals away from the fast flowing water. They had to drink slowly, to ensure that they did not swallow too much too fast. The men would bring their mounts back later for a second chance to satisfy their thirst.

Lifting his gaze, Hathor studied the barbarians who had retreated reluctantly before him. Just over half a mile away another hill rose up to the east. The enemy fighters had ridden up the slope that ridged the sky. From there, they stared down at the Akkadians. A few still brandished their bows or lances, while other expressed their anger by shouting what must be curses in his direction. If what Eskkar said were true, these fighters hated to retreat, especially after a challenge by those they called dirt eaters.

They could shake their fists and wave their weapons as much as they wanted. All that mattered was that Hathor's men had the stream, and if anyone wanted a drink of water, they would pay for it with their blood.

The brief encounter between the two forces had taken only moments. The flight of arrows launched by the barbarians had wounded two horses, and Hathor doubted the shafts of his own riders had done any better, especially shooting uphill, always a difficult shot.

His men might bask in the glow of their small victory, but Hathor needed to hold this position until Eskkar and the rest of the Akkadians arrived. Handing his horse over to one of his men, Hathor paced the length of the stream. From its origin in the northern cliff wall, the Khenmet flowed in a nearly straight line for almost four hundred paces before it disappeared into another maze of impenetrable rocks and steep, gray crags.

He knew the stream travelled underground for more than two miles before it emerged from a cleft in the rocks as a waterfall, its clear waters then plunging several hundred paces to a rock-filled canyon below. From there the water flowed south, slicing its way through more cliffs and crags, and still inaccessible to a horse or wagon.

And while a man might risk his neck and clamber down the canyon's walls to slack his thirst, by the time he regained the land above, he'd be as thirsty as when he started.

Even worse for the barbarians, the caravan of wagons and livestock would have to be left behind, as the terrain to the south was far too rough. If the Alur Meriki did not cross the stream here, they would be forced to travel nine or ten miles over treacherous cliffs and rocky ground to the south before the stream reemerged and gave them a place to access the water.

But those ten miles would take several days to traverse, and leave them no better off than they were now. They would face another four or five days of rough travel just to get back to the trail, leaving them still short of water for the rest of their descent from the mountains. No, the Alur Meriki would water their herds and ford here, or turn back toward the east and retrace their path.

Hathor let his eyes sweep the terrain. He'd been here before with Eskkar, but that was more than a year ago, when Eskkar first hatched the idea of an ambush. With a handful of riders, they spent almost twenty days exploring the pass and hills that marked the likely Alur Meriki migration trail, until they found this place. Hathor remembered how Eskkar's eyes had widened in satisfaction at the find.

"A good place to give battle," Eskkar had said. They remained at the Khenmet most of a day studying the land before moving on to the east.

Only when they had discovered all the possible watering places within four or five days ride did a satisfied Eskkar and his men turn their horses' heads toward Akkad.

As soon as he and Hathor returned, they met with Ismenne the Map Maker. From their descriptions, she sketched out the all the land from Aratta to the Khenmet, laying out the routes and the Alur Meriki migration path. Once completed, the planning for this expedition had begun.

Hathor took another look at the stream, less than forty paces wide. The water splashed noisily from a cleft between two large rock formations, both tall and formidable. While not particularly wide or deep – Hathor guessed that he could throw a stone from one bank to the other – it gave the Akkadians another advantage besides a place to quench their thirst. But for a horse charging through the chilly waters, the current would slow both horse and rider, and make them an easy target for his archers.

Draelin, still leading his horse, strode over to stand by his commander. "Where do you want the men?"

Hathor turned away from studying the stream to gaze at the north rock wall rising above him. "I want the men closest to the cliffs. Have them form a defensive line starting from there."

"We don't have enough men to hold the length of the stream."

"I know, but if they overrun us, we can keep our backs to the cliff, and our archers can control the crossing."

It wasn't much of a defensive plan, but it would have to do. "Picket the horses in the little hollow in the cliff," Hathor ordered. "That should give most of them some protection from the barbarian arrows."

"We're going to fight on foot?" Draelin sounded dubious at the idea.

"Oh, yes, at least until Eskkar gets here." Hathor lifted his gaze once more toward the enemy hilltop. "If the barbarians arrive in force, they'll overwhelm us if we try to match them on horseback."

"I'll settle the men in," Draelin said, his eyes already searching the ground for the best possible fighting position.

"And see if we've got anyone who knows how to climb," Hathor said. "Eskkar claimed a fit man could scale that cliff. A pair of eyes up there would be useful."

Draelin's mouth opened as he stared up at the seemingly sheer cliff. "I'll ask. Maybe some fool will volunteer, but don't expect me to try it. I'd just fall and break my neck."

Hathor laughed. "I wouldn't attempt it either. But Eskkar will have a few slingers with him who can do it, I'm sure. Wait until morning before you ask anyone to try. It'll soon be too dark to see anything." He turned his gaze back across the stream to where the Alur Meriki watched. "I wonder what they're thinking about?"

"Nothing good for us," Draelin said. "I just hope Eskkar gets here by tomorrow."

"If he doesn't, we're all going to be dead."

Neither man worried about that. The earth would have to open up and swallow Eskkar and his men before he let anything stop his march to this place.

The two commanders trudged back to where their men waited, holding the halters of their mounts.

"Subcommanders! Everyone!" Draelin's voice echoed against the cliff. "Every tenth man, collect the horses and move them into that cleft. The rest of you, form a line twenty paces from the stream, every man a step apart. Once you've taken your position, put down your bows, and we'll all start carrying rocks from the stream. I want to scatter a layer of rocks between us and the stream, to slow down any charging horsemen. Everyone, keep your swords with you at all times."

Hathor nodded approval. Plenty of work still remained to be done. To make matters worse, there would be no fire, as the bare ground this close to the mountains held little in the way of trees or bushes. With the coming darkness, the Alur Meriki might try to attack, or even attempt to steal or stampede the horses. The tired Akkadians would get little sleep tonight.

—⚬—

At midmorning the next day, Bekka returned to the hilltop once again and stared down at the invaders. They kept busy, and except for a line of sentries, ignored the hill to their east. Bekka, meanwhile, cursed the slow gathering of his fighters.

The number of warriors under his command had grown slowly since yesterday, as the men he had dispatched to collect the Alur Meriki raiding parties had rejoined his force. At least twenty members of his clan had come back, and another fifteen or so had not yet reported. At last count, Bekka had close to seventy fighting men under his command.

The dirt eaters remained in their protective half-ring, with their horses bunched up in the gully behind them. Every man kept his bow and weapons at hand, and Bekka had no doubt they knew how to use them.

A shout made him turn to the east. He saw Kushi galloping his horse down the adjoining hill, across the flat space, then scrambling up the slope to join his clan chief.

"Chief Bekka," Kushi began, then had to catch his breath. "Chief Chulum and his warriors are here."

Bekka could not hold back a brief frown. He'd known that Chulum and the warriors of his Serpent Clan rode closest to his position, but with a little luck it might have been one of the other chiefs who arrived first. Chulum, five years older than Bekka, had risen to command of the Serpent Clan only five or six years ago, and he'd done it by sheer strength of will. No man questioned his fighting skill or courage, but he'd yet to prove himself as a wise leader.

His name, Chulum, meant "stone," and the members of his clan muttered among themselves, though not when Chulum might overhear, that he'd been aptly named.

"How many riders with him?"

"All of his clan, I think," Kushi said. "Ninety, perhaps a few more."

Bekka gritted his teeth at the news.

The sound of hoof beats echoed over the hills, and Bekka saw a mass of riders cresting the hill behind him. He watched as riders climbed over the crest and began the descent. It was a good way to count them. When the last man started down, Bekka's count reached ninety-four.

Chulum, at the head of his force, rode straight toward Bekka.

Bekka resigned himself to the coming encounter, knowing there would be trouble. The situation was awkward. As the leader of warriors in this part of the countryside, Bekka should take command. But being the older chief and with a superior number of warriors, Chulum would expect to give the orders.

Once again, Bekka swore under his breath at the bad luck that dogged his steps. Then he had time only to get control of his emotions as Chulum rode up to his position.

"Chief Bekka." Chulum gave the merest nod to acknowledge Bekka as an equal.

"Chief Chulum." Bekka returned the nod with as much enthusiasm. "It is good to see you."

Taller and broader than Bekka, Chulum had thick arms that could strangle an ox. He carried no bow, but had two lances slung over his right shoulder. "These are the dirt eaters in our path?" He had already turned his attention to the narrow valley below.

"I think they are Akkadians, probably sent by the traitor Eskkar. They are . . ."

"You should have stopped them before they reached the stream."

Bekka ignored the insult. "They have a hundred men and . . ."

"Dirt eaters." Chulum cut him off. "It matters not. With your men and mine, we have more than enough to finish them."

Bekka kept his voice under control. "I think we should wait. More warriors are on their way. And I've sent riders to Thutmose-sin."

Perhaps the mention of the Great Chief's name would restrain Chulum's eagerness. "Meanwhile, the invaders have no place to go."

Chulum shook his head. "Thutmose-sin is not here, may not be here for days. Besides, my men need the water. We rode hard when we got your message." He turned to his commanders, waiting in silence behind their leader, and listening to every word of the exchange. "Prepare the men to attack."

Orders were bellowed, drowning out Bekka's reply. Chulum's men readied weapons and started forming a battle line. Some of Bekka's own men, caught up in the excitement, joined in. Bekka attempted to order his own men to hold fast, but already the shouts of the warriors preparing for battle drowned out his efforts. Without challenging Chulum, Bekka could not stop him. Swearing again, Bekka resigned himself to the attack.

Chulum never looked back. He kicked his horse into position in the front of the line even before all of Bekka's warriors formed up. Bekka tried to reach Chulum's side, but too many riders were jostling about, blocking the way. The horses caught their riders' excitement, and added their whinnies and snorts to the din.

Warriors gulped the last of their water and readied their weapons. Meanwhile, Chulum unslung his two lances and held them up, one in each hand. A loud roar went up from his men and echoed out over the valley, as bows and lances were thrust upwards.

"Warriors! Destroy the dirt eaters! Attack!"

Bekka swore again, a mighty oath that should have made the gods strike Chulum down from his horse. Nevertheless, Bekka drew his sword and put his heels to his horse's flanks. Nothing could stop Chulum's warriors now, and all Bekka could do was join in the fight and hope for the best.

——⊶⊷——

"Not wasting any time, are they." Hathor studied the movements on the hilltop.

"The sooner they come, the less time our men will have to worry." Draelin nocked an arrow to his bowstring. "Too bad I don't have my war bow. It's not doing much good hanging over my door in Akkad."

Hathor shook his head at Draelin's eagerness. The smaller cavalry bows had shorter range and less stopping power. Still, at close range, their bronze tips would take a man down. Hathor unslung the lance that had chaffed his shoulder for the last eight days, then loosened his sword in its scabbard.

His men were drawn up about twenty paces from the stream, in a half moon formation, with the opening facing the northern cliff. The horses remained in the gully. Ten of the strongest soldiers attended to them, each man responsible for hanging on to ten horses.

The animals, tethered together, would need to be restrained once the attack began, and more than a few were going to be struck by arrows. No matter how many wounded animals panicked or bolted, the rest of the horses had to be held fast. If they all broke loose or stampeded, Hathor's men would be left on foot.

The Egyptian didn't waste any words exhorting his men. They understood the need to hold the stream. Besides, if they tried to retreat, the barbarians would cut them to pieces.

The Akkadians settled into their positions. Each man knelt on the ground, on one knee, with his two quivers of arrows before him. The smaller bows, designed to be used from horseback, could still be used effectively in that position. Kneeling made every bowman a smaller target, with each archer separated from his companions by a good pace on either side. That allowed enough room to work the bow properly, and swing it from side to side if necessary.

Hathor moved to the center of the line, where the brunt of the attack would likely fall. Draelin stood thirty paces to the right, in the more exposed position. The barbarians would try to envelop their enemy on the south side and break through to the horses. Hathor had given Draelin command of the men. As an experienced archer, he would know when to loose the first volley.

A din of noise erupted from the enemy's position and floated over the stream. To Hathor, it sounded as if every barbarian had given voice to his war cry. Then the warriors started down the hill. Hoof beats added to the fury of sound that echoed off the cliffs and washed over the Akkadians. As soon as the barbarians reached the base of the hill, they put their horses to a full gallop.

As he watched their progress, Hathor made a rough count of their number. He grunted in satisfaction. They didn't have enough men to break his position.

"Ready arrows!" Draelin's bellow, too, boomed out against the cliff behind him, but every man heard the order.

Already the first few barbarian shafts flew into the air, arching upwards. Hathor didn't bother to try and watch their approach. He'd seen men dodge one shaft only to be struck down by another. Best to stand in one place and cover his chest and neck with the small shield he'd carried all the way from Akkad. And hope the gods of war stood by your side to brush each deadly shaft away.

"Shoot!" Draelin's command started the defense.

The Akkadian bowstrings slapped against the leather arm protectors, as almost ninety shafts flew into the air, aiming for a point about eighty paces on the far side of the stream. They flew high, then arched down, arriving just as the front line of warriors reached the same patch of ground.

Hathor saw a few riders go down, but only a few. The first of the barbarian arrows landed, taking their toll on the Akkadians. Draelin kept shouting orders, but the men had little need for direction. They whipped shaft to string, bent the bow to their ears, and let fly with a speed that the barbarians, trying to shoot from the back of a moving horse, couldn't match. Hathor guessed his men were loosing at least three shafts for every two from the Alur Meriki.

By now the Akkadian shafts were held level with the ground. The barbarians, with several gaps in their line, reached the stream with a rush. Mounted, they presented a large target for every Akkadian archer, as a strike to the horse was almost as effective as a killing shaft in a man's chest. Both usually brought the rider down, possibly to be trampled by those behind him, or just stunned by the hard ground.

A huge water spray flew up into the air, as the galloping horses plunged into the stream. For a moment the flying water almost hid the enemy horses as if behind a protective curtain. The Akkadians never ceased loosing their arrows. Hathor heard the scream of animals in pain, and the shouts and war cries of the enemy, but the quick flowing water slowed the horsemen despite their best efforts to urge their animals across.

Horses staggered and plunged to their knees. A few crashed sideways into the water, the impact of their bodies knocking more spray into the air. Others rose up on hind legs, whinnying in pain. Barbarian riders, dead or wounded, splashed into the water.

Other riders could not control their wounded mounts. Many horses lost their footing on the wet and treacherous rocks that formed the bed of the stream, and tossed their riders into the cold water. By now every Akkadian had emptied one quiver and started on the second.

The charge faltered, then stopped in midstream. To continue forward invited a handful of arrows in the chest. The chaos in the water turned it into a killing zone.

For a few moments, the attackers struggled to hold their position, exchanging shafts with the Akkadians, but in the stream, the horsemen couldn't guide their horses and shoot at the same time. The moment any rider urged his horse forward, arrows hummed through the air to strike at man and beast. Soon wounded or daunted riders whirled their mounts around, scrambling back toward the bank, desperate to escape the deadly flights of arrows launched at them from close range.

Hathor noticed one rider in the second rank, waving his sword and urging his men onward. Hathor stepped back, extended his right arm to the rear, and with a single long stride hurled the lance toward the middle of the stream, giving it just enough arc to clear the first rank of enemy fighters.

The lance struck the rider's mount at the base of the neck, and the animal screamed in pain at the death blow. The beast stumbled and staggered to its knees, and the rider disappeared into the frothing water. The killing shafts continued to fly. The rest of the attackers turned back, hanging low over the necks of their horses as they fled for the safety of the far side of the stream.

Many warriors had lost their mounts. Now they scrambled on foot, stumbling over the loose stones that bordered the bank. Hathor saw a good number of those running had taken wounds, Akkadian shafts protruding from arms and legs.

Hathor shifted his attention to Draelin. Only on the southern part of the stream, away from the Akkadian position, had a number of the barbarians managed to cross. A few of them still exchanged arrows with the Akkadians. As more of Draelin's men turned to meet this threat, and with the main force stopped by the water, those barbarian warriors soon whirled their horses and raced back across the stream.

The Akkadians jeered them on, and laughter rose up at their frantic retreat.

"Keep shooting, damn you!" Draelin's bellow rose up over the excited shouts of his men.

Hathor strode over to his second in command, still launching shaft after shaft at the fleeing warriors. Only when his arrows could no long reach the retreating barbarians did Draelin halt his efforts.

"Well done, Draelin." Hathor clapped him on the back. He raised his voice and made sure every man in his command could hear. "Well done, Akkadians!"

A ragged cheer answered. Draelin could only nod, his chest rising and falling as he gulped air into his chest.

Both men glanced around. Now it was time to take stock of their own losses.

"I doubt they will be back any time soon," Hathor said, "but make sure the men are ready."

"Recover your arrows!" Draelin bellowed the order, and the cry went up and down the line, as the Akkadians surged into the water, looking for the dead and wounded, to pluck the shafts from their bodies. The barbarian arrows, too, would be scooped up and used against their former owners.

Afterwards, while Draelin regrouped his men, Hathor inspected the little encampment. He paced up and down the line, praising the men and their efforts, all the while counting the dead and wounded. The barbarians had inflicted plenty of damage, though not as great as he had expected. Nine men lay dead or dying, and another sixteen had taken wounds.

All the injured were carried to the space just outside the gully that sheltered the men's mounts. Those who could would relieve the ten able bodied soldiers who'd tended the horses. The dead bodies were carried to the rear, to be buried later, when time and events permitted.

A quick check of the horses revealed that only three had been struck by arrows. One of the handlers had taken a shaft in his arm. The horses remained skittish, pawing the ground or whinnying nervously. The scent of blood hanging in the air and the excited chatter of the men kept them from calming down.

The barbarians had fared much worse. Hathor's soldiers were already across the stream, many for the second time, collecting weapons and loot, and killing any wounded barbarians still alive. Two men, on Draelin's orders, took a count of the enemy dead.

The Akkadians didn't remain on the far bank long. Soon arrows arced down toward them, as angry Alur Meriki fighters let fly from the base of the hill. But almost all the shafts fell short, the distance too far for the small size bows. The laughing soldiers splashed their way back across the stream, all of them clutching their new possessions.

When Draelin trotted over to where Hathor stood, he had a grin on his face. "Thirty four dead, and maybe another ten or fifteen washed down the stream. Plus about forty horses. They'll think twice before they try that again."

"Probably another thirty wounded, maybe more." Hathor had fought in many battles. Usually the number of dead equaled the number of wounded. Ninety Akkadian archers had loosed at least one quiver, twenty shafts, into the enemy's ranks. The more proficient archers had shot another five or six. All together, at least two hundred and fifty arrows had struck the mass of barbarian warriors.

The smaller shafts might not be as deadly, but a wounded enemy was not likely to be back in action any time soon. A fighter weakened by loss of blood, or in too much pain to control his horse, tended to be less effective. Dead or wounded, the Akkadians had taken a lot of the barbarians out of the fight. And while the loss of so many horses might not mean much to the barbarians with their large herds, those mounts would still need to be replaced.

"I've ordered the men to distribute all the remaining arrows equally. We may need every shaft." Draelin gestured toward the still celebrating fighters. "Then I'll put them back to work carrying rocks. That should calm them down."

Hathor laughed. The men would be swearing at him soon enough. He glanced around and lowered his voice. "If Eskkar and the rest of the men don't get here before the full horde of the barbarians arrive, we'll need more than rocks and arrows."

⸺⸺

Up on the hill, Bekka sat on a stone and stared down at the dead and dying below. Another of his men, skilled in the ways of the healer, knelt on the ground beside him. He finished bandaging his leader's wounds with the damp shreds of Bekka's own tunic.

Bekka's horse had been killed beneath him by a flung lance, and the plunge into the chilled water had stunned him. Or some horse had kicked him in the head. Only the courage of one of his clan brothers had saved him. The man had dragged his dazed commander onto the back of his horse, turned around, and raced for safety.

Both of them had taken wounds in the flight. Bekka, clinging to the man's back, had taken two arrows, one in the left arm, and a glancing shaft that had ripped a gash in his right thigh. He forced the pain from his thoughts.

"Get me a horse, a good one." Bekka pushed himself to his feet. His head hurt, either from the fall into the water or the rage in his heart. The growl in his voice made his men jump to find him a suitable mount. This fight might be over, but Bekka still had work to do. His right leg hurt more than the wound in his arm, and he accepted the help of two of his men in climbing on the strange and skittish stallion.

He settled onto the animal's back with a sigh, and sat there a few moments, to calm his new mount. When the horse settled down, he took a moment to make sure both his knife and sword slid freely in their scabbards.

A glance around showed the extent of the disaster. Men sat on the ground, staring at nothing, weapons dumped beside them. Many of his fighters had taken wounds. Others appeared stunned at their defeat. Some hung their heads, unwilling to speak, embarrassed by the shame of their failure. Bekka had no idea how many warriors had fallen, even those from his own clan. That, too, could wait.

"Kushi, come with me," Bekka ordered. "You are now a leader of forty."

His newly promoted subcommander had his own bloody bandage across his chest, but he seemed fit enough. Kushi swung up onto his horse, hiding any pain that he might feel.

Bekka guided his horse across the top of the hill, then down about thirty paces to the place where Chulum's clan had gathered to lick their wounds and count their dead and missing. Bekka picked his way through the dismounted men, ignoring their grunts of pain as they tended to their injuries.

Chulum had survived the battle, damn the luck, though he now wore a bloody bandage wrapped around his forehead, and a second one around his left hand. Chulum, too, had found a new horse, and he remained astride as he listened to the reports of his men.

The wounded Serpent Clan warriors ignored Bekka's approach. Those still fit to fight glanced at him with little interest. The shock of defeat weighed heavily on their hearts. Chulum's men had led the way and taken the brunt of the losses, but Bekka didn't concern himself about that.

Chulum saw Bekka's approach, and his right hand moved closer to the hilt of his sword.

Bekka ignored the gesture. He slowed his horse and stopped it beside that of Chulum, facing him, their right knees almost touching. Bekka stared at the leader of the Serpent Clan.

"Your men should have taken their flank," Chulum said, breaking the silence with an angry shout. "We were almost across. If you had . . ."

Bekka kicked his horse's right flank, at the same time easing up on the halter. The horse, as well trained as any Alur Meriki mount, moved toward the right, pushing against Chulum's mount and forcing it to take a step backward. At the same time, Bekka's right hand flashed down, not for his sword, but for his knife. Before the startled Chulum could recover control of his horse or draw his sword, Bekka had lunged forward, extending his arm to its fullest, and thrust the knife deep into Chulum's right side.

Not a killing blow, but Bekka kicked a second time at his horse, and once again the animal responded, this time shoving Chulum's mount with enough force to stagger the animal. The sudden lurch tipped Chulum from his horse, and he fell heavily onto the hard ground, Bekka's knife still protruding from his side.

Bekka slid his good leg over the neck of his horse and dropped to the ground, ignoring the sharp pain that lanced up his injured leg and made him clench his teeth. Bekka's sword slid from its scabbard, as Chulum struggled to his knees and fumbled for his sword, blood already staining his right side. With a quick move, Bekka raised his weapon and struck, striking Chulum in the shoulder blade. The blow knocked Chulum back to the ground and wrenched a cry of pain from his lips.

"You disobeyed the order of your commander!" Bekka put all the force of his body into the shout. He wanted to make sure everyone heard his words. The warriors all around him had gone silent, though he heard the faint rasp of bows against shafts. At least a handful of Chulum's warriors had drawn their weapons. Only one had to let loose and Bekka would be dead.

Caught up in his own rage, Bekka didn't care. "You disobeyed my order to wait for Thutmose-sin." Again the words bellowed across the hilltop. "Because of your stupidity, many of your men and mine are dead, slaughtered for nothing. And the dirt eaters are now laughing at all of us."

Bekka raised up his sword again, this time using both hands. The blood streaked blade swung down, and this time it landed exactly where Bekka aimed. The thick bronze cut deep into Chulum's neck, nearly slicing through and unleashing a burst of bloody spray that pulsed for a few moments before Chulum's heart ceased beating.

"Men of the Serpent Clan," Bekka shouted, whirling the sword around to include all the warriors, "you will obey my orders!"

"Put down your weapons," Kushi bellowed, following Bekka's lead. He, too, had drawn his sword. "Obey your new clan leader."

The Serpent warriors exchanged glances. Chulum's leadership had garnered him few friends. One by one, the warriors lowered their weapons, letting bows go slack or half-drawn swords slide back into their sheaths.

Bekka knelt down, ignoring the pain in his leg, and cleaned his sword on Chulum's tunic. Now was not the time to show weakness. When he finished wiping the blade, Bekka jerked his knife from Chulum's side, and cleaned that, too. Then Bekka straightened up, returned his weapons to their scabbards, and turned to face the warriors.

"You will obey my orders until Thutmose-sin decides what to do with you." He extended his right arm and swept it around, encompassing all of Chulum's men. "Any one of you who disobeys a command from me or Kushi, or from any of my commanders, will be handed over to Thutmose-sin for judgment. Do you understand?"

They did. If Chulum had indeed disobeyed the Sarum's orders, he deserved his death. If not, the Alur Meriki High Council would sort it out. When clan leaders fought, the common warrior preferred to stay out of it. Meanwhile, no warrior wanted to face Thutmose-sin's fury, especially not after this defeat.

Bekka surveyed the sullen warriors one more time, as if searching for any sign of disobedience. He saw only sullen looks, and no one met his gaze. "Good. Kushi, take charge of these men. Count the dead and wounded, and report back to me."

It took all his strength and he had to grit his teeth, but Bekka managed to swing himself back onto his horse, refusing to let the pain from his wounds show on his face or in his movements.

He had survived another battle. Now all he had to worry about was the same danger he's just used to threaten the Serpent Clan. Thutmose-sin's anger might soon be directed first and foremost at Bekka.

8

Bone weary, the men trudged along, over, and through the foothills. Just after midmorning, Eskkar and his men crested the last hilly obstacle between them and the Khenmet. He had hoped to reach the stream yesterday before dark, but the men carried too much weight on their shoulders.

At least twenty times along the way, Eskkar had cursed himself for not bringing more pack animals. Another twenty added to the thirty he had started with would have made a difference.

All that didn't matter now. Eskkar halted A-tuku and watched as his men stumbled by, all of them grateful there were no more cursed hills to climb. He could see Hathor's position below, the men spread out along the stream. A line of alert guards surrounded the camp, most of them watching the east. Eskkar could also see the bodies of men and horses scattered between the far side of the stream and the base of the next hill.

Shading his eyes, Eskkar squinted toward the hill on the far side of the stream. Twenty or thirty mounted Alur Meriki scouts stared back at their Akkadian counterparts. He had no idea how many warriors might be encamped behind the hill. That too, no longer mattered. All that mattered was that Hathor's cavalry had reached the Khenmet and held it against the warriors.

He knew the details of yesterday's fight from the pair of scouts Hathor had dispatched to find Eskkar, and help guide him in.

Hathor rode up the hill to join his commander. "Good to see you, Captain."

"Not as glad as I am to see you alive." Eskkar always tried to keep his emotions under control, but this time he didn't bother to hide his relief. He gestured toward the enemy. "Any more attacks?"

"No. More barbarians are arriving, but we gave them a belly full of arrows in yesterday's skirmish. Whoever led that attack was a fool."

"We may not be so lucky next time. When the whole Clan gets here, their war leaders will know how to mount an attack."

"Any trouble on the way in?"

Eskkar shook his head. "No, but a few of their scouts watched us from the hilltops. They never came close. Must have seen Mitrac's men with their long bows."

The two men rode down the hill and into the camp. Eskkar swung down from A-tuku and stretched, forcing the stiffness from his muscles. He led the bay to the stream and let it drink, then handed the animal over to one of his guards. The horse might object to strangers riding it, but had learned to accept grooming and care from Eskkar's personal guards.

Meanwhile, a crowd of Hathor's men had bunched up around the just arrived pack animals, and soon seven or eight sacks containing stale bread, dried apples, figs, and dates, all foods that traveled well, were ripped open to feed Hathor's hungry men.

Eskkar strode over to where Drakis and Alexar stood with Draelin, staring across the stream. Using his bow, Draelin pointed out the various points of attack. Soon Mitrac, Muta, and Shappa joined the group.

Eskkar listened as Draelin recounted the fight, explaining how the Khenmet's flowing water had slowed the charge and disrupted the barbarians' ability to control their mounts and use their bows. Each of the commanders had questions, but by then, Eskkar knew everything he needed to know. Ignoring the conversation, he focused his attention on the enemy hilltop.

Ten or twelve new barbarian riders had joined the others on the crest. They sat on their horses and stared at those who had dared to block their path. Every one of them would want vengeance for their unburied dead still lying on the ground.

The talk died down, and the men turned to their leader. Eskkar set aside his thoughts.

"Well, we're here now, with our men and supplies intact. All of you have done well. Now the hard fighting will start."

Eskkar let the sobering words sink in for a moment. "Alexar, Mitrac, take your subcommanders and prepare for another attack, and this time it will be with every man they have. See how you can best arrange the men, and if there's anything we can do to make our position stronger." Alexar knew how to build a stout defensive position, and then defend it. "Lay out as many stones as you can. We've plenty of those, if nothing else."

Alexar had worked with old Gatus on defensive positions until he died, and then with Bantor. And Mitrac's bowmen would find the best positions to cover the approaches.

"Shappa, take your slingers and study the cliffs." Eskkar gestured toward the towering rock face. "See if you can get a few of your men up there. I don't want the barbarians to take the high ground and start shooting arrows down at our men. The more men we can put up there, the better."

Shappa stared up at the steep rocks. "I hope we brought enough ropes, Captain."

"If any of your men threw theirs away on the journey, let me know. They'll go up first, and without any ropes."

The slingers had brought plenty of rope with them, along with a few hammers and some bronze chisels. Eskkar knew Shappa would not report any of his men who had discarded their ropes. The master slinger would deal with such an offense himself.

Eskkar turned to Hathor and Muta. "As soon as Alexar stakes out his position, you'll station your horsemen. The barbarians may try to get some of their riders behind us, if they aren't already moving into position. We may need to fight on two fronts. If they don't attack our rear, assign your bowmen to stand beside the others facing the stream. Make sure that both you and your commanders know Alexar's plans."

The Akkadian leaders, mounted on their horses, would present an easy target for any enemy bowmen. If Hathor and Muta were killed, their subcommanders must know what to do. In battle, confusion reigned, and once soldiers stopped fighting to ask for orders, the battle would be lost.

Eskkar nodded in satisfaction as his commanders moved off and the camp stirred itself with activity. There remained much to prepare before the next attack, but his commanders knew what to do. All of them were veterans of at least one major battle. If they wanted to live through the next few days, they would make sure their men were ready.

—⸘⸘⸘—

Thutmose-sin guided his best stallion, a tall and rangy gray, up the slope. He'd ordered the standard bearers, and other trappings that indicated the presence of the Sarum, to remain behind and out of sight. When he reached the crest, only two bodyguards attended him, accompanied by the three chiefs invited to join him.

Once atop the hill, Bekka led the way along the crest, until the four clan leaders reached the best position to examine the force of dirt eaters below.

Only moments ago, Thutmose-sin had ordered the survivors of Chulum's Clan to be merged with that of Bekka's. No one, not even Chulum's kin, voiced any opposition. Chulum had acted like a fool or a loud talker on his first raid, and Bekka had done well to kill him, saving Thutmose-sin the trouble of having to deal with the man. Still, because of Chulum's stupidity, the Alur Meriki had lost many irreplaceable fighters.

After making the decision vindicating Bekka, Thutmose-sin had spoken to the remaining warriors in Chulum's clan. That action had elicited many angry looks, and Thutmose-sin had taken time to make sure the Serpent Clan understood their position. They had disgraced themselves before a force of dirt eaters, and for that offense, their clan was no more.

Thutmose-sin set all those thoughts aside as he settled his horse alongside Bekka's and stared down at the stream. He saw the bodies, men and horses, lying where they'd fallen two days ago. The death smell, held at bay by the cooler air of foothills, hadn't spread through the basin yet, though there would be plenty of flies buzzing about and feasting on the ripe flesh. "No arrows in the bodies."

"No, Sarum. The dirt eaters recovered them, along with the weapons and anything else of value from our warriors." Bekka made no excuses for not preventing it.

Thutmose-sin understood. Looting the bodies and collecting the weapons of the fallen would have been the first order of business for the dirt eaters. As long as men had been fighting, the living always took from the dead.

He lifted his gaze to the stream. The glistening flow glinted in the sunlight. Already his riders lacked enough water for their mounts, and the men's dry mouths would soon be protesting as well. The Akkadians had plenty of water, and doubtless enough food for a few days.

The southern end of the stream, where it disappeared beneath the rocks, had already been turned into a latrine. Two soldiers stood there, side by side, talking as they pissed into the waters.

"How many are there?" Thutmose-sin had heard the number already, but it might have changed since yesterday.

"Just over a thousand men, Sarum."

"Damn that Eskkar," Thutmose-sin muttered. "How did he get so many men here without our learning of his movements?"

"My scouts have already reported in," Bekka said. "They back-tracked the Akkadians and found their trail, coming straight from the west, right along the crest of the foothills."

The last place the Alur Meriki expected to find anyone approaching them. Too late to worry about that now.

Instead, Thutmose-sin examined the enemy force across the stream. First he studied the horsemen, all apparently skilled with the short curved bow that once marked only the Alur Meriki. Then his eyes picked out the accursed Akkadian archers that had slaughtered his men at Orak, recognizable by the longer bows they carried.

Thutmose-sin next turned his gaze on the spearmen, what the dirt eaters now called infantry. They carried true spears, not lances, each one as thick as a man's wrist and longer than the tallest warrior.

He gave but the briefest of looks at the company of slingers, who even from here looked more like boys than men. Still, the Akkadians had selected a carefully chosen force to fight in this particular place, and Eskkar must have some plan for the slingers.

"Any signs of confusion, fear, any quarrels in their ranks?"

"None, Sarum." Bekka kept his voice respectful. "These men are under strong discipline. When we charged, they took their positions and stood their ground. Not a man turned to flee."

Thutmose-sin shifted to face Urgo and Altanar, the other two chiefs who had accompanied him. Urgo had not spent so much time on a horse's back in months, and the old man's pain, though he tried to hide it, showed in his clenched jaw. But Thutmose-sin knew he would need the old fighter's experience, especially his knowledge of the land.

"What do you think, Urgo?"

The experienced warrior shook his head. "First there were eleven. Then they became a hundred. Now they are a thousand. They spread across the pass from end to end. Any more men would only be in the way, not worth the food they would need to eat. This Eskkar of Akkad has chosen this place, this time, and these men to offer us battle."

Thutmose-sin frowned at Urgo's words and what they implied.

"The outcast Eskkar seems confident of victory," Altanar said, after a long silence, "if he brings so many dirt eaters to this place. Although he blocks our way, he, too, is trapped here, cut off from his supplies. He cannot have brought much food with him. We could starve him out in eight or ten days."

"Yes, if we could last that long." Urgo reached behind to massage a sore spot on his hip. "Meanwhile we have not enough water to fill our bellies, let alone our horses. And what will our women and children drink? Already their water skins hang flat from the wagons. In one day and half of the next, they will arrive here, desperate for water."

Yesterday the clan leaders had met and decided to move forward, not back. No one believed that a force of dirt eaters could prevent the Clan reaching the water. Once again Urgo had urged them to turn the caravan around, but that choice was too bitter for any of the others to stomach.

And now, Thutmose-sin realized, it was too late to change his mind. Even if he gave the order to retrace their path, half and maybe more of the Alur Meriki would never reach their last watering place.

"What do you say, Bekka?" Thutmose-sin gazed at the man beside him. "You've been watching the dirt eaters for more than two days, and fought them. What do you think?"

"I say we must drive them away from the water. I know that many of us will die, but at least we will die with honor. To turn back without a battle . . . to refuse to fight dirt eaters, how could we face our women and children again?"

Urgo shook his head. "We know Eskkar has two or three times this number of fighters at his command in Akkad. By now, a second horde could be marching toward this place from the south. Even if we drive these dirt eaters away from the water, if we kill every one of them, how many warriors will we have left to face the next force of soldiers Akkad will send against us? Who will defend our women and children and wagons then?"

"We do not know if there are more coming," Altanar countered. "Our scouts have seen nothing. If the Akkadians come, we can attack them in the foothills. These dirt eaters fight well in a fortified position, but on the march, out in the open, they may not prove so formidable."

"Your scouts may have seen nothing, but that does not mean they are not coming." Urgo shook his head again. "We did not see these dirt eaters approaching until it was too late."

"The Council has made its decision." Thutmose-sin didn't want to go over the old arguments again. "But no matter what, we need every warrior we can put on a horse to finish Eskkar and these dirt eaters. If more Akkadians are indeed coming toward us, the sooner we destroy those in our path and secure the water, the better."

He turned to Bekka. "Your men are more rested. Dispatch riders to collect every band of warriors. I want every warrior from every clan here as soon as possible."

"Yes, Sarum."

Even as Thutmose-sin gave the order, he wondered if this was not exactly what Eskkar wanted him to do. The Sarum let his gaze roam up and down the ranks of the Akkadians. Two men, taller than most, stood together, staring up at this very hilltop. One of them likely was Eskkar himself.

Without thinking, Thutmose-sin touched the scar on his forehead. The next time he met Eskkar in battle, no broken blade would be enough to stop Thutmose-sin from killing the traitor. Of that, he was certain.

"Is it him?" Alexar strode over to join Eskkar and Hathor, craning his neck and shading his eyes as he stared across at the enemy hill. None of the Akkadians had ever seen the dreaded Thutmose-sin, except for Eskkar.

"I think so," Eskkar said. "If it's not, then whoever it is has taken charge."

"The one on the end." Hathor pointed toward the right. "I recognize him. He was one of the leaders in the attack."

"Four clan chiefs together. They're making their plans while they gather their men." Eskkar turned away from the hill. "By now they've figured out that they have to fight. Let's just hope they don't come up with anything better than charging at us from across the stream."

Eskkar glanced toward his own soldiers. "How soon before we are ready?"

"Not long," Alexar said. "The men still need some time to recover from the march. Meanwhile, the slingers are busy chipping away at the cliffs, and the rest of the men are cursing at me for making them carry rocks. By the end of the day, we'll be as ready as we're going to be."

Water-polished stones from the stream, some larger than a melon, were being scattered over both sides of the waterway, with twice as many on the Akkadian side. If the barbarians succeeded in crossing over, the stones would make it difficult for a charging man to keep his footing. It would be yet one more obstacle to overcome before the enemy could come to grips with the Akkadians.

"They've known about us for almost four days," Eskkar said. "It will take them at least the rest of the day, and probably tomorrow, to assemble enough warriors for another attack. And Thutmose-sin knows by now that he's going to need every one if he wants his horses to drink from the stream."

"Then I'll have time to rest the men. All that walking has taken its toll." Alexar rubbed his hands together in anticipation. "I'll even make sure they do a little training."

"You sound like old Gatus." Eskkar grinned at his infantry commander. "Always eager to make his men sweat."

Alexar laughed. "Well, Gatus would be happy to be here and see what we've done."

"He would be proud of these men, and of all of you," Eskkar agreed. "The veterans tell the new men stories about how hard training was in the old days, and how easy the recruits have it today."

Gatus had been dead for more than eight years, yet many of the men still spoke of him as if they'd suffered one of his tongue lashings only yesterday. Eskkar, too, missed the old warrior, who had befriended Eskkar and Trella early on, and remained loyal to the very end. At least he had died as he wanted, in his sixtieth season, fighting with his companions.

"Let's hope his spirit is watching over us." Alexar took one last look at the enemy hilltop. "I think we're going to need him."

⸺◆⸺

Thutmose-sin spent the rest of that day and half of the next on the hilltop, watching the Akkadians, while he waited for the remainder of his forces to arrive. His enemy kept busy. Gangs of dirt eaters moved rocks from the base of the cliff, the stream bed and the water itself. They scattered these in a wide belt along the bank, creating an obstacle for ten paces as the ground sloped up and away from the flowing water.

With the west side of the stream littered with the smooth river rocks, they repeated the process on the east bank. Then, to further stymie the Alur Meriki warriors, they started piling more stones on the far side, to provide their bowmen with some protection, at least for their lower legs.

The speed of the Akkadians impressed him. In less than a day, they created a barrier on the west side of the stream that would slow any charge. Any horses that managed to make it through the rocks and across the stream would find even more dangerous footing on the Akkadian side. Nor would his bowmen shoot their arrows effectively while guiding their mounts through the water's current and past the field of stones.

In yet another affront to the Alur Meriki, the hated Akkadian archers set up some target butts. Thutmose-sin watched as groups of bowmen took turns practicing with their long bows, launching the heavy shafts that could bring down a horse at close range, let alone stop a man. Those tall bowmen with their brawny arms would launch two or three arrows before his warriors rode into range.

Nor were the archers the only ones practicing. Groups of slingers flung stones at the cliff face. He could see the puffs of stone chips fly off the hard rock wall. Small of stature, they looked like boys at this distance. Some had used ropes to scale the cliffs on the west side of the stream. From those heights, they would hurl their missiles at any approaching warriors. More important, they ended Thutmose-sin's idea of sending a band of his fighters to slip over the north end of the stream, clamber through the rocks, and catch the Akkadians unaware.

The steepness of the south cliff, where the flowing water disappeared into the ground, prevented even Akkad's slingers from using it to advantage. No enemy could work his way through those rocks, to attack from behind.

Thutmose-sin didn't fully understand the purpose of the Akkadian slingers. He'd used a sling himself as a boy. But somehow the traitor Eskkar had created a whole class of fighters using what Alur Meriki warriors considered a toy for women and children. Scattered across the cliff, or mixed in with the rest of Eskkar's fighters, they would no doubt add to the killing of his men. Otherwise, the traitor would not have brought them, instead of more bowmen or spearmen.

The Alur Meriki had never faced slingers before, and while he doubted they would be as dangerous as archers, they might take their toll. What effect they would have on the battle remained to be seen.

The foot soldiers, spearmen as they were called, presented another unknown. Thutmose-sin knew his warriors had ridden down bands of dirt eaters armed with spears in the past, but the Akkadians had brought two hundred of these fighters to this place, and they, too, were an unknown.

Even at this distance, he could see the spearmen moving back and forth as they practiced, thrusting with their spears from behind shields. The spears looked to be both thick and long, and the bulky shields appeared solid enough to stop an arrow or turn a sword stroke.

For Thutmose-sin's warriors scrambling up from the stream and picking their way through the rocks, the spears would be a daunting weapon to face. A powerful thrust could impale a rider before he could bring his sword to bear. Nor would horses willingly charge a bristling line of sharp spear points.

Of course if his warriors could ride back and forth, launching their arrows, the spearmen would be cut down soon enough. But the Akkadian archers and slingers would make sure that tactic failed.

The six hundred horse fighters Thutmose-sin counted also looked dangerous. If they had truly learned how to shoot a bow from the back of a fast moving horse, they presented a threat as dangerous as another steppes clan. Their presence ended any hope of sending an Alur Meriki force of warriors to the Akkadian rear.

However many Thutmose-sin dispatched on the two day trek, they would only find themselves facing these horsemen after a long ride, and the Alur Meriki would be that much weaker on this side of the stream. Scouts on the cliffs would see his warriors coming in plenty of time for the Akkadians to shift their soldiers and counter the attack.

Man for man, Thutmose-sin had no doubt his warriors were superior. They had, after all, learned to ride almost as soon as they could sit on the back of a horse. But Eskkar had chosen his place of battle well. Most Alur Meriki tactics relied on movement and skill with a horse. Those would be less effective in this enclosed pass through the foothills.

And if Eskkar had trained and prepared his men for a steppes battle, Thutmose-sin had to respect their strength. They'd out-fought his warriors before.

The odd mixture of forces Eskkar had established on the west bank worried Thutmose-sin. He didn't know how effective they might be in a combined effort. On an open plain, the Alur Meriki could hurl their entire force at a single point, and nothing could withstand that. But here, the cursed stream with its desperately needed flowing water prevented the warriors' best tactic.

Midday had just passed when Bekka returned from his duties and rejoined his Sarum on the crest. A fresh bandage covered his thigh, now marked by only a trace of blood.

"The last of our men have arrived, Sarum. There can't be more than a handful who haven't ridden in."

Thutmose-sin turned away from the enemy camp. He'd seen all he needed. "What is the count now?"

"Over twenty-two hundred warriors," Bekka answered.

That included more than four hundred old men and young boys, fit to ride and capable of holding a sword, called up from the caravan. These would take their station in the front ranks, to take the first rush of arrows from the Akkadians. Many, if not most, of the old and young would sacrifice their lives to allow his seasoned warriors to close with their enemy.

"Then it is time to prepare." Thutmose-sin rose and swung onto the back of his horse. "Ride ahead and summon the clan leaders."

As Bekka rode off, Thutmose-sin took one last look at the Akkadians. Obviously they didn't have more than a few days supply of food, and by now the first stirrings of hunger might be making itself felt.

The invaders had dragged a few dead horses from the stream and gutted them. That would give each man a fistful of raw meat, since the bare ground held little in the way of firewood. Too much uncooked flesh made men sick, but it would take several days for that to happen.

Meanwhile, his own men had nearly emptied the last of their water skins. The thirsty horses, who could scent the water just over the hill, would soon be more than restive. At last Thutmose-sin turned his horse's head aside, and followed Bekka's path back to camp.

When Thutmose-sin reached the area set aside for the gathering of clan leaders, he gazed in satisfaction at the men waiting there. Bekka, Urgo, and Altanar had been joined by Suijan, Narindar, and Praxa. Bar'rack arrived last. Accompanying Bar'rack were the warriors who guarded the caravan, along with the old men and boys. He also brought a pack train loaded down with all the arrows, lances, and other weapons normally stored in the caravan's wagons.

Thutmose-sin settled himself on the ground beneath the great standard of the Alur Meriki. Each of its feathers, ox-tails, and leather loops represented a particular clan, or commemorated a victory or conquest, some of which no one any longer remembered.

The clan leaders followed their Sarum's example. Each was attended only by one of his most trusted or senior subcommander. Thutmose-sin studied their faces as they settled into their places.

All the leaders looked grim. Each had ascended to the hilltop and stared at the Akkadians in silence. Even the fools and loud talkers among the warriors realized that this would be no easy victory.

More than twelve years had passed since the mighty assault on Orak had decimated the Alur Meriki. Almost four years later, seeking revenge for that defeat, the Clan, at the urgings of the Sumerians, had launched a night attack on Akkad's walls. The leaders of the Great Clan had split into two factions over the attack, and Thutmose-sin faced the most serious threat to his rule.

He'd objected to that attack, but a large force of his warriors chose to join with those willing to battle Akkad. Fortunately for Thutmose-sin, the attack had failed, and most of those opposing him died, trapped and cut down within the walls of the dirt eater's city.

Yet the stupidity of the attack had also taken its toll, both in lost warriors and honor. The Great Clan had not yet regained the strength it boasted before the first attack on Orak. Now Thutmose-sin and the Alur Meriki faced a desperate battle, and for the first time, one not of their own choosing. Every clan leader sitting in the circle knew how much was at stake.

"For almost two days I have studied the Akkadians." Thutmose-sin chose not to use the usual name of dirt eaters. Whatever low beginnings these men from Akkad might have had, they had turned into fighters, and the sooner his clan leaders and warriors accepted that fact, the better.

"They are well prepared to face us, and they have used the time to strengthen their position. They show no fear. They may not have food for more than a few days, but they have the water. A hungry man can still fight. A warrior weakened by thirst is not as strong. We must drive them away from the stream, and soon. Another two or three days, four at the most, and we will all be opening the veins and drinking the blood of our few surviving horses to stay alive."

He let the words sink in, as he glanced around the circle. No one challenged his assertions.

"So we must make a choice, right here and right now, about how to fight and how to drive them away from the water. If we fail to do that, the Alur Meriki may be finished as a people. And let me not hear loud talk about wiping these invaders out to the last man. I would let the Akkadians ride away tomorrow unscathed, if we could somehow secure the water for the caravan."

Thutmose-sin turned to Bar'rack. "How soon before the caravan reaches this place?"

"I made sure the wagon masters understood the need for speed. We marked the trail, and the caravan will travel as far as it can into the evening. It should be here by midmorning tomorrow."

"Good." Thutmose-sin did not feel comfortable about leaving the caravan undefended and so far behind, but it couldn't be helped. "When they arrive, the path to the water must be free."

He glanced around the circle of warriors. "We've already wasted two days gathering our strength. Now it is time to plan the defeat of these Akkadians."

Murmurs of approval greeted Thutmose-sin's words.

"To kill these dirt eaters, we must come up with a new way to fight. We cannot waste our warriors' lives by charging across the stream. Chulum's foolishness at least convinced our men of that. The first to die will slow our approach, and leave the survivors easy targets for their archers. Even if we are successful, too many of our men will die. Since that is so, I believe we should attack at night and on foot. There will be little moon, and we should be able to get close to the stream before we launch our attack."

"On foot and at night!" Suijan shook his head. "No warrior with any honor would agree to such a battle plan! Better to die on a horse, under the sun and sky."

The man's outburst surprised Thutmose-sin. Suijan had proven himself to be strong fighter and wise beyond his years. "You have been here less than a day, Suijan." Thutmose-sin kept his temper despite the man's angry words. "Let us ask Bekka, who has not only been here the longest, but who has actually ridden against these invaders."

Bekka shifted his body while he collected his words, surprised at being asked to offer his opinion ahead of his elders. "I think the dirt eaters are waiting for us to charge across the river. One hundred of them stopped our charge before we reached midstream. Struggling through the water, not one warrior got close enough to throw a lance. I thought Chulum and I had wasted our men's lives. Now I agree with our Sarum that we have learned from their deaths. If we ride against them on horseback, we will be destroyed."

"How can you be certain that an attack at night will succeed?" Praxa, the oldest of the clan leaders after Urgo, leaned forward, his eyes shifting from Bekka to Thutmose-sin.

"I cannot be certain," the Sarum replied. "But at night, the long bow-men of the Akkadians will not be able to see us, nor will they have a large target to aim at. Eskkar has taught these men to aim for the horses. If we hug the ground as we approach, we may be able to cross the stream and close in on them."

"How deep is the stream?" Altanar's question showed support for his Sarum.

"Only above the knees, and a little deeper in the center." Bekka answered without glancing at Thutmose-sin. "There it might reach mid thigh for a few steps.

"It will slow down our men." Altanar kept his voice even. "But it would also slow down horses, who will be fearful of the depth of the water. At least we can tell the men what to expect."

"And whatever slingers or bowmen the Akkadians have on the cliff will be of little use," Bekka went on. "Once we close in, they will have no targets."

Thutmose-sin waited for a moment, but no one offered anything else. "Urgo, you have not spoken. What would you recommend?"

Every eye turned toward the old warrior. He, too, took a moment before he replied.

"I agree that a mounted attack would fail, and with heavy losses. Eskkar will have planned well for just such an encounter. But an attack at night will be almost as bad. Do you think Eskkar will not be expect-ing this? Besides, our warriors are not used to fighting in the dark, while the dirt eaters have shown themselves to be good fighters after the sun goes down. Do not forget the lessons of Orak. At the great siege, we tried several attacks at night, and they all failed, but the dirt eaters raided our horses in the dark. And when Rethnar tried to slip into the city at night during their war with Sumer, his men were trapped and slaughtered like sheep in a killing pen."

No one wanted to be reminded of Rethnar's failure. At least he had the good fortune to get himself killed during the attack, which had saved Thutmose-sin the bother of doing it.

Or Bar'rack might have done it. He had ridden with Rethnar in that battle and fought in the Akkadian city. Afterwards, when the survivors collected themselves, Bar'rack had searched through the surviving and shattered warriors, naked blade in hand, calling out Rethnar's name and demanding a challenge.

"What you say is true," Thutmose-sin conceded. "But I see no other path to follow."

"There is another way, perhaps two," Urgo went on. "First, we can try to . . ." he had to pause to remember the word seldom used by the Clan, "to negotiate with Eskkar. Perhaps he can be persuaded to depart. Villagers like gold and horses. We can offer them to the Akkadians."

"Buy our path to the water!" Even for Altanar, that course of action bordered on the unthinkable for a warrior. "Never!"

"You will buy the water from that stream, paying for it in the blood of our fighters and our horses." Urgo shrugged, unperturbed by the passion of Altanar's response. "If that is not acceptable, then I suggest that we turn the caravan around, and return to the last watering place. Many will die, the old, the young, the weak, and most of the herds, but much of the caravan will survive, as will many of our strongest horses and warriors. Meanwhile, Eskkar cannot remain in this place long. His thousand fighters and half as many horses need food and grain. In a day or two, once we are well on our way, the Akkadians will leave this place. Once they do, they will be vulnerable to attack by our warriors. And for once Eskkar is a long way from the safety of his walled city."

"To fight and die is surely more honorable than a . . . retreat." Praxa had nearly uttered the word "cowardly," which no one dared say of Urgo.

"Perhaps Urgo is right," Thutmose-sin spoke quickly, before tempers flared. "If we can talk to the Akkadians, perhaps we can trade horses and gold for passage."

"We've no gold here," Altanar said, "unless we strip every ring, necklace, and arm bracelet from our warriors."

"How many horses would we offer?" Suijan's voice held a trace of resignation.

"A hundred, three hundred, it makes no difference," Urgo said. "In three days we'll lose that many and more to thirst."

"Why should this Eskkar trust us to deliver the gold and horses?" Bekka's tone indicated that he, too, preferred not to face the Akkadians.

Thutmose-sin already knew the answer to that one. "I, perhaps all of us, would have to give our oaths as warriors."

A sigh of despair greeted his words. No warrior dared to break such an oath, even one given to a dirt eater. But no one spoke. Even for proud fighting men now reduced to offering horses for water, the idea of giving their solemn oaths to dirt eaters would take time to swallow.

"And if the traitor spurns your offer?" Bar'rack's angry voice told everyone what he thought of the prospect.

Not "our" offer, but "your" offer, Thutmose-sin noted. "If we can save the lives of our warriors, we must try. Or we can turn the caravan around, as Urgo suggests. Who else is in favor of that?"

The clan leaders glanced at each other, but no one spoke. Retreating without a fight, refusal to accept the dirt eaters' challenge, no, the leaders of the Alur Meriki were still not ready to consider that.

"Then we will first try and bargain with the Akkadians." Thutmose-sin shook his head and took a deep breath. "Meanwhile, prepare your men for the night attack. Unless anyone has another plan?"

He glanced around the circle. No one appeared satisfied, but neither had anyone a better idea. Before he could end the council and send them to their duties, Bar'rack spoke again.

"There may be another way," Bar'rack said. "I could challenge this Eskkar to fight, warrior against warrior. If I kill him, we agree that his men can depart in peace. If he kills me, then we can give them the horses."

Thutmose-sin frowned. All of the clan chiefs knew Bar'rack had sworn the Shan Kar against Eskkar.

"I know of your bravery, Bar'rack," Urgo said. "But Eskkar will not fight you. He commands an entire city and thousands of fighters. No such leader would accept a challenge to fight someone of lesser status. It is likely he does not even know your name. If you offer Eskkar a challenge, he will ignore it."

Bar'rack flushed at the gentle rebuke, but said nothing.

"No, Eskkar would not fight you," Thutmose-sin agreed, breaking the silence. "Still, he might take such a challenge from me. But we will hold off on that challenge for now."

—⊶⊷—

The messenger darted through the ranks, running as fast as he could to find Eskkar and deliver his message. Eskkar thanked the soldier, but he'd already seen the huge cross-pole totem that symbolized the might of the Alur Meriki and the power of its leader. Now placed atop the hill, the white streamers formed of clan tokens and animals symbols floated in the light breeze.

"What does it mean?" Alexar stood beside Eskkar as they stared at the enemy hilltop. Warriors were filling the crest, but their leisurely movement didn't appear to portend an attack. Some of the Alur Meriki riders had even dismounted, and now stared down at the enemy that denied them water.

"It's the great Alur Meriki standard, representing all the clans and all their victories. There are even a few yak tails brought down from the steppes," Eskkar said. "It also means that Thutmose-sin is on the crest."

By now Hathor, Mitrac, and Drakis had reached his side, all of them staring open-mouthed at the sight. Part of the barbarian ranks parted, and three warriors rode over the crest and started down the slope, walking the horses with unusual care down the incline. They stopped at the base of the hill, well out of range of the Akkadian long bows.

"Is one of them Thutmose-sin?" Alexar couldn't keep the excitement out of his voice.

"Those are all chiefs," Hathor said. "Look at the horses."

"Could be," Eskkar said. None of the three warriors carried a bow or lance. "I think they want to talk, to meet face to face. They'll wait there until they see three of us move toward them."

"Why? What is there to talk about?"

Alexar's blunt words brought a smile to Eskkar's face. "Well, there's only one way to find out." He turned and strode over to where his horse stood. Eskkar's long sword rested on the ground beside the animal. Eskkar gathered it up and slung it over his right shoulder, then tested it to make sure it drew easily.

"I'm going with you," Hathor declared.

One glance at his horse commander told Eskkar that nothing would deter the Egyptian from accompanying him. Besides, Hathor's grim demeanor would strike fear in any warrior's heart.

"Come, then." Three barbarian chiefs meant an equal number of Akkadian leaders could meet them in the center of the battleground. Eskkar considered only a moment. "Mitrac! String your bow and find yourself a horse. I want you with me."

A chorus of disappointed groans rose up at Eskkar's choice.

"By the gods, Eskkar, don't take Mitrac," Alexar said. "Even he can't use his bow from horseback. Let me come with you."

Draelin and Drakis joined in the protest, each suggesting he should accompany his leader.

"Only three can face them," Eskkar said. "And I want to send a message."

He waited until Mitrac had strung his bow, slung a fat quiver of arrows over his shoulder, and climbed onto the back of a horse. Then Eskkar led the trio through the ranks. He guided his stallion into the stream, letting A-tuku choose its path through the rocks, Hathor and Mitrac following.

Eskkar halted in the middle of the water. A-tuku snorted at the chilly flow, but lowered his head enough to gulp a few mouthfuls of water.

Hathor, too, paused to let his horse drink. "That should send another message."

When all three horses had slacked their thirst, Eskkar started forward. The three riders splashed onto the opposite shore and let the horses pick their way through the scattered stones. After another twenty paces, Eskkar paused again.

"Do you want me to count their numbers?" Mitrac had taken his station at Eskkar's left.

Eskkar glanced up at the hilltop. Warriors filled the ridgeline from end to end, two and three deep in places. "No. I'm sure Alexar has his men getting a count."

Not that it mattered how many warriors the Alur Meriki could field. The Akkadians would have to fight them all.

They waited, but the Alur Meriki didn't advance. They seemed to be conferring among themselves. It didn't last long, and the three started toward the Akkadians.

"Nice and steady," Eskkar said, touching his heels to his horse. "Just match their pace."

Step by step, the two groups walked their way toward one another. The gap between them narrowed, until the Alur Meriki halted.

"They're just in range," Mitrac commented, his eyes gauging the distance. "My archers can reach that far."

Eskkar shook his head. "The minute they see a shaft in the air they'll turn and gallop away." He touched the halter against his horse's neck, and the three resumed their slow pace.

When the distance closed to ten paces, Eskkar eased A-tuku to a stop, and the enemy warriors did the same. Mitrac and Hathor remained on either side, about two paces away from their Captain, leaving each with enough space to use their weapons.

Eskkar studied the three chiefs facing him. In the center, wearing the gleaming bronze medallion that signified the leadership of the Alur Meriki, was Thutmose-sin. He rode a powerful looking gray stallion.

Though Eskkar couldn't recall the man's face, he recognized the powerful emblem of the clan. As a youth, he'd seen it hanging on the breast of Maskim-Xul, father of Thutmose-sin. And in the nighttime fight outside Orak's walls, Eskkar had glimpsed it again on the chest of Thutmose-sin, gleaming in the light from the raging fires.

The second warrior wore a fresh bandage on his thigh and another on his arm. Despite the wounds, he seemed calm enough, betraying no emotion either by his face or body movements. That one, Eskkar decided, would be dangerous.

The third and youngest chief struggled to control his anger. While Eskkar didn't have Trella's skill in reading people's faces, he recognized raw hatred when he saw it. Eskkar returned his gaze to Thutmose-sin.

"You are Eskkar of Akkad, what was once known as Orak. I am Thutmose-sin, leader of the Alur Meriki. This is Chief Bekka," he nodded to the bandaged warrior on his left, "and Chief Bar'rack."

Eskkar acknowledged their names with a nod. "I am Eskkar of Akkad. This is Hathor, commander of my cavalry, and this is . . ."

"We know the Great Slayer of warriors," Thutmose-sin finished. "He is Mitrac the Archer. Many of our women have cried out into the night and cursed both his name and his arrows."

Even before the siege of Orak, Mitrac's shafts had killed many warriors. During the siege Mitrac and his deadly bow had killed or wounded an uncountable number of the enemy. No single man had ever slain so many of the Alur Meriki. No wonder they knew his name and cursed his existence at their cooking fires.

"He gives insult by bringing the Slayer before us," Bar'rack said, not bothering to conceal his hatred. "Even an outcast should know that bows are forbidden when warriors meet."

"Control your tongue." Despite giving the rebuke, Thutmose-sin betrayed no trace of anger toward his commander for speaking out of turn.

Eskkar smiled. So that was what had prompted the brief discussion when they had first seen him and his men ride out.

He considered Bar'rack's outburst. It seemed odd for the Sarum of the Alur Meriki to bring a young clan leader with him, one who could not control his emotions. Eskkar finished his examination of the three clan leaders before he answered. "We have met once before, Thutmose-sin, on the night of the great burning."

"My sword shattered against your blade," Thutmose-sin said, "or I would have killed you."

Eskkar shrugged. "Perhaps. But you are the one who bears the mark of my sword on your forehead. If the wagon had not burst into flame, I would have killed you."

Thutmose-sin frowned at the memory. Though the years had faded the scar, the force of Eskkar's pommel had indeed left its mark, and not only on Thutmose-sin's body. "The custom of meeting before battle forbids the carrying of bows."

"Your customs mean nothing to me." Eskkar kept his voice calm, almost placid, another piece of useful advice from Trella. Let your words carry the message, not your voice or face, lest you reveal too much of what is in your heart. "If Mitrac frightens you, I can send him back to my men."

That elicited a second, deeper frown from Thutmose-sin, while Bar'rack's lips formed a thin line across his face. Only Bekka remained unmoved, almost unconcerned.

Eskkar kept his face impassive as the warriors swallowed the insult. "What does the leader of the Alur Meriki wish to say?"

"Your men hold the water." Thutmose-sin once again had his voice under control. "Our women and children will soon arrive here. They need water for themselves and their herds."

"The water of this stream belongs to Akkad, as all of this land now belongs to Akkad. If you want water, you will have to find it somewhere else." Eskkar didn't bother to add, or fight for it.

"We have come too far to turn back," Thutmose-sin said. "And a battle between us will leave many dead on both sides. If you abandon this place, we will let you depart in peace."

"We are not ready to depart," Eskkar said. "In four or five days, we may wish to move on. If you wait until then, you may have your water."

Thutmose-sin knew that in four more days, the Alur Meriki wouldn't have any warriors who could fight or horses to carry them. "If you leave now, we will give you gold, as well as many horses, at least one hundred."

The Alur Meriki were indeed desperate. Eskkar shook his head. "You want to burden my men with gold and have them tending a horse herd when you attack? The moment your warriors' horses finished drinking they would ride to attack us. No, keep your gold. If you want water, turn your horses back toward the east and leave this land."

"So you came here only to challenge the Alur Meriki." Thutmose-sin's voice now betrayed his anger.

Trella's advice once again proved its worth. The calmer Eskkar remained, the angrier Thutmose-sin grew.

Eskkar leaned forward and rested his left hand on the neck of his horse, who bobbed its head contentedly at the touch. "I came here to end once and for all time the raids and attacks against the farms and villages and herds of this land. If that means I have to destroy the Alur Meriki . . ." He shrugged again, the gesture so familiar among steppes warriors.

Silence met the blunt words. At least now, there would be no compromise, no turning back for either side.

"Then you will never leave this place alive." Thutmose-sin's voice betrayed his hatred.

"That may be. But even if we are defeated, the might of the Alur Meriki will be broken here forever. Never again will your warriors ride freely though our lands. And while we fight, more forces from Akkad approach. How will you stop them?"

There were no more soldiers coming, but Eskkar knew Thutmose-sin couldn't be sure of that.

"You *are* a traitor to your kind." Thutmose-sin clenched his fist, unable to contain his rage any longer. "Your father killed my half brother. For that you and your clan were declared outcast. Now you shall pay for that deed as well."

Eskkar had never heard the whole story of what had happened the night his parents died. To learn that his father, Hogarthak, had killed a clan leader before his own death, now made his memory all the stronger. "Then my father died as a brave warrior doing his duty. I will honor his memory."

"And I will kill you myself." Bar'rack moved his horse a few steps closer. "I've sworn the Shan Kar against you, Eskkar of Akkad, to avenge my brother's death. He died in the valley north of Orak, ambushed by you and the Ur Nammu scum. If you have any honor, you will take the challenge I offer you, and fight me man to man, here and now."

So that was why Thutmose-sin brought the young warrior. To see if he could goad Eskkar into accepting a challenge.

At Bar'rack's advance, Hathor let his horse take one step forward, ready to block the way, and moved his hand closer to his sword's hilt. Mitrac shifted his bow, which had been resting across the back of the horse's neck, and let it hang down at his left side. Despite what many believed, he could nock and shoot a shaft from a horse if he had to.

"I accept no challenge from unweaned loud talkers." Eskkar remained relaxed on A-tuku.

"Then you refuse to face me? The leader of Akkad has grown old and soft, afraid to fight."

"What else does Thutmose-sin wish to say?" Eskkar ignored the angry warrior and let disdain show in his voice. "Or does the Great Chief of the Alur Meriki have no control over his men? Does he not honor the truce of his own calling?"

"Enough talk, Bar'rack." Thutmose-sin ordered. "Return to my side." He waited until the warrior backed his horse into position. "If you will not take our horses or our gold, then it will be war to the death."

"If you fight, my men will take the gold from your warriors' bodies." Eskkar let the force of his voice show for the first time. "And there will be many riderless horses to be collected."

"Then it will be war," Thutmose-sin repeated. "I will see you on the battlefield."

The Sarum jerked the head of his horse around, and set his mount to a canter. Bekka also turned away, but Bar'rack paused to spit on the ground. "The next time we meet, Eskkar, you will die." He whirled his mount around with such force that it reared up for a moment, before its front hooves crashed to the earth once more, then burst into a gallop.

Eskkar watched the warriors depart. "Now they're committed. They have to fight."

"Let's get out of here." Hathor glanced around. "I don't like being exposed like this." He guided his horse back toward the west.

Back across the stream, Eskkar and his commanders prepared their men. At any moment the barbarians could ride over the crest and launch an attack. The Akkadians stood close to their weapons and assigned positions.

The easy talk and occasional laughter died out. Everyone now understood they faced a fight to the death. But as the afternoon lengthened and no attack materialized, Eskkar turned to Alexar.

"Either they don't have enough warriors yet, or they're coming tonight."

"They've had plenty of time to gather their men," Alexar said. "And they've got to be running low on water. They'll come tonight, or at first light."

Eskkar swore. "Damn them, I thought they'd attack today. Now we'll have to keep the men alert all night."

"They've had a day to rest," Alexar said, unperturbed at the prospect of an all night vigil for his soldiers. "Every other man will keep watch during half the night, while the others get what sleep they can. If barbarians come, we'll be ready."

"Shappa!" Eskkar's voice soon brought the leader of the slingers trotting toward his commander.

"Yes, Captain?"

"The barbarians may attack tonight. Prepare a force of skirmishers to cross the stream after dark. I want to make sure we know when and where the enemy is coming."

The slingers, mostly young men and boys, and all too small to make a good spearman or archer, had proven themselves in the war with Sumer. Since those days, they had learned to take on many roles, and one of the most important was that of scouting out enemy positions and intentions. Their small stature made them difficult to see in the dark, and they could creep through the night with hardly a sound.

Their slings made almost no noise, and they prided themselves on their skill with the long, curved knives they carried. Those sharp blades could hamstring a horse and send it crashing to the earth. Every one of Shappa's men carried twenty perfectly round bullets made of bronze in their pouches, and the slingers could launch their missiles fast enough to keep pace with any archer.

"I'll send out sixty men." Expecting the order, Shappa had already made his preparations. "I'll spread them out in a curve just over the stream. And I'll have those with the sharpest eyes on the cliff. From up there, they may have enough moonlight to see men moving."

Eskkar nodded. "Barbarians don't like fighting at night and they hate leaving their horses behind. They won't be skilled at moving through the darkness."

"You don't think they'll try and cross the stream on horseback?" Alexar didn't sound so certain.

"No, not at night. The horses would balk and whinny and make too much noise. The barbarians will come on foot if they come tonight."

"Let's hope your luck holds, and they come tonight." Alexar sounded relieved. "If they find another source of water, they might just decide to starve us out."

9

The silvery stream glistened in the faint moonlight, its gurgling passage a soothing murmur of endless repetitions as it flowed along the boundary of the Akkadian camp. To Shappa, however, the sound was only another distraction. His men were out there, on the enemy side of the stream, while he remained safe, surrounded by the Akkadian host.

Crouched down in the dark, Shappa swore at the responsibility of command. He wanted to be with his men, crawling around on the rocky ground, listening for the slight sounds of the enemy moving toward them. Instead, as commander of Akkad's slingers, Shappa had to send others out to risk their lives, when he, with all his heart, wanted to be at their side.

If he had told Eskkar that he wanted to join his skirmishers across the stream, Eskkar would probably have let him go. Afterward, assuming Shappa survived, the King would have selected someone else to take command of the slingers.

Foolish courage, as Eskkar often reminded everyone, did not always win battles. A commander had a higher responsibility to his men, all his men. That responsibility demanded that Shappa stay behind, where he was most needed and could do the most good.

Tonight Shappa's main duty was not to fight, but to get the reports of his scouts, assess the information, and relay his conclusions to Eskkar and the other commanders. Not to mention Shappa might have to dispatch more slingers if necessary.

Still, he was eager to fight. He wanted to prove to all of Akkad, once and for all, the value of his men. In their hands, the sling became a powerful weapon, especially at close range. But in the last five years, he'd trained them to move through the darkness without a sound, and to strike and withdraw unseen.

Now those skills would be put to the test. The duty of his skirmishers was to first gather information, then disrupt and harry the enemy's forces until the more powerful fighting units of Akkad could be brought into play. In the blackness of night, Shappa's slingers would be even more effective.

These Alur Meriki warriors might be fearsome fighters on a horse, but Shappa doubted they would do as well at night and on foot.

Shappa had learned all the skills of a night hunter at an early age. He'd grown up on a farm just a day's journey from Akkad. As the youngest son in a family of six, he seldom got enough to eat, and soon became skilled at hunting for food among the night creatures, if he wanted to eat well. Rabbits, rodents, small game, birds, even a young deer, anything that moved after the sun went down soon fell victim to his expert sling.

Tonight Shappa envied his companions, most of them with less than sixteen seasons, who now risked their lives facing the hardy and ferocious barbarians. They might be afraid deep inside, but the bravado of youth easily overcame that, and he felt confident they could handle themselves.

A glance into the night sky showed the waxing moon still rising. Its dim light marked the dark hulk of the cliff to the north. Shappa had positioned men with the keenest night vision on the massive stone towers that rose up over the stream. He had to stay in contact with those above, making sure that news of any enemy movement they spotted reached the King's ears.

Nevertheless, Shappa grimaced in frustration, as he touched the leather sling at his belt. It was going to be a long night.

———

In the Alur Meriki encampment, Thutmose-sin sat beside a small fire. Its low flames did nothing to warm the small circle of clan leaders gathered around it. Only a handful of glowing fires marked his warriors' camp. Wood and anything else that would burn was scarce in these foothills, and the few clumps of horse dung dry enough to burn had already gone up in smoke. His guards had done well to collect even these few twigs to light their Sarum's meeting.

On the other side of the hill lay darkness. The Akkadians had no camp-fires, and only the stream remained faintly visible in the dim moonlight. The sun had disappeared from the western sky some time ago, and the deep shadows from the cliff walls soon covered the landscape between the two forces. And hiding, Thutmose-sin hoped, the number and movements of his men.

Urgo arrived last, leaning on a stick as he limped his way to the edge of the fire to join the other war chiefs.

Thutmose-sin glanced up. "Is everything ready?"

"Yes, Sarum." Despite his misgivings, Urgo had worked with all the clan leaders to prepare the attack. "Bekka and Altanar will lead their clans and attack along the southern edge of the stream. When they are in position, Suijan, Narindar, and Praxa will move forward and launch an arrow storm at the center of the dirt eaters' battle line. They will empty their quivers and then attack. After that, it will be up to you."

"After Suijan has begun his attack against the center," Thutmose-in said, "I will lead the rest of our men against the northern part of the line."

The cliff anchored the northern and apparently strongest end. If the dirt eaters believed the main attack was to the south, they would likely move some of their men down the line to face that threat.

"We will not fail you," Suijan answered for the others.

Thutmose-sin studied their faces. "Make sure your men do not attack until Bekka and Altanar are in place and have begun the assault. If you move too soon, the enemy will not shift any of their men. Remember, we want them to think our attack is concentrated at the south."

The southern part of the Akkadian line appeared the weakest, or at least the most exposed. If Thutmose-sin had more time, he would have sent a few hundred horsemen south to circle around the Akkadian camp. But that couldn't be done in one day. The earliest those riders would be in position would be the following night, and tonight he knew he would need all his warriors.

"We will give you time to get into position, Sarum," Suijan said.

Once the battle began, Thutmose-sin and Bar'rack would lead their men, over six hundred fighters, forward. They would stay close to the northern cliffs. The warriors would creep and crawl through the darkness, to get as near as possible before being seen.

The noise of the fighting should mask any sounds they made. With only a short distance to cover, they would swarm across the stream and break into the enemy's line.

"Make sure the leaders of ten and twenty understand what is to happen." Thutmose-sin hardened his tone. "There are to be no foolish charges, no loud talking. This battle must occur step by step, like three separate blows of the smith's hammer on the forging stone."

He turned to Bar'rack. "Are your men assembled and ready?"

"Yes, Sarum. And Urgo and I have instructed your men as well. Our warriors will fight bravely together."

Thutmose-sin smiled at that. It had been many years since the Sarum of the Alur Meriki had waded into battle at the head of his clansmen. "We will, indeed. And Urgo will remain behind, with fifty warriors. He will send them in wherever they are needed."

He turned toward his old friend. "Remember, Urgo, dispatch your men only if victory hangs in the balance. Do not waste their lives if the battle goes against us."

"I will follow your orders," Urgo said.

Thutmose-sin nodded. Urgo understood the value of each and every Alur Meriki warrior. He would not waste their lives foolishly. Thutmose-sin had another reason for leaving the old warrior in the rear. If Thutmose-sin were killed in the attack, Urgo would provide the voice of reason and wisdom in the Council, hopefully as the next Sarum.

"Then it is time. Start moving the men."

—◆—

As soon as night covered the ground, Markesh, second in command of the Akkadian slingers, said his farewell to Shappa. At the head of his men, Markesh led the group of sixty skirmishers across the stream in a single file. They crossed over at the northern end, as close to the cliff wall as possible. The shadows there blocked the moon's rays, and the slingers took advantage of the deeper darkness.

Like all the men chosen for this expedition, Markesh was short and slim. He moved with care through the water, crouching over and ignoring the chill that numbed his feet and lower legs. He took his time wading across and made sure he didn't make any unnecessary splashes that might reveal their presence in the water.

The tinkling stream covered what little sounds the slingers made. Their dark tunics helped conceal them as well. The archers, spearmen, and cavalry of Akkad's fighting men all wore tunics the color of wheat, the natural tint of the linen.

The slingers, at Trella's suggestion, wore garments dyed a light brown. At night, the slingers were almost impossible to see, and even during the daylight, when they hugged the ground, they tended to blend in with the sands or rocks of the landscape.

Once across, Markesh waited on the far side of the stream and counted his men. When the last of them had reached the opposite bank, they formed into three groups. Markesh took the first group of twenty, the one that had the farthest to go. He led the way, hugging the ground and crawling on his hands and knees.

One by one, his men followed after him, like a long snake slithering soundlessly over the rocks. Markesh kept the stream on his right, but slowly he angled away from the water, into the deeper darkness.

Shappa and Eskkar had warned him that the likeliest point of attack remained the southern end of the stream, and Markesh insisted on taking that position himself. If the barbarians tried to creep up under the cover of darkness, he would encounter them first. His orders were to stop them if he could, or delay them as much as possible. In any case, he had to send back knowledge of their strength.

Like the rest of his men, Markesh carried only his sling, twenty bronze bullets, and his sharp knife. The long curved blade made for a dangerous weapon at close range. When combined with the quick reflexes of agile young men, the well-trained slingers could defend themselves even against a sword. At night, creeping along on the ground, they could strike like a deadly serpent.

Though he made almost no sound, Markesh covered the ground quickly. At least, he decided, he wouldn't have to crawl back. More likely he'd end up with an arrow in his back as he tried to retreat across the stream.

He had no trouble finding his way. The stream on his right glistened in the moonlight, and marked the line of the Akkadian defenders. Still, Markesh breathed a sigh of relief when he reached his first position, about sixty paces from the water. A slight rise in the ground concealed his prone body, and he lifted his head to stare into the darkness.

Glancing to his left, he saw nothing, which meant that the rest of his men had settled into their positions. He waited a few more moments, to give his men time to settle down.

One last look around, and he whispered the order to move out. Taking care not to make the slightest sound, Markesh and his men crawled away from the safety of the stream, straight toward the Alur Meriki position. The entire line of slingers would take their station on him. If all went well, they would crawl another hundred paces toward the enemy, then settle in to await the dawn.

If the barbarians attacked tonight, they would be in for an unpleasant and hopefully unexpected surprise. They would be expecting their enemy to be beyond the stream, not right in their path. Regardless, Markesh had his orders. Identify the point of attack, send word back to Shappa and Eskkar, and slow down any assaulting force. He took some pride in knowing that he would probably be the first to meet the Alur Meriki attack.

Standing just behind the ranks of spearmen, Eskkar and Mitrac watched the slingers move into position. Eskkar's eyes had lost the keenest of his youth, and his ability to see into the night's shadows had suffered as well. It took some time to discern the crawling men. If they made any noise, he couldn't hear it over the gurgling of the stream, and he doubted if any Alur Meriki could either.

Then the line of skirmishers vanished. "I can't see them any more."

The moment he uttered the words, Eskkar swore under his breath. Of course he couldn't see them. They weren't supposed to be seen. He hated revealing his nervousness by making foolish statements.

"They've moved away from the stream," Mitrac said. "I can just make out the last of them disappearing toward the hill."

Eskkar gritted his teeth, grateful for the darkness that hid his frustration. Still, the master bowman Mitrac, raised in the vast distances of the northern steppes, had better eyesight than most men.

"Now we wait." Only the growl in his voice betrayed Eskkar's tension.

"I'll go check on my bowmen," Mitrac said, no doubt glad for the excuse to leave the King's brooding presence.

All the Akkadian archers, including Hathor's men, sat on the ground, their weapons ready. The men tried to rest, catching a few moments of sleep when they could, but always prepared for battle. If the barbarians attacked, arrows would be flying everywhere, and every man who wielded a bow needed to be ready.

Eskkar had already made his own preparations, donning the bronze plates that formed a layer of protection across his chest and back. A bronze helmet lined with leather fitted snugly on his head, with flanges on each side that extended down to cover his temples, and reached nearly to the back of his neck. Eskkar had first worn the armor at the battle of Isin, more than eight years ago.

Since then, he always wore the helmet and chest plates when he practiced his swordsmanship. The extra weight and bulk tended to slow him down, and forced him to work his muscles harder on the exercise ground.

At least twice a year Trella made sure the bronze laces and shoulder straps fit perfectly. She understood that the more natural his movements, the more likely he would survive.

Tonight he felt grateful for the added protection. Unlike most of his men, who would be kneeling or crouched over, Eskkar would be standing upright and moving up and down the line. The small shield he'd brought with him from Aratta would help, but he couldn't depend on that alone. Arrows would be plummeting from the darkness, and the more protection, the better.

Like most soldiers, Eskkar had his own personal fear. Some men envisioned a sword piercing their bellies, others trembled at the thought of a blade in their groin. For Eskkar, it was the vision of an arrow striking him in the eye, carrying his death on its point. He shrugged the gloomy image away, and concentrated on his duty.

Moving along the line, he reached Hathor's position at the center of the Akkadian position. The Egyptian had no bow, but close to his hand five lances had been thrust into the ground. Hathor could fling the slim, bronze-tipped weapon with the best of his men, whether from horseback or standing on the ground. He, too, had a shield slung over his shoulder.

Eskkar resisted the urge to ask if Hathor's men were ready. If any of them weren't, Hathor would have told him. "Can you see anything?"

Another stupid question had slipped past Eskkar's lips.

"Nothing, Captain. It's as black as a demon's cave out there." Hathor keep his eyes on the far side of the stream. "If anyone's out there, I hope the slingers find them."

Eskkar grunted. "Damn all this night fighting."

From the hill that overlooked the Alur Meriki camp, Bekka moved his men forward, creeping down the hill and hugging the darkest shadows. Over two hundred warriors followed behind him, each making their way as best they could while trying to make as little noise as possible. Progress remained slow, however, and he heard the muffled curses mixed with the faint clink of bronze weapons scraping over the rough ground.

The distance from the hill to the stream, only a short ride on horseback, took much longer than expected for men on foot. By the time Bekka reached the halfway point, he knew the first part of Thutmose-sin's plan had already gone astray. He and his men would be late getting into position.

Every twenty paces, Bekka lifted his head and looked toward the Akkadian camp. At last he glimpsed the silvery gleam of the stream, now less than two hundred paces away. He thought he could hear the water rushing along. Dropping to his knees, he continued his slow march forward, his men following his example.

Despite the noise from the stream, Bekka decided the Akkadians would hear them coming long before his men got into position. Many of the extra fighters assigned to Bekka's command consisted of old men and young boys. Both lacked the hard discipline of mature warriors. They would fight and die bravely enough, but it was too much to expect them to move silently.

Bekka swore under his breath at the too frequent noises behind him. To his ears, it sounded as loud as a mounted charge. Once again he wondered if the war gods had determined to claim his soul tonight. He cursed the Akkadians for drawing him and the Alur Meriki into this night fight.

Thoughts of death, something no warrior should acknowledge, had lurked in Bekka's thoughts since Thutmose-sin had selected him to ride out and meet with Eskkar. The leader of the Alur Meriki had picked Bekka, one of the youngest chiefs, instead of the older and wiser leaders like Suijan or Praxa. Thutmose-sin hadn't bothered to explain his choice, and his curt voice when he announced his decision had silenced any questions from the others.

Still, Bekka had seen the looks on the other chiefs' faces. Bekka might have been at the stream longer than any of the chiefs, but that seemed like a weak explanation. Bar'rack's selection was merely to test Eskkar's willingness to be drawn into a fight.

Bekka pushed these thoughts from his mind. Whatever Thutmose-sin's reason, it no longer mattered. Bekka's duty demanded that he do his utmost in the attack, and he knew how slim the odds were that he would survive the coming encounter.

Though no one expected the dirt eaters to be sleeping at their posts, Bekka hoped to catch them at least slightly off guard, giving the attack a chance to succeed. Besides their bows and swords, most of Bekka's force carried lances, more useful weapons at close range.

Fifty paces behind Bekka, Altanar would be guiding his own clan and half of Bekka's, keeping three hundred warriors ready to support Bekka's attack when it began. Altanar's men would rise up as one and launch the first volley of arrows, arching them high to avoid striking Bekka's men, to break the ranks of the dirt eaters. Or so Bekka had told his men. The thought of taking an arrow in the back from his own kind didn't appeal to him.

He swore again at the slow progress. The plan that had seemed reasonable enough around the council fire now appeared fraught with danger. Bekka's forces leading the attack were going to take heavy losses.

He just hoped they succeeded in their task. A warrior's main duty was to fight, but Bekka hated the thought of dying for nothing. He and his men had to buy enough time for Thutmose-sin and the brunt of the Alur Meriki forces to launch their assault.

That meant that Bekka and Altanar had to keep fighting until their Sarum attacked. Bekka had no doubts about the fighting ability of these Akkadians. He'd seen them prepare to attack his warriors on the hill, and their cold efficiency in cutting down the riders in the steam. Win or lose tonight, Bekka knew it was unlikely he would survive.

—◁▥᠊ᡶ▥᠊

As Markesh had instructed his slingers before they left camp, they settled down in a rough line about a hundred and fifty paces beyond the stream. Overhead, the faint sliver of the moon moved slowly across the night sky, its journey the only way to tell that most of the night had night already passed.

Dawn was not far off, and Markesh almost convinced himself that there would be no nighttime attack when he first heard the muted scrape of bronze on stone, or perhaps a bow dragging along the ground, faint sounds that grew ever louder, and more frequent.

He remained motionless, his eyes closed so that he could hear better. Soon the little telltale noises grew louder, and Markesh guessed that a sizeable enemy force was moving toward him. Despite their attempts to keep silent, the Alur Meriki could not muffle all the sounds of their approach.

At last Markesh opened his eyes and nodded in satisfaction. As he expected, the Alur Meriki might be fearsome warriors, but they lacked experience in this kind of fighting. The slingers, however, had prepared for an encounter like this, and they could move in near silence. While the rest of Eskkar's army practiced by day, Markesh and the others like him spent half their time training at night.

The wait seemed endless, as Markesh heard the clumsy movements of the enemy approaching his position. Still, those sounds were not yet loud enough to be heard on the Akkadian side of the stream.

Lying flat on the earth, Markesh's heart beat rapidly in his chest, and his mouth felt dry, though he had gulped plenty of water before setting out.

He wasn't afraid, not really, but excitement threatened to overwhelm him. Then he glimpsed a dark hump of a shadow moving toward him. Markesh wondered if the approaching enemy could hear his heart pounding in his chest.

He gripped his sling, and took a deep breath. A faint whirr sounded less than five paces to his left. One of his men had struck first. The smack of the bronze ball striking flesh wasn't loud, but the gasp of pain from the warrior carried over the ground.

Markesh rose to his knees, and spun a missile toward the still-approaching shadow, now less than twenty paces away. A muffled oath marked the bullet's strike, but Markesh had already ducked back down, and slipped another missile into the sling's pouch.

All around him, Markesh heard the soft but continuous whirring that marked each throw of a sling. Not every cast scored a hit, but the throws continued, as the slingers hurled missile after missile at any and every approaching shadow. The effect on the warriors proved all that Markesh could expect.

⊸ᴍ◦ᴍᴍ⊷

Bekka heard the unseen missiles striking all around him. His men were under some kind of attack, but he could see no one. Only when a stone glanced off the earth, its impact kicking dirt in his face, did he understand what was happening. The Akkadians had moved their slingers, dismissed by the Alur Meriki warriors as a feeble fighting force, into the ground between the stream and Bekka's position. And now these boys were striking at his warriors with deadly force and at close range.

Neither Thutmose-sin nor any of the other clan leaders had foreseen this. Bekka swore at his own stupidity. Of course the Akkadians would have scouts out in the land beyond the stream. Clenching his teeth, Bekka squirmed forward and hugged the ground.

He'd covered only a few more paces when he realized the plan had broken down. All surprise had vanished with the loud groans of Bekka's wounded. This invisible enemy had to be swept aside, or they were going to stop the attack before it even reached the stream. Bekka lifted himself to one knee. "Warriors! Attack! Attack!"

He matched his own words. Leaping to his feet, he rushed toward his unseen attackers, sword in one hand, shield in the other. His warriors, as frustrated as their clan leader at this invisible and silent enemy, rose to their feet, let loose their war cries, and charged after their leader. In a moment, two hundred warriors raced through the darkness, as heedless of the slingers before them as of the treacherous ground underfoot.

The night erupted with the battle cries of the Alur Meriki. So far no arrows had come from the Akkadians. A few paces ahead, Bekka now glimpsed men fleeing toward the stream, and guessed these must be the slingers, running for the safety of their lines.

From behind, Bekka heard the first flight of Altanar's arrows hissing their way toward the Akkadian position. Then Bekka's own men began to fall, some crashing to the ground on either side, and he heard their curses as the sharp, bronze-tipped Akkadian arrows smacked into their flesh.

Something hummed past his ear, but Bekka kept moving. Twice he stumbled over the loose rocks the Akkadians had scattered on the bank, but both times he regained his footing. Then he reached the stream, and splashed into the chilly water.

The force of the current slowed him down, but Bekka lunged forward. Younger and more agile warriors surged ahead of him, kicking up plumes of cold water. Several fell on the slippery footing and crashed headlong into the water. Others went down and failed to rise. Death had taken them. Bekka heard the curses of the wounded join with the war cries of his men.

Breathing hard, he staggered onto the far side of the stream. By now Bekka could see the white blurs that marked the faces of the enemy. Already a few of his men flung themselves onto the Akkadians.

Then Bekka reached the enemy line. With a savage whirl, he knocked a spear aside and swung his blade with all his strength. A scream of pain burst into his face. More of his men surged out of the water and reached his side, cutting and hacking with their swords, others thrusting with their lances. Shouts of rage mixed with the cries of the wounded. He glimpsed men falling all around him, and wondered when the arrow or spear tip would rend his own flesh.

The Akkadian line sagged for a moment, but it held, and as fast as Bekka could swing his blade, another sword or spear thrust at his breast. Arrows shot at such close range ripped into his men, turning war cries into screams of pain. Twisting and dodging, he fought back. At the same time, he urged his men to break through the enemy's line.

While the front lines of both forces fought grimly, archers on both sides kept pouring shafts into the ranks. Altanar's warriors continued shooting their arrows as they charged forward. Bekka cursed as one of his fighters stumbled to the earth, an arrow in the back of his neck. The two forces had closed together, and Altanar's bowmen had little to aim at.

Bekka might be struck from behind by his own kind, the worst way to die. He crouched down as he fought. The Akkadian archers launched shafts so fast that most of his men were killed or wounded even before they could bring their swords into play.

A spear burned along his left side, and Bekka stepped into the thrust and shoved the point of his blade into the spearman's face. Then the crush of warriors pushed him forward and up against the front rank of the Akkadians. Bekka voiced his battle cry as he struggled to free his sword arm. They were going to break through the enemy's line. He could feel it.

Another Akkadian spear thrust at his belly. He shoved it aside with his sword, but before he could react, the thick edge of a shield smashed into his forehead, knocking him backward. As Bekka struggled to regain his footing, a sword cut into his right arm, sending a wave of pain through his body and making his own weapon slip from his fingers.

A strong arm caught Bekka by the shoulder and dragged him back, away from the carnage of the line. Then Bekka's feet felt the cold water of the stream. All around him warriors were falling back, away from the battle line and their Akkadian pursuers.

Bekka shook himself free and took a step back toward the Akkadians.

"It's over," Unegen shouted. "The attack has failed."

Bekka glanced to his left and right. Unegen pulled him back into the water, and in a moment, they had joined the others, moving as fast as they could. Arrows still hissed into their midst, and Bekka waited for the one that would strike him down and take his life. Then they were across the stream, stumbling through the rocks and back into the dark shadows.

Bekka ran as hard as he could, gasping for breath. Then he flung himself behind a rise in the ground. Unegen, gulping air into his body, dropped to the ground beside him.

"We failed." Bekka uttered the bitter words.

"At least we're alive," Unegen said.

"Yes, at least we're alive," Bekka answered. "For now."

———————

From the northern end of the warrior advance, Thutmose-sin watched the attack. For some reason, Bekka had started his assault early. The center force had also pushed its way forward and into the stream and launched their attack, and now the far side of the water roiled as men charged up the bank and flung themselves at the hated dirt eaters. He couldn't see much, but the noise of the conflict had risen, the echoes bouncing off the cliffs and hills and adding to the din.

"We must attack now!" Bar'rack had moved to Thutmose-sin's side. "The warriors have not broken the line."

"It's almost time. Get back to your men," he hissed. "Await my signal."

Thutmose-sin lifted himself from the ground, to get a better look at the fighting. The splashes in the stream had almost ceased, so he knew all of Bekka's warriors had crossed the water. He glimpsed Akkadians moving behind their line. If the dirt eaters had shifted their fighters, it was indeed time to attack.

"Bar'rack! Warriors! Attack! Attack!"

He rose to his feet and raced toward the stream, voicing the age old battle cry of the Alur Meriki, the undulating wail that had never failed to strike terror into the hearts of their enemies.

———————

Up on the cliff face that overlooked the northern end of the stream, over twenty slingers clung to the steep sides, crouching in crevices or kneeling on tiny ledges scarcely wide enough for a foot hold. Luka, a leader of twenty, commanded these men. When the attack began at the far end of the stream, they'd moved from their hiding places into more open positions, finding their footing and seeking advantageous outcroppings where they could use their slings. They were more exposed, but they could fight more efficiently.

Even before the attack, Luka had seen the ground, nearly thirty paces below, slowly shift. Looking down, he glimpsed movement everywhere, and what looked like a mass of shadows writhing across the rocky ground directly beneath him. It took a moment before he realized that a large number of Alur Meriki were creeping toward the stream.

When the attack began, he'd expected the barbarians below him to rise up and join their companions. However these warriors held back, either waiting for orders or for some other unknown reason. Whatever held them back, Luka stayed his own hand. He wanted clear targets for his precious bronze bullets, and didn't want to waste a single one on what might be a shadow.

A voice from the shadows below shouted something in the barbarian tongue. Instantly the ground came alive, as a mass of men rose up and raced toward the stream. For a moment, Luka stared open-mouthed at the warriors, surprised at their numbers. How could so many men have gotten so close to the stream? He had paid too much attention to the attacks on the rest of the line.

"Now! Throw!" Luka's words launched the first wave of stones. He spun his own weapon, hurling a bronze bullet into the moving mass of men below him. Before the sling had completed its revolution, he had a second missile in position. His left hand caught the still moving leather pouch, and the loose cord whipped up as he seated the stone. Another savage snap of his wrist and shoulder sent the second heavy pellet toward the barbarians below.

His few men could not hope to stem the flow, but by now arrows from the Akkadian ranks at the base of the cliff began shooting as well. The barbarians loosed their own shafts as they charged. Screams and curses floated up into the air from both sides of the attack. Luka ignored them all as he worked his sling.

Despite the battle rage, years of training kept the stones flying from his weapon. He soon realized the warriors below showed no interest in the handful of slingers atop the cliff, so Luka and his men stood upright and hurled their missiles with even greater force at the barbarians now splashing across the stream, shouting their unnerving war cries.

From his place behind the archers, Eskkar heard the barbarian war cries, and saw the mass of Alur Meriki warriors charging toward the stream. He'd already dispatched some of the northernmost men to help out in the center and southern part of the defense line, and there was no time to get them back. Eskkar drew his sword as the first wave of barbarian warriors burst into the water, their churning feet sending splashes high into the air, almost as if asking the water to conceal their movements.

At least he had no need to bellow orders. The archers and cavalry men loosed their arrows as fast as they could. Many launched ten or more arrows before the first wave of the enemy charged up from the stream and hurled themselves at the Akkadians.

But the barbarians found more than archers waiting for them. Akkadian spearmen stood there. They had not formed the solid ranks they preferred. Eskkar hadn't brought enough of them for that. But every fourth man in that part of the line carried a shield and a spear, and the sharp tips of their weapons glistened in the moonlight.

None of the spearmen waited for the Alur Meriki to reach them. Nearly every spearman impaled a warrior with his first thrust, stepping forward with a long stride and using their bodies and extending their arms to ram home the long weapon, often brushing aside an enemy sword or lance.

Some of Eskkar's spearmen lost the use of their weapon with that first kill, as dying men and clinging flesh clamped themselves on the weapons. But the Akkadians, trained for that occurrence, too, and drew swords from their scabbards even as they took a step back and raised their shields up to their eyes.

With their shoulders lowered behind the shield, the spearmen stood firm, hacking and jabbing at their enemy. Unlike the Alur Meriki warriors, who preferred to swing their swords overhead and in a downward arc, Gatus had trained the Akkadians to hold their swords low and thrust up, taking a step forward at the same time, and aiming for belly wounds.

When the barbarians swung their swords, the spearmen took a step back, then moved forward and lunged again. That gave the spearmen another advantage, as they could execute two or more thrusting attacks for every overhead swing of the enemy warriors.

Meanwhile, behind and between the Akkadian ranks, arrows shot at eye level, both from the longbows and the shorter cavalry weapons, wreaked deadly damage on the charging attackers.

Eskkar glanced up and down the line. He glimpsed Hathor, his supply of lances expended, wading into the line, sword in hand. Mitrac had started with three quivers of arrows, and he still loosed his shafts, their powerful sting searching out the most ferocious barbarians, and probably killing a man with each arrow.

Despite the Akkadians' efforts, the northern portion of their line weakened under the ferocious onslaught, but Shappa arrived, returning from the southern end of the battle line. He brought fifty or so slingers with him. He'd collected Markesh's men after they regrouped back on the Akkadian side of the stream, and now led them at a run to the northern end of the line. Unable to use their preferred weapons against such a crowded mass, the slingers carried their long knives in hand.

Wherever the line of defenders appeared weak, Shappa shoved his men forward to reinforce those points. Young and fearless, they relied on their quickness and agility to avoid their stronger and larger opponents. While his men lacked the size and weight to battle a warrior face to face, they could slip in, strike low, duck under any enemy thrust, and dart back as they'd trained, taking a man down with a thrust to the thigh, stomach, or groin.

The barbarian attack slowed, devastated by the hail of arrows at such close range, and the hail of stones that descended from the cliff. Meanwhile, the Akkadian line recovered and hardened. The spearmen were difficult to bring down, and they used their shields as effectively as their swords.

Akkad! Kill! The Akkadian war cries grew louder and stronger, giving strength to Eskkar's men.

Even the Alur Meriki could not break such a defense. By now more than eight hundred archers and bowmen had each emptied at least a quiver of arrows into the barbarian horde. Their surge halted.

Eskkar sensed the moment had come. "Spearmen! Attack! Drive them back!"

He pushed his way through the archers and flung himself into the line. His long sword swung down, knocking aside a blade and striking deep into a warrior's shoulder. His bronze helmet and chest plate turned aside an enemy's sword thrust.

Using his small shield as adroitly as any of his spearmen, Eskkar pressed forward, using his shoulder to knock another man back, and

smashing the thick ball of bronze that formed his sword's hilt into the face
of another.

All the Akkadians were shouting now, matching the barbarian war
cries in volume, as they moved forward and forced the warriors back. The
defenders sensed their opponent's wavering.

The Alur Meriki had done their best, but the relentless storm of arrows,
accompanied by stones flung at them from above, had killed or wounded too
many of Thutmose-sin's warriors to enable the attackers to overwhelm Eskkar's
line. Not enough warriors had survived the crossing to break the Akkadian ranks.

Pushed back a few steps by the Akkadians' advance, it took only
moments before the retreat turned into a rout, as the warriors turned and
fled back through the water. Only a few arrows hissed through the air during their retreat. Many of the archers had dropped their bows and taken up
swords to contain the assault, while others had expended all their shafts.
Splashes roiled the waters of the stream, masking the violent sounds of
men cursing and shouting in their rage.

Then the splashes died away. Gradually the water resumed its normal
gurgle, as the Alur Meriki disappeared into the darkness, heading back
toward their own hill.

Now the cries of the wounded ascended into the night, the awful sound
as injured men on both sides writhed in pain, most of them knowing that
death would soon take them. Ignoring their cries, Eskkar halted at the edge
of the stream, breathing hard. Some of his men had splashed into the water.
He raised his voice and bellowed.

"Everyone! Back to the line! Back to the line!"

Holding his shield before him, Eskkar backed away from the stream,
glancing frequently to make sure of his footing. Bodies and loose stones,
both now covered in blood, might still send a man tumbling to the ground.

His commanders and leaders of ten and twenty repeated his order.
Soon all the Akkadian survivors were back in their original position. Every
man gulped air as fast as he could, chests rising and falling.

Swords and spears now seemed almost too heavy to hold, and more
than a few were dragged along the ground as the suddenly exhausted
men stumbled back. Some realized for the first time that they had taken
wounds. Others, still caught up in the battle fever, continued to hurl curses
at their enemies.

Many Alur Meriki dead remained in the stream, their bodies snagged on rocks or jammed fast against other bodies. One by one, those floated clear of whatever obstruction held them, and drifted away. That, too, lasted only a few moments, before most of the dead were swept downstream, and water ran clear once again.

Only a handful of bodies, those caught on the rocks, still bled into the cold water. The ground between the Akkadian line and the stream remained littered with the dead and dying, along with a collection of swords, lances, bows, and other enemy weapons.

"I don't think they'll be back tonight." Hathor, breathing heavily, had reached Eskkar's side.

Eskkar shook the battle fury from his thoughts. "The rest of the line? Are they . . ."

"We held them all the way," Hathor said. "These must have been the pick of the attackers. None of the others fought as hard or lasted as long as these did."

Eskkar could still hear the sounds of the warriors retreating. At least they'd stopped shooting arrows toward the Akkadian side of the stream. "I'll see to the men."

Eskkar moved down the line, speaking to his soldiers, talking with Alexar and the other commanders along the way. Before he reached the southernmost part of the line, Eskkar had spoken with almost every leader of ten and twenty he encountered, asking them how they'd fought, and making sure they aided their wounded. He knew his men would remember his concern.

Many men had received a wound, either an arrow or the thrust or slash of a sword. Some of these lay on the ground, tended to by their companions. The piteous cries of the wounded, the aftermath of every battle, fanned the anger of the survivors.

The dead, most with arrows still protruding from their bodies, were dragged to the rear. They would have to wait until sunrise before they could receive whatever burial rites his men could offer.

By the time Eskkar had moved up and down the line twice, the sky in the east had begun to lighten. Dawn approached, and very likely another attack. Nevertheless, the water yet glistened in the faint moonlight, and it still belonged to the Akkadians.

10

The sun had risen over the hills without Thutmose-sin noticing. He sat on a small boulder, his hands hanging at his sides, staring at the ground between his feet. The stunned survivors of the attack surrounded him, but he neither saw nor heard them. For the first time in his life, Thutmose-sin was alone.

More than twenty years ago, Thutmose-sin had stood on the bank of the Tigris and swore to his ancestors that he would never allow the dirt eaters to grow strong enough to threaten the Alur Meriki and their way of life. Now that day had arrived, and he had failed in his duty. Nothing he could do, nothing he could say, would diminish the defeat that he and his people had endured.

His gods had abandoned him, giving their favor to an outcast. They had not even permitted Thutmose-sin an honorable death in battle, and with at least a shred of honor. Instead, he would have to endure the unendurable.

The moans of the injured penetrated the dark cloud of his thoughts. He lifted his head, and tried to comprehend the disaster that had overtaken his people. What he saw wrenched at his heart. Truly, he wished his body lay dead on the battleground.

Those wounded but still able to walk cursed their cuts and slashes as they waited their turn with the healers, who bandaged as many as they could. Those who had survived the battle uninjured or with only minor wounds sat scattered all around, heads down in shame and humiliation.

Once again, Alur Meriki fighters had suffered defeat at the hands of the hated dirt eaters, led by a renegade from their own clan.

Thutmose-sin's fighters had spearheaded the final assault and taken the worst of the casualties. He awaited the final tally of dead and wounded, but knew the numbers would tell a grim story. A healer already had tended to his Sarum's wounds, binding up a deep cut on his left arm from an Akkadian spear, and a sword thrust that had grazed his ribs.

Neither injury had prevented him from fighting, until what must have been a stone from a sling struck his head, dropping him to his knees, and stunning him.

By the time he'd shaken the weakness from his head, the attack had already failed, and Thutmose-sin's personal guards, the few who survived, dragged him to safety back across the stream and into the sheltering darkness.

He glanced up as a horse approached. Urgo slid down from his mount, taking his time. Thutmose-sin saw that the old warrior had taken an arrow in the leg, adding to his afflictions, when Urgo led the reserves into the conflict in a futile attempt to turn the tide. Bar'rack and Bekka, on foot, followed behind him. Bloody bandages decorated both men. The two chiefs had fought hard, but failed to break the Akkadian line.

"I've taken the count of the dead and wounded." Urgo dropped to the earth beside his Sarum and closed his eyes for a moment of comfort.

"How many?" Not that Thutmose-sin cared any longer. This defeat ended his rule over the Clan. It would have been kinder for his guards to have left him behind, to be hacked to death by the dirt eaters along with the other wounded unable to crawl away.

"Three hundred and forty dead," Urgo said. "At least that number wounded. Many of them will die, even if they reach the wagons. Altanar is dead, as is Narindar and Praxa. Suijan is badly wounded, and can fight no more today."

Four clan leaders dead or unable to fight. More than one warrior in three dead or wounded. For the first time, Thutmose-sin heard their moans rising up all around him. From their youngest days, warriors were taught not to show pain, but some wounds were too severe for even the bravest to resist.

"We will have to attack again," Bar'rack said, breaking the custom of not speaking until the eldest clan leader had finished. "At least this time we'll ride into battle like warriors."

The first criticism of his leadership, Thutmose-sin noted. Of course, if the night attack had succeeded, no one would have dared say anything. "How many dirt eaters did we kill?"

"It's hard to say." Urgo stretched out his leg and grimaced. "But not many. Perhaps a hundred, maybe more. Their archers cut down many of our men before they crossed the stream."

Six dead or wounded warriors for every dirt eater. Thutmose-sin had attacked at night to prevent just such a disaster, and it had still befallen him. In his anger, Bar'rack spoke the truth. They would have done as well to attack at dawn on horseback. At least they would have died with more honor than crawling on their bellies.

"Who gave the order to retreat?" Thutmose-sin lifted his brow, expecting Urgo to answer.

"I did." Bekka's voice sounded firm and unapologetic. "I've lost nearly half my men. The dirt eaters weren't going to break, and I saw no sense in the rest of us dying on their spears."

"You should have kept fighting until you broke their ranks!" Bar'rack's accusing voice revealed his anger.

Bekka eyed his detractor. On another day, Bar'rack's criticism might have resulted in a challenge. But not today.

"No, Bekka was right to stop the slaughter." Thutmose-sin spoke quickly to avoid the quarrel. "Eskkar spoke the truth. Even if we broke their ranks, it would have meant the end of the Alur Meriki."

"When will we be ready to attack again?" Bar'rack raised his voice, his rage and humiliation clear to all. "We need the water more than ever. Soon we will lose control of the horses."

The animals had scented water for two days now, but been held from reaching the stream. Many had not tasted more than a mouthful of water for longer than that. Another day, and no amount of rope would hold them from breaking free and rushing to the stream.

"An attack in daylight will mean the end of the Alur Meriki," Urgo said. "The Akkadians will break our charge, and then our women and wagons will be at their mercy. Another day or two without water, and our surviving warriors will have no strength to resist them."

"Are we to do nothing then?" His hands clenched into fists at his side, Bar'rack could barely control his anger and frustration. "Will we just sit here until thirst kills us in front of our women?"

"What do you suggest, Urgo?" Bekka sat down beside the old warrior.

Thutmose-sin understood the implication. Bekka, too, had signaled his lack of confidence in his Sarum.

"We need to find a way to deal with Eskkar." Urgo kept his voice calm. "He was one of us once. He will not want to see the women and children die a slow death from lack of water."

"No! We must attack now." Bar'rack's contorted face flushed red. "Either we achieve victory or we die in battle."

"Silence!" Thutmose-sin climbed to his feet. "You must not fight among yourselves. Whatever you decide to do, you must be in agreement."

"And what do you suggest?" Urgo spoke before Bar'rack could again vent his rage.

"I will make one last attempt to talk to Eskkar," Thutmose-sin answered, "to challenge him to a fight to the death. If he refuses to fight, then I will ride against his forces and kill as many as I can before I die."

His words stunned them into silence.

"No matter what happens, I am no longer your Sarum. Choose another as soon as I am gone. Urgo, you will take command of my clansmen."

Thutmose-sin called for his horse. The last of his guards led the big gray over, and Thutmose-sin swung onto the animal's back, ignoring the pain in his side. He settled his sword into place across his back, snatched a lance from one of the warriors, and rode off.

No one, not even his guards, followed him. Most didn't even bother to lift their heads as he passed through their midst.

—◈—

"We must have a new Sarum." Bekka didn't even wait until Thutmose-sin had disappeared over the hill.

"I will take command of the Alur Meriki." Bar'rack voice rose up loud enough to be heard by those near them. "If this is to be our last fight, then we must die with honor."

"No. I chose Urgo as our new Sarum." Bekka's words carried a force that caught both Urgo and Bar'rack by surprise. "Now is not the time for another slaughter of the Alur Meriki. Urgo will find another way."

"Urgo is too old . . ."

"Urgo is wise." Bekka rose to his feet. "The Alur Meriki need wisdom now if we are to survive. Unlike you, I am not so eager to see my women and children dead in their wagons." He turned to the old warrior. "Will you accept the name of Sarum?"

"Yes." Urgo offered his hand to Bekka, who helped lift him upright. "And Bekka will be my war chief."

Bar'rack's eyes flashed from one to the other, his teeth bared in disgust. "So the coward and the old fool join together. No warrior will follow a fool into battle."

"Summon your clan, Bekka," Urgo ordered. "Tell every warrior the news. The sooner they know who leads them, the better."

Bekka nodded. He understood what must happen. Bar'rack had to be prevented from ordering the warriors to follow him in another attack.

With an oath, Bar'rack spun on his heel and walked away. Bekka went in the opposite direction, both men seeking out his horse, and leaving Urgo behind. Once mounted, Bekka rode through the dispirited warriors, shouting the news and ordering his men to pass the word.

As the news spread, Bekka looked around for Bar'rack, and saw him pacing his horse away in silence. Bekka did not notice that Bar'rack rode not toward where his clansmen sat, but toward the top of the hill, following the path taken by Thutmose-sin.

—◦◦◦—

"Captain! Wake up." Hathor shook Eskkar's shoulder a second time. "There's a rider coming."

Eskkar pulled himself to his feet. After a long day, a sleepless night, and a hard fought battle, he'd hoped to get a few moments rest. A glance at the gray clouds that stretched overhead and blocked the morning sun told him he'd slept only a few moments. A few drops of rain fell from the sky, scattering themselves on the ground.

"One rider?" Eskkar felt a sudden breeze against his face that pushed the rain aside. He rubbed the sleep from his eyes. Hathor wouldn't have roused him for a single warrior.

"Just one, but I think it's Thutmose-sin. At least it's the same gray stallion."

A look toward the enemy lines showed a single horsemen picking his way to the bottom of the hill. As Eskkar watched, the warrior brought the horse into an easy canter. By now Eskkar had reached the front ranks of his men. He stared at the approaching rider.

"That's Thutmose-sin, all right. And carrying a lance."

Mitrac stepped to the King's side, his great bow already strung, waiting for the order to shoot. "He's almost in range."

Eskkar shook his head. He felt curious at the rider's steady pace toward the Akkadians as did the rest of his men. All had climbed to their feet, shifting positions and shading their eyes against the rising sun, wondering if this portended another attack.

Thutmose-sin reached the place where the chiefs and Eskkar had met yesterday, but he kept riding toward them.

"He's in long range now, Captain," Mitrac said. "I can have twenty archers ready to shoot. One of us will bring him down."

"No." This time Eskkar used his command voice, the tone that brooked no argument. "Tell your men to hold their arrows."

A hundred and fifty paces from the stream, Thutmose-sin halted his horse. He hefted the lance over his shoulder, then threw it in a high arc toward the Akkadians. The slim missile dug into the earth about seventy or eighty paces short of the stream. Then the stallion reared up on its hind legs, thrusting its front hooves at the Akkadians before crashing down to the earth.

"I am Thutmose-sin, Sarum of the Alur Meriki." The powerful voice, full of authority, rolled across the stream and echoed off the cliff. "I come to challenge Eskkar of Akkad to fight me to the death. If he is not afraid, let him come forth and face me with a sword in his hand."

"By the gods," Hathor muttered. "Is he mad?"

"No, not mad." Eskkar understood what must have happened. "He's ready to die. By now his warriors have abandoned him. He led them to defeat, and he cannot rule them any longer."

"Then let's kill him now," Hathor said. "Mitrac's archers can finish him off. One volley will do it."

Eskkar considered it. He had nothing to gain by accepting Thutmose-sin's challenge. And the warrior was offering nothing for victory or defeat. The time for that had passed. Only a warrior's honor remained.

"You're not thinking of riding out there." Alexar, too, had wakened from a brief sleep and joined the other commanders. "If he's desperate enough to throw his life away, let Mitrac's archers finish him."

"Perhaps you're right." Movement on the hilltop caught Eskkar's eye, and he saw warriors filling up the crest of the hill.

"Look!" Alexar pointed toward the hill. "They're getting ready to attack again."

But the distant warriors made no hostile moves. No bows or lances waved in the air, no shouts of bravado.

"They know he's a dead man,' Eskkar said, "but Thutmose-sin is carrying what's left of their honor."

By now warriors covered the hilltop, some on horseback, but most on foot. Not as many as yesterday, but probably every warrior who could walk or drag himself onto the back of a horse was up there, waiting to see how Thutmose-sin would be treated.

Eskkar made up his mind. He couldn't let this challenge to his honor go unmet. Besides, if he ordered Thutmose-sin shot down like a wild dog, the barbarians would fight to the death, and many more Akkadians would die. Perhaps there might be another way.

"No one is to shoot at that man. No one, do you hear?" Eskkar made eye contact with each of commanders, to be sure everyone understood his words. "Hathor, send for my horse. I'm going to meet him."

"Are you as mad as he?" Hathor demanded. "There's no reason . . ."

"Yes, there is, and maybe a good one. This is about more than honor. Do as I ask."

Eskkar slung his sword over his shoulder. One of the soldiers had cleaned it after last night's fighting, but Eskkar checked to make sure the blade drew easily. Another soldier ran up to him, leading A-tuku.

Esskar checked the halter himself, making sure the rope was firmly in place, but without undue stress on the animal's head. He patted the stallion on his neck, and let the horse nuzzle his face. His life might depend on his mount in a few moments. Satisfied, Esskar swung himself onto the horse's back and let it paw the ground as it adjusted to its master's weight.

"Give me a lance," Esskar ordered. "And no matter what happens, do not kill Thutmose-sin. His warriors will fight to death if he dies in dishonor. Even if he kills me, his own warriors will finish him."

Before Esskar could get the horse in motion, the leader of his Hawk Clan bodyguards, Chandor, stepped forward and grabbed the halter. "My Lord, I cannot let you do this. Let me ride out and kill this man for you."

Another of Esskar's personal guard, a grizzled veteran named Pekka, grasped the other side of the halter. "My Lord, Lady Trella ordered us to stop you from taking risks like this. She insisted . . ."

Esskar's face hardened, and he stared at the man. The soldier blanched at the force of Esskar's determination.

"Please, My Lord, I meant no offense." Pekka shrank back and released the halter.

Even here, hundreds of miles from Akkad and in the middle of a battle, his wife exerted her influence and his men showed their respect for her wishes. "Stand aside, both of you. This is not some foolish challenge. I need to do this, and only I know what must be done."

He spoke the words with force, in a tone that few dared to resist or argue against. Before either of them could think about what to do, Esskar touched his heels to his mount, and the powerful animal moved forward. Chandor's hands slipped from the halter, as he lowered his head.

"Alexar! Mitrac! Hathor! Make sure everyone obeys my command." Esskar called the order over his shoulder. "No one is to leave the ranks."

Without waiting for an acknowledgment, Esskar paced his way down toward the stream, taking his time. This was dangerous and he wanted time to think. Thutmose-sin had nothing to lose. For him, victory or death were the same. Not that the warrior expected to survive. Even if he killed Esskar, Thutmose-sin must know that the Akkadian bowmen would cut him down. All he wanted was one last chance for revenge, and to die with honor.

Again Esskar halted the bay in the middle of the stream, letting A-tuku slurp a few noisy mouthfuls before pulling up on the halter. He allowed the horse to choose its path across the stream and a few paces beyond. Then Eskkar hefted the lance in his right hand, leaned back, and hurled it toward the Alur Meriki lance jutting into the air. Eskkar's missile landed just beside that of Thutmose-sin, a good throw. The challenge had been made and now accepted.

Once again, Eskkar touched his heels to his horse, and let the animal pick its way through the rocks. Bodies lay strewn everywhere, the dead lying face down, many with arrows in their back. Others stared sightlessly into the sky, arrows protruding from their wounds, blood trails and pools marking the ground. Flies buzzed low over the bodies, and carrion birds swooped down from the sky.

Step by step, Eskkar moved forward. He reached the place where the lances had dug themselves into the earth and halted. Thutmose-sin now paced his horse forward, giving Eskkar time to study both man and animal.

Thutmose-sin was a dangerous fighter. Eskkar knew that from personal experience. But Eskkar had practiced much since that night battle at the fire wagons outside of Orak, and his skills had increased. Both men were much the same age, so that wouldn't matter.

After last night's fight, Thutmose-sin would be more weary than Eskkar, and while his wounds might be minor, they, too, would weaken him. No, the approaching rider might be a deadly opponent, but the big gray stallion warranted as much concern as its master.

No matter how much time Eskkar had spent training A-tuku, Thutmose-sin's horse had seen many more fights. A huge brute, it stood at least a hand and half taller than A-tuku. It would respond to its master's slightest touch.

Eskkar's mount looked sleepy and slow compared to the gray. But A-tuku's appearance was deceiving. The bay, too, would respond to Eskkar's commands, and no other horse in Hathor's cavalry, no matter what its size, had stood against it.

At least in training, Eskkar reminded himself. A-tuku had never fought a battle, while the gray must have many such encounters.

Thutmose-sin stopped about fifteen paces from Eskkar. "I didn't think you would dare come out to face me. You escaped my sword once, but this time you will not be so lucky. You should have let your archers cut me down."

Eskkar shrugged. "That would have given strength to your warriors. Now they will watch you die at my hand. You led them to defeat last night, and with your death, they will once again know defeat. They will not have the stomach to face us again."

A grimace of rage twisted Thutmose-sin's face. "No, my warriors will see me slay you, the mighty Eskkar of Akkad, and they will take courage." Without haste, he reached up and drew his sword.

Eskkar made no move toward his weapon. "Tell me of the death of my father, Hogarthak. I have never learned the truth of what happened that night."

A look of surprise come over Thutmose-sin's face, and he lowered his sword. "Why should I tell you anything?"

"What can it matter after all these years," Eskkar said, his voice still calm. He had not drawn his sword.

"It doesn't. Nothing matters now." Thutmose-sin took a deep breath. "I was not there the night my older brother, Seluku, died. But after our fight at the fire wagons, I asked the elders what had happened to your family. It seems my father, Maskim-Xul wanted to absorb the warriors of the Hawk Clan into his own. I suppose your clan leader Jamal had grown in influence or done something to make my father jealous. My father ordered Seluku, his war chief, to challenge Jamal at the Council Meeting. Your father was there, a leader of twenty, attending his clan leader."

"I didn't know that," Eskkar said. "My father never returned to his wagons after the day's ride."

This time Thutmose-sin shrugged. "My brother offered the challenge to Jamal, and the old man, stung by Seluku's insults, accepted it. But Seluku chose not to fight himself. He ordered his guards to kill your clan leader. They attacked, and your father guarded Jamal's back. When Jamal took a wound and dropped his sword, Seluku stepped forward to deliver the killing blow. Your father exposed his own back, and struck from underneath Jamal's arm before your clan leader fell. Hogarthak drove his blade into Seluku's stomach, and then was killed by the other guards. My father flew into one of his rages. Seluku was dying the slow death, crying out in pain, so my father ended Seluku's life himself. Then he ordered everyone in Jamal's family and yours to be put to death. Somehow you killed a guard and escaped."

Eskkar took a deep breath. So that was how it happened. He'd suspected something like that all these years, but at least now he knew the truth. Not only had his father died honorably, but he had slain the son of the Great Chief, Maskim-Xul.

"Is there any more to tell?"

"No, only that your mother clawed out the eyes of another guard before she died. Your brother and sister were slain as payment for my brother's death. You should have died that night as well. Instead you ran away and became a dirt eater. Now you have the blood of your own kind on your hands."

That night, Eskkar had seen his brother and mother die, but had been too busy fighting for his life to really know what was going on.

"Then my father died with honor, defending his clan leader."

Thutmose-sin laughed, a bitter sound wrenched from his belly. "Seluku was a pig, and I despised him. Your father's deed made me Sarum five years later. So I suppose I should thank him for that."

"And now I've ended your rule as Sarum," Eskkar said. "So the circle is complete. With your death, my father's spirit will be satisfied." He lowered his shoulder and slid the long sword from its scabbard.

"We will see whose spirit lives on with honor, outcast!"

Eskkar never saw the movement or word that launched the gray forward. One moment the horse had been standing there stolidly, the next it was charging at full speed. Eskkar reacted almost as fast. A kick of his heels as he thrust the halter forward, and A-tuku jumped into motion.

The normal reaction was to turn slightly to the left, so that each rider's sword arm could strike freely. But Eskkar nudged the halter to the right. A-tuku leapt in front of Thutmose-sin's charging stallion, and Eskkar swung the long sword across his body to strike at his onrushing enemy's left side.

Caught by surprise, Thutmose-sin barely whipped his sword over to his left, and while he parried the blow, the force of Eskkar's cut almost knocked the warrior from his mount.

A cheer arose from the Akkadians at the stroke, while on the far hillside, the Alur Meriki line shifted uneasily at the exchange. Both riders wheeled their horses around and charged again. Thutmose-sin's blade rose up in the air, but Eskkar leaned forward along A-tuku's neck, sword extended like a lance.

Yesterday, Eskkar had taken the measure of the leader of the Alur Meriki, and Eskkar decided he had a few finger width's in height, and perhaps even more in the length of his arms. With his sword held high, Thutmose-sin had to strike early to knock Eskkar's blade aside as the two fighters hurled past each other. It took the full strength of Thutmose-sin's blow to deflect Eskkar's weapon.

Another cheer arose from the ranks of Eskkar's men, as the two riders wheeled to face each other a third time. But this time, they were too close to get the horses to a gallop. The two fighters came together, and the clash of bronze on bronze echoed from the hills.

Once, twice, three times each man struck at his opponent or parried the other's attack, before the two were forced to ride apart to maintain control of their mounts. This time Eskkar had to yield ground to recover, as Thutmose-sin's stallion, despite its size, proved quicker in these short turnings.

A-tuku, however, snorted in anger. The big gray had tried to bite A-tuku's neck. The two fighters separated, opening a gap of about twenty paces before they gathered themselves for another attack.

"Straight at him, A-tuku," Eskkar muttered, just loud enough for the bay to hear his words. "Show that stallion what you're made of."

Once again Thutmose-sin launched the attack, and Eskkar kicked his mount forward. He let A-tuku take two good strides, then turned him to the right, as he had in the first encounter. He held his course just long enough for Thutmose-sin to recognize Eskkar's intent. Thutmose-sin turned his to the left, to keep Eskkar on his right side.

But Eskkar jerked the halter back, and A-tuku's move to the right lasted only the briefest moment. A-tuku shifted his stride and lowered his head. The fighters were too close to each other for either to turn aside.

The two horses met in a mighty collision. Both A-tuku and Eskkar had trained for this type of attack, and the bay's right shoulder struck hard into the stallion's forequarters. The gray, knocked to a standstill, cried out at the force of the contact and staggered back on his haunches.

Expecting the collision, Eskkar, his legs gripping the horse's sides with all his strength, had managed to hang on to his seat, his halter-hand clinging with a death grip to A-tuku's mane. But Thutmose-sin, his wild swing coming within a hand's breath of Eskkar's head, was flung off his mount and landed hard onto the earth.

A-tuku recovered his footing and needed no urging to move to the attack, launching himself directly at the unhorsed man. Before Thutmose-sin could get to his knees, Eskkar's sword was descending, a powerful stroke made even stronger by the horse's movement.

Thutmose-sin managed to get his sword up, but Eskkar's weapon scarcely slowed as it brushed aside Thutmose-sin's blade. The finest bronze weapon in Akkad, swung with all of Eskkar's strength, struck the warrior's left shoulder and bit deep into flesh and bone.

Thutmose-sin's cry of pain echoed off the cliff before it reached the hilltop. Eskkar's momentum took him past his enemy, but he quickly wheeled A-tuku around.

Eskkar's blow had knocked Thutmose-sin once again to the ground. This time blood covered his left shoulder, running freely down his chest. The man still clutched his sword, however, as he struggled to his knees.

Eskkar slid down from his mount and strode across the bare ground. He didn't want to risk an injury to A-tuku by attacking someone so low to the ground. Thutmose-sin might be wounded, but he could yet strike a heavy blow.

As Eskkar approached, he saw the extent of Thutmose-sin's wound. A glimpse of white revealed the bone in the warrior's shoulder, and a strip of flesh hung from his arm. With so much blood spurting from the wound, nothing could save him. He would be dead soon.

"You're dying, Thutmose-sin. You should have trained your horse better. Now I will avenge my father Hogarthak, and my kin."

"Then come and finish me if you dare, you . . . outcast!"

Eskkar raised his sword up. Thutmose-sin struck upwards, aiming at his enemy's groin, but Eskkar had expected it. He twisted aside, and his sword whirled down and struck at Thutmose-sin's right arm, the sharp edging cutting into the man's hand. The weapon tumbled to the ground.

Eskkar never let his sword stop moving. The blade whirled up and swung down in a sideways motion, and at the bottom of its arc, driven by all the strength in both of Eskkar's arms, it sliced through Thutmose-sin's neck with a spray of blood, sending the Sarum's head rolling across the hard ground.

A roar erupted from the Akkadian line. Men jumped and waved their weapons. "Eskkar! Eskkar!" The deafening cry echoed from the cliff. Eskkar took a deep breath, then reached down and slid the big copper medallion from the Sarum's body and stuffed it into his tunic. Suddenly the cheers from the Akkadian line changed in intensity. Eskkar glanced up toward the hilltop.

A lone rider raced down the hillside in a reckless display of horsemanship. This one clenched a bow in his left hand, and even as he descended, Eskkar saw him fit an arrow to the string.

A-tuku stood waiting only a dozen paces away, chewing on a lonely tuft of grass. Eskkar could leap astride and reach the safety of his men before the rider could get close enough to launch an arrow. But Eskkar recognized the horse. It belonged to Bar'rack, the clan leader who had sworn the Shan Kar against his hated enemy.

Eskkar made up his mind. The lances that he and Thutmose-sin had hurled to show their defiance stood close at hand. Eskkar ran toward them, shifting his sword to his left hand. The drumming hoof beats changed as the warrior's horse reached the base of the hill and increased its speed. Head down, Eskkar covered the last few paces.

Without stopping he ripped the Akkadian lance from the earth and flung himself to the side, back toward the way he'd run. An arrow hissed through the spot where Eskkar had been only a moment ago.

As Bar'rack fitted another shaft to his string, Eskkar charged toward him, reaching back at the same time with his right hand and tightening his grip on the weapon. Before Bar'rack's bow could come up, Eskkar's lance flew through the air, flung with all his strength. The bronze tipped lance struck the charging horse, now less than twenty paces away, full in the chest.

The animal took two more strides, stumbled, and fell to its knees, less than five paces from where Eskkar stood. The arrow launched by the warrior flew wide, as Bar'rack was pitched from the dying horse's back. He landed heavily, rolling once, the bow flying from his hand.

Stunned, Bar'rack tried to regain his feet as he tugged clumsily at his sword. By then Eskkar had reached him.

"Your brother died with honor, but you will die like a coward, and your kin will not mourn your passing." Once again the big sword descended and bit deep into flesh, a showering of blood marking the place where the blade impacted the side of Bar'rack's neck. The warrior fell, and lay twitching on the ground, still alive, bleeding to death.

Esskar stared at him. Before Esskar could regain his breath, Bar'rack's body went limp, the man's sword still half in its scabbard. Taking his time, Esskar wiped his bloody blade on the dead man's tunic. Then he walked back to A-tuku and swung astride. He forced himself to take a deep breath, though he felt his heart race within his chest from the battle fury. He had truly avenged his father's death.

"We did it, A-tuku." He patted the animal on the side of the neck. "We defeated the best the Alur Meriki could send against us. Never again will they doubt the strength of our men or of our horses."

Overhead, the last of the dusky rain clouds had faded away, and suddenly a wide swatch of sunlight streamed down from the sky, bathing the patch of ground where Esskar stood with its warmth. A good omen, Esskar thought, to mark the death of Thutmose-sin.

A glance toward the enemy hill showed the Alur Meriki warriors looking up, and the faint murmur of their words drifted toward him. They, too, saw the omen and understood. The gods had given their approval to Esskar's victory.

Another shout from the Akkadians turned Esskar's head back toward the enemy's hilltop. Two riders were descending, but this time at a slow and measured pace. Neither carried bow or lance, and one lifted his right hand high in the air, to show that he carried no weapon.

"Now what do these two want, A-tuku?"

A-tuku snorted in reply, and lowered his head once again to tug at the stubborn clump of tough grass.

—⬥—

From the hilltop, Bekka and Urgo watched Thutmose-sin's final moments. Every Alur Meriki warrior knew of their Sarum's prowess, but it seemed that this Esskar had dispatched their ruler with both skill and a display of better horsemanship.

"That bay didn't look that powerful," Bekka remarked, sitting on his horse beside Urgo. "I think Thutmose-sin made the same mistake."

They both turned to stare when they saw Bar'rack disobey his Sarum's final order, and dash down the hill, blind in his hatred.

Urgo shook his head. "Bar'rack is a good clan leader for one so young, but his Shan Kar has driven reason from his head. If he kills Eskkar, we are doomed. The Akkadians will never leave the stream until we are all dead."

"He will not get close enough," Bekka said. "The archers will . . . by the gods!"

Both men stared open mouth as the King of the Akkadians raced across the field to where the jutting lances protruded from the earth. A few moments later, they saw the long sword, reflecting a gleam of sunlight, swing down to end the life of another clan leader.

Silence swept across the hilltop. Until now, the Alur Meriki warriors had offered many reasons for their defeat at the Akkadians' hands. Now one man, even one who once had belonged to the Clan, had struck down two of their leaders with apparent ease. No longer could any warrior dare impugn such a fighter's honor.

"At least it is finished." Urgo raised his voice. "Pass the word. No warrior is to leave the hilltop." He waited a moment as the order spread out to either side. "Come, Bekka, ride with me." He touched his horse's neck with the halter, and the animal started down the slope.

Bekka joined him. Neither man said anything, both concentrating on guiding their respective horse. Urgo led the way, and Bekka suspected that he did so to conceal the grimaces of pain from his body. Bekka knew the old warrior could ride for short stretches on level ground, but a steep slope such as this amounted to agony with each step.

"He waits for us," Bekka said, as they reached the level ground.

"He has no fear," Urgo agreed. "Which means that he probably won't order his archers to strike us down."

Bekka had been thinking about that as they stepped past the ragged line of long shafts angled skyward that marked the extreme range of the powerful Akkadian bows.

"It's not that I'm afraid, Urgo, but you have lived many years, while I still have more children to father." He could see a wide line of Akkadian bowmen formed up along the edge of the stream, and Bekka recognized the Slayer of Warriors, bow in hand, standing at their center. A hundred shafts could rain down from the sky upon them at any time.

Urgo snorted with amusement. "Today, tomorrow, death will take us sooner or later if we don't get our people to the stream."

The new Sarum of the Alur Meriki and one of his few remaining clan leaders approached Eskkar's position. The Akkadian King sat on his horse, facing them. His face revealed no emotion, no boastful signs of a victorious fighter.

"What are you going to say?" Bekka knew little of negotiations or serious talks between leaders, let alone enemies.

"What we must. The only thing that will save the Alur Meriki from destruction."

11

Eskkar had collected A-tuku's halter and stood beside his mount, watching the two warriors walk their horses toward him. Satisfied that their slow pace indicated peaceful intentions, he swung astride his horse and moved a few paces toward them. That would take A-tuku away from the flies, as well as show the approaching horsemen he didn't fear them.

While he waited for the two to draw near, Eskkar glanced up at the sky. The mountain sun had broken through most of the dreary clouds of morning. The bright sunlight brought back a memory. His father, Hogarthak, always muttered a prayer to the gods for the warmth of the sun.

Today, the day Eskkar had never really believed would arrive, had come. Today he avenged his family. When Eskkar met his own fate and descended into the underworld, he could stand before his father with honor. And for Hogarthak's bravery to his clan leader, Eskkar knew his father would command a seat of importance close to the gods. His spirit could now rest in peace.

Eskkar brought his thoughts back to the two riders. He recognized Bekka's stocky form. The other chief, with long wispy gray hair floating in the light breeze, seemed uneasy on his horse. But the older man led the way, with Bekka obviously deferring to his companion's years. As they drew close, Eskkar saw that neither wasted a glance at the headless body of Thutmose-sin.

The old warrior halted his horse within a single stride of Eskkar's bay. All three animals stretched out their necks, sniffing at each other, tails swishing away the flies summoned by the freshly spilled blood. More sunlight rent the last of the fading clouds, and shone down on the Akkadian position. The gods had clearly spoken, and they had given their favor to the fighters from Akkad.

The gray haired warrior studied Eskkar's face for a moment. "I am Urgo. For now, I am Sarum of the Alur Meriki."

Eskkar searched his memory, but he had left the clan many years ago, when he was fourteen. He couldn't recall a warrior or chief named Urgo. In those days, there had been twelve clan leaders forming the Great Council. This Urgo was old enough to have been one of those, but he might have risen in the ranks since then.

"I am Eskkar." He nodded to Bekka. "Do you wish to talk, or have you also come to challenge me again?"

"The time for challenges is past." Urgo rested both hands on the base of his horse's neck and leaned forward, as if seeking relief for an injured back. "The women and children of the Alur Meriki need the water you guard. I ask you, as warrior to warrior, to not take your vengeance out on them. If you must destroy our warriors this day, so be it. But after the battle, I plead for mercy for our women, our old, and our young."

Eskkar studied their faces as Urgo spoke. Trella had taught him to read the subtle signs that often passed over men's visages, and he recognized the small hints that indicated Urgo was in pain, possibly much pain. Bekka, who had bloodstained bandages wrapped around his right arm, chest, and left leg, betrayed no sign of weakness.

Eskkar sensed something else in the younger man's calm exterior. Bekka had fought hard, but he, too, realized the time for battle had passed.

The Alur Meriki had indeed grown desperate. Eskkar's men, their demeanor, their willingness to fight, and their steadiness during the attack, had delivered a chill into the hearts of these brave warriors. With their advantage in numbers gone, they knew they faced hardened fighters. Though the Alur Meriki would never admit it, deep down in their hearts, they knew they could not win.

A glimmer of an idea caught hold in Eskkar's thoughts. When he finally spoke, he addressed his words to Urgo.

"You speak of mercy, but for many years the Alur Meriki have shown none to the villagers and farmers of this land. Why should I now offer any to you?"

"What you say is true, Eskkar of Akkad. But once you were Eskkar, son of Hogarthak, of the Alur Meriki. I knew your father as a brave and honorable man. I watched him fight and die with honor. Are you so eager now to take revenge on your own kind? You have killed many hundreds of our men since the days of Orak. How many more will it take to satisfy you? How many would Hogarthak want to die?"

Urgo wanted peace, Eskkar decided. More than that, he wanted to preserve the Alur Meriki from destruction. The hastily conceived idea in the back of Eskkar's mind took hold and grew. The risks would be great, but he much preferred a bold gamble. He would have liked more time to think it through, but knew this moment might not come again.

Moving with care, Eskkar raised up his right leg and rested it across A-tuku's neck. The gesture left him vulnerable should either of the warriors attack, but it also proved the courage needed to display such strength. Up on the crest of the hill, the watching warriors would see and understand.

"My father's spirit is satisfied with the death of Thutmose-sin. His father killed mine, so that blood debt is paid. But my brother, my sister, my mother, what of them? How will their deaths be avenged?"

"They cannot," Urgo answered. "Still, over the years Thutmose-sin lost three of his sons, killed at the hands of your fighters. Now his wives and children will mourn his loss. But if you need to take your revenge on Thutmose-sin's family, I will send them to you. You can kill them, or keep them as slaves."

Neither choice interested Eskkar. Instead, the plan developing in his mind fell into place. With luck, it might come to be. Nevertheless, there was only one way to find out. He turned his gaze to Bekka.

"What do you say to this, Bekka?"

The warrior met Eskkar's eyes for a moment, apparently surprised at being asked his opinion. Then, taking his time, Bekka lifted his right leg up and onto the neck of his horse. To those watching, he and Eskkar might have been old friends taking a moment of rest after a long day's ride, both too lazy to dismount.

"I have only been a clan leader for four seasons," Bekka said. "So it is not my place to speak against Urgo's wisdom. But it may be that the fighting between Akkad and the Alur Meriki should come to an end. Akkad has won the long conflict. Even if we attacked your forces and destroyed all of them, those of us who survived would be too weak to defend themselves and our wagons against our enemies."

And you have many enemies, Eskkar thought. But now was not the time to remind these proud men of that.

"Akkad, too, still has enemies who would test our swords." Eskkar paused, searching for the right words. "But it may be possible for there to be peace between us. Are the Alur Meriki willing to accept such a peace?"

"Yes."

Urgo hadn't hesitated. No more bargaining, no more threats. Just the single word that might save the Alur Meriki from annihilation.

"I agree with my Sarum," Bekka said. "What is it that we must do?"

Eskkar wished Trella were here to negotiate with them. She would know the right phrases to smooth the way. All the same, he would have to do his best. He had, after all, sat through hundreds of seemingly endless bargaining sessions with greedy traders and gold-loving merchants, arguing over every copper coin or slight to their honor. Nothing here could be worse than that.

"If the Great Clan wishes peace, then they must accept the following. First, a thousand warriors to fight under my banner when I summon them. They will have their fair share of any loot when we battle my enemy. Bekka will be their leader, and on that day, he will swear his allegiance to me on his sword and on his honor as a warrior in front of his men. It may be two or three years before your fighters are needed, but then they must place themselves under my command."

"With so many warriors gone, the Alur Meriki will be vulnerable." Bekka offered it not as a challenge, merely an observation.

"I understand. When I summon you, your people may place themselves under the protection of Akkad, in our northern lands. They will be safe there, and I will see that they have what they need while your warriors are gone."

Bekka turned to Urgo, who nodded approval.

Urgo met Eskkar's gaze. "It will be done."

"Second," Eskkar went on, "the Alur Meriki must swear to never again raid the lands of Akkad, or wage war against the Ur Nammu. Like Akkad, the Ur Nammu have suffered greatly from the wrath of the Alur Meriki. Every warrior must swear on his sword and his honor, and with open hands. There must be no pebbles held to deny the oath."

Some warriors considered that a pebble clutched in one hand rendered an oath meaningless.

Urgo smiled. "You are wise, indeed. Agreed. Akkad and the Ur Nammu will be considered as friends."

The Alur Meriki hadn't considered anyone their friends for as far back as anyone could remember, but Eskkar decided not to bring that up, either.

"Third, I will need three hundred war horses. One hundred now, two hundred next year."

Urgo shrugged. "After last night, we have many extra horses. Agreed."

"Fourth, the Alur Meriki must free all their slaves. Many of those have been captured in these lands."

"That can be done," Urgo said. So far the only thing of real value Eskkar had requested was the horses. The slaves were a useful luxury, nothing more.

"And last, I want all the members of my father's clan, Jamal's Hawk Clan, to be given the chance to join my standard. They must be permitted to make the choice freely."

For the first time, Eskkar saw surprise on Urgo's face.

The old man took his time before replying. "I don't know who they are, or even how many of them are left alive," Urgo said. "It has been many seasons since the Hawk Clan's banner flew in the sky."

Over thirty years, Eskkar guessed. But this was something he wanted to do for his father, Hogarthak.

"That may be," Eskkar said, "but I will make the offer myself to your warriors. And you and Bekka will make sure that they are free to leave the Clan."

"It can be done," Urgo said.

"And I want the family of Thutmose-sin protected and cared for. All of them. They are mine by right of conquest, but you will place them under your standard, Chief Urgo. They are not to be harmed or suffer any shame."

The dead Sarum's family meant nothing to Eskkar, but many would take offense at any harsh treatment to Thutmose-sin's family. Instead, Eskkar's generosity would be appreciated. Not to mention he didn't need Thutmose-sin's children growing up eager to avenge their father's death, and waiting for an opportunity to strike.

"Agreed." Urgo obviously had little sympathy or interest for his former Sarum's wives and children. "That is all you . . . request?"

"Yes." Another wild thought jumped into Eskkar's mind. "And I will speak to all your warriors myself."

For the second time, Urgo displayed surprise. "How will . . . when will you do this?"

Eskkar glanced up at the sun. Midmorning had just passed. From all the morning's activity, he would have thought the sun about to set. "At midday. Bring your warriors to the bottom of the hill. I will come to you then."

"Our warriors are angry," Bekka said, obviously not so much concerned for Eskkar's safety but he knew what would happen if the Akkadian leader were killed. "Some have lost kin, and others may not like to hear your words. In their anger, they may not listen to our words to hold their vengeance."

Both clan leaders knew a single arrow could end the last chance of the Alur Meriki.

Urgo considered this for a moment. He turned to Bekka. "It is dangerous, but wise. Eskkar must speak to our warriors himself, if this peace is to work. They may not listen to us, but they must listen to the man who defeated them."

Urgo sighed, and shifted his gaze to Eskkar. "I will speak to them first and tell them of the bitter herbs they must taste. I believe they will hold their anger."

Once again Urgo had cut straight to the heart of the matter.

"King Eskkar understands the use of power as well as the need for courage," Urgo went on. "Is there anything else?"

"No." Taking care not to disturb A-tuku, Eskkar shifted his leg off the animal's neck. He shook the halter and added a touch from his left heel. A-tuku picked up his head and turned to the left. Eskkar put him to a canter, which he sensed would be more dramatic than simply walking the horse back to his men.

As he rode, Eskkar let out a long sigh of relief. Once again his luck had held. Sooner or later, Eskkar knew it would run out. He just hoped it would last for the rest of today.

— — —

On the Akkadian side of the stream, Hathor paced up and down, his dour countenance hiding his concern for his friend and King. Hathor owed much to Eskkar, and the two had grown close over the fifteen years since Eskkar had spared Hathor's life. It would be bad enough if his friend were killed in battle. Hathor didn't want Eskkar getting himself killed doing something foolish. Hathor preferred another battle rather than face Trella in her grief.

Hathor would follow his Captain and friend into the very teeth of the enemy, and he had done so at the Battle of Isin. To stand here and watch Eskkar take a foolish challenge from a defeated enemy had been bad enough. Hathor would have met the leader of the Alur Meriki with a shower of a hundred arrows. But Eskkar had given strict orders, and Hathor trusted his commander enough to follow them.

All the Akkadians had rejoiced when Eskkar took Thutmose-sin's head. Hathor had led the cheering himself for the few moments before the second warrior attacked. Eskkar could have avoided battle by riding back to the stream, but stayed instead and slew his opponent, once again proving his courage against a mounted foe armed with a bow.

Those moments of worry during the brief fighting were nothing compared to what Hathor endured during the long conference with the two barbarian chiefs. Expecting treachery at any moment, he stared open mouthed when Eskkar relaxed so much that he shifted his leg over the horse's neck. The long talk between the three dragged on and on, and finally Hathor could stand the tension no longer.

He strode down the rank of soldiers until he reached the position where Alexar and Mitrac stood. Mitrac had a shaft fitted to his string, though he held the bow at his side.

"How long will they talk?" Hathor made no effort to conceal his concern. "Has Eskkar lost his wits, to meet with his enemy like this? Sooner or later, they're going to kill him."

"I've known him for almost twenty years, since he came to Orak," Alexar said. "He's risked his neck at least ten times that I know of. It's some barbarian code of honor that he still holds to, despite all they've done to him over the years. All the same, he usually knows what he's doing, and with these barbarians, he may be on to something. Those on the hill aren't getting ready for another attack."

"Look, he's coming." Mitrac gestured with his bow, and the three of them watched as at last Eskkar rode back toward the lines. During the desperate fight with Thutmose-sin, Mitrac had twice raised his bow, ready to shoot if Eskkar fell, but each time Mitrac lowered his weapon.

When Eskkar splashed across the stream, his soldiers roared in approval, shaking swords and spears into the air. The chant of "Eskkar!" sounded again and again, bellowed from close to a thousand throats. He raised his arms to silence their voices, but the sound didn't subside even as he swung down from his horse. Commanders and leaders rushed to surround him, many clasping his shoulders in relief.

"You will get yourself killed one of these days." Alexar shouted to be heard over the din. His smile softened the rebuke.

Eskkar took a deep breath. "Silence!" He used his command voice, and the cheering slowly died away. He glanced around for a moment, to make sure he had his men's attention.

"There won't be any more fighting. They're going to give us everything we want." That elicited another even more thunderous shout. For a brief moment, Eskkar basked in the admiration of his companions, before he raised his hands and ordered them to keep quiet again.

He quickly told them what the warriors had agreed to. His commanders listened in stunned silence, while the soldiers clustered around their leaders renewed their cheering. Every one of them had been expecting a another bloody assault before the morning ended. Now it appeared that they might all get home alive.

Everyone had a question. When the excited soldiers finally calmed down, Eskkar told them the rest of the agreement.

"I'm going to ride into their camp. I want to speak to the warriors. For the last forty years, they've heard only their clan leaders and Thutmose-sin. It's time they heard another voice. This Urgo seems willing to listen to something new."

Alexar shook his head. "I don't believe this. You're going to ride into their camp, to talk to them? You'll never get out alive."

"Alexar's right." Hathor, too, couldn't believe what he heard. "This is beyond courage. The battle madness has taken your wits."

"There is some danger," Eskkar admitted. "But if I can turn aide the hatred of those warriors, no clan leader will ever be able to renounce the agreement. Think of it, a thousand warriors at our command." He lowered his voice, so that only Hathor and Alexar could hear. "Remember, the Elamites are coming."

"I'm going with you," Hathor said. "And we'll bring twenty horsemen."

Eskkar considered the idea. "A warrior chief is expected to bring his second in command with him whenever anything of importance is discussed."

"Good," Alexar said. "I'll go with you, too."

"No, this time I think it would be better for Hathor to accompany me. And the fact that he is an Egyptian and someone from another land who fights for Akkad may impress the warriors. I'll take him and two Hawk Clan guards. That will be enough. The rest of you will wait here."

Nevertheless, all his commanders urged him to reconsider, or at the least to take more men. But no amount of arguing could change Eskkar's mind. Finally he glanced up at the sun. "Enough talk. The time for the meeting is almost at hand, and I still have some things to prepare."

—◁▥◍▥▷—

At the appointed time, Eskkar led the way across the stream. Though he hadn't worn it during the fight with Thutmose-sin, Eskkar now wore his bronze breastplate, knowing that it would impress the warriors. His soft brown cloak, a gift from Trella, hung down his back. Like the breastplate, the fine garment would create a favorable image in the warriors' eyes.

No other Akkadian possessed such an article of clothing. Eskkar's long hair had been combed and tied back neatly with a thin strip of leather.

Before leaving, Eskkar had plunged into the chilly water of the stream to cleanse himself of the dust and blood spatter, and his guards had seen to his horse. While the sleepy looking beast would never look impressive, at least the animal's coat shone after a quick splash in the stream and a good brushing. Eskkar's sword had been cleaned and oiled, and once again slid easily in its scabbard.

"Ra's beard!" In times of stress, Hathor often called up the old gods of Egypt, instead of Marduk or Ishtar, the main deities of Akkad. "I can't believe we're doing this. Are you sure this is a good idea?"

He rode at Eskkar's left side, with the Hawk Clan guards, Chandor and Pekka, following behind. Both soldiers looked grim, each convinced they were going to their deaths at the hands of the barbarians.

The sight of what awaited gave weight to Hathor's remark. The Alur Meriki had drawn their warriors up in ranks at the base of the hill. He guessed at least a thousand mounted fighters sat on their horses and watched as the Akkadians approached. Many displayed rough, blood-stained bandages.

Filling the hill behind them stood the women and children of the Alur Meriki, rising up almost to the crest. Apparently the caravan had reached the camp late this morning. Anyone who could walk or ride had abandoned their wagons and climbed the hill to watch their warriors meet with the hated dirt eaters.

Eskkar guessed that close to four thousand warriors, old men, women, children, and slaves stared in fascination at the four Akkadians riding slowly toward them. Led, of course, by the hated outcast Eskkar who had defeated their sons, husbands and fathers.

To his surprise, Eskkar felt no pangs of anxiety as he rode toward the massed horde of Alur Meriki. They were, after all, his own people. They had not declared his family outcasts, only the Sarum, now long dead, and Thutmose-sin, his son, carried on the blood feud.

While such feuds could span generations, fueled by the slightest of incidents, such quarrels could also end abruptly under the right circumstances. That knowledge had determined Eskkar's decision, and now he had to trust to his instinct to see him through.

Twenty paces in front of the horsemen, Urgo, Bekka, and another clan chief waited.

With scarcely a glance at the grim warriors crowded behind their leaders, Eskkar rode up to the three chiefs, halting when his horse's nose practically touched Urgo's mount.

"Greetings, Sarum of the Alur Meriki." Eskkar raised his voice, so that many of the Alur Meriki could hear. Hopefully, they would appreciate the sign of respect. "This is Hathor, from the land of Egypt. He commands my horsemen."

Hathor inclined his head to show respect to Urgo's rank.

The guards needed no introduction. Eskkar hoped they had their faces under control. He had warned them not to show any signs of fear. Now was not the time to look weak.

"Greetings, Eskkar of Akkad." Urgo acknowledged Hathor's greeting with a nod, and gestured to the warrior on his right. "This is Suijan, leader of the Fox Clan."

Eskkar nodded politely. Suijan's left arm hung in a rope sling, and though he kept his face impassive, he could not conceal the occasional pain he struggled to control. But for such an event, every chief that could sit on a horse would ignore his wounds to partake in this meeting.

Neither Suijan nor Bekka displayed any signs of hostility. All three appeared more interested in Hathor. His tall frame and bald head were as impressive as the scars that marked his body. No doubt they had seen few if any Egyptians in their wanderings.

"Bekka and I have spoken with Suijan, and he, too, has agreed to your requests." Urgo glanced over his shoulder. "I have told our warriors what you have asked for, if there is to be peace. They have accepted it, and will swear the oath of friendship. You said you wished to speak to our men."

"I do." Eskkar reached into his cloak. A pocket on the inside held the copper medallion, taken from the body of Thutmose-sin, that for generations belonged to the Great Chief of the Alur Meriki. Eskkar drew it forth, and held it up for all to see.

"I return this emblem to the people of the Alur Meriki."

Eskkar's powerful voice echoed off the cliffs. His words, spoken in the language of his youth, easily reached the top of the hill. He leaned forward and handed the medallion to Urgo. As the new Sarum accepted the token and donned the polished copper, Eskkar guided his horse forward, moving past the three clan chiefs, until he stood between them and the host of warriors.

He took a deep breath. All of them needed to hear his words. "Warriors of the Alur Meriki. I am Eskkar, once of the Hawk Clan. As a boy, I rode with my father and with our warriors in the service of my Clan."

The name of the Hawk Clan had not been spoken aloud in many years, and in truth, probably most of the young warriors had never heard of it until after this morning's battle. Nevertheless, many of the older men would have heard rumors and stories about the outcast boy who had grown into a leader of the dirt eaters.

For the first time, they saw Eskkar face to face, wearing his gleaming bronze breastplate, long sword jutting from his shoulder, and the cloak flowing easily down his back. Seeing him stand before them, not one doubted his role as a leader of fighters and a leader of men. And if there were any doubt as to his prowess, the deaths of Thutmose-sin and Bar'rack had ended those forever.

Eskkar shifted the horse and moved slowly down the line. "My clan leader was Jamal, and my father, Hogarthak, served him faithfully. The father of Thutmose-sin, Maskim-Xul, and his son, Seluku, killed Jamal by treachery. My father honored his oath to Jamal and fought to save his clan leader. My father Hogarthak slew Seluku before he died."

Watching their faces, Eskkar knew that he'd caught the interest of more than a few warriors. Even those with hatred on their faces put that aside for the moment.

"For doing his duty, Maskim-Xul ordered my family slain. My mother, my brother, and my sister died that night. That night, I, too, killed my first man, the warrior who slew my younger brother."

Once again Eskkar paced his horse closer to the warriors, moving further down the line. He wanted as many warriors as possible to see him close up. As he paced A-tuku along, his eyes sought the faces of the men in front of him. Most were stoic, a few twisted with hate, but now many more showed interest. This story, he knew, would have been told only in whispers.

"I took my father's horse and fled the Clan, while Maskim-Xul sent warriors to hunt me down. But I escaped his reach, and I swore that someday those who murdered my father and my family would pay that debt with their blood."

Turning A-tuku around, Eskkar trotted back past the center of the line. He wanted every warrior to see and hear his words.

"Today I have taken my vengeance. Thutmose-sin died at my hands in payment for the life of Hogarthak, my father. My blood oath is satisfied. The women and children of the Alur Meriki have nothing to fear from my soldiers. We will stand aside and let your wagons pass, to drink from the stream in peace. But first, I want to speak to those warriors who once belonged to the Hawk Clan. Those men may think that our Clan died that night with Jamal, but I have kept it alive."

He swept his arm up and pointed to his two guards, sitting stoically on their horses just behind Hathor. "The Hawk Clan has been reborn in the land of Akkad. See the emblem on my chest, and on the clothing of my guards. Once again the Hawk Clan boasts the bravest of the brave. They are the fiercest warriors among my soldiers and lead the way in every battle. I am called the King of Akkad, but the name I hold most proud is Leader of the Hawk Clan."

By now the warriors glanced about, looking at each other, wondering about Eskkar's words. Even the faces once twisted with hatred had softened, curious in spite of themselves.

"I know that after Jamal's death, his Hawk Clan warriors were scattered in disgrace among the other clans. Today, I ask those that wish to return to their true Clan to join me. Your women, your wagons, your horses and possessions, all will find a place of honor in my service. The people of Akkad have many enemies, and I need brave warriors both for battle and to teach the villagers how to ride and how to fight. For accepting that duty, you will be treated with honor for the rest of your days, and your sons will once again ride into battle under the Hawk Clan banner."

By now murmurs arose from the ranks, as warriors turned to those beside them, some asking questions, others answering. Heads swiveled to and fro. Eskkar sat motionless, waiting, while the warriors absorbed the impact of his words. As Trella reminded him, there is a time to speak, and a time to let others speak.

His eyes searched the warriors' faces, but no one moved. The Hawk Clan of Eskkar's youth had been one of the smallest, and over the years many warriors would have fallen in battle or resigned themselves to their fate. Still, there must be one or two who felt the rancor about the treatment of the Hawk Clan. Just as he was about to give up hope, a voice called out.

"I will join Eskkar of the Hawk Clan!" An older warrior, a bloody bandage on his right arm attesting to his courage, stepped his horse from the rear ranks, pushing his way through the lines until he stood in the open space facing Eskkar.

"I am Mutaka, once a member of Jamal's Hawk Clan, and a friend to Hogarthak, a wise warrior who died bravely defending our clan leader. Now I return to my true clan, if Eskkar will accept my sword in his service."

Eskkar allowed himself a grunt of satisfaction. He guided his horse closer to that of Mutaka, stopping close enough so that their left knees almost touched. Eskkar stared into the face of Mutaka for a moment.

"I remember Mutaka of the Hawk Clan, who visited the wagon of my father many times. Though the Mutaka I remember had much more hair on his head."

A faint ripple of laughter spread across the ranks.

"I remember the oldest son of Hogarthak," Mutaka replied. "Then you were but a boastful boy who trusted too much to his fighting skills and not enough to his wits." He lifted his arm to encompass all warriors on the hill. "We see that you have not changed much."

This time the laughter flowed freely, and many riders shifted on their mounts at the exchange. Eskkar allowed himself a smile. One warrior, that was all he'd hoped for. One would be enough.

"Then I welcome Mutaka and the wisdom of his years to my service," Eskkar said.

Another warrior weaved his way through the crowd, then another. Soon five veterans, all of them mature in years, had left the mass of Alur Meriki horsemen to cluster at Eskkar's side. He welcomed each of them in turn, learning their names, and clasping arms in the sign of brotherhood.

Well satisfied, Eskkar returned to where Urgo waited. "I will accept these five warriors into the Hawk Clan. They will help form a bond between our peoples."

The three clan leaders had listened to Eskkar's exhortation in silence. There was, after all, little they could say or do.

Urgo, Bekka, and Suijan turned to face the crowded hillside. Each held up both their hands, palms outward, and swore the oath of friendship to Akkad. When the leaders finished, Urgo called on every warrior with honor to repeat the pledge. Every warrior raised his open hands and repeated the oath. When the voices faded away, Esskar nodded in satisfaction.

"Urgo, Sarum of the Alur Meriki, from this moment there is peace between the people of Akkad and the Great Clan. Now I will return to my men. We will break camp, and move away from the stream."

Turning toward Mutaka, Esskar raised his voice. "Members of the Hawk Clan, I welcome your return."

He lowered his voice, so that only the three chiefs could hear Esskar's next words. "I think we should all do everything we can to avoid any fighting between your warriors and mine."

"You are indeed wise," Urgo said. "And I see you know the ways of power."

"As do you, Urgo. Will you make sure that Mutaka and the others leave in peace, with all their belongings. When they are ready to depart, send them to me."

"I will see to it," Urgo said. "It is not every day that a new clan is born. Or should I say, reborn."

"Then today is indeed a good day," Esskar answered.

He nodded to Hathor, and the Akkadians turned their horses aside and headed back to the stream and their camp.

Hathor moved to Esskar's side. "Captain, you are either the luckiest person alive or a damn fool. I'm still waiting for an arrow in the back."

Esskar laughed. "We'll need to get you a breastplate for the next battle."

As they rode back to the stream, another cheer erupted from his men. They might not understand all that had transpired, but they understood well enough that there would be no more fighting, and that they would be returning home to their wives and children.

Esskar considered what he had accomplished – a decisive victory over the Alur Meriki, one more than enough to convince them to accept peace on his terms. The Akkadians had lost men, but in return Esskar had gained the promise of a thousand warriors for the coming fight against the

Elamites. And the additional horses Urgo promised would enable Hathor to add another two hundred or more fighters to his cavalry.

Men would say that Eskkar's luck had aided him again, but he knew luck had little to do with this victory. The Alur Meriki had brought defeat upon themselves. They had kept their eyes to south, when Eskkar and his soldiers had come from the west. Nor had they taken precautions to secure the water before their arrival. And most of all, they had underestimated Akkad's power, and failed to prepare for a real confrontation.

It was, Eskkar knew, a hard lesson. All warfare, to some extent, is based on deception. Akkad had seemed a distant threat, and Trella's rumors, carefully fed to those greedy traders who dealt with the barbarians, had placed the city's soldiers far from the northern frontier

The Alur Meriki would not make the same mistakes again, and Eskkar felt satisfaction that he had turned aside at least part of their hatred. Now it was time to make a true peace with them, to make sure this conflict never arose again.

The ongoing relationship with the Alur Meriki would be difficult, but Trella would find a way to help them and in so doing, gradually turn them to Akkad's side. She would also find a way to make sure the peace held. All and all, Trella would be pleased about his arrangement with the Clan. Eskkar suspected that she would be less happy about his two fights and his riding unprotected into the Alur Meriki camp.

Eskkar sighed. He did not look forward to that part of their coming discussion.

12

Twelve days after the battle, and just before sunset, a weary but still jubilant Eskkar rode through the gates of Akkad at the head of a column of one hundred horsemen. Messengers had reached the city days earlier, to announce his latest battlefield success. Nevertheless, as word spread through Akkad at the sight of the approaching cavalry, the inhabitants clogged the lanes from the city's main gate to the Compound, hoping to catch a glimpse of the King as he returned. The sight of his tall figure riding A-tuku elicited cheers from the throngs that nearly blocked the riders' path.

Many of Akkad's denizens had kin in the northern parts of the country, and they rejoiced in the knowledge that friends and family would be spared any further raids from the Alur Meriki. Others in the crowd had lived through the desperate siege of Orak, and even more through the attack on the city during the war with Sumer.

Relief showed on the faces of those who had survived that attack. For villagers who once shook in terror at the mere mention of the barbarians, this success meant so much more.

To celebrate the victory over the Alur Meriki, Eskkar had again donned the bronze breastplate and his luxurious cloak, with the image of a fierce hawk stitched across his shoulder, for his entrance into Akkad. He knew the armor and garment would impress his own people as much as it had the barbarians. The gleaming metal caught the last rays of the sun as

A-tuku cantered through the twisting lanes of the still-growing city and its cheering inhabitants.

Abandoning his usual reserve, Eskkar waved his hand at the cheering throng eager to catch a glimpse of their king and deliverer.

A-tuku reflected the spirit of its rider, and its hooves kicked clods of dirt into the air as it snorted and pranced its way through the press. Some of the crowd's exuberance came from the effect of too much ale or wine. Many had started drinking early, not waiting for the official three days of feasting to begin. Still, everyone wanted to celebrate the soldiers' bravery and give thanks to the Goddess Ishtar for the city's good fortune.

Eskkar felt as much satisfaction as his subjects. The strategy he and his commanders had developed had worked even better than anyone expected. Battles rarely went as planned, but this clash had succeeded beyond Eskkar's most optimistic expectations. Not only had the threat from the Alur Meriki vanished, but Eskkar had gained a new ally for the coming war with the Elamites.

And within the Great Clan, the remnants of the once-disgraced Hawk Clan would increase his influence among his father's people, as well as a handful of warriors sworn to serve him. In the future, these older warriors would help facilitate the exchange of goods and information between the two peoples.

To strengthen the new alliance, Eskkar knew Trella would soon have gifts and supplies moving toward the Alur Meriki. Not that he expected any sudden show of harmony between the two hereditary enemies. But the seeds of mutual respect had been planted. It would take years, perhaps many years, but at last the chance to build a bond between villagers and steppes warriors existed.

And he now had one thousand warriors at his command! Such a force, used properly as light cavalry and aimed at the right target, would be more devastating than two or three times that number of Akkadian trained horsemen.

Eskkar swung down from his horse in the courtyard of the Compound with a smile of satisfaction on his face. Almost every one of the household servants and guards had turned out, to greet his arrival with words of praise and congratulations. As always when he returned from a hard day's ride, Eskkar strode through the courtyard to the well at the rear of the house, to cleanse the dust and dirt from his body.

With the Tigris so near, many of the wealthier residents had dug their own wells, and Eskkar and Trella's dwelling was no exception. Their well was surrounded on two sides by the Compound's walls, while the house formed the third barrier. A large bench offered seating, and two small trees provided shade for the tiny garden during the day. In Eskkar's Compound, the water source provided a private area where the Lord and Mistress of the house could relax or bathe in relative seclusion.

Tossing his sword and belt to one of the servants, he stripped off his rank garments and kicked them aside. Another servant poured the first of many buckets of cold water over his naked body, while one of the women handed Eskkar a square of linen, which he used to scrub the grime and horse smell from his body.

It took ten buckets before Eskkar finally felt clean, and told the servant to stop. Picking up another piece of linen, Eskkar dried his face and chest. Trella joined him, carrying a clean tunic and a larger, more luxuriant drying cloth. The servants, smiling broadly, respected their wish for privacy, and left them alone.

"By the gods, you grow more beautiful each day." The words slipped from Eskkar's mouth without volition. He stroked her long, thick hair for a moment, before taking her face in his hands. Nearly thirty days had passed since his departure, and to his stirring manhood, it seemed even longer. He took her in his arms, and held her close.

"Welcome back, Husband. You've done well." For a fleeting moment, she pressed herself against his naked body before stepping back and handing him the fresh garment.

Eskkar had shared his life with Trella long enough to know when something was amiss. His pleasant thoughts about a relaxing romp in their bed chamber before supper faded.

He slipped the tunic on, ignoring the soft feel of the fine garment. "What's wrong?" He reached out and grasped her by the shoulders.

"There's been an . . . incident with Sargon."

"Is he alright?"

She shook her head. "No, nothing like that. Come upstairs where we can speak in private."

So it was serious. Eskkar followed her into the house. Inside, he noticed the suddenly somber expressions on the faces of their personal servants. Those who spent their days within the residence would, of course, know all about the problem, whatever it was. Servants always knew about such things, usually before the master or mistress.

In their quiet chamber, Trella closed the door. She went to the table, where servants had placed fresh food and drink. Two thick candles already burned, lighting the room and holding dusk at bay.

"Sit, husband. You must be tired." She picked up the wine pitcher, and half-filled a cup, adding water to weaken the strong drink.

Eskkar ignored his usual chair and instead slumped onto the long bench, covered by a soft blanket, and stretched out his long legs. It was a bad sign when Trella poured his wine.

"What trouble has Sargon gotten himself into this time?" The question wasn't an idle one. He knew it must be something important for Trella to bring it up at once.

"Corio will be here shortly, demanding to see you. One of his daughters, Sestana, she has thirteen seasons and was just initiated into the rites of the women. She was . . . injured by Sargon."

His fist tightened on the cup and he took a long sip from the cup. "What happened?"

Eskkar was well acquainted with another of Corio's daughters, Ismenne, who visited the Compound each day to work with Trella and the other commanders in the Map Room. But the master builder had sired many children from his two bountiful wives, and Eskkar couldn't recall a face to match the name Sestana.

Trella slipped into the chair beside the bench, and took Eskkar's hand. "Sargon and Ziusudra were visiting at Corio's house, to spend some time with one of his sons."

The last of Eskkar's good mood vanished. He straightened up and set the wine cup down so hard that the table shook, and a splash of red splattered across the wood.

"I ordered Sargon not to have anything to do with Ziusudra," he said. "I told him . . ."

"I know, husband. You must stay calm." She tightened her grip on his hand. "Sargon had slipped away from his teacher and gone to visit

Ziusudra. They spent a good part of the morning drinking wine, before heading to Corio's. They had more wine there, with Corio's boy. The house was nearly empty, except for a few servants. Somehow they encountered Sestana and she joined them. They offered her wine, and I think she drank some. Then Ziusudra and Sargon tried to force themselves on Sestana."

"Damn that Ziusudra." Even the boy's name grated on Eskkar's nerves.

Trella continued the story. "Sestana struggled, and . . . one of them struck her, and split her lip. Her clothing was torn, but she resisted. When a serving woman arrived, summoned by the commotion, she saw Sargon straddling the girl, holding his hand over her mouth. At the same time, Ziusudra held her shoulders down."

Eskkar gulped the rest of his wine. "He raped her." The words sounded harsh in the quiet of their chamber. Not just the chamber, he realized. The whole house had gone silent, aware of what was happening in the upper chamber.

Trella shook her head. "No, Sargon hadn't quite reached that point. The housekeeper screamed so loud that the guard at the front door ran inside. By the time he arrived, Ziusudra and Sargon were leaving. The guard recognized Sargon, of course, but didn't think to stop him. So the guard waited there with Sestana and the housekeeper. By then, both of them were screaming. They sent for the girl's mother, and she and Corio arrived together."

"I've told him, ordered him countless times to stay away from Ziusudra." Eskkar's voice held a hard edge. "He's nothing but a worthless fool."

"I know."

Neither of them had to say anything else about that. Ziusudra, a year or so older than Sargon's fourteen seasons, was Akkad's leading mischief maker. Handsome and daring, he'd been involved in every kind of trouble and prank imaginable.

His father, a wealthy merchant named Ningal, doted on his only son. Money, clothes, jewels, Ziusudra possessed them all, and displayed them at every opportunity. Girls and even women old enough to know better looked with favor on his handsome face and golden hair. Nearly every boy in Akkad idolized him, including Sargon.

"Where is Sargon?"

"He's in the guard's quarters, probably sleeping off the effects of the wine. I ordered the commander of the Hawk Clan guards to keep him there."

Sargon's chamber, which he shared with his younger brother, Melkorak, was on the main floor. Their sister Zakita, two seasons younger than Sargon, had another room, one she shared with the matron who attended her. Just across the courtyard from the main structure was a row of small rooms, used by the Hawk Clan to quarter some of the Compound's guards, or serve as visitor's lodgings.

"And the girl . . . Sestana? Are you sure he didn't rape her?"

"Corio's wife examined her. Aside from a cut lip and a bump on her head, she's unhurt. Frightened, of course. Still, this incident will reflect on her reputation and hopes for a good marriage. Otherwise, I'm sure she'll be fine in a day or so."

Eskkar's first thought was that any maiden who allowed herself to cavort with men unsupervised should suffer a serious stain on her reputation. It could have been worse.

His second thought was to go downstairs and have the boy whipped. Raping a virgin, according to Akkad's laws, was punishable by death. Trella and the King's Justice, Nicar, had written the law only a few years ago. Attempted rape, including injuring a young woman in the process, would be almost as bad.

"Corio can insist Sargon be punished. He can demand . . ."

"I spoke briefly to Corio, Husband. Of course he wants to see you. The blood is still hot in his veins, but he will calm down by tomorrow. By then he will not want to press this matter too hard. In a few days, Sargon can apologize. Perhaps I can convince Corio to accept some payment as restitution."

"No, don't insult him. Corio has no need of gold." As Akkad's Master Builder and the man who built the walls that saved the city, Corio possessed more wealth than most of the city's merchants and traders. "His honor will demand more."

"He values your friendship, Eskkar. He will not want to lose that."

"There is friendship, and there is blood." He stared at her. "How would you feel if one of his sons did this to Zakita? Would you accept a few gold coins to satisfy her honor?"

"No, my husband, I would not." She pressed his hand again, then released it. "I agree something must be done with Sargon. This wildness must end. He could have been killed by Corio's bodyguards."

Eskkar bit back the words that nearly reached his lips. *Better if the boy had died.* No father should ever wish for such a thing. Still, for more than a year, Sargon had brought them nothing but trouble. Willful, disobedient, lazy, and now taken to drinking wine and ale early in the day, with others just as wild and shiftless as himself.

"Then it will end." Eskkar pushed himself to his feet and went to the door. Out on the landing, he called down to the guard and ordered Sargon brought to the upper chamber.

Back inside the Workroom, Eskkar turned to Trella. "What do you think I should do?"

"All day I have been thinking about what to say when you asked that question. My heart says to forgive him. But as your eldest son and the heir to the Kingdom of Akkad, Sargon is bringing disgrace to our family. Until today, the people have smiled at his foolishness. Now many will think he is dangerous, and likely to bring the wrath of the gods down on their city. As leaders of Akkad, we cannot allow such thoughts to grow in their minds. If they believe we are too weak to control our son and their future king, then they will soon think as little of us as they do of Sargon. When that happens, they will look to others to take our place."

Footfalls sounded on the stairs. Then Sargon stepped into the room. Unlike his father, Sargon stood only of average height, and his frame, while sturdy enough, appeared closer to that of a counting house clerk than a soldier. Wide-spaced eyes made him look older than his years. Despite his detention, someone had combed and arranged the long brown hair, and his tunic appeared fresh and clean. Sargon must have summoned one of the servants to attend him.

Eskkar jerked his head at the guard, who hurriedly closed the door. Eskkar waited while the guard descended the stairs, treading more heavily than usual, no doubt to make sure that the King could hear his descent.

"Welcome home, Father." Sargon acknowledged his mother with the slightest bow. "Congratulations on your latest victory." The voice held the tiniest trace of insolence.

Eskkar decided it might just be the lingering effects of the wine. He leaned back against the edge of the table. "Perhaps I should have stayed away a few more days. By then the King's Justice might have sentenced you to be stoned to death in the market."

Sargon swaggered to the table and scooped up a handful of grapes. "Nicar would never do such a thing. Nor would Corio demand it, once he calmed down."

The boy spoke the truth. Nicar, the dispenser of the King's Justice, would have stayed his hand from that punishment. And while Corio might shout and bluster for a few days, even he would not want a serious breech between his house and the King's. Sargon was no fool, Eskkar granted his son that. "And what should I do in their stead?"

Tossing a grape into his mouth, Sargon stepped away from the table. "Nothing happened, Father. Besides, Sestana told me she wanted me to take her. She'd been drinking wine before we got there. Then she changed her mind."

"And after you finished with her, Ziusudra would have taken his turn as well. Your friend knew better than to rape the girl first. He was willing to let you have all the blame."

Drunk or sober, virgins of Akkad's noble families were not debauched without serious consequence. Disgraced, Sestana's bride dowry would have vanished, and the embarrassment to Corio's House would have had other lingering effects. Eskkar set that thought aside for a moment.

"More important, you disobeyed both your mother and me. You left your teachers, and joined with Ziusudra, despite our orders. What should be your punishment for that?"

Sargon met his father's gaze. "I promise I will attend to my studies. But I already know more than most of the Noble Families about how to rule a city. There will be plenty of time to study when I am King."

"Ah, then you think you will rule Akkad someday?"

Sargon seemed to realize that his words might sound presumptuous. "Not for many years yet, I'm sure, Father."

"And if I decide to choose your brother Melkorak as my heir?"

Melkorak, Eskkar's other son, had five fewer seasons than Sargon.

Sargon shrugged, unconsciously imitating his father. "Melkorak is too young. And he is slow to learn the symbols. He will not be strong enough or wise enough to command the City."

Leaving only you to rule when I am gone, Eskkar thought. "You press too hard on my patience, Sargon." He turned to Trella. "And what do you suggest we should do with our son?"

Trella, sitting so quietly that she had almost faded from the room, fastened her gaze on Sargon. One of the candles illuminated her face, and Eskkar caught the glint of anger in her eyes and in the tension of her lips.

Her look startled him for a moment. He hadn't seen that expression for . . . almost fifteen years, since the night Trella had helped him fight Korthac. She'd saved Eskkar's life by stabbing the Egyptian usurper in the leg, slowing him down just enough so that Eskkar could defeat him.

When Trella spoke, however, her voice remained calm. Whatever emotions she felt about her son remained locked in her heart, but Eskkar recognized the signs of anger, the signs of a woman and mother pushed too far.

"Perhaps we should ask Ziusudra. Sargon listens to his counsel." She turned away from Sargon to face Eskkar.

"You should know, Husband, that Ziusudra has a loud voice, and when he talks many hear his words. Yesterday he suggested that you were lucky to survive this battle with the Alur Meriki, and that you might not be so fortunate in the next encounter. He also told Sargon that the Kingship of Akkad was his for the taking. I wonder what he meant by that? Perhaps if Ziusudra spent a session with the torturers, they could obtain the explanation."

Sargon's eyes widened. Obviously it had never occurred to him that Trella's agents might be spying on him. "He never said that! I swear he . . ."

Eskkar pushed off from the table, covering the distance between himself and his son in two long strides. For a tall man, Eskkar could move with both speed and agility, a fact that had surprised his enemies and saved his life more than once. Before Sargon could react, Eskkar's hand clamped on his son's shoulder with such force that Sargon gasped in surprise and pain.

Jerking his arm, Eskkar shoved Sargon so fiercely that he staggered across the room and slammed into the wall, hard enough to send the sound throughout the house.

Eskkar never stopped moving. He caught Sargon as he bounced off the wall, and this time his right hand fastened around his son's throat. "You call your mother a liar to her face!"

The grip tightened. Sargon clasped his hands on his father wrist and tried to loosen his grip, but far bigger and stronger men had failed to move that arm.

Sargon's face turned red, and he gasped for breath. He dropped his right hand to fumble with his tunic. But before he could draw the dagger from beneath his garment, Eskkar caught Sargon's wrist with his left hand and squeezed. Sargon cried out as the bones in his wrist ground together. The blade clattered to the floor.

"Damn you!" Eskkar twisted his shoulders and flung Sargon back into the center of the room. The boy stumbled and went down, landing awkwardly on the plank floor, his head within the shadow of the table.

The door burst open. The guard, summoned by the noise, took one step into the room, his hand on the hilt of his sword. His eyes darted around the room, seeking any sign of danger.

Eskkar's frown froze the man in mid step. "Fetch the commander of my guards. At once! And find my Hawk Clan guards, the two who returned with me."

"Yes, My Lord." The soldier looked grateful for any excuse to leave the room. He turned and raced back through the door, his heavy sandals pounding on the stairs.

Sargon twisted on his side, and started to rise, but Eskkar clamped his foot on the boy's chest, pinning him to the floor. "Move and I'll crush your ribs." A shift of Eskkar's weight brought a gasp from Sargon.

Chandor and Pekka arrived together, rushing up the stairs and into the chamber. Saruda, the commander of the Compound's guards, followed them into the room.

Eskkar's glare halted all three just inside the chamber. "Saruda, my son Sargon is to be placed in the smallest of the guest quarters. He is to see no one, speak to no one. That includes the servants. You will not obey any of his orders, and you will ignore any requests. If you fail in this duty in the slightest, I'll have you hung from the city's walls. Do you understand me?"

Over the past few months, perhaps even longer, the guards had grown accustomed to taking orders from Sargon. That practice had to stop.

"Yes, My Lord." Saruda glanced down at the boy. "Of course."

Eskkar turned to the other guards. "You two will remain in the chamber with Sargon. I give you the same orders as Saruda. No one is to see him or talk to him. And he is not to speak with you. If he does, for each word he utters, I order you to punch him as hard as you can in the stomach. If either of you fails to obey my orders, you'll both wish you'd never been born."

Eskkar glanced at the guards and his son. Then he turned to Trella. She remained seated on the bench, expressionless, her face drained of color. She met his eyes and nodded.

"Get him out of here."

The moment the door closed behind them, Eskkar whirled and returned to the table. He wanted to strike something, someone. Instead he pounded the surface with the heel of his hand. "Damn him to the pits." Taking a deep breath, Eskkar regained control of his emotions. He filled his cup with wine, and gulped half of it, spilling a mouthful on his clean tunic in the process.

"My son!" The bitterness grated on his tongue. "I taught him everything but honor."

"That cannot be taught, unless the pupil already has the seeds within him." Her eyes closed for a moment. "But perhaps it is not too late for Sargon. You know I have never approved of your idea of sending him to the Steppes People to learn the ways of war. Perhaps I was wrong. Perhaps it is time for him to learn honor the hard way."

He stared at her. "Then he will have one last chance to learn it. Tomorrow he will accompany me to the north. I will take him to Subutai of the Ur Nammu. Maybe he can teach our son what I have failed."

Trella's eyes closed at Eskkar's words. She knew what they meant, and she did not protest. Her son would likely die in the north. "You have not failed, Eskkar. It is I who have put up with Sargon's bad habits far longer than I should. Now I will have to bear the responsibility for that."

Eskkar sat beside her. Taking her in his arms, he felt her tremble against him, as she rested her head on his shoulder. After a few moments, she regained her composure.

"Now the gods will decide his future." Trella's voice had regained its decisiveness.

Eskkar had more faith in Subutai than any gods, but decided to keep that thought to himself.

Loud voices sounded through the door, coming from the common room below.

"Damn every demon, now what?" Eskkar strode to the door, flung it open so hard that it slammed against the wall, and stared down into the house's main chamber.

Corio stood there, his path blocked by one of the household guards. "Eskkar! I demand to speak to you. Right now!"

The last man in Akkad Eskkar wanted to see. He considered sending the outraged girl's father away, but decided that he respected Corio too much to avoid him. Besides, if Eskkar sent him away, the man's anger would only increase. "Come on up, Corio."

A moment later, the Noble Corio, his face red with anger, stomped into the room. "Eskkar, do you know what your son has done?"

Eskkar held up his hand and shook his head. "Save your words, Corio. If you're not satisfied with what I intend for the boy, you can use my own knife to cut off his balls."

13

That night and the next day strained Trella's resolve. She had to set aside her own sorrow and worries to deal with her husband, who alternated between the darkest gloom and a burning fury. In his anger, Eskkar wanted to ride out of Akkad the next day, but Trella pleaded with him to wait a few days.

"I want to prepare some things before you go," Trella said. "And you need time to select your men and ready your supplies. It may be a long journey, and you should get some rest. Also, I want to prepare gifts for the Ur Nammu. That may help them receive Sargon more favorably."

Grudgingly Eskkar agreed to the delay.

That time stretched out to four days, during which Trella prepared for Eskkar and Sargon's departure.

"There is much you will need, my husband," she said, more than once. "Traveling will be difficult, so it is better to take our time."

She saw how Eskkar hated each day of waiting. Trella understood his dilemma – he feared that he might weaken in his resolve, and release Sargon from his confinement, to give the boy yet one more chance. On several occasions Eskkar turned to her, the anguish plain on his face. Eskkar's unspoken plea was that she would change her mind about Sargon's banishment.

Those moments wrenched at Trella's heart. She had acquiesced to Eskkar's decision, but her love for her son shook her resolve. If she weakened the slightest, Eskkar would rescind his orders. But though the decision tested her strength of will, Trella refused to relent. The boy was counting on them doing just that. But Sargon had created a crisis that must be resolved, once and for all.

She and Eskkar had labored for too many years to establish their place at the top of Akkad's hierarchy. They had gambled their lives more than once, and endured too much danger, to risk everything now on a wayward son. As he was, Sargon would never be a good or wise ruler. And the fact that he would keep company with one who spoke against his father's rule was damning of itself, far worse than anything Sargon could have done to Sestana.

All Trella's efforts to ensure their rule could still come to naught if Eskkar died without a suitable heir. With a weak son, several of the nobles and even some of the soldiers might be tempted to put themselves forth as the next King of Akkad.

In her heart, she doubted that their oldest son would ever fill the role of heir. And despite Sargon's claims that he would change, she'd seen youths such as this before. She knew that her son's shiftlessness would only increase as he grew older. Those who took to drinking too much ale so young rarely abandoned the habit as they grew older.

Trella dared not let the years pass, hoping that Sargon would outgrow his wildness. With the danger from the Elamites approaching, the need for a suitable heir had grown even more urgent.

Better to remove the boy now, give him this one last chance, before he grew old enough to cause more serious trouble. Despite the pain it brought her, Trella knew Sargon had to go the Ur Nammu. He needed the hard training, both physical and mental, that Sargon had failed to receive in Akkad, with its ever-present temptations.

Sargon, of course, only added to Trella's woes. She visited him several times each day, and at every opportunity to speak he pleaded for another chance, another opportunity. He swore that he would drink no wine, that he would attend to his studies, and obey his teachers. Again and again, Sargon pleaded his case, and as the days passed without setting out on the journey, Trella saw that her son's belief that they would relent increased.

Both father and son underestimated Trella's resolve. She needed a suitable heir to the city, someone who could rule one day, and accept Trella's guidance.

"The time to resolve this problem is now," she told Eskkar. "Akkad has enemies within and without, all waiting for us to show the least sign of weakness. Many harbor hatred in their hearts toward us. You, because you were born a barbarian, and I because I was a slave. While I love my son in spite of his foolishness, others might use him to threaten us or our family. We must also think of Melkorak and Zakita."

That thought, in the end, kept her determination strong. Trella had other children to consider. Nor was she too old to have another child. If Melkorak did not yet display the sharp mind needed for a ruler, at least he would accept his mother's guidance. As would Trella's daughter, Zakita, who possessed keen wits. Both would play significant roles in Akkad's expansion in the coming years. No, she would not risk their futures to save Sargon's.

Both Trella and Eskkar remembered that the boy had lied, and they remembered, too, that he had reached for the knife he'd worn under his tunic. Any son who dared raise his hand against his father might be put to death. Exile from the family would be considered a mercy.

So the days passed. Eskkar fell back into what he did best, choosing his men and horses, and deciding what to take with him. Trella agreed that he should take Chandor and Pekka, his bodyguards, of course, along with twenty of Hathor's best horse fighters, ten of them already Hawk Clan.

Hathor had insisted on accompanying his king, but Eskkar refused, unwilling to waste Hathor's time on such a mission. Eskkar did accept Draelin, one of Hathor's senior men, to be his second in command. Six pack horses would accompany the riders, burdened with supplies for the trip and gifts to the Ur Nammu, most of those selected by Trella herself.

On the morning of the fifth day, in the pre-dawn darkness, Trella stood in the Courtyard. A crackling torch provided the only light. Outside in the lane, the horsemen, many still rubbing sleep from their eyes, waited to begin the journey. Eskkar had insisted on an early departure. Trella knew her husband wanted none of the city's inhabitants to witness the spectacle of the king leading his troublesome son into exile.

"Do not blame your father," Trella said to Sargon, who stood before her. "He . . . both of us believe this is for your own good. In my heart, I am certain that you will return to us."

"You cannot do this to me, Mother. I am your son. You need me here."

The words sounded well enough, but Trella heard the anger hidden in them. Her son still could not believe his parents would go through with his punishment.

She reached out and touched his cheek. "You must endure this, Sargon, for your own good. Just remember that I love you, and will pray for your swift return."

Sargon brushed her hand away. "Then I have no mother, no father! No mother would banish her own son." The boy's loud words echoed throughout the Compound. The servants and soldiers averted their eyes at the hurtful words.

Eskkar, seeing to his horse a few paces away, strode over. "If you raise your voice again, I'll have you gagged."

Sargon glared at them both, then turned away.

Eskkar gave the order to move out. He led his horse out of the Courtyard, with Sargon following, with two Hawk Clan guards on either side.

Stretching her legs to keep up, Trella accompanied them to the main gate, now called Ishtar's Gate by the people. She gave Eskkar a brief farewell, and tried to say something encouraging to Sargon. But again her son turned his face away.

Tight-lipped, Trella climbed the guard tower steps just as the sun's first rays of light topped the hills to the east. She watched from the wall as her husband and son rode out. Tears streaked her cheeks, but Trella refused to brush them away. The last time she felt such grief was when she watched her mother and father die, both murdered before her eyes. As she stared, Eskkar put his horse to a canter, and the soldiers matched his pace.

The moment Eskkar and his men passed out of sight, Trella brushed the tears from her face. She turned away from the wall and spoke to the leader of her four Hawk Clan guards, waiting patiently a few steps away.

"Send a messenger to Ningal the merchant. Tell him that the King would be grateful if Ningal would attend him at the Compound at mid-morning. And he is to bring his son, Ziusudra, with him."

That problem, too, needed to be resolved, though she had already taken the first steps.

At the appointed time, Ningal the merchant, and his wayward son, Ziusudra, arrived at the Compound. As they climbed the steps and entered the upper chamber, no doubt the merchant expected to hear angry words from King Eskkar, followed by some sort of fine as punishment.

The passage of time had lessened the impact of the assault. Even Corio, Sestana's father, had controlled his rage, though he administered a savage beating to his own son for his part in the drunken attack. Of course Ziusudra was no longer welcome at Corio's house. But after the first two days with no word from the King, Ziusudra assumed the worst of the storm had blown over, and resumed his usual ways, as the city's gossip turned to other matters.

As two more days passed without any summons, father and son smiled at each other and relaxed. But that idea disappeared the moment Ningal saw the reception that Trella had arranged.

Trella and Annok-sur sat behind the large table, flanked on either side by a Hawk Clan guard. Bantor, the Captain of Akkad's Guard, sat at the end of the table. Behind him, Hathor, the city's cavalry commander, leaned his sparse frame against the wall.

No scribes or servants hovered nearby, but more important, Nicar, the King's Justice, was absent. Befitting their status as wealthy and influential citizens, any of the city's important traders expected to plead their case in the presence of Nicar. Ningal's complacent mood vanished as he took in the hard faces of those arrayed before him.

The door to the chamber closed, as Ningal moved into the center of the room.

"I received a summons from the King." Ningal glanced around, as if expecting Eskkar to join them from the other chamber.

Eskkar's planned departure had remained a secret, known only to those soldiers and servants within the Compound. The less anyone knew about his goings and comings the safer he, and Trella, too, would be.

She stared at Ningal, observing the worried look that he no doubt thought he was concealing. Ningal's fine tunic, soft leather sandals, and etched belt did little to enhance his rotund body. The merchant had eaten far too many fine meals, each one accompanied by the most expensive wines.

A weak man despite his successes, ruled by his appetites and desires for wealth. He had fathered only one child, Ziusudra, though he possessed several wives and an extensive collection of nubile slave girls.

Ziusudra, tall and handsome, looked nothing like his father, and Trella wondered if Ningal had, in fact, sired the boy. Her sharp glance examined their ears, and noted that father and son did not resemble each other in that feature. Perhaps some sturdy household slave had taken advantage of one of Ningal's absences to slip into his wife's bed and cuckold his master.

Not that it mattered any more. The father's laxity and the boy's deviousness and subtlety had brought this punishment upon their family.

Ziusudra, mistaking the brief silence, favored Trella with his best and most sincere smile.

"Eskkar is not here." Trella did not intend to waste any more of her words or her time. "Ningal, you are being banished from Akkad, you and your family. You have three days in which to depart. And you will make a payment of two hundred gold coins to the King before noon today. Or one hundred if you do not wish for Ziusudra to accompany you. In that case he will be put to death for treason."

As she spoke, Trella turned her gaze to the son, the ambitious boy who had twisted Sargon to his own purposes.

The smile had left Ziusudra's face. "I've committed no treason!" Ziusudra had grasped the import of her words even faster than his father. "Your own son can swear to that."

Ningal's mouth fell open in shock, and it took a moment before he could speak. "Banishment! For a youthful prank, a prank instigated by your son? And two hundred gold coins? Such a fine is unheard of." Even for a man as wealthy as Ningal, that much gold would be a serious hardship. "I protest! Lady Trella, I demand to see the King's Justice. This is not allowed and . . ."

Hathor pushed himself away from the wall and stepped across the room. Before Ningal could react, Hathor grabbed him by the throat, the powerful muscles in his arm rippling under the dark skin. At the same time, the Egyptian drew the short sword he always carried.

When the sharp blade pressed against Ningal's stomach, a gasp of panic escaped from his mouth. He tried to shrink away, but Hathor merely tightened his grip.

"The penalty for treason against the King is death." Trella kept her voice firm, letting it reach through Ningal's fear. "And if you have forgotten, treason is not resolved by the King's Justice, only by the King. So if you continue to argue or protest, Hathor will kill you and your son right now. I can collect the gold from your household myself."

Far tougher and braver men than Ningal had withered under Hathor's ruthless gaze. The merchant, lips protruding and his face now bright red, attempted to speak. Hathor released his grip on the man's neck, and shifted his grasp to the front of the man's richly woven tunic. But the tip of his sword remained firm against Ningal's soft stomach.

"I . . . I will pay! Please don't kill me. I will leave the city, I swear it!"

With a snort of disgust, Hathor released the man. Ningal would have fallen, but Ziusudra, his eyes wide with shock, caught his father's arm and held him upright.

"That is wise, Ningal." Trella's voice still hadn't risen. "There is another condition. Neither you nor your son will say anything to anyone about this matter. There will be no mention about the fine, no explanations about why you have decided to leave Akkad. You will just leave the city. The first time I hear talk about what has happened here today, that will be your last day of life. Do you understand?"

Ningal nodded. His lip trembled, and his eyes remained wide with fear.

"After you leave, you will not take up residence within two hundred miles of Akkad. If you do, then your treason will be proclaimed, and a bounty set on both your heads. Perhaps a hundred gold coins for each. You do understand what that means, don't you, Ningal?"

For that much gold, a hundred men would set out to find the merchant and return with his head. And no city, no ruler within the Land Between the Rivers would offer succor to Ningal, not for any sum. The wrath of Akkad was too well known to take such a risk, not when it would be just as easy to seize Ningal's possessions for themselves and then turn him over to Akkad for the reward.

"I do . . . Lady Trella. I will . . . I do."

"Good. Then you may depart. My guards will accompany you home, and remain at your side until the gold is delivered. Do not waste their time. Leave us."

Numbed, the merchant nodded and turned to go, still clutching onto his son's arm. His unsteady gait showed his shock.

Trella waited until father and son had left the room and descended the stairs. "Thank you, Hathor, and you also, Bantor."

Bantor rose and stretched. "For what? I still think you should have killed him. That would have satisfied Corio, too."

"Come, Bantor." Hathor slid his sword back into its scabbard. "We've got enough to worry about."

Bantor glanced at his wife in resignation, and shook his head. The two commanders departed, taking the guards with them.

As the door closed, Trella breathed a sigh of relief. "I'm glad that's done."

"Bantor is right." Annok-sur shook her head. "You should have killed them both. And confiscated all their goods."

"No, this way is better. Eskkar and I agreed on this. Better not to give Sargon another reason to hate us." She refused to consider the possibility that she might never see her son again. "Besides, time and uncertainty will work in our favor. You have set everything in motion?"

"Yes. Derina left yesterday for Lagash. She will be in place by the time Ningal arrives. The fool does not even know that he goes where we want him to go."

Everyone knew that the merchant had kin in the city of Lagash to the west. And that place lay just outside the two hundred miles that Trella had specified. Where else would Ningal go to restart his ventures?

"And Derina's box is ready?"

"Almost. She will make a stop or two along the way, to gather what she needs. When Ningal arrives in Lagash, he will be searching for household servants. Derina's cooking skills will make her the obvious choice. She understands she is to wait two or three months before serving her special mushrooms."

And that would be the end of Ningal and Ziusudra. They would die by poison in a distant land, and no connection to Akkad would ever be established. Nevertheless, many would guess the truth, and even more would respect the long reach of Trella's power. Most of all, the boy who had poisoned her son's thoughts would die in agony of poison himself, a fitting end to a short and wasted life.

14

At about the same time that Ningal and Ziusudra learned their fate, Sargon slid from his horse and stretched his stiff legs. He hadn't ridden a horse for at least ten or twelve days, though Eskkar had told Sargon often enough that he should ride every day. Now, with his father pressing the pace, Sargon's lack of endurance showed itself. Eskkar obviously had wanted to get as far from Akkad as possible before stopping. Though Sargon knew how to ride, he'd never covered so much ground without stopping to rest.

The soldiers milled around, talking among themselves while easing their own muscles, though none of them showed any signs of weariness. No one paid much attention to Sargon, except for Chandra and Pekka, his father's bodyguards, who had ridden at Sargon's side during the journey. They, too, had received their orders – to keep a close eye on the King's son.

Sargon felt tempted to tell them not to bother. He knew better than to try and run away. Any of these men Eskkar had chosen for this expedition would have little trouble catching Sargon, binding his hands, and leading him back. He didn't intend to give his father that satisfaction.

Instead Sargon tossed his horse's halter to Chandra and sat on the ground. Though surrounded by twenty men, he remained as alone as if he were still imprisoned in his room. The soldiers ignored him. They knew of Sargon's banishment, and that knowledge made them keep their distance. No one wanted to get caught between the King and his son.

The guards meant nothing to Sargon. He thought as little of them as they did of him. Simple creatures, they did as they were told.

Sargon glanced up, to see Eskkar striding toward him.

"We've a long ride ahead of us, Sargon." Eskkar kept his voice low, and his words cold and flat. "Don't give the soldiers any trouble. If you try and run away, they'll hunt you down. When they find you, they'll break one of your legs, to make sure you don't try it again. So unless you want to face a long and painful ride with a broken leg, do as you're told."

Sargon glared at his father, but said nothing.

Eskkar met his son's gaze for a moment, then turned away and raised his voice. "Mount up. Let's get moving."

At that moment, Sargon's last glimmer of hope, that his mother and father might be testing him vanished, dispelled by the grim look in Eskkar's eyes. His father never spoke much, but when he did, especially in that tone of voice, Eskkar meant what he said.

Sullenly, Sargon mounted his horse – not his own horse, just some nag the soldiers had given him – and started moving. Four guards accompanied him, two in front and two behind. Two of them had ropes slung over their shoulders, which Sargon knew would be used to restrain him if he attempted to slip away.

Sargon's fist tightened around the halter rope, and he fought the urge to take his anger out on the horse. He hated the soldiers, hated all of them, especially Chandra and Pekka, his father's efficient bodyguards, both loyal members of the Hawk Clan.

The fact that Sargon was the heir to the kingdom meant nothing to them. Their loyalty lay with the King, not his son. They were too stupid to understand that Akkad's future lay with Sargon, not his father.

His horse needed little guidance. The animal followed those ahead of it, so Sargon had plenty of time to brood. He remembered his mother's goodbye, uttered just before they left the courtyard. *This is not the end,* she said, leaning forward and kissing his cheek, *only the beginning.* After those brief words, she moved away, to linger much longer as she whispered her farewell to the king.

Sargon glimpsed her once more, as he rode through the gate and left the city. A glance back toward Akkad's walls revealed her, bathed in the first rays of dawn, standing atop the tower, watching the company of toughened fighters depart. But her gaze, Sargon knew, was directed at her husband, not the son that she had condemned and banished.

He decided that he hated his mother even more than his father. Despite Eskkar uttering the shocking words that he would take his son to the Ur Nammu, Sargon blamed his mother for his banishment.

Angry as his father might be, his mother always found a way to talk him around to whatever she wanted, most of the time without Eskkar realizing he had changed his mind. His mother ruled the city, if not directly, then through her husband. And the city of Akkad always came first in her thoughts, far ahead of any concerns for husband or son.

A fury of silent rage swept over Sargon. They both should have been more concerned about him, the future ruler of Akkad. Instead they had condemned him.

Sargon stared at Eskkar, riding at the head of the column, his shoulders hunched forward, as if brooding on his decision. But his father said nothing further to his son the rest of the day, and the grim soldiers guarding Sargon took their lead from their King. Sargon didn't bother trying to talk to them. He knew they had orders which forbade them to listen to his words, let alone obey any of his requests.

Only Draelin, his father's second in command, exchanged words with Sargon when they halted at midday to rest the horses. "Don't feel bad about riding that horse. After a few days, you can switch to one of the pack animals. They're all good stock."

Sargon didn't bother to answer. Men like Draelin, despite his rank of commander, meant nothing, less than nothing. Simple soldiers, every one of them. They obeyed orders without question, just as they would obey Sargon's commands when he became king.

He should be the one giving the orders. Even Ziusudra agreed that Eskkar's time to rule had come and gone. The city no longer needed a warrior king, someone ready to pick up a sword and do battle. Even his father's latest venture had involved him fighting, one foolish barbarian against another.

If only Eskkar had fallen in the battle. The soldiers would still have returned victorious, and Sargon would be the city's ruler.

But, no, his father's famous luck had spared him once again. And of course, Eskkar had to come back to the city on the same day as the trouble with that stupid cow Sestana. Her arrogant father, worse luck, was one of the few in the city who could make demands on the King. Even so, a few days later, and the prank would have been forgotten.

Then a mere slip of the tongue had betrayed Sargon and sent his father into one of his rages. Again and again Sargon relived that moment. He could still feel his father's hand on his throat, choking the life from his body. At that moment, Sargon thought he was going to die. If only he could have reached his dagger. Then it would have been his father lying dead on the floor.

With Eskkar dead, no one, not even his mother, could have stopped him from taking the kingship. Sargon was the oldest son and the rightful heir. His popularity with the people of Akkad would have lifted him, the city's first true-born Akkadian, to the highest power. Even Trella, his mother, would have yielded to the will of the people. His brother Melkorak was too young, and his sister didn't matter.

Trella would have turned to Sargon out of necessity. Either her son would take charge of the city, or some favored son of the nobles would, leaving her with nothing. And once Sargon had the power in his hands, he would make sure his mother changed her ways, or she would have found herself banished from Akkad.

If only Sargon could escape and return to Akkad. Ziusudra and his father Ningal would help. They had spoken often about Sargon's eventual ascent to the kingship. With their backing, and that of others who Ziusudra assured him had grown tired of Eskkar and his barbarian rule, the soldiers would bow down and accept Sargon as their king. If only . . .

Instead he rode north, and each jolting stride of the miserable horse took him farther away from any chance of ruling. And always the grim Hawk Clan guards remained alert. They had their orders and they knew their business.

That night, exhausted, Sargon fell asleep on the hard ground, placed as far away from the horses as convenient, though he felt too weary to even think about escaping. In the morning, after a quick breakfast of already stale bread, the journey continued. Sargon's muscles protested, but he knew showing weakness in front of these men would not help. Gritting his teeth, he concentrated on controlling his horse.

The soldiers, meanwhile, talked and laughed as they rode. Over and over, they discussed Eskkar's battle at the stream against the Alur Meriki. Despite Sargon's lack of interest, he heard every detail of every part of the struggle, and the role each man had played in the conflict. The simple Akkadian soldiers remained in awe of his father.

To them, this journey meant nothing more than a chance to earn some extra coins, enjoy a ride through the countryside, and get away from Akkad for a while. Occasionally one or another would break into a song, with the rest joining in. Sometimes the rough words they sang poked fun at the King, as if the ruler of Akkad were a fair target for their jests.

Sargon had listened to many soldiers' songs before, but he had never heard such disrespect shown by common soldiers to their King. In Akkad and the nearby training camps, the men kept such coarse words to themselves. On the march, it seemed, loose discipline prevailed.

His father never complained about the lack of respect. In fact, Eskkar often joined in with their foolishness, acting as though he were nothing more than a common soldier himself, instead of their ruler. In Sargon's mind, he heard the caustic comments Ziusudra would have uttered at such an embarrassing and humiliating spectacle.

The miles rolled by beneath the hooves of their horses. For the rest of that day and the next, Sargon clung to the forlorn hope that his father might yet change his mind and turn the column around, admitting that the whole journey was nothing more than a final test to force Sargon to his parents' will. Sargon's mind went over what he would say when that happened, how much he would apologize, and how much he would swear to be a dutiful son.

And he would promise anything, everything his parents wanted. Trella's spies might have heard some of Ziusudra's comments, but one talk Sargon felt certain that no one had overheard remained in his mind. For the right amount of gold, Ziusudra claimed, even a king could be slain by the right man. Ziusudra intimated that he knew just such a man.

By the fourth day, that slender hope had vanished. Even mounted on a better animal, Sargon knew he could not escape. Five or six riders would each take an extra horse, and they would run him down, long before he could reach the city's walls or disappear into the countryside.

Even if Sargon succeeded in making it to Akkad, Bantor's soldiers or Annok-sur's spies would soon find him. And with each passing day, Ziusudra might become more unwilling to risk his father's fortune to succor his friend.

Sargon thought often about his friend, sitting in their favorite ale house, probably with a girl on his lap. Ziusudra always managed to enjoy himself.

More days passed, and the weather grew cooler. When they made camp on the twelfth day, Draelin appeared and handed Sargon a cloak unpacked from one of the supply packs.

"Your father wants you to have this, Sargon. It will be getting colder at night as we move north."

Sargon accepted the cloak, but turned away from Draelin without saying a word. Sargon refused to bow to his father's will. Sargon had already decided he would speak to his father as little as possible.

The cloak, a fine one made by one of his mother's servants, served Sargon well that night. In the morning the journey continued, each day taking the caravan farther and farther north, through country so rugged and desolate that the riders seldom encountered anyone.

When the scouts began riding back and forth, searching for the Ur Nammu, Sargon let his hope return. He knew little about the small clan of barbarians that lived in the mostly empty lands north of Akkad. His mother had a weakness in her heart for them, and Eskkar considered them important allies, though how a handful of ignorant nomad horsemen could be of value to Akkad escaped Sargon.

In the war against Sumer, the Akkadians had raised an army of more than five thousand men, more than enough to defeat and tame the Sumerians and their allies. What could a few hundred barbarians matter against such a force?

By now thirteen days of hard riding had passed. Although well-mounted, the troop had traveled a vast distance. Sargon knew his father and the soldiers had only the most general location of where the small clan of steppes warriors might be found, and the last four or five days included much searching and scouting, all of which required caution on the part of the soldiers.

Far enough from home that even the name Akkad meant little or nothing to the inhabitants, the few people living in these lands remained fraught with fear. Any large party of armed men warranted suspicion, and more than a few farmers or herders fled in fright at first sight of the Akkadians.

Sargon watched with interest when they did cross paths with a band of marauders, about fifteen well armed men, all of them mounted, who watched their progress for half a day. To the soldiers' disappointment, his father ignored the bandits.

Eventually they abandoned any ideas of raiding Eskkar's party. The six pack animals promised little reward when balanced against the heavily armed Akkadians and their greater numbers.

None of the soldiers appeared the least concerned, and Sargon soon realized that raiders such as these had little stomach for a tough fight, one that promised only hard knocks and empty purses even if they were successful. All the same, Eskkar ordered extra guards on duty each night, to protect both the horses and the camp. Sargon, of course, had no such duty to perform.

After another day of fruitless searching, Sargon started to believe that they were not going to find the wandering clan, and that his father might soon be forced to return to Akkad. Then Eskkar's troop sighted a small band of five riders, outlined on top of a hill almost a mile away.

Though yet at a great distance, Sargon heard Draelin claim he could see yellow strips dangling from their lance tips. Sargon couldn't be sure, but his father ordered the large yellow pennant broken out. Lifting that standard and waving it back and forth brought a reaction.

Two of the riders guided their mounts down the slope, heading for the Akkadians, the other three warriors holding back. If this were a trap, they could escape to the north and gather their clan.

With much care, the two riders approached. Meanwhile, Eskkar ordered his men to dismount. Sargon, at the back of the caravan, stared helplessly, hoping these were not the Ur Nammu. His last dream of returning to Akkad turned to ashes when one of the horsemen gave a shout, and urged his horse forward, calling out Eskkar's name. The rider had recognized Akkad's leader.

Sargon watched the barbarian pull his horse to a stop beside Eskkar. The scout, a powerfully built man with long black hair, carried a curved bow with yellow feathers dangling from the tip. A sword slung across his back, the hilt jutting over his shoulder, and he had a quiver of arrows hung on his left hip. His sturdy horse looked more like a wild beast, with a shaggy gray coat and wild eyes.

The two Akkadian columns tightened up, the horses nose to tail, and even Sargon could hear what was said.

"I did not believe it was you, Eskkar of Akkad. I am Unkara of the Ur Nammu."

"Your eyes are good, Unkara," Eskkar answered. "Forgive me for not recalling your name."

"I was just a young warrior when I last saw you, Chief Eskkar. You are far from your lands."

"And you wonder what has brought me so far north to these empty lands?" Eskkar laughed. "I wish to speak with Subutai. I trust he is well?"

Sargon understood the importance of the question. Men died, not only in battle, but from disease or accidents. A dead clan leader might change the situation.

"Subutai is more than well," Unkara answered. "Our camp is but a day's ride from here. I can guide you to him. And I will send a rider on ahead, with word of your coming."

Sargon caught the implication in those words, too. Subutai might have no use for a visit, or might want time to organize a war party.

"That would be good," Eskkar said. "These lands are unfamiliar."

"These lands are dangerous," Unkara agreed. "There are many roaming bands of fighters crossing through this territory, and none of them have any use for strangers. We hunt them down when we get the opportunity. Most have learned to avoid the reach of our riders."

Eskkar nodded in approval. "We saw one such band. Still, we will be grateful to ride beside you and your men, Unkara. It will speed up our journey. We're running low on food."

"Follow me, then." The barbarian whirled his horse around and dashed away, to rejoin his companions.

Eskkar gave the order, and the Akkadians moved forward again. Sargon followed more slowly, until one of his guards smacked the palm of his hand against the rump of Sargon's horse.

Startled, Sargon almost slid off the horse's back. Instead he kicked his horse forward, taking out his anger on the dumb brute.

Like a slave, he would soon be handed over to uncouth barbarians living in smoke-filled tents and sleeping with their horses and dogs. The meanest slave in Akkad would live a better life. Once again, Sargon cursed the injustice that had brought him here.

The final leg of the journey took longer than expected, as the Akkadians pack animals slowed the usual rapid pace of the warriors. Midafternoon of the next day had passed before the caravan crossed over the crest of a hill and Sargon saw the Ur Nammu encampment. Its tents nestled between the protecting arms of two long ridges extending down from a steep hill.

Despite his gloom, Sargon stared down at the barbarian camp. About four hundred horses grazed in the shelter of the hills. Tents, some made from animal skins, were pitched haphazardly along the banks of a meandering stream, and Sargon could see smoke rising from several campfires.

The camp's inhabitants stopped whatever they were doing and watched the strangers approach. He could see children running about. A few cattle and a small herd of sheep grazed a quarter mile downstream of the tents.

The barbarian Unkara shouted something to Eskkar, and then rode on ahead. Sargon saw his father turn to Draelin.

"You've never dealt with the Ur Nammu before," Eskkar said. "Our men will be quartered a short distance away from their camp. You must make sure that none of our soldiers leave that place, or do anything to give offense. Otherwise . . ."

"I understand, Captain."

Eskkar gave the order, and the little troop started down the hill. Before they reached the bottom, Sargon saw two riders heading toward them. One was Unkara.

Eskkar halted his men and waited until the two barbarians arrived. Sargon heard the name "Subutai" several times, and decided the leader of the Ur Nammu himself had ridden out to meet the Akkadians.

Sargon stared at this barbarian, who would soon be his master.

Subutai, about the same age as Eskkar, appeared fit. Tall and sinewy, Subutai had a broad forehead and deep brown eyes. A wide mouth filled with strong white teeth flashed when he smiled. Hard muscles covered his chest and his legs were thick and powerful. Only a few strands of gray in his hair gave evidence to his years.

After a brief discussion in the language of the steppes peoples, Eskkar told Draelin to take the men and follow Unkara to a campsite about a half mile from the tents of the Ur Nammu. Eskkar and Subutai left the Akkadians and rode toward the main camp.

No one paid any attention to Sargon, so he followed Draelin. No doubt his father wanted to talk in private with the barbarian chief. Sargon felt certain his presence would be the main topic of the conversation, like a head of livestock offered for sale, or a new slave, fresh on the auction block.

15

A chill wind blew down from the hills as Eskkar dismounted in front of Subutai's tent. Gray clouds had rolled in from the west, obscuring the sun. Subutai, arms crossed over his bare chest, ignored the brisk breeze. He motioned toward the tent, and led the way inside.

Ducking beneath the flap, Eskkar found himself facing one of Subutai's wives, Petra, if Eskkar remembered right. She had built a small fire, so the interior would be more comfortable for her husband's important visitor.

Layers of blankets and horsehides covered the ground, except in the center, where a ring of stones surrounded the smoky fire. A small hole at the top of the tent was supposed to let the smoke escape, but from the haze in the air, Eskkar doubted it was working today. Two small chests comprised the tent's only furnishings.

"Wine and water for our guest." Subutai's words sounded inviting enough, and he managed a friendly smile for his visitor. "He's had a long and hard ride." He gestured toward a colorful blanket. "Come. Sit at our fire."

Eskkar bowed in appreciation and eased himself down, shrugging the long sword off his shoulder and dropping the weapon carelessly at his side. The two men sat cross-legged on blankets, facing each other over the crackling blaze.

One of Subutai's daughters entered the tent and helped Petra fill the cups. The young girl shyly served Eskkar a cup of wine, then returned in a moment with a water pitcher. He allowed her to pour a generous amount into the wine.

Polite conversation followed, as each man inquired about wives and children. Subutai announced that he had two new sons and a daughter. Soon the tent flap moved back and forth as the proud mothers displayed their offspring. Eskkar, as a leader of warriors, touched each child on the forehead, to give them strength and bring them luck.

At last, after refilling their cups with fresh wine, the women and children left the two men alone. Subutai waited until the tent flap settled into place.

"So, Eskkar, what brings you this far from your city? Whatever it is, it must be important."

Eskkar took a long sip from his cup. "First, I bring good news. My soldiers and I defeated the Alur Meriki in battle. Thutmose-sin is dead."

Startled, Subutai spilled wine from his cup, ignored it, and stared at Eskkar. "Dead? Are you sure?"

Subutai insisted on hearing the whole story, and Eskkar obliged. A lengthy discussion followed. Eskkar explained the details of the secret march, Hathor's battle to secure the stream, and the night attack. The duel with Thutmose-sin took longer to relate than the actual fight.

When Eskkar finally finished, Subutai rocked back and forth for a moment. "It is hard to believe. Thutmose-sin ruled for so many years. Thousands have died because of him, and many hundreds of Ur Nammu warriors. He nearly destroyed our Clan. And now he is dead, and by your own hand. We owe you and Akkad a great debt."

"I thought you would rejoice at these tidings."

"Later, perhaps." Subutai shook his head. "But first I must look into my heart."

Subutai wanted to know where the battle happened, and why that stream was chosen. Eskkar explained, using directions and landmarks that would have been incomprehensible to anyone who hadn't spent their life on a horse. Then he went into the details of the peace arrangement.

Even Subutai's inscrutable face showed surprise at the news. "So the Alur Meriki accepted your terms? They will honor the peace?"

"Yes, I believe they will keep it. And they've sworn to leave the Ur Nammu alone," Eskkar repeated. "I assume that you won't want to challenge them."

"No, even with their losses, they still far outnumber us. If they do not search us out, we will bide our time."

Blood feuds between steppes clans could endure many generations, and the Ur Nammu had no intention of ending theirs. Subutai's father had died in his son's arms, from an Alur Meriki lance.

"Still, this is good news," Subutai declared. "We will take our herds and turn to the southwest earlier than we planned, before we once again return to the lands north of Akkad. That should keep us out of their path."

With that rough timetable, Eskkar guessed the Ur Nammu would not touch Akkad's borders for at least two, perhaps three years. The Ur Nammu might still be able to help Eskkar face the Elamite invasion.

"If you stay out of their way," Eskkar agreed, "they should honor their oaths, provided your warriors do not attack them."

"We will speak more about that later," Subutai said. "And you will need to retell the story of your battle for my warriors, no doubt many times. They will have many questions. Now, though your news is most welcome, what is the real reason that brings you to my tent?"

Eskkar took another sip of wine, already well into his second cup, more than he usually drank. Subutai was no fool. Sooner or later, news of the battle with the Alur Meriki would have reached him. Or Eskkar could have dispatched a messenger to carry the news.

"The reason for my searching you out involves my son, Sargon. He is at the camp with my men."

Subutai's eyes widened, no doubt in surprise at this breach of manners, but he said nothing. Nonetheless, Eskkar knew the heir to the kingdom of Akkad should have been seated at his father's side during a meeting such as this, not left behind with the other Akkadians. How else could a young leader learn the ways of command?

Eskkar waited a few moments while Subutai worked it out. "Sargon has become . . . a trial to Trella and myself. His wildness brought him into the company of those whose thoughts . . . they represented a danger to the city. He's spent too much time in idleness and drinking and not enough learning how to rule. Nor learning how to live with honor. I thought . . . I hope . . . that if my son spent time with your warriors, if you took him into your clan for a time, he might yet grow into manhood and learn the ways of honor."

Subutai kept his gaze on the fire. He knew how difficult such words were for any father to believe, let alone utter the thought to another. "Such a thing has been done in the past, in the days of my father. But if I accept Sargon into the Ur Nammu, it might be many years before he can return to Akkad."

"I understand." Eskkar reached out and poked the sticks deeper into the fire, keeping it going. He, too, preferred to not meet Subutai's eyes.

"And if he does not accept our ways? If he is injured or killed, then what?"

"Then he will be dead. Better that than for him to live with dishonor." Eskkar met Subutai's gaze. "I know the danger he will face. But if he cannot accept this chance, then it is better that he not return to Akkad."

"I see. Then my heart is heavy for my friend Eskkar. And for Trella. Did she . . ."

Subutai caught himself. One did not ask a warrior what his wife thought about the raising of his son. Despite all that Subutai knew about Trella's influence, a son remained the property of his father, and the duty and responsibility of raising him belonged only to the head of the family.

Eskkar didn't care. "Yes, Trella agreed with this decision. She knows that we need a strong heir to follow us, to rule in our place, and to carry our line down through the ages. If Sargon cannot be that son, then it is best that finds his own path."

Once again Subutai stared into the fire for a few moments. "I will accept your son, Sargon, into the Clan. But I do not think it wise that I should take him into my own family. It would . . . it might make things more difficult for your son. If you agree, I will select another warrior to look to Sargon's training."

Subutai, Eskkar realized, was offering him a final chance to back out. Probably Subutai didn't want the responsibility of a wayward son he might end up having to kill, let alone explain an accidental death. Such an occurrence might bring an end to their friendship. Better another be given the responsibility.

"The choice is yours, Subutai. I am sure you have many suitable warriors to choose from. When this is over, no matter how it ends, Trella and I will again be in your debt, Subutai."

"As I am in yours, Eskkar of Akkad, and doubly so for killing Thutmose-sin." Subutai took a deep breath. "I will speak to Sargon myself later. Meanwhile, I will think about this, and about which warrior to choose."

Eskkar finished his wine. He wanted another cup, but that could wait until he returned to his men. With a heavy heart, he bid his host goodnight, got to his feet, and left the tent.

A young boy stood apart from the tent, patiently holding A-tuku's halter. As Eskkar swung astride, he felt a relief that the most difficult part of the ordeal had ended. Now he just had to face his son, Sargon, and give him the bad news.

⸺◦⸺

Huddled in his cloak, Sargon sat alone, away from the warmth of the soldiers' fire. By now even his guards had ceased watching him. If he tried to flee, they or the barbarians would gleefully hunt him down.

Despite that knowledge, Sargon couldn't keep his mind away from somehow trying to escape. But those thoughts always brought a host of fears, and Sargon refused to give up all hope. After all, anything could happen. On the way home, his father could be attacked by bandits, or thrown from his horse and killed. Such accidents happened often enough. No, better to wait and see what the future held.

The sentry on guard called out. "The King is returning."

Sargon lifted his head at the words. Not that his father's coming and going from the barbarian camp meant anything to Sargon. The two hadn't exchanged more than a handful of words since the morning of their departure from Akkad. With his eyes shaded by the cloak's hood, Sargon watched his father arrive at the Akkadian camp, swing down from his horse, and hand it over to one of the guards. The King brushed past the soldiers with scarcely a nod, and headed straight for his son.

Sargon kept his head down and remained on the ground, though he should have risen out of respect for his father.

Gritting his teeth, Eskkar considered ordering the boy to stand. But that would only add one more humiliation for Sargon to bear. Instead, Eskkar settled on the ground across from his son.

"I've spoken to Subutai. He's agreed to take you into the Clan, but not in his own tent. He's picking a warrior to see to your training."

Sargon's determination to keep silent vanished. "Then I'm to be a slave to some filthy barbarian?"

The anger, bottled up so long in Sargon's breast, spat the words at his father. Sargon watched Eskkar's jaw tighten. The King had never been very good at concealing his emotions.

"You will not be a slave. In fact, how you are treated will be up to you. It will be difficult, but you must earn the respect of your new family. If you do, then in time you will be able to return to Akkad."

"I will never return to Akkad!" Sargon practically shouted the words in his father's face. A few of the soldiers, startled by the outburst, glanced at the two for a moment, before turning their eyes away and pretending they hadn't heard anything. "I will die here among these ignorant barbarians! Banished by my mother, murdered by my father."

Eskkar stared at his son for a moment. "It is true you may die. No man knows what the gods have in store for him until it is too late. But that is why you are here. It is not yet too late for you. We thought . . . I thought we had trained you well, taught you the ways of honor. It may even be my fault that you turned away from us. All that no longer matters. Whatever fate brought you here, you must learn to make the best of it. Here you will learn honor, or die."

"Then when you return tell my mother that I am dead. Tomorrow, the next day, I will die, and probably even before you get back to Akkad. Tell her that, and see how much her son's death matters compared to her precious city."

His father's jaw clenched again. Harsh words against Trella never failed to arouse him.

Eskkar rose to his feet. "I will be leaving in a day or two. But I will not carry any such message to your mother. If you want to tell her hateful things, you'll have to do it yourself."

His father turned and stalked off into the night, away from the soldiers, and away from the barbarian camp.

Sargon watched him go. His father could brood alone in the darkness for all Sargon cared.

The anger still burned in Sargon's heart. His scheming mother was as bad or worse than his fool of a father. But perhaps Eskkar had said one true thing. There still remained a chance that one day Sargon could hurl those same words into his mother's face. As long as that chance remained, Sargon decided he would do whatever it took to stay alive.

After all, these barbarians were simple people. It should be easy enough to deceive them, pretend to accept whatever concept of honor they believed in. Do whatever they asked, grovel in the dirt at their feet if need be. It might take a few months, but in time, they would accept him.

Then he would find a way to escape and return to the Land Between the Rivers. With a horse between his legs and a sword for protection, Sargon felt certain he could make his way to other cities, other places he could go. And perhaps when the time was right, he would return in triumph to Akkad.

Sooner or later the Ur Nammu would turn in that direction. All he needed to do was be patient until that time came. Then his friends and companions within Akkad would help him. Ziusudra had plenty of gold. With his friend's help, Sargon would strike out on his own, and find a place to live for a time. Someplace where the names Eskkar and Trella meant nothing.

Perhaps Ziusudra would call upon the man he claimed to know, the one brave enough, for the right amount of gold, to kill even a king. After all, Sargon reasoned, however much gold was needed would only be a loan.

Once he became King of Akkad, all the wealth of the city would be his. That thought brought a grim smile to Sargon's face. Yes, he would deal with these simple barbarians and await his time.

16

In the morning, Sargon awoke to find the encampment full of activity and himself the last one to arise. Though the sun had risen not long before, he saw the place where Eskkar had spread his blanket empty. His father must have left, to return to the tents of the Ur Nammu.

Before long, young barbarian children wandered over, to stare with big eyes at the newcomers with their odd clothes and strange ways. Yesterday, to Sargon's surprise, he learned that two of the Akkadian supply sacks contained gifts for the children.

Draelin and two of his men smiled at the shy children and waved them into the camp. Before long, a few of the braver boys and girls crowded around Draelin.

Sargon stared as Eskkar's commander distributed the pack's contents, taking his time and drawing out the suspense. Soon the children's shrill voices turned to happy laughter, directed as much at Draelin as the gifts they eagerly accepted. These included a good quantity of small copper knives for the boys, suitable for carving soft wood.

Some of the girls received necklaces of polished stones, strung together with a strip of leather. Others received lengths of brightly dyed linen, which could be used either as a scarf against the cold, or worn across the body for decoration.

The Akkadian commander made sure that no child received more than one present. Soon even the youngest of the Ur Nammu children had summoned enough courage to approach the strangers and extend an empty hand. Naturally, there were more children than gifts, so those who arrived late returned to the camp empty-handed and envious of their companions' good luck.

Sargon refused to join in the gift-giving. His mother had prepared these trinkets, no doubt considering them a small price to pay to obtain a measure of good will. When the last of the children had finally departed, Draelin and his two helpers picked up and carried two more sacks across the grassland to the Ur Nammu camp. These contained offerings for the women.

Those gifts, Sargon guessed, would disappear even faster than the children's. When Draelin returned just after midmorning, each of his men carried a large wineskin. The commander handed one over to the smiling soldiers, but held the other back for the evening.

Sounds of revelry floated over the meadow from the Ur Nammu. Cheers and shouts erupted, separated by long silences. Curious in spite of his desire not to converse with anyone, Sargon called out to Draelin when he walked nearby.

"What's going on over there?"

"Your father is telling Subutai and his people about the battle with the Alur Meriki. The Ur Nammu can't believe their good fortune. They'll be safe from the Alur Meriki, for a time, at least. That's why they're celebrating. They know they won't be hunted when the Alur Meriki come through these lands."

"But the noise . . . it's been going on all morning."

"Aye, and probably the rest of the day and all night, too. Your father will be telling and retelling the story for the rest of the day. He had to sketch a map in the dirt, so that they could see where everyone fought. Every warrior has a handful of questions. If I could speak the language better, I'd be over there helping explain, too."

With a shock, Sargon realized that he would be expected to speak the barbarian tongue when the soldiers departed. Two years ago, Eskkar had attempted to teach him the dialect of the steppes people, but Sargon had not tried very hard to learn it.

Like most inhabitants of Akkad, Sargon saw no need to learn the barbarians' crude language. Of course he had studied the various dialects and symbols of Sumer and the other cities in the Land Between the Rivers, as well as the language used on the trade routes. His mother had insisted on that, but those were little more than variations of the Akkadian tongue and easily grasped.

Now Sargon wished he'd paid more attention to his father's urgings. The smattering of steppes words Sargon understood would not allow him to converse with his new clan. Not only would he be alone, but he would have to depend on others to speak. The sooner he could escape the barbarian camp, the better.

As the celebration in the Ur Nammu camp continued, Sargon watched as small groups of grinning warriors galloped out, bows in hand, to hunt game for the evening feast. A few waved at the soldiers as they rode by. In the afternoon, a handful of Ur Nammu women from their encampment dragged over a pair of bleating sheep and enough firewood to get the cooking started.

By the time the flames caught, Draelin's men had gutted and skinned the bleating animals, and already had the still-bloody carcasses turning on spits.

The soldiers of Akkad would not be allowed to mix with their allies in the main camp, but Sargon knew his father would see to it that they enjoyed their own feast. By now the Akkadians knew they would depart for home in the morning, more than enough reason for the men to enjoy a fine meal and a few mouthfuls of wine.

Just before sundown, the noise from the barbarian camp finally died down, as warriors returned to their tents and wagons. Sargon stared at the Akkadian cooking fires, watching the smoke tendrils rise into the sky, the sheep revolving on the spit, and soldiers taking turns to keep the meat cooking evenly. Even quartered, it took a long time to cook a whole sheep, and Sargon guessed the sun would be well below the horizon before the meat cooled enough to be eaten.

A shout from Draelin turned Sargon's head, and he saw his father, Subutai, and another warrior approaching.

Both Ur Nammu warriors looked fierce. Subutai had a powerful build, and Sargon saw the thick muscles that bulged on his chest and arms. The other, much younger, stood a hand's width taller, but with a slim build, narrow hips, and more delicate features. Both wore their hair tied back, in much the same fashion that Sargon's father preferred.

Eskkar called out to his son. "Sargon! Come, join us." Eskkar's words carried to all the soldiers.

Every one within earshot paused to watch what would happen next. Even the men turning the spits forgot their tasks, wondering if the wayward son would dare to disobey his father in front of the warriors.

Part of Sargon's mind told him to ignore his father's command, but he knew Eskkar would likely just order Draelin and the others to drag him over. While he didn't care what his father or these barbarians thought, Sargon didn't want to embarrass himself in front of the soldiers. Better not to have such a story told in Akkad, that the son of the King needed to be carried like a child to meet his destiny.

Sargon gritted his teeth. There was nothing to be gained by waiting. He climbed to his feet, his heart beating faster as the dreaded moment approached, and followed his father's order. The three men stopped at the edge of the camp.

Still, the command in his father's voice rankled Sargon, and he took his time walking through the camp until he stood before his father and the strangers.

"Walk with me, Sargon."

Eskkar placed his hand on Sargon's shoulder and guided him away from the camp. The warriors followed behind. About fifty paces away, a small circle of stones marked a place where the Ur Nammu children had played during the day. Eskkar sat on a rough slab, and his companions found places to sit facing him.

"This is my son, Sargon of Akkad."

The two warriors nodded in acknowledgement.

The older one spoke first, using the language of Akkad. "I am Subutai, leader of the Ur Nammu. This is Chinua, one of my chiefs and third in command. He fought with your father at the great battle before the city of Isin, though Chinua had only sixteen seasons at the time."

The serious looks on their faces silenced the angry words that Sargon had in his mind. He bowed to show respect. "Greetings to the Great Chief of the Ur Nammu." Sargon remembered enough to give the proper greeting.

"Your father tells us that you do not yet speak our language," Subutai said. "Until you learn, we will talk in the language of the . . . villagers."

Sargon nodded his head in gratitude.

Eskkar spoke. "Subutai is a wise leader of his people, and three times we have battled the Alur Meriki together. I have asked him to teach you the ways of the warrior, and he has agreed. But since he leads the Clan, Subutai has many duties and little time to spend training a young warrior. Chinua, a most worthy warrior, has offered to guide you in the ways of the Ur Nammu. He will teach you how to ride and how to fight."

"Your father is a mighty warrior." Chinua's gentle voice contrasted with the harsher tongue of his leader. "I followed him on the great charge into the ranks of the Sumerians."

Sargon saw his father smile at the memory. "The moment I gave the order to attack," Eskkar said, "Chinua raced to the front. His was the first arrow to strike at the Sumerians."

Chinua laughed, too. "That arrow fell short, as I remember. It was my first battle, and the blood raced in my body."

Almost nine years had passed since that battle, and yet his father and Chinua spoke of it as if it had been fought yesterday. Sargon nodded. He didn't know what to say.

"Chinua will take you into his household," Eskkar went on. "You will be treated as one of his own sons. There will be many lessons to be learned before you can be considered a warrior, but you have the battle skills, and your wits are quick to learn. Your courage and your strength will be tested, but I am sure you can master their way of living and fighting. When that day comes, you can return with pride to Akkad."

"Yes, Father." Sargon had to clench his teeth to hold in his rage. Whatever Sargon uttered would be meaningless. Eskkar had set these events in motion. This Chinua would now rule Sargon's life.

Once the Akkadians departed the camp, the barbarian would have the power of life and death if he should so chose. Sargon would be alone. He wondered what instructions his father had given these men in private.

"We have prepared a great feast in your father's honor," Chinua said. "The women labored all day to prepare it, and there will be plenty of food and wine. You are welcome to come with us and sit beside your father and the leaders of the Ur Nammu."

The words sounded honest and respectful, and Sargon guessed they came straight from Chinua's heart. But Sargon couldn't . . . wouldn't sit beside his father and pretend that all was well while these barbarians heaped praises upon Eskkar and his latest deeds. Sargon couldn't bear such a night of endless humiliation.

"I thank you . . . Chinua." Sargon hoped he pronounced the warrior's name properly. "But I would prefer to spend the night with the soldiers. It will be my last chance to be with my own kind."

If either Subutai or Chinua thought Sargon's refusal odd or disrespectful, neither let their face betray their feelings. And while Eskkar could usually control his emotions, Sargon saw a flicker of anger twitch at his mouth.

"Then you will enjoy the celebration with your own warriors." Subutai's words showed no resentment. "There will be many more meals for us to share in the future."

Subutai rose to his feet, and Chinua followed. "We will return to our camp. The meat should be well cooked by now, Eskkar, so come as soon as you can."

The two clan chiefs strode off, leaving father and son together.

"You insulted Subutai by not joining him at the feast."

Sargon heard the rebuke in his father's voice. Sargon, his fists clenched, felt his lips tremble. "They are your friends, not mine. When you are gone, I will have to live with all of them, sharing a tent with four or five others, all of them stinking of horse sweat."

"This is the path you have chosen. So be it." Eskkar stood and stared down at his son. "Before we left Akkad, your mother told me not to weaken in my resolve. She said I would be tempted to change my mind and bring you back to the city, to give you one more chance. I was proud when you answered Subutai with the proper respect. But your mother was right. I see your heart is still blind with anger. You will have to rise above it, if you ever wish to return home."

"I have no home. I have no father or mother. You are both dead to me. And even if I survive this fate, I will never return to Akkad. Tell that to your wife."

Sargon rose and stalked away in the growing darkness, leaving his father standing there. Sargon would eat by himself tonight, though surrounded by the soldiers of Akkad. But in the morning, Eskkar and his men would be gone, and Sargon realized that, for the first time in his life, he would truly be alone.

Manuscript

The next day, just after midmorning, Sargon stood by himself in the remains of the Akkadian camp. The soldiers had gathered their weapons and collected their horses. With nothing more to do, they waited impatiently for the command to depart, all of them no doubt eager to return to Akkad.

Sargon paced back and forth, his hands limp at his sides. His father had spent most of the morning first making sure the men had readied themselves for the departure, then galloping to the Ur Nammu camp for one last talk with Subutai. Whether by chance or on purpose, Eskkar returned just as Draelin finished his final inspection. With the Akkadians standing by their horses, Eskkar had little time to spend with his son.

Their parting was as impersonal as it was brief – neither had anything else to say to the other. Sargon took some small consolation that at least his father would never torment him again.

"Mount your horse, Sargon, and ride with me to the camp."

His father's voice sounded hoarse, probably from drinking too much wine. The talking and singing had continued long into the night, and this morning more than a few soldiers had sore heads. Sargon had fallen asleep before his father returned.

Sargon's horse awaited, and the soldier attending it gave him a friendly smile as he handed over the halter.

"I've already given Chinua a sack containing your sword and knife." Eskkar brusque words sounded cold and distant. "And there are some things your mother wanted you to have."

Sargon didn't answer. He swung onto the horse and grudgingly guided his mount beside his father.

"Is there anything you want to say? Any message for your mother?"

"No." Sargon hadn't wanted to speak at all, but that single word escaped his lips. Let his parents suffer the tiniest pain for what they'd done to him.

Swearing under his breath, Eskkar touched his heels to his horse, and cantered over to the Ur Nammu camp. The Ur Nammu warriors had already returned to their usual routine. A small crowd of mostly women and children stood around in scattered groups, to watch the men from Akkad depart.

Sargon followed his father, though at a slower pace. He saw no need to rush. Eskkar reached the outskirts of the camp where Chinua stood, and then waited, his jaw clenched, until Sargon guided his horse to a stop facing them.

"Sargon, try to remember what I've taught you. Chinua will take good care of you." For a moment, Eskkar hesitated, as if he wanted to say something more.

But his father had nothing else to add to his goodbye. Sargon watched as Eskkar wheeled his horse around and headed out. Draelin already had the Akkadians on the move, and his father put his horse to a fast canter to catch up. A few soldiers glanced back toward Sargon, but not his father.

"Sargon, come walk with me," Chinua said. "My sons will tend to your horse."

Sargon dismounted. Chinua took the horse's halter and called out something in his own tongue. A young warrior, perhaps a few seasons older than Sargon, jogged over and accepted the horse.

Chinua led the way back toward the circle of stones where they had spoken last night. A handful of young boys had already reclaimed the place, but Chinua ordered them away with a wave of his arm. He settled himself on the same slab Eskkar had taken yesterday.

"Sit."

The single word carried the man's authority in a way no command of Sargon's father ever had. Sargon eased himself down facing the warrior and studied his new master.

Chinua appeared far too young to be third in command over all these warriors. If he had indeed fought at the battle of Isin at sixteen, he could not even have reached twenty-five seasons.

"Your father has told only myself and Subutai that you do not understand the warrior's code, that you lack the honor and respect a son should display toward his mother and father. That secret will remain between us."

Chinua kept his eyes fixed on Sargon. "As far as my sons and the other warriors will know, you are here only to learn the ways of the warrior. Do you understand?"

"Yes."

"Many young men your age already ride with our fighters. Some have even fought against our enemies. The others work the horses, help around the camp, and make themselves useful. They are also given the chance to improve their own skills with sword, bow, and lance. Even more important, they must train their horses and learn to ride well. After a year or two of accompanying our men, or whenever Subutai thinks they are ready, these young men are accepted as warriors. Only then can they take a wife, and take part in the life of the Clan."

No words seemed to be called for, so Sargon merely nodded.

"Despite your age, you are not ready to ride with the warriors. No young man is permitted to ride with the warriors unless he is trained and prepared to fight in support of his kin and his clan. So, Sargon, first you must prove you can handle a horse. Then you must learn to use your weapons, the ones you choose to fight with, sword, lance, or bow. If a warrior cannot master the bow from horseback, he will pick the lance or sword as his main weapon."

"I can use both a sword and a bow," Sargon said.

"Perhaps." Chinua rubbed his chin for a moment. "You know your father never mastered the use of the bow. He told me that he left the Clan when he was too young, before he could master that skill. Though I believe he would have been too tall. I've seen Eskkar fight. A sword fits his hand very well."

Sargon nodded, but said nothing.

"But that matters not," Chinua said. "Until you master these skills, you will practice with the younger boys. My son," Chinua glanced toward the boy still holding Sargon's horse, "will help you. Your training will be long and hard, but no different from what Ur Nammu young men receive from their fathers. All the same, I expect you will find much of it difficult."

Sargon found the young clan leader's words reassuring. He'd expected the Ur Nammu to be little more than savages, but Chinua spoke with a calm wisdom that belied his years. But it really didn't matter. Sargon intended to leave as soon as he could, and the sooner Chinua accepted that, the better.

"I . . . I thank you for your effort, Chinua, but I do not believe in your ways, or even the ways of my father. In Akkad, we no longer have need of such skills. The days when a ruler needs to go into battle himself are past. Now men of wealth pay others to protect them and fight for them."

"And you have much wealth," Chinua agreed. "Even so, Subutai and I have promised your father that we will try to teach you the code of the warrior. But I will not waste my time or even that of my son if you will not learn. So this is what I will do. The moon will be full," he glanced up at the sky, "in two more days. When three more full moons have risen in the night sky, if you wish to leave the Ur Nammu camp, you may take your horse and depart. You may go wherever you wish, even return to Akkad if that is what you want. I do not think that would be wise, but there are many villages and cities in the Land Between the Two Rivers, and even more beyond."

For the first time, Sargon felt a glimmer of hope. All he had to do was wait for . . . less than ninety days, and he could simply ride away from all this. Chinua was right. There were other places, other cities.

And sooner or later, Eskkar would die. He was old, after all, already in his middle forties. Many men were dead by that age, and with his father's willingness to take risks, it might not be long before Sargon could return to Akkad. Then he could claim his birth right and accept the welcome of the city's inhabitants.

Chinua must have understood Sargon's feelings by the expression on his face. The warrior rose to his feet.

"But until the third moon is full, you will work hard to master the skills of our fighters. If you do not, you will be punished. And if you try to leave before I give you permission, we will hunt you down. And then you will suffer the same penalty as the slaves and those who disobey our laws – your legs will be broken, and you will work as a slave for the rest of your life."

Sargon also stood, and his own determination hardened. "I will obey your orders, Chinua, until the third full moon. Then I will take my leave and depart."

"Good. The sooner a task is begun, the faster the time passes. My son, Garal, awaits us, and your horse is ready. He will take you for a ride. That is how all warriors begin their training." Chinua turned and started back toward the camp.

That didn't sound too bad. Sargon already could ride as well or better than most of Akkad's soldiers. His father had seen to that. Ninety days would pass soon enough, and he would be on his way back home, or to wherever he decided home would be. Lagash would be the closest large city, and it was far from Akkad. Yes, Lagash would be his home for as long as his father remained alive.

17

With a few rapid-spoken words that Sargon didn't understand, Chinua gave Garal his instructions and left the two young men alone. Sargon turned to Garal, who didn't look much older than Sargon. Only average in height, Garal's black hair hung down to his shoulders. A small but jagged scar ran from his right eyebrow halfway to his ear.

Nothing about Sargon's teacher appeared impressive, except for the powerful muscles in his arms. Sargon would have recognized the mark of an archer even if Garal didn't have a bow slung across his chest and a quiver of arrows on his hip. A sword, almost as long as the one Eskkar carried, jutted up over his right shoulder.

Garal handed Sargon the halter to his horse. Then with an ease that impressed Sargon, Garal swung onto the back of a rangy, spotted stallion, and said something in the Ur Nammu language.

Sargon shook his head in confusion. Garal repeated the word. "Teneg!" This time he pointed to the horse. "Teneg."

Obviously Garal did not speak the language of the Land Between the Rivers. Still, Sargon realized what he meant. Without attempting to match the ease of his instructor, he climbed up onto the back of his horse.

"Utga!" Garal jabbed his finger toward Sargon. "Utga Oruulah!" This time he touched his heels to the horse, which broke into a canter.

Swearing at this foolishness, Sargon followed after the young warrior, already fifty paces ahead. How could he learn anything, if Garal couldn't even speak the language of Akkad? Sargon urged his horse along the same path. He had no idea where they were going. He had no water skin, no weapon of any kind, so they couldn't be going far.

But obviously Garal expected Sargon to ride. Gritting his teeth, Sargon kicked his horse into a faster pace, and gradually caught up with his new mentor, until he rode only a few strides behind.

The horses swept through the thick grass that sighed beneath their hooves as the two young men rode west. To the north stretched the snow-capped peaks of the Zagros Mountains. To the south, the hilly plains extended into the distance, gradually leveling off into the woodlands and meadows where isolated herders tended their flocks.

For the rest of the morning, Sargon matched his guide's movements. Garal varied the pace, dropping from a canter to a walk, or sometimes a trot, depending on the ground. A few times he put his horse to a gallop, but not for any length of time. Mostly Garal rode, as Sargon soon learned, at the usual pace of the steppes warriors, cantering for a good length of time or until the horse began to tire, before falling back into a quick walk to let the animal catch its breath.

As the sun reached its highest point in the sky, Sargon wondered where they were going. Already they'd traveled many miles from the Ur Nammu camp, moving at a much faster pace than what his father and the Akkadians usually set. Already Sargon's leg muscles and backside protested the constant movement, though Garal seemed unaffected. Finally Sargon decided he'd ridden far enough. He eased his horse to a stop.

Hearing the cessation of Sargon's hoof beats, Garal also slowed, then halted. Twisting astride his mount, he waved his hand, Obviously urging Sargon to continue. "Utga!"

Sargon shook his head. "No. My horse needs to rest."

Though the horse had not been ridden yesterday, Sargon had sensed the animal growing tired, while Garal's mount still seemed as fresh as when they'd started out. His father always claimed that the steppes tribes bred the strongest horses, and Sargon decided that it must be true.

Garal turned his stallion around and trotted back to Sargon. He approached on Sargon's right, and halted his horse close enough for their knees to touch. With a quick movement, his right arm stiffened, catching

Sargon in the chest with the flat of his hand. The powerful blow caught Sargon unprepared, and he tumbled from his mount. He landed heavily on his shoulder.

"Utga." Garal pointed to the horse, then swung his arm around until it pointed once again in the direction they had been traveling. "Utga."

Furious at himself for being caught by surprise, Sargon pushed himself to his feet. "No! No utga! Rest first."

With a supple movement Garal slid down from his horse. He strode three paces over to where Sargon stood. Again, Garal's right arm snapped forward. Sargon raised his own hands to defend himself, but the blow landed so quick, and with such force, that for the second time Sargon tumbled backwards to the ground.

"Utga." Garal's voice held no emotion.

Sargon's rage boiled over. No one had ever struck him like that. Even in his training with Akkad's soldiers, he'd always had time to prepare himself. But Garal had struck twice without a flicker of expression in his eyes, both times catching Sargon off guard.

Flushed with anger, Sargon leapt to his feet and swung his fist at Garal's head. The warrior scarcely seemed to move, but he shifted slightly and the fist missed Garal's head by a few finger widths. This time Garal smacked the palm of his hand against Sargon's ear as he lunged forward.

Already off balance, the blow sent Sargon tumbling to the ground for the third time. His ear felt as if someone pounded a drum inside his head. His anger and rage hadn't diminished, but took longer to get to his feet, and this time he swayed as he drew himself up. The blow to his head had affected his balance, and he stood there a moment, trying to prepare himself.

Garal pointed to Sargon's horse. "Utga."

Sargon clenched his teeth. Garal had still not raised his voice or even looked angry. Nor had he raised his hand to the long sword that hung from his shoulder. Sargon no longer cared. The anger and frustration he'd endured for the last twenty days swept over him. Shaking his head to clear his thoughts, Sargon advanced slowly toward his nemesis.

This time Sargon remembered his training, and even his father's advice. *Move carefully, don't extend yourself or leave yourself off balance.*

If you're stronger, close with your enemy and bring him down. If he's more
powerful, keep your distance and strike hard at his head or stomach.

Garal didn't seem particularly stronger. The two were of much the
same size and build. But Sargon remembered the sudden force and power
of the blow that had toppled him from his horse. All the same, he was
determined to get in close with Garal no matter what, and strike at least
one blow. Lowering his head, he feinted to his right, then shifted left, lashing out with his fist for Garal's impassive face.

The warrior twisted his body in reaction to Sargon's feint, but when
the real attack came, Garal simply ducked underneath the blow. Meeting no resistance and caught with his arm extended, Sargon lurched
off balance again. Garal slid his right arm around Sargon's neck and
yanked hard. At the same time, he shoved his right hip into Sargon's
side.

Sargon's feet left the ground, and he slammed into the earth on his
back, his whole body bouncing upon impact with the ground. The force of
Garal's maneuver was as powerful and quick as it was unexpected.

This time, Sargon lay where he'd fallen. His head and neck hurt, and
the breath had fled his body. His eyes refused to focus. When his thoughts
cleared, Sargon pushed himself up on his elbows.

Garal led Sargon's mount back to where Sargon lay stretched out on
the ground. He dropped the halter beside Sargon's hand. "Utga."

Muttering an oath to Marduk that would have offended his mother,
Sargon climbed unsteadily to his feet. It took him three tries to climb onto
his horse. By the time he had control of his mount, Garal had swung onto
his own steed and waited patiently.

"I know, utga, utga," Sargon muttered grimly. He gripped the mane
with his left hand, and touched the halter to his mount's neck. The animal
moved forward.

At least, Sargon decided, the horse had gotten a brief rest, which was
more than its rider could say for the delay. Garal set the pace at a canter,
no doubt to make it easier on Sargon's still spinning head.

It was well after midday before Garal raised his arm to signal a halt.
Sargon felt exhausted. They had ridden most of the morning and part of
the afternoon. Looking around, Sargon saw neither stream or well, nor any
place where they might find something to eat.

Garal tied his horse to a bush and took a long look at the entire horizon, no doubt searching for any possible sign of danger. Satisfied, he stretched down on the ground, lying in the shade of the same bush that tethered his animal.

By now Sargon had no strength left to complain. He managed to fasten his horse to the bush, though he knew his father would never have approved of the sloppy tie. Between the effects of the long ride, and his occasional collisions with the earth, Sargon couldn't hold back the sigh of relief as he dropped to the hard earth.

The stress of the last few days caught up with him, and he slipped into a light sleep. He woke when Garal's foot shoved into his leg. "Utga." He pointed to the sun, which Sargon realized had moved to the west and started its descent. The hottest part of the day had passed, but plenty of daylight remained.

At least Sargon knew better than to argue or complain. He pushed his protesting body upright, every muscle complaining at the slightest movement. Garal waited on his own mount, watching Sargon struggle with his horse. Once again, it took two tries before he could get himself astride. Without a word, Garal turned to the west and started off at a fast walk.

They continued westward for the remainder of the day, making only two brief stops to refresh the horses. As dusk arrived, Sargon searched the land ahead of them for any signs of life, a house, a tent, a stream, even a grassy hill. But nothing presented itself, only the same monotonous landscape they had traversed all day. Hunger gnawed at his stomach, and his mouth was as dry as sand.

When Garal at last gave the sign to halt, the darkness was nearly complete. He tied his horse to a fallen tree lying on the ground, and this time he inspected Sargon's tie as well, redoing it to make certain that the knot would stay firm as the animal moved and pulled on it. Satisfied, Garal pointed to the ground.

"Rest."

Sargon understood that word. He slipped to the earth, and once again could not hold back a groan of relief as he eased the long day's burden from his stiff muscles. Every part of his body felt sore from the constant riding, and his neck still hurt.

Without any difficulty, Garal sat cross-legged and stared off into the distance. He didn't appear any different than he looked that morning, not at all tired, hungry, or thirsty.

The two had no water, and of course nothing to eat. If Sargon had a bow or even a sling, he might have tried to bring down something to eat, but exhausted as he was, Sargon knew he wasn't likely to find, let alone kill, any game. But his thirst had grown all day, and now he could scarcely swallow without forcing himself.

"Water." He knew that steppes word for that, of course. "Water."

Garal shrugged, that same annoying gesture Sargon's father used so often. "No water tonight. Tomorrow. Midday." The young instructor had to repeat his words several times before his pupil understood.

Sargon's mouth felt even drier than it had a moment ago. No water until tomorrow! No food, no fire, and now no water. This couldn't be happening. Sargon had never gone so long without food, let alone water.

And there was nothing he could do about it. Garal carried neither pouch nor water skin with him. If Sargon departed at dawn tomorrow, he would have to ride all day before he returned to the Ur Nammu camp, supposing, of course, that he could find his way back. That assumed that Garal would let him go. More likely, the barbarian would kill him.

With a shock, Sargon realized he had forgotten another one of his father's teachings. Sargon had failed to notice, let alone memorize, any landmarks that might show him the way back. He knew the general direction, and the sun to guide him, but with only those, he might miss the camp by ten miles, if he couldn't follow their tracks back to his new home. He should have paid more attention to his surroundings. Instead Sargon had spent his time nursing his bruises and raging at Garal's back.

"Sleep now. Ride in morning."

With those few words, Garal stretched out on the ground, shifted his body a few times to settle in, then closed his eyes. It didn't take long before Garal's soft snores sounded over the dry camp. His sword lay beside him, and Sargon stared at it. He considered waiting until Garal had reached a deeper sleep, then creeping over the few paces that separated them. With the sword in his hand, one good swing would end his humiliation.

For a time, that idea tempted him. Of course, Garal might wake up, and the sword might prove as useless as Sargon's fists had earlier. Even if he killed the warrior, he would still have to find his way back, and Chinua would find his son's body sooner or later. No, the thought of what the barbarians did to those who offended them didn't appeal to Sargon.

With a muffled curse, he laid down on his side, his back to Garal, and tried to get some sleep. The hard ground pressed against his stiff and sore muscles. Frustrated at every turn of today's events, and with his throat feeling as dry as a cup of sand, sleep didn't come easily. When at last Sargon did slip into a fitful sleep, dreams filled with anger at his father for abandoning him haunted what little rest he could manage.

18

Sargon woke in the predawn with Garal's foot pushing against his ribs. It took a few moments before the harsh words penetrated, and by then the pressure of the warrior's foot increased enough to roll Sargon over onto his side.

"Get up. Ride."

Without waiting, Garal strode to his horse, unfastened the halter, and swung himself up. "Ride."

Sargon's anger rose, but he knew there was nothing he could do. The sooner they got to water, the better. Swearing under his breath, he reached his horse and fumbled with the halter. The animal was skittish. Like its master, it had grown accustomed to being fed and watered each day. It took all of Sargon's agility to keep a grip on the animal's mane and climb onto its back.

As soon as Garal saw Sargon astride, the warrior turned his mount toward the west and set his horse to a canter. Sargon decided that he might as well vent his anger at both Garal and his own misfortune aloud. The barbarian didn't understand the Akkadian language anyway. Sargon cursed his companion as an ignorant savage and one that Marduk and Ishtar would soon send to the burning pits below for punishment.

Sargon's anger soon faded, to be replaced by a parched throat that seemed to have rubbed itself raw from lack of water. He felt the weakness in his body, and the slowness of his movements. His lips felt parched and dry. He'd never imaged that a single day without water could weaken him so.

No wonder his father had defeated the Alur Meriki so easily. And today, his nervous and thirsty horse required even more attention than it had yesterday.

Garal's horse exhibited none of these problems. The warrior tried to set the same pace as he had yesterday, but by midmorning, Garal realized the Akkadian mount needed more frequent periods of rest. Once Sargon had to fight to keep control of the animal, when it shied at a bush tumbling across their path. The result of their slower pace saw midday come and go, with still no sign of water. Of course there was nothing to do but keep riding.

By now Sargon could barely keep his seat, and the ground seemed to waver under the horse's hooves. Thirst had sucked the strength from his body, and his youthful vigor had vanished many miles back.

In the end, it was the horse that saved Sargon from tumbling ignominiously to the ground. First Garal's mount, then Sargon's, caught the scent of water ahead. Both animals responded with a second effort. Still, they had to traverse more than a mile before they reached the water.

No river or even a stream, only a small sinkhole of brackish water, surrounded by a wide border of mud. Animal tracks and droppings covered the ground, indicating the water was drinkable. Sargon didn't care. His horse forced its way through the soggy ground and thrust its nose deep into the water. Sargon slid from its back, landing on his stomach, with his face in the water.

He drank and drank, lifting himself up every few moments to catch his breath. Water that he once wouldn't have bothered to piss in now tasted as sweet as anything that came from his parents' well. When he could force no more liquid into his stomach, Sargon pushed himself to his knees.

He saw Garal kneeling at the water's edge, dipping his hand into the water. The barbarian clearly hadn't suffered as much from thirst as Sargon had. Even Garal's horse had already stopped drinking, while Sargon's mount continued to slurp at the muddy water.

Not that Sargon cared. He lay down in the mud again and drank some more, drank until he started coughing and had to stop. When he crawled away from the water's edge, he felt satisfied, his stomach full for the first time in two days.

By then Garal had led his mount away, and tied its halter to a low bush that had sprouted nearby. The warrior sat on the ground, his face as impassive as when they had first departed the camp.

Chagrinned, Sargon dragged his mount from the water. He knew the animal shouldn't drink too much, or it might sicken.

With a start, Sargon realized the same thought applied to him. He wiped his hand across his mouth, tasting the foul mud on the back of his hand. Looking down, he saw that his legs and tunic had turned black from the wet earth that clung to him.

"Rest. Then we ride back."

Sargon eased himself down to the ground. The water had filled his belly, and his hunger had vanished, for the moment at least. He stared at his surroundings, a dreary landscape of occasional clumps of grass scattered among the sand and rocks, with a few bushes here and there. Nothing to see, and obviously nothing to eat. Sargon wondered how long Garal intended for them to rest.

The answer came soon enough. With a sudden pain in his stomach, Sargon felt his insides heave. He barely got to his knees before the burning liquid shot from his lips, as he hunched himself over, his hands clutching the ground. The retching continued, on and on, until Sargon felt as if he had expelled every last drop of water that he'd consumed.

When the heaving finally stopped, Sargon found himself gulping air and panting like a dog. Looking around, he saw that Garal had climbed to his feet.

"Ride. Drink first." The warrior gestured with his hand as if scooping water from the ground. "Three only."

With the last of his strength, Sargon returned to the water's edge. His throat burned from the contents of his stomach. All the same, he followed Garal's instructions, taking only three scoops of water into his hand, and drinking each handful slowly so as to ease his burning throat. When Sargon finished, Garal had already mounted. "Ride. Home."

"Yes, ride, damn you." Sargon's rage had returned. He swore to himself that he would extract vengeance on this man if it were the last thing he ever did.

Somehow he managed to mount his horse. Sargon faced another long ride back to the camp, and he hoped he would survive it. He comforted himself that at least they would have food and fresh water there.

The ride back to the Ur Nammu encampment took almost two full days, and by the time Sargon saw the smoke trails from the camp leaning their way into the sky, he could barely keep his seat on his horse. Hunger, something completely unknown to him, had weakened his muscles and made thinking difficult.

At the same time, a raging thirst consumed him. His eyes wandered, and at times he found his head nodding against his chest. For the first time in his life, Sargon had gone almost three days without food. Those same three days included plenty of hard riding and almost no water. Nothing in his life had ever prepared him for such hardship.

By the time he approached the outer line of tents, only a grim determination kept him on the horse. Fueled by his rage toward Garal, who seemed unaffected by either hunger or thirst, Sargon refused to quit. Better to die on his horse than to give the filthy barbarian the satisfaction of seeing Sargon fall to the ground and crawl in the dirt.

Sargon's weary mount, in as bad shape as its master, headed straight for the stream. The trembling animal pushed its way through the line of bushes, staggered into the water, and lowered its head to drink. Sargon tried to dismount, but his hand slipped from the mane and he slid feet first into the stream. For a few moments, he just lay there, letting the cool liquid wash the heat and dirt from his body. Then he remembered to drink, and once again he buried his face into the sweetest drink he'd ever tasted.

This time, however, he knew better than to overfill his stomach. Sargon wanted no repeat of yesterday's vomiting. When he pushed himself to his knees, he heard Garal's harsh Ur Nammu gutturals, and found three warriors, including Subutai and Chinua, standing behind him. Dimly, Sargon realized that word of their approach had reached the clan's Sarum, and the Ur Nammu leader had walked to the stream to see for himself how well the Akkadian's first lesson had gone.

Garal spoke rapidly and at length to Chinua, using his hands expressively to convey some additional meaning. Subutai, arms folded across his chest, stared at Sargon, who lay half in and half out of the water, his already filthy tunic covered with fresh mud. The third warrior, shorter and stockier, watched from the edge of the stream, his face impassive.

Ashamed of being on his knees, Sargon staggered to his feet with the last of his strength, leaning on his horse to help. His hunger had returned, but he refused to beg on his knees for food in front of the Ur Nammu clan leader.

Subutai solved that problem. "Come with me, Sargon. You must be hungry." He turned to the other warrior. "Perhaps you could help him, Fashod."

That would be the third man. The name meant nothing to Sargon, but he saw Fashod smiling at him.

"Yes, I will bring him." Fashod stepped into the bubbling water and wrapped a powerful arm around Sargon's waist, ignoring the wet and filthy garment. "Three days without food weakens any man, especially one from the city of Akkad."

Despite himself, Sargon sagged against Fashod's broad shoulder, letting the warrior take much of his weight. In that way, the man half-carried Sargon through the camp. Along the way, curious onlookers paused in their tasks to stare at the weak-kneed Akkadian youth. Sargon didn't care, and they soon reached Subutai's tent.

The smoke from a small cooking fire couldn't mask the scent of the crisping meat, speared on small sticks thrust into the glowing coals. Fashod eased Sargon to the ground beside the fire.

An old woman of about thirty seasons tended the blaze. She smiled at him, then plucked a stick from the fire and handed it to him. The tempting smell made Sargon lose control, and he thrust the meat into his mouth, biting hard and ignoring the burning against his tongue.

Clutching the stick in both hands, he bit off another chunk from what he realized was the hind leg of a rabbit. In four ravenous bites, Sargon stripped the meat to the bone.

The woman, meanwhile, spoke to a young girl, who filled a cup with stew from the copper cooking pot. She knelt beside him, offering Sargon the thick liquid.

"Wait before you try that." Fashod dropped to the ground across the fire from Sargon. "It's hot."

Despite Sargon's unfamiliarity with the language, he grasped Fashod's meaning, if not all of the words. Sargon tossed the bone into the fire, accepted the cup from the girl's hands, and raised it to his lips. Careful of his still smarting tongue, Sargon restrained himself and took only a small sip, grateful for Fashod's warning.

By now others had joined the meal circle, each of them reaching to the fire and selecting the nearest stick. Garal kept up most of the conversation, obviously telling the three warriors about their ride. Occasionally Subutai or Chinua would nod in approval or agreement. Out of politeness, they ignored Sargon's filthy tunic, his arms and legs still streaked black with mud.

Sargon didn't care. He soon drained the cup, and the girl reappeared again to refill it for him. While she did so, he took the last stick from the fire, waved it in the air to cool, and started chewing. Only when he finished the second cup of stew did the pain in his stomach start to ease.

Though he wanted to keep eating, Sargon forced himself to stop. He'd already eaten more than any of the others. Besides, he didn't want to throw up again, and he knew too much food taken too fast would only make him sick.

"We have never met." Fashod spoke now in the Akkadian tongue, when he saw that Sargon had gotten control of himself. "But I fought with your father three times, and twice with your Egyptian, Hathor. Eskkar is indeed a great man. And now he has defeated the Alur Meriki. In all my life I never thought I would live to see this day."

Now Sargon recalled hearing the name of Fashod, as Subutai's second in command. He had not been present at Eskkar's arrival or departure. The words of praise for Sargon's father meant nothing. Sargon had heard the same words, or some variation, all his life. To these simple barbarians, his father was a great man. No doubt any man who could fight well was considered great.

"I am sorry that I did not greet you properly." Sargon's voice sounded hoarse. He hadn't spoken more than a handful of words all day. However, he knew how important it was to have friends among the warriors. "I'm sure my father was saddened that you were not here to meet him."

"Garal says that you did well on the ride," Chinua said, joining the conversation. "He says that if you had a stronger horse, you both would have returned before midday."

Fashod laughed. "Not many villagers could have done as well, Sargon. Your father would be pleased."

"Tomorrow he will have a better horse," Chinua said. "I will give him one of my own, while I turn his over to my sons to build up its strength."

"Is Garal ready to ride out again?" Subutai's polite question was more of a statement. No doubt every clan member always considered himself ready to ride.

Garal nodded. "Yes. This time I will take Sargon toward the mountains. We may even see signs of the Alur Meriki."

That brought a frown to Subutai's face. "Take care where you go. The Alur Meriki cannot be trusted."

"Yes, Sarum. I will not venture too far north."

Sargon's thoughts, slowed by the food now filling his belly, realized that the warriors were talking about another ride.

"Tomorrow? But I need time to rest, to . . ." His voice died out as he saw another frown cross Subutai's brow.

The conversation stopped. Sargon glanced around, and realized no one was meeting his eyes. Obviously he had shown weakness in front of these warriors.

Subutai ended the silence. "With a fresh horse, you will have plenty of time to rest. Now you should go and sleep." He gestured to Garal, who immediately stood. Sargon, who still wanted another cup of stew, forced himself upright, trying not to betray the stiffness in his body.

Garal led the way from Subutai's tent, through the camp, until they reached Chinua's dwelling place. To the rear of the tent, two blankets had been spread on the ground. Garal pointed to one. "Sleep. Tomorrow ride."

Sargon didn't have the strength to protest. He sank to the ground, jerked part of the blanket over his chest, and rested his head on his arm. With his stomach full of food and water, he fell asleep in moments, a deep, unbroken sleep that lasted throughout the entire night.

19

Garal and Sargon rode their horses out of the camp a little after sunrise. Traveling at an easy canter, Sargon had to admit, Chinua had spoken the truth last night. The horse he'd led over for Sargon's use might not be anything special by Ur Nammu standards, but the powerful beast had no trouble keeping up with the fresh mount Garal rode.

Chinua's women had arisen even earlier than their men and prepared a quick meal for them both. Sargon was glad to see that this time, he and Garal each carried a water skin, a blanket, and a small sack containing the flat bread and dried meat the barbarians preferred. At least for today, Sargon wouldn't be starving.

In addition, Garal bore two extra items – wooden swords, similar to the ones used in Akkad's own training.

Obviously Garal intended to expand his pupil's training. Sargon's muscles were stiff, and his backside sore from the previous days, but Garal showed no concern for Sargon's condition. As before, Garal kept the horses moving at a good pace, stopping only when the animals needed rest.

Another difference in today's ride was that Garal rode alongside his pupil. Sargon wondered why, until the first time he reached for the water skin.

"No. No drink." He shook his head, then pointed toward the sun with his hand, then swept his arm up to indicate midmorning. "Drink."

For a brief moment Sargon considered ignoring the command, but the memory of Garal knocking him off the horse ended that thought. Besides, Sargon had drunk just as much water from the stream before they departed as Garal, and Sargon's pride refused to allow himself to drink before his teacher.

The idea of Garal being his teacher held more truth than Sargon expected. As they rode, Garal started pointing out various details of the landscape, pronouncing the word and insisting that Sargon repeat it correctly. Bush, tree, grass, dung, rock, boulder, Garal spoke the name of each with care, repeating it as often as necessary.

When Sargon made a mistake, Garal patiently corrected it. Except once, after Sargon grew frustrated and refused to answer. Then Garal simply smacked the heel of his hand against Sargon's upper arm.

The unexpected blow almost knocked Sargon from the horse. As soon as he regained control, Garal continued the lesson as if nothing had happened. Nevertheless, Sargon's arm ached painfully, which motivated him to concentrate.

They rested at midmorning and again at midday, each time drinking deeply from the water skins. The lessons continued until Sargon's mind could hold no more. By then, half the afternoon had passed. They reached a small stream lined by a long wall of bushes. Sargon noticed faint hoof prints on the ground, and guessed this place served as a convenient watering hole.

"Halt. Camp here."

Gratefully, Sargon slid down from the horse. He knew he was expected to care for the horse before taking care of his own needs, so he did, leading it to the water, and washing the animal down as it drank. Only when the horse willingly lifted its head from the stream did Sargon lead it out of the water and fasten its halter to an exposed root of a willow tree. Then he quenched his thirst from the gurgling stream.

If Sargon thought that the time for rest had arrived, that idea soon vanished.

Garal untied the wooden swords that he had bundled inside his blanket. Tossing one to Sargon, he pointed to a flat spot twenty paces away from the horses.

The heft of the sword in Sargon's hand banished the tiredness from his body. Unarmed, he might not be a match for Garal. But with a sword,

Sargon knew things would be different. He had, after all, practiced many hours with Akkad's best instructors, including his father.

Garal raised his weapon. "Fight."

Sargon needed no further urging. He hefted the sword, getting a feel for the weapon. Its weight appeared a little different from what he'd practiced with. This blade was longer, and the wood itself seemed heavier, the grip cruder. But those differences were slight enough.

Sargon started with a feint, swinging the sword high as if for an overhand stroke, then shortening the arc and thrusting forward with all his strength. Garal parried the stroke, catching Sargon's thrust above his sword's hilt and deflecting it just enough to send it past Garal's arm.

If the wooden tip had landed against Garal's chest, the warrior would have been knocked down at the least, possibly even injured.

At the same time Garal stepped into the thrust and rammed the hilt of his sword against the side of Sargon's head.

When Sargon regained consciousness, he found himself flat on his back staring up at the sky. His head hurt, and he felt a small trail of blood, along with a good sized lump, just above his temple. Groaning, he pushed himself up on his elbows and glanced around.

Garal, never one to waste a moment, busied himself preparing a fire. He'd obviously had time to collect a large pile of dried wood, and now worked on arranging the sticks so that the fire would draw easily.

When he heard Sargon stirring, he glanced over and smiled. "Good. Good thrust. Too slow."

Sargon had a little difficulty with the word 'thrust' but he figured it out as he got to his knees. By then Garal had picked up his sword once again. Sargon's own weapon remained where it had fallen.

Garal raised his weapon as before. "Fight."

Sargon shook his head. He wasn't ready to face the warrior again. His head hurt, and his knees still felt weak.

"You fight. Or I fight."

Garal took a step toward him, the menace plain in the way he gripped the wooden sword. Wincing against the pain throbbing in his head, Sargon picked up his own weapon.

This time, however, Garal only wanted to spar. He attacked and withdrew, giving Sargon time to react and defend. Round and round they went, kicking up grass, sand and dirt, the dull thump of wood against wood repeating itself. One stroke caught Sargon on his right hand, a painful blow across his fingers that knocked the blade from his hand. Garal backed off and waited until his opponent could reclaim his weapon and grip it properly.

Sargon used the time to remember what his trainers and his father had taught him. Watch where you step. Keep your guard up at all times. Don't commit until you're sure. Never waste your strength on blows that can be easily parried. At all times, watch your opponent's eyes and his shoulders.

These and all the other lessons he had learned returned, and for a time, Sargon held his own. But he soon felt his arm growing weak from the strain. The sword had grown heavy in Sargon's hand. It might only be made of wood, yet it could still inflict pain and injuries.

Garal halted when it became apparent that Sargon could do no more. "Good. You will get better. Learn to watch your enemy's body, not his eyes. You will fight better."

"At my father's training camps, we were taught to watch an opponent's eyes."

"Body move before eyes reveal. Tomorrow, watch body."

Sargon recalled his father once saying much the same thing. Perhaps there was something to it after all. "I will."

"Good. Rest now. Eat."

They sat facing each other across the fire while they gnawed at the bread and solid chunks of meat packed in a bit of rag at the bottom of the sack. Sargon's appetite made him wolf down the food, and he ignored the taste, or lack of it, anxious only to get the nourishment into his body. When the meal ended, the language lessons resumed.

"Ground. Blanket. Stream. Sandal. Laces." These words and more were forced into Sargon's vocabulary. By the time Garal felt ready to turn in for the night, Sargon had learned more Ur Nammu words in a single day than he had ever mastered in Akkad.

In the morning, they finished the last of the food, watered the horses, and rode out. In addition to his weary leg muscles, now Sargon's right arm complained as well, from all the sword practice. But it soon loosened up, as Garal stopped at midmorning for more practice, and repeated the effort at midday, and again in the middle of the afternoon.

Meanwhile the language lessons never ceased as the two young men rode side by side.

By the time they returned to the Ur Nammu main camp that night, they were communicating in simple sentences, and Sargon felt proud of his progress. Nothing like an encouraging blow from your teacher to keep you focused, though Garal had not needed to repeat that motivating part of his lesson today.

After caring for the horses, Sargon followed Garal's example and plunged into the stream, to wash away the horse smell and clean his tunic. Their garments still damp, they returned to Chinua's tent and ate their supper.

Tonight, that warrior made sure the language lesson continued. No Akkadian was spoken, forcing Sargon to concentrate if he wished to understand what was said. Though much of the men's talk escaped him, he caught words and phrases whose meaning he knew. The language of the steppes people turned out to be much simpler than Akkadian.

Once again, an exhausted Sargon fell asleep as soon as his head rested on the earth. In the morning, a young boy about six or seven seasons woke him, laughing at the stranger who slept after the sun had cleared the horizon.

Day after day, the training continued. Long rides with little food and water, to toughen his body, with plenty of sword practice and language lessons during the day. After seven days, Garal took him on a four day journey, and they rode up and down the distant lands to the west. By this time Sargon could speak the language well enough to converse, and his command of Ur Nammu words grew each day.

A wooden knife now hung from Sargon's leather belt, and the wooden sword projected over his right shoulder, just as it often did with his father. They practiced with sword and knife, and Garal now added regular sessions of unarmed fighting.

"A warrior never knows when he will need to fight, or what weapons will be at hand. You must master them all."

As the days passed, possible weapons included sticks, rocks, dirt that could be thrown into an enemy's face, anything that could cut or bruise or cause pain. They even practiced throwing stones at targets.

Each night a weary Sargon wrapped himself in his blanket and fell
asleep in moments. Every morning, his muscles ached and complained,
but little by little, they grew stronger. His thighs now gripped his horse's
sides firmly, and his arms no longer complained with every movement.
The wooden sword felt lighter in his hand with each session.

Nevertheless, every night before he closed his eyes, Sargon counted
the days remaining until he could depart. He would survive this, and he
would ride away, to be free of these simple people and of his parents
forever.

⟨⟨⟨⟩⟩⟩

By now sixteen days had passed since Eskkar's departure and the start
of Sargon's training. On each of those days, from sunrise to sunset, Sargon
had labored on his riding skills and weapons practice, with every spare
moment devoted to learning the Ur Nammu language.

That night as he sat at Chinua's campfire, eating and listening to Garal
and Chinua's other sons speak about the day's activities. Sargon suddenly
realized the talk had turned to him.

"Garal says you are ready to ride with the warriors," Chinua said. "A
scouting party is riding out tomorrow, to scout the lands to the southwest.
The Clan will be moving that way soon. Fashod will lead the band. There
will be much that you can learn."

Sargon nodded. Whatever he thought of the idea mattered little anyway.

"Garal and two of my clan are also going. And Timmu will accompany them, to help care for the horses. You can ride alongside Timmu."

Timmu, seated only an arm's length away, was Chinua's oldest natural son, with eleven seasons. By now Sargon knew that Chinua had four
sons and three daughters of his own, from his two wives. But Chinua once
had an older brother, who had died at the hands of the Alur Meriki more
than twelve years ago. Since that day, Chinua had raised his only nephew,
Garal, as if he were his own son.

Barbarians made little distinction between such offspring. Garal had
fifteen seasons, close to Sargon's age, but had only a few months ago
been accepted into the warrior ranks. In Chinua's eyes, that made Garal

the perfect teacher for Sargon. Still young enough to enjoy his youth, but strong and capable enough to have proved his valor as a warrior.

Timmu might have only eleven seasons, but he was tall for his age and sturdy enough, though he yet had many years ahead of him before he finished growing. The boy tried to conceal his excitement at the idea of his first expedition riding with the warriors, but the smile on his face couldn't be held back.

"You do not have to go, Sargon," Chinua said. "If you feel you are not yet ready . . ."

Sargon didn't mind. Riding with the warriors would at least be a change of pace, something to speed up the passage of the days.

"No, Chinua, I am ready. It will be an honor." He bowed in acceptance, the proper response for any invitation from the head of a family and one of the clan leaders.

"Then sleep well tonight. Fashod will lead out the warriors just after dawn."

When the meal ended, Sargon prepared his blanket for sleep. Most of the others would sit around the fire talking, check on their horses, or walk along the stream with their women, to enjoy themselves for a time under the open sky.

As he threw himself down, Chinua appeared. "You will need this." He dropped Sargon's knife, the one his father had brought with him from Akkad, onto the ground. "Only warriors can carry a sword or bow, but anyone who rides with warriors is expected to have a knife, and know how to use it. Garal says you will carry it well."

"I will, Chinua. And my thanks to both you and Garal."

In the midst of a camp filled with armed warriors, any of whom could probably cut him down in moments, the presence of a knife shouldn't mean much. Nonetheless, Sargon found it comforting to have his own weapon close at hand. The blade was a good one, bronze, ordered by his mother from Akkad's master sword maker, and similar to the one his father wore at his waist.

The reminder of his father brought back another memory. When Eskkar was even younger than Sargon, he killed his first man with a knife. In a way, that stroke had started Eskkar down the path that eventually took him to the kingship of Akkad. Perhaps there was a lesson in that after all.

Before dawn, Timmu woke Sargon. "Hurry, we must eat and look to our horses."

By now Sargon had learned to come awake at the slightest touch. A few morning kicks from Garal had taught him that lesson. Timmu's mother had prepared food and supplies for them both, and she had tears in her eyes as her oldest son snatched them from her hand and darted off, eager to begin his first ride with the warriors.

Again Sargon remembered his manners, and thanked the woman before he, too, rushed off into the first light of dawn to find his horse.

The sun had just lifted above the horizon when Fashod rode out of the camp. Twelve warriors followed him. Timmu, Sargon, and another boy named Meeka brought up the rear. Sargon soon learned that was where they were expected to remain. Fashod traveled fast, and Sargon found himself grateful for all of Garal's strenuous rides.

As they rode, Timmu warned Sargon about the slightest lapse of obedience. "We are both sons of a clan leader, so we will not be beaten unless we fail to obey. Nor will either of us end up as sleeping companions, for the same reason. At least not on so short a ride as this."

Sargon grunted at hearing that, and fingered his knife. He didn't intend to share anyone's blanket. Nevertheless, despite Timmu's youth, the boy knew the ways of his clan. Sargon decided to heed his companion's words, and to give no offense to anyone.

Timmu and Meeka might be good riders, but Sargon, being older, had the stronger body. His horse knew its business, and clearly didn't enjoy riding behind the others. Sargon had no trouble keeping up with the warriors. At midmorning the scouting party took its first rest, and Sargon got his first shock.

While the warriors sprawled out on the grass, the boys were expected to rub the horses down and keep them secure. It took all three of them to accomplish this, with the result that the boys – and Sargon knew he was considered to be nothing more – got almost no rest for themselves.

"Is that all we're going to do," Sargon asked Timmu when they once again rode side by side. "Care for their horses?"

"There is more, much more," Timmu said. "We must gather wood for the cooking fires, make sure the horses are safe, prepare the campfire, and do the cooking. And anything else any of the warriors wants us to do."

Apparently the horse boys were expected to do everything. They cleaned the game the hunters brought down with their arrows, washed and groomed the horses at least once a day, sometimes oftener if a warrior became unduly concerned about his mount. They were also expected to search for and carry firewood and dried dung back to the camp.

"And what will the men be doing while we work?" Sargon had wondered about the mission. What did the party expect to find?

"The men will search for any signs of danger to the Clan." Timmu spoke as if he had vast experience with such things. "They will look for good hunting grounds and possible camp sites. Some riders will range far ahead, searching for anything of value."

Gritting his teeth, Sargon held back his words. So now he'd become nothing more than a servant to a bunch of barbarians riding over the countryside. Garal's lessons would have been better than this. Regardless, Sargon knew better than to complain. Several times he saw Garal glancing behind, checking up on how his charge performed his duties. Sargon realized that any mistakes he made would reflect more on Garal and Chinua than on himself.

Swearing under his breath at this new situation, Sargon knew he would just have to endure it for the next two or three days. By then they should be back at the Ur Nammu encampment, and Sargon could resume his lessons with Garal.

Instead, the scouting expedition lasted ten grueling days, at least for Sargon and the other horse boys. Fashod and the warriors appeared to enjoy themselves. They rode in a wide arc to the west, often breaking up into smaller groups. At times, they left the horse boys behind, or sent them on ahead to prepare a camp.

Aside from riding and hunting, and occasionally practicing with their weapons, Sargon noticed the warriors did little work.

"In Akkad, we would be considered slaves," Sargon said to Timmu at the end of the tenth day. "We're lucky they don't beat us every night, merely for their fun."

Just before midafternoon of the tenth day of the scouting trip, the warriors returned to the main camp. Fashod and the others exhibited the usual signs of excitement and eagerness to be home. Sargon and Timmu were so tired that they could scarcely guide their horses to Chinua's corral. Timmu explained that they were no longer expected to take care of the other animals. Once the group returned to the camp, the warriors' kin would see to that.

The moment he'd finished with his horse, Sargon threw himself into the stream, luxuriating in the chance to get clean again. Timmu had to call him several times before he climbed out of the water, ignoring the chill in the air.

Chinua's household prepared a small feast for Garal and the returning horse boys. The family's largest pot was filled with rabbit meat, along with leftovers of a deer taken in yesterday's hunt. The women added a generous helping of wild vegetables, whatever they had managed to find. It all went into the pot, along with a handful of spices, some of which Sargon recognized as coming from Akkad.

By the time Sargon got back from the stream, the tempting odors wafted over Chinua's camp site. Sargon gratefully took his seat on the fringe of the fire, next to Timmu, who had already started recounting each day's adventure to his father.

Sargon understood that for Timmu, the ride was one of several rites of passage the boy would be required to complete before he could consider himself a warrior. For Sargon, the trip had accomplished nothing.

"And you, Sargon, did nothing exciting happen to you?" Chinua's interest appeared sincere.

"I did kill a rabbit with a rock."

Everyone smiled at that. "Fashod says that you did well, that you rode as well as any of the warriors."

So Chinua had sought out the trip's leader as soon as he returned. Or perhaps Fashod had come to Chinua's tent.

"My backside is not as sore as it usually is," Sargon admitted.

Chinua chuckled. "Then tomorrow Garal will continue your training." He turned to one of his daughters, a girl of eight or nine seasons and nodded. She scrambled to her feet and ran inside the tent, to reappear almost at once. In her hands she carried a bow and a quiver of arrows, which she handed to her father.

Chinua passed them to Sargon. "Now that you have learned to ride, you must learn to shoot a bow and arrow."

Sargon ran his hands over the bow, his excitement plain. To hold a real weapon in his hand after so many days with nothing but a wooden sword or knife. He'd seen the warriors practicing their archery as they rode, often taking time to charge a particular tree or hill, shooting arrows as they rode at a gallop and shouting their war cries. A deadly weapon indeed in the hands of a skilled marksman. Of course, the horse boys were forbidden to touch any of the warriors' weapons.

"Even your father admits he never mastered the bow from horseback," Chinua said. "Though I saw him charge the Sumerians with a lance in his hand."

Sargon felt pleased to hear of his father's weakness. "He told me once that he left the Clan too soon, before he'd had time to master the bow. And that he was too tall and broad to use one efficiently from the back of a horse."

"Then you will have something to show him when you return," Chinua said. "It is always well when a son exceeds his father."

20

For the first time since he'd reached the Ur Nammu camp, Sargon fell asleep looking forward to the morning. He slept with the bow at his side that night. As usual, Garal awakened him just after dawn. Sargon climbed to his feet, rested and refreshed. Perhaps Garal's foolishness about keeping the bow close mattered after all.

They washed up at the stream, then returned to the tent, where the women handed each of them a strip of dried meat. The sun had scarcely cleared the horizon when Garal led the way to the farthest end of the camp, far enough from the tents so that they would be undisturbed. The warriors had established an area there, to practice their bowmanship.

Sargon took stock of the barbarian archery range. Unlike the large targets used in Akkad, he found a series of tall stakes driven into the ground. A thick sack full of dried grass and weeds hung from each one, dangling about the height of a man on a horse. Each stake stood apart, at least twenty paces from its neighbor.

Examining the ground, Sargon saw the tracks of many horses, and realized the warriors must use this place regularly. This early in the morning, however, the field remained empty.

Under Garal's direction, Sargon started by shooting at a stationary target. He had drawn the powerful Akkadian long bows on many occasions, but he'd never mastered the weapon. He was just tall enough, but the stiffness of the bow taxed his strength. His father's archers spent a good part of every day drawing and loosing at least a hundred arrows.

That built powerful muscles in their arms and chests. As the trainer often declared, a bowman must be able to stand and draw his shafts all day long, if necessary, and in the heat of day and the thick of battle. That onerous requirement explained why most of the Akkadian archers were tall, with broad chests and well-muscled arms and legs.

The shorter horseman's bow Garal had given him, however, with its horn tips, thickened grip, and sharply curved limbs, was a different matter all together. Meant to be used from the back of a horse and at close range, its draw was much shorter than that of the longer bows of the city. Sargon knew he could use this weapon well enough, especially after the last twenty days of riding and training.

Garal carried his own bow as they walked up to the nearest target, but Sargon struggled under the weight of four quivers of arrows.

"We will lose some shafts," Garal explained. "Once an arrow flies into the grass or sand, it often disappears. Others will break when they impact the target, or shatter if they strike a rock. These shafts are not the best our old men and women make. Those are kept for battle. But these will do well enough for us."

Everyone in the camp worked at something. Those men too old, or unable to fight or ride made weapons, mostly lances, bows, and arrows, scraping and carving most of the day. The Ur Nammu had few skilled in working with bronze, but Akkad filled that void, providing them with bronze swords, knives, and lance heads.

Sargon examined the shafts in one of the quivers. All had bone tips set into the shaft and bound with thread. Few looked straight enough for accurate shooting. The feathers that steadied the arrow in its flight looked jagged and uneven.

Garal halted twenty paces from the first post, and told Sargon to begin. Dropping the quivers to the ground, Sargon strung his bow, set his feet, and launched his first shaft. It struck the dangling grass sack, making it rock back and forth.

"Good," Garal grunted. "Again."

After launching twenty or so arrows, Sargon's right arm started aching, and his left trembled as he struggled to keep it rigid. Some shafts flew wide of the mark. Nevertheless, Garal declared himself satisfied with Sargon's efforts.

"Your teachers in Akkad taught you well. You know how to take aim and to release smoothly. That is good. But you must nock and aim faster. On horseback, everything happens at once. One moment you are out of range, the next you are too close. Often you get only one chance to launch a shaft."

To demonstrate, Garal slung a quiver over his shoulder. With a smooth motion, he whipped an arrow from the quiver, nocked and drew the bow in the same motion, and released the shaft. Without pausing he plucked another arrow from the quiver, and another and another, until he emptied his quiver of missiles, sixteen arrows in all.

Sargon stood there with his mouth hanging open. None of Hathor's warriors or even Mitrac's archers had ever shot so many shafts so quickly. Even Mitrac himself, Akkad's master archer, had never accomplished such a feat. And every one of Garal's arrows struck the target.

The warrior led the way to recover the shafts. "Your fingers must grow used to nocking the arrow to the bow. You must do this without looking down, as that will disturb your aim."

They practiced until midmorning. By then, Sargon's arms had turned to water, and he felt even more tired than if they had worked out with swords.

"Time to get our horses and ride," Garal remarked. "We will each carry our bows and one quiver."

They returned to the camp, drank at the stream, then collected their horses and rode out. Sargon carried his bronze knife, along with the wooden sword slung over his shoulder. He carried the bow in his left hand, with the quiver fastened to his waist on his left side. In battle, Sargon's left hand would also have to hold the halter and guide his horse, assisted by pressure from the rider's knees. The right hand, of course, remained free, ready for sword, lance, or to draw the bow.

Most of the warriors carried their weapons in this manner, though some replaced the bow with a pair of lances. Aside from his Akkadian tunic, Sargon looked and rode like any Ur Nammu warrior.

Garal set a fast pace as they raced around the camp, crossed the stream, and headed east. They galloped up and down gentle hills covered with grass, jumped gullies, and wove their way through large collections of boulders, pausing only long enough to rest the horses when they needed it. The ride ended where the morning had started, at the archery range. This time the two men remained mounted.

"The horses are too tired for much more." Garal patted his mount's neck as he spoke. "But they can still serve to give you some more practice." He started at the same twenty paces. Slipping an arrow from the quiver, he loosed it at the target, followed by five more, all launched with the same speed. "We'll take turns. Now you shoot a few."

Sargon found himself fumbling with the quiver. Sitting astride the horse, the quiver didn't hang straight down, so the arrows rested inside at an angle, which made them harder to grasp. When he finally nocked one to the bow, he realized the bow could not be held straight either. The halter, which still had to be grasped, interfered with his grip, and his left thigh forced the bottom of the bow out to the side. Sargon's first arrow flew wide of the mark. His next one, which took even longer to nock, also missed the target.

"It is difficult at first," Garal said. "Keep trying."

Gritting his teeth, Sargon emptied the quiver, while his bored horse pawed the ground. At least the last few shafts struck the target.

The two men climbed down and recovered their arrows.

"Now let's try it at a walk," Garal said. He guided his horse to a spot about fifty paces from the target. "A skilled warrior would have already shot two shafts by the time he reached this point. Set your horse to a walk, and we'll see how many arrows you can put on the target."

The moment the animal started moving forward, even at a plodding walk, Sargon found the entire process had doubled in difficulty. The horse's movements jiggled the quiver, even as it made Sargon's leg shift slightly, forcing him to fumble when he extracted a shaft and nocked it.

Determined, he kept shooting, loosing the arrows as fast as he could yank them from the quiver. Nevertheless, he managed to only get off ten shafts before the horse halted in front of the target.

Sargon glanced at Garal, who said nothing. He didn't have to. Half of the Akkadian's shots had missed the target.

Garal broke the silence. "We'll collect our arrows and try again."

And again and again, until the pain and weakness returned to Sargon's arms. But his last effort showed improvement, as he put fourteen arrows into the target, and missed only two.

"Enough archery for today," Garal said, glancing up at the sky to see how much daylight remained. "Another ride will do the horses good, too."

A final quick gallop through the countryside brought them back to the camp well before dusk. "Now it's time to practice your sword play."

This was the first time that Sargon had done any training inside the warriors' camp. After tending to the horses, they washed the dust from their faces, and drank from the stream. They walked back to Chinua's tent and found themselves an open space nearby. Garal put down his sword and took up a wooden one. "Let's begin."

The session began, but this time with a crowd quickly forming to watch the performance. Women, children, even a few old warriors, appeared as if by magic, attracted by the thumping of the wooden blades, to watch the young Akkadian match his skills with one of their own.

Aware of the growing audience, Sargon exerted himself, defending attack after attack by Garal. With the sweat pouring from his face, Sargon matched strokes with his instructor, but Garal seemed to grow stronger with each clash of the swords.

Soon a stroke slipped past Sargon's guard, a stinging blow on his upper arm that, if the swords had been real, would have probably severed the limb.

Garal ordered a brief rest. Sargon, breathing heavily, glanced around, and saw that about thirty people had formed a rough circle around the two men. He heard comments, most of which he didn't understand, exchanged between members of the crowd. Half a dozen warriors watched also, but they stared in silence.

They were, Sargon realized with a shock, studying both antagonists, just in case they ever had to face either of them in a fight.

The practice resumed, but it didn't take long before Sargon's lack of endurance made itself evident. His offense vanished in moments and his defense began to weaken. Garal, stronger to begin with, seemed to grow in strength with each attack. Stroke after stroke slipped through Sargon's guard.

In the end, his weary legs made him stumble as he failed to block one of Garal's simple overhead strokes. The thick wood of the sword landed almost unimpeded on the side of Sargon's head.

When he recovered consciousness, Sargon found himself where he had fallen, though someone had placed a blanket under his head. Two women were tending him, one still dabbing at his head with a damp rag. Both smiled as he lay there embarrassed and trying to gather his wits.

"No more today," the older woman said, smiling and giving his head a final pat. "Time to eat soon."

The other woman – Sargon realized she was only a young girl – had wiped his chest and face with another wet rag. He thought he'd seen her before, though not at any of the tents belonging to Chinua or his neighbors.

She returned his gaze. "I am Tashanella." Her husky voice sounded older than her years. "My father is Subutai, leader of the Ur Nammu. He wishes you to join him at his campfire tonight."

Sargon pushed himself to a sitting position, assisted by both women. The movement made the blood rush to his head, and he nearly passed out again. When the dizziness faded, only Tashanella remained kneeling at his side, holding his arm.

"It is best if we go now," she said. "My father does not like to wait, and he sent me some time ago. I arrived while you were still fighting with Garal."

He touched his head. His right ear felt hot, as if it were going to burst into flames. "It wasn't much of a fight."

"Yes, I saw. He could have fought much harder. Such encounters often end with broken bones."

Sargon didn't need to be reminded of that. For the first time, he gave the girl a closer inspection. Young, perhaps yet a maiden waiting to be initiated in the women's rites, she spoke with a certainty that seemed older than her years.

Her eyes, large and dark brown, regarded him with as much interest. Long brown hair hung straight down her back and reached halfway to her waist. A smile formed on her lips, revealing even white teeth.

"I know he could have fought harder." Sargon found himself staring into her eyes.

"I am glad he did not," she said. "Otherwise I would have to drag you back to my father's tent."

Despite his throbbing head, Sargon managed a smile. He pushed himself to his feet, and the girl's strength helped him remain upright. He stood there for a moment, until he felt certain that he wasn't going to fall. The girl, however, still held onto his arm.

"I can walk." He realized he had forgotten her name. "What is your name?"

"Tashanella." She dropped her hand, turned away, and started walking.

Sargon followed her across the camp until they reached Subutai's tent. Tashanella opened the tent flap and held it so that he could enter. Ducking, Sargon slipped inside the tent and heard the flap drop behind him.

Subutai sat cross-legged on a folded blanket. "Sit." He motioned to a blanket set opposite his own. "You were fighting?"

Sargon bowed his head in respect before sinking onto the blanket. "With Garal."

No need to explain that they had been practicing. The Ur Nammu language used the same word for sparring and fighting. Subutai knew the difference. Sargon would be dead if the fight had been for real.

"Garal is almost as good with a sword as his bow. Someday he will be one of our greatest warriors."

"He is . . . a good teacher. Is that not as important as being a great fighter?"

Subutai nodded. "You are learning our language. And, yes, someday being a good teacher may be as important as being a strong warrior, but that day has not yet come. Meanwhile, you have already answered my question about your progress. Since you speak our language well enough, I would like you to take your evening meals with me from now on."

Not sure what to make of that request, Sargon hesitated. Subutai had asked him politely enough, but a suggestion from the clan leader carried the same force as one of Eskkar's commands to his soldiers.

That rankled Sargon. He felt almost the same anger toward Subutai as he did toward his father.

Subutai misunderstood the hesitation. "It has nothing to do with Chinua. But at my campfire, you will learn how the clan leaders make decisions, how they speak and plan for the future. The ways of leading are difficult to teach. Better if you watch and see for yourself."

This time it took a moment before Sargon translated the more complex phrases. Not that it really mattered. Giving affront to the Ur Nammu clan leader didn't seem wise. "As you wish, Sarum."

"Good. We will begin tonight. You will sit at my left hand." He rose to his feet, a smooth movement that took him from sitting to standing with little effort. "My wives are already waiting."

Honored guests sat at the left side of their host. Sargon, still feeling the effects of Garal's sword, took twice as long to get to his feet.

He followed the Sarum outside the tent, where a few warriors stood around the campfire. Waiting until Subutai sat, Sargon slipped to the ground beside him, but a little to the rear. He'd seen the same situation at Chinua's evening fire, though he had never sat beside the warrior.

In the western sky, the crimson sun had touched the horizon. The cooking fire had already served its purpose, and now only low flames curled and crackled from the embers. Subutai took his place at the head of the rough circle that formed around the campfire.

His grown sons had their own tents and families, and only two younger boys about Sargon's age were present, watching their elders. On Subutai's right sat Fashod, the second in command, or what the Ur Nammu called a leader of one hundred. Although Sargon knew that title had little to do with the actual numbers of warriors under his command.

Subutai's wives, Petra and Roxsanni, and their daughters began ladling out the evening's meal. The simple fare was no different from what Sargon had eaten at Chinua's tent. The customary stew of mixed vegetables and small game, usually rabbit, came first. But tonight one of the family's hunters had bagged a wild sheep, so the thick smell of roasted mutton hung over the camp site.

Every family member had his own eating bowl, and visitors were expected to arrive with their own. Before Sargon could decide how to handle the situation, a girl appeared at his left and thrust a bowl into his hands. He lifted his gaze and saw Tashanella, as she handed a second bowl to her father. Tashanella gave Sargon the briefest glance before returning to her mother's side.

Fashod lifted his bowl in the gesture of thanks to his host, and immediately began eating, so Sargon copied his gesture of respect.

After a few swallows, Fashod spoke. Either he was speaking slower out of consideration for his guest, or Sargon's knowledge of the language had improved. The second in command ran through the day's events, the reports of the scouts, the condition of the horses, even an argument over a horse between two men who had nearly come to blows.

No one else spoke, and Sargon guessed that the first order of business must be the report of the day's activity. He took another sip of the stew, and enjoyed a pleasant surprise. Either the Sarum's wives, being older, were better cooks than Chinua's wives, or Subutai's women had received the choicest cuts of meat and the freshest vegetables. Soon Sargon was scooping the last of the stew out of the empty bowl, using his fingers to get the last shreds of meat.

"You know I am one of the twelve warriors who fought with your father in our first battle together?"

Sargon realized that Fashod had directed that comment toward him. "No, I did not know that." Now would come a long tale about his father's battle skills and fearless courage.

"That was before you were born. It was I who first scouted the way toward Akkad. Your people called it Orak then. I remember when the few of us who survived reached the village, with its high walls still being built. Your mother came out to us, and gave us food and drink with her own hand. She directed her women to care for our wounded, and her healers saved many of our youngest, including my own daughter."

His mother had probably calculated the value of each basket of food, and weighed it against any possible return. "I did not know that, Fashod."

"It's true," Subutai added. "My son also was near death, and my first wife," he gestured to the smaller circle of women and children eating their own meal, "nearly died as well. The Ur Nammu Clan would have probably starved to death and disappeared from the earth without your parents' help."

"Your people have repaid that debt many times," Sargon offered. "Even in the war with Sumer, I knew Chinua and Fashod rode with my father."

Subutai shrugged. "That was as much to train our own warriors as to help Eskkar. Even without our help, he would have defeated the Sumerians."

"Still, we did help," Fashod said, unwilling to concede that their effort hadn't amounted to much. "And we led the charge against the desert rabble, though they outnumbered us greatly. I remember that many of them turned their horses away in fear when they heard our war cries."

Fascinated in spite of himself, Sargon leaned closer. "Tell me about the battle." Of course he had already heard it many times, told by Hathor and many others, as well as his father.

This time Sargon heard a different side to the story of the great battle. Fashod had ridden with Hathor in the remarkable raid that circled almost all of the Land Between the Rivers. Akkad's soldiers still told the tale nearly every night in the ale houses.

Now Fashod described that ride, told how the need for speed and secrecy caused them to rush toward their enemies as fast as the wind. The Ur Nammu had provided the scouts for the campaign.

Fashod told of the attacks against the desert tribes, the fall of Uruk, even the wild ride to Isin the day before the deciding battle. And after that bloody encounter, where they broke Sumer's army, Hathor and Fashod led their men south, all the way to Sumer's gates, to carry the war back to those who had started it.

By the time Fashod finished, the fire had grown cold, and the full dark of night had arrived. Sargon glanced around the circle. Many others from nearby tents had moved in to surround their leaders, edging close enough to hear the story of the Ur Nammu's greatest victory. No doubt they, too, had heard it many times, but Fashod related the adventure with the easy skill of an accomplished storyteller.

For the first time, the battle truly came alive to Sargon. Now he could genuinely appreciate the final desperate charge against overwhelming numbers, picture the arrows arcing through the sky, see the lances hurtling toward the enemy, even hear the shouts of the warriors, the thunder of the horses, and the cries of the wounded and dying.

"Each time he tells the story," Subutai said when Fashod finished, "he kills a few more Sumerians."

Everyone laughed, a satisfying sound that nevertheless gave praise to the brave men who fought that day, and to the memory of those who had fallen in battle.

"Now it is time to rest," Subutai said, ending the evening meal.

Everyone was on their feet. The women collected the food bowls and picked up the discarded scraps, to keep the night creatures away from the tents.

As Sargon stood, Subutai leaned close to him. "You will make a good warrior someday, Sargon. When the need arises, you will heed the war call bravely. My sight tells me this is true."

The Sarum, of course, was supposed to be able to foretell the future. No doubt his ignorant followers all believed it. Nonetheless, Subutai's tone told Sargon that the Ur Nammu leader believed every word he had just uttered.

"Then I hope I will be ready when the time comes," Sargon answered.

"Put your trust in the teachings of Chinua and Garal," Subutai said. "Then you cannot fail."

Sargon nodded, grateful for the kindly words. As he started back toward Chinua's tent, Sargon glimpsed a figure standing a few paces away, watching him. By the time Sargon realized who it was, Tashanella had vanished into the shadows.

21

For the next six days, Sargon and Garal spent at least half their time riding across the countryside, and the remainder practicing with weapons. The long days of hard work now yielded results. Sargon's skill in controlling his horse improved, even as the muscles in his arms and legs grew firm.

Whenever they stopped to rest the horses, out came the wooden swords. By the sixth day, Sargon could hold his own. No longer could Garal risk giving Sargon the slightest opening. Both men considered it a poor session if Sargon did not score at least one 'fatal' strike against his instructor.

Garal believed the sword and bow the most important, but he didn't neglect the lance and knife. When Sargon's arm grew weary of drawing the bow or holding the sword, Garal would switch to the lance.

They took turns, riding at the target at ever increasing speed, and hurling the lance. When Sargon mastered the basics of that, they would ride together, side by side, yelling war cries, and throw their lances at the same moment.

The hardest skill to master remained shooting the bow from the back of a galloping horse. Sargon swore a hundred oaths at missed targets, dropped arrows, broken bowstrings, and embarrassing times when the bow simply slipped from his hand.

Three times he lost control of his horse and fell heavily to the ground, to Garal's amusement. Nevertheless, Sargon felt his confidence grow with each wild charge.

Whenever Sargon grew frustrated or complained, Garal brushed aside his complaints. "You have it easy. A real warrior has to practice his skills whenever he can. Much of his day is spent riding and scouting and hunting, following the Sarum's orders. Since you've been here, the camp has not moved. When the Ur Nammu journey to another place, then the warriors have to work the horses, help pitch the tents, load the wagons. Every man in the camp would be grateful for an opportunity to hone their skills like this."

"When is the camp going to move?"

"Not for another thirty or forty days," Garal replied. "And we will not move far, just a few miles farther downstream. This country is still well stocked with game, there is thick grass to feed the horses and herd animals, and the stream provides plenty of good water. But first, in two days, Chinua will lead a large scouting party to the southwest, to check on the next campsite. You and Timmu will probably both join us."

The only rest Sargon enjoyed, before he dropped wearily to his blanket to sleep the night through, was the obligatory evening meal at Subutai's tent. The good food helped relax him after a long day, and by now Sargon looked forward to it.

After that first night, Sargon brought his own bowl, and it was always Tashanella who took it from his hand and filled it from the pot. After a few meals, he realized that the portions he received were as choice as those given to Subutai. Sargon couldn't tell if that was because of his status as an important guest, or Tashanella's doing.

One of Subutai's wives usually attended her husband, but on several occasions Tashanella also served her father. She didn't seem to be the eldest daughter. By the plain garment she wore, Sargon guessed that she must still be too young for the women's rites.

Ur Nammu fathers, in much the same way as those in Akkad, married their daughters off as soon as they reached puberty. No one, barbarian or city dweller, wanted to deal with the problems a young girl turning into a woman created.

Those who delayed marriage for their daughters too long often regretted that decision. Better to get them married off, out of the household, and under their new husband's authority. A baby or two would quickly subdue a girl's hot emotions.

Sargon raised the question with Garal one day during their morning ride. "Chief Subutai's daughter, Tashanella, seems different from the other girls in the camp."

"She is." Garal turned to give Sargon a long look. "Do not concern yourself with her. When she passes through the rites, she will be married to some brave warrior, or at least one who can afford such a prize."

"What makes her such a prize?"

"She is the Sarum's daughter, but the women say she possesses much wisdom. Some day she may even become one of the Gifted Ones."

It took a few moments before that idea translated. "What's a Gifted One."

"A woman wise in the ways of the Clan, one who can be invited to sit in on the Sarum's Council. They are rare, and the Ur Nammu have not had such a one in many years. You would be wise to give no offense to her. Tashanella is her father's favorite, and he is quick to anger where she is concerned."

"Maybe you should take her for a wife yourself."

Garal laughed. "She will not be given to any young warrior, let alone one who has never fought in a battle. No, she will belong to an old and seasoned warrior, one who probably already has too many horses and too many wives."

For the first time, Sargon realized that Garal, too, had never fought in battle. For the last thirty days, Sargon had struggled to keep up with the warrior. Garal was less than two seasons older. That thought was soon replaced by another. If Garal was so strong, how would Sargon match up against an older and more experienced fighter?

Unbidden, Sargon thought of his father. Even now when Eskkar had grown old, few men in Akkad were willing to face him in combat. Of course, his father's famous luck and reputation might have much to do with that unwillingness. Or perhaps Eskkar's frequent long rides and the almost daily practice with his sword had something to do with it.

"Is not your mother," Garal interrupted the silence, "I have forgotten her name, one of the Gifted Ones? That is what Subutai's wife claims. She has met several times with her."

His father, and now his mother. Sargon shook his head. Even out here in these desolate lands, he could not escape their presence.

"My mother, they call her Lady Trella, is the wisest and most cunning person, man or woman, in Akkad. She rules the city even more than my father, so I guess you could say she is one of the gifted."

Garal grunted at the unflattering description, but said nothing.

That evening, at Subutai's tent, Sargon once again handed his empty bowl to Tashanella. It was returned filled to the brim, and he thought the girl's hand lingered for a moment on his as he accepted it.

He smiled up at her. Sargon knew warriors, even visitors at another man's tent, did not thank their women for serving them. Nevertheless, he nodded his appreciation.

Tashanella flashed the fleetest of smiles at him, before moving away. For the rest of the meal, Sargon's attention drifted again and again to the women's circle. Of course he could not stare at her, but the longer he studied the girl, the more interested he became.

He could not guess her age. Slim as a willow tree, Tashanella appeared yet a maiden. Still, her loose dress concealed much, and Sargon wondered just how ripe was the body that hid beneath the garment. He felt a stirring in his loins, a rare sensation since he had left Akkad.

Later that evening, after he returned to Chinua's tent, Sargon approached Garal. He often sat and spoke with the young warrior before they slept. The animosity Sargon had first felt for Garal had gradually faded away. Now they were more like companions who could trust each other.

Usually Sargon wanted to know more about the next day's activity, and tonight he managed to ask a few questions about the morning before he asked what was really on his mind.

"How many seasons does Tashanella have?" For once he was glad that he couldn't see Garal's face in the dark.

Surprised by the sudden change in the conversation, Garal had to think for a moment. "I think she has thirteen, no, maybe fourteen seasons. Why do you ask?"

"No reason. Just that she seems old enough to be married."

"She will be, soon."

Sargon knew that most girls went through Ishtar's rites between the ages of thirteen and fifteen, though some took longer. Even so, it was not uncommon for girls to be married off even if they had yet to undergo the rite of passage into womanhood. Even maidens could provide relief for a man's needs.

"I don't think you should be casting eyes at Tashanella while you're at the Sarum's camp. You may be a visitor here, but that kind of offense . . ."

"Do not worry," Sargon said. "All I want to do is get through the next fifty days with my head on my shoulders."

By now Garal knew all about Sargon's pact with Subutai.

"You are still keen to leave the Clan as soon as you can?"

"The Clan is your home, your family, not mine. I no longer have a family of my own. I will have to find a new place in the world, one as far from Akkad as I can."

"Then you'd better get some sleep," Garal said. "We have another long day tomorrow."

⸺◦⊶⦿⊷◦⸺

Two days later, Sargon rode out of the Ur Nammu camp just after dawn. Chinua and fourteen warriors led the way, while Sargon and three other horse boys brought up the rear. Timmu, Chinua's son, rode beside Sargon, and the younger boy grinned excitedly at the prospect of accompanying the men again.

From his evening meals at the Sarum's tent, Sargon understood the need for this trip. In the last month, Subutai's outriders to the west had encountered small groups of people fleeing toward the lands traversed by the Ur Nammu. The Sarum wanted to know more about these people, including why they fled whatever lands they came from, and even more important, who might be pursuing them.

Subutai had ordered Chinua to go out with a small band of warriors and collect whatever information he could. Sargon and Timmu, Chinua's son, found themselves included in the group.

Not that Sargon concerned himself with Chinua's orders. The trip held no excitement for Sargon. Whatever the value to the Ur Nammu,

Sargon had done this before, and this venture promised more days of hard work, with little to be gained. Even though Garal rode with the party, Sargon guessed that the warrior would have little time for any training.

Though the clan's women had packed extra food, Sargon knew the men would be living off the land, and that part of each day's journey would be devoted to hunting the evening's meal. If the hunt came up empty, then every rider would sleep on an empty stomach, and in the morning belts would be tightened. The horse boys, of course, would eat last, even if the hunt were successful. If not, then they would be as hungry as the men.

Chinua led the warriors almost due west, and they covered the ground at the deceptively easy canter that made the miles pass swiftly beneath the horses' hooves. The tall green grass brushed the bellies of the horses as they swept along, much like a boat racing through the waters of the Tigris. Scattered groves of trees, mostly poplars and a few white oaks, broke the monotony.

Sargon, like everyone else, carried a small sack of grain to help his horse keep up its strength, as well as a second pouch of dried meat and fruit prepared by the women. In addition to his personal supplies, Sargon and Timmu struggled under the weight of their other burdens. Between them they carried three cooking pots and several sacks of supplies, to be shared among the warriors.

It was, Sargon decided, like riding a fully loaded pack horse and about as pleasant. The other two boys, Makko and Rutba, considered themselves far superior to the younger Timmu and the outsider Sargon. Both ignored Sargon and Timmu as much as possible, unless some opportunity arose to give them orders.

Makko and Rutba, both about Sargon's age, boasted they would be admitted into the ranks of the warriors soon after Chinua's expedition returned to the Ur Nammu camp. Naturally they treated Sargon and Timmu as if they were children, and expected them to do as much of the menial work as possible.

Nevertheless, Sargon had no choice, and by now he knew better than to complain or sulk. If there were one thing warriors despised more than a dirt eater, it was anyone who complained about his daily tasks.

Everyone was expected to work hard. If some, through favor or fortune, received easier assignments, that was just the luck of the gods. All Sargon cared about was that by the time the trip ended, he would be so much closer to taking his leave of the Ur Nammu.

Makko's father, Skala, also rode with the party, as a leader of five and third in command under Chinua. To Sargon's eyes, both father and son appeared much the same – dour, thickheaded, and built like an ox.

"You're right," Timmu whispered, just as the afternoon sun began to settle toward the horizon. "Makko does look like an ox."

Sargon struggled to control his laughter. Makko rode only a few paces ahead, and in spite of his hard head, might have a good pair of ears. "Don't let him hear you," Sargon warned. "He'd snap you in two with one hand."

Timmu snorted. "Only if he could catch me."

With little to do during the ride, Sargon used the time to extend his knowledge of the Ur Nammu language. Timmu enjoyed pointing out anything new, and correcting Sargon's mistakes. Since Timmu chatted almost non-stop, Sargon's understanding of the language increased. If nothing else, the practice helped pass the time.

"Only another ten or twelve days, and we'll be back in camp," Sargon said. Two cooking pots and an extra food sack grated annoyingly against his right leg as he guided his horse through a sandy stretch of ground. "At least the sacks will be a little lighter each day."

"By this time next year, I'll be taking my last trip as a horse boy," Timmu declared.

"Not you! You'll need another five or six seasons." The two had become friends, and Sargon could laugh with the boy. "You're too small to be a warrior."

The boy had just started his growth spurt, and by next summer, Sargon guessed Timmu would be almost as tall as his father.

For Sargon and Timmu, the actual traveling was the easiest part of the day. They merely had to keep pace with the men. Neither was burdened with weapons, only their knives. Even Sargon's wooden sword had been left behind. If Garal or one of the other warriors decided to help him with his training, they would have to make do with sticks or what they could find along the way.

By sundown of the third day, Chinua's party had covered more than a hundred miles since leaving the Ur Nammu camp. When their leader finally gave the command to halt for the night, Sargon noticed more than a few of the warriors stretching to ease aching muscles.

Thanks to his incessant riding since his arrival, Sargon felt no discomfort. Still, he gave a sigh when they stopped riding. Now his real work would begin.

Two warriors remained on their horses, riding out to give one last sweep of the immediate countryside for any game that might be around. Nothing had shown itself during the day's ride, and if the men failed to bring anything down, the entire party would eat little of substance tonight. That meant the horse boys would have to make do with even less. Sargon expected to sleep this evening with his appetite unsatisfied.

Tonight was a dry camp, so there would be no water to wash down the horses. After the men secured their mounts, Sargon and Timmu brushed them down with clumps of grass to loosen any dirt that had settled under the hair. Then they used a bit of rag to flick off any remaining dust and smooth down the animal's coat. Last they used their fingers to straighten the horse's mane, and eliminate any tangles.

The animals stood quietly during the grooming, knowing they would be rewarded with a handful of grain.

The horses tended to, Sargon and Timmu busied themselves setting up the camp. Makko and Rutba had gone off to search for firewood, though Sargon guessed the lazy pair would return with only a few sticks. Of course Timmu and Sargon would be expected to collect more to keep the cooking fires burning.

Timmu had offered to gather some kindling, so Sargon knelt on the grass and started shoving stones together to make a fire ring. One of the warriors approached. "Where is Makko?"

Glancing up, Sargon saw the dour-faced Skala, Makko's father, standing over him. "He's gathering firewood."

"Find him. Bring him to me." Skala crossed his arms, as if expecting his son to rise up from the ground.

Without a word, Sargon climbed to his feet. He knew it would do no good to protest, though of course Sargon would be berated if the campfire wasn't started soon. He glanced around, not sure of what direction Makko had taken. Puzzled, Sargon turned again, trying to remember when he'd last seen Makko, when Skala's fist landed on his cheek.

Caught by surprise by the unexpected blow, Sargon crashed to the earth, his head glancing off one of the fire stones.

"When I give you an order, you will obey it!" Skala reinforced his words with a kick that landed on Sargon's thigh and pushed him over onto his stomach.

Dazed, Sargon took a moment to clear his head. His face felt on fire. The fist had landed high on his cheekbone and sent a wave of pain through his head. Never in his life had Sargon been struck like that. Rage flooded through his body, driving the pain away. He twisted to his side and lurched to his feet, facing Skala. Without thinking, Sargon jerked his knife from his belt.

At that moment, Timmu rushed into the space between them. He flung himself on Sargon, wrapping both arms around his friend. "Put down the knife! Put it down!"

Over Timmu's shoulder, Sargon saw that Skala had drawn his sword and taken a step forward.

"Get out of my way." A flush of hatred raced through Sargon's body, rage that burned twice as hot as any feelings toward his father. Sword or not, Sargon intended to kill Skala or die in the attempt.

"No! You must not do . . ."

Sargon threw Timmu to the side. Skala had raised his sword and moved to attack, and the big warrior would just have likely killed Timmu or anyone else in his way. Sargon jumped back as Skala's sword swung down. The blade flashed by Sargon's face, the point diving almost into the grass.

Before the angry warrior could regain control of his weapon, Sargon twisted aside and lashed out with the knife, the sharp tip grazing Skala's forearm.

The stroke, delivered off balance and at full extension, didn't amount to much more than a deep scratch. As Skala whirled his blade around in a sweeping cut, Sargon leapt back, and the stroke just missed gutting Sargon's stomach. On the balls of his feet, Sargon waited knife in hand for the next attack.

"STOP! Do not move. Drop your weapons." Chinua's shout halted everyone, and every man in the camp turned toward Skala. "I'll kill the next one that moves."

The camp went silent. The warriors set aside whatever they were doing, and moved quickly to watch the conflict.

Even Sargon, still blind with rage, heeded Chinua's words. Timmu again rushed to Sargon's side, and grasped his friend's knife hand with both of his. "Put down the knife! You must put down the knife!"

At the force of Timmu's words, Sargon released the knife, letting it drop to the earth.

Skala, his face flushed with anger, raised his blade. A horse boy had drawn a knife on him. Not only that, but had actually wounded him.

"Do it, and I'll kill you."

Chinua spoke the words in a matter-of-fact tone, and Sargon realized they were not directed at him, but at Skala, whose rage now exceeded his own.

Chinua stepped in front of Skala, their faces only a hand's width apart. He said nothing, just stared into Skala's face.

However Skala's rage still controlled him. Every man in the camp could guess his thoughts. He would kill Chinua first, then finish with the boy.

A twanging sound made Sargon and the others glance to the side. Ten paces away, Garal had strung his bow and let the string snap back into position instead of easing it to the full tension. Before the bowstring ceased quivering, Garal nocked an arrow and drew the weapon, the arrow-head pointed at Skala. Chinua was kin, after all.

Only Chinua hadn't turned his head toward the sound. When he spoke, his words so soft that Sargon and the others could barely hear them. "Are you offering me a challenge, Skala? You know what that means."

A warrior was forbidden to challenge his leader while on the clan's business. Anyone who did so without the gravest of reasons risked death or worse when the offending warrior returned and faced his Sarum.

For a moment, Skala hesitated. Obviously he didn't enjoy the thought of Garal's arrow in his back, and every rider in the party knew all about Garal and his skill with the bow. Either that, or the thought of facing his commander man-to-man didn't appeal to him.

"No, Chinua. I meant no offense." Skala stepped back and sheathed his sword. "This fool of a boy angered me by his disobedience."

Sargon's anger flared up again. "That's a lie!"

Chinua held up his hand, but didn't take his eyes away from Skala. "Keep silent, Sargon, or I'll have you beaten."

Skala's face flushed an even darker crimson, as he absorbed yet another insult to his honor. Now a horse boy called him a liar in front of his peers.

"I demand the right to kill the dirt eater! My honor . . . "

"Your honor will suffer greatly if you attempt to kill our guest. The Sarum's guest, I would remind you. Not to mention that you would shame your honor to kill a mere horse boy. And did you forget Subutai's order, not to use the words "dirt eater" in his presence?"

Sargon hadn't known that. The phrase was used by every warrior to refer to any and all farmers or villagers.

"He cut my arm. He . . ."

That was too much for Timmu. "You struck him from behind! I saw you! He did nothing to offend you."

Skala glared at Timmu, but decided now was not the time to challenge his commander's son. He faced Chinua. "He was slow to obey my order. He failed to . . ."

"And you knocked him to the ground," Chinua interrupted. "He lost his wits, and you received a scratch on your arm. Or is it anything more than a scratch?"

Every eye went to Skala's arm. Blood still dripped down his wrist and hand. To Sargon, it looked a lot worse than a scratch.

Skala gave it a quick glance and shrugged, his warrior's pride refusing to acknowledge any discomfort or pain. "This . . . this is nothing."

"Good. Have the healer bind it up, and we will get back to our supper."

Garal stepped forward. He still held the bow in his left hand, the arrow nocked on the string. "Timmu, where is the wood for the fire?"

"Makko and Rutba went to collect it."

Everyone glanced around. Makko and Rutba, alerted by the noise, had raced back to the camp. They slowed to a halt, and stood there, breathing hard, twenty paces away. Each carried a handful of twigs, barely enough to get the fire going, but not enough to sustain it.

Chinua brushed past Skala and strode over to where they stood. "You went out for firewood as soon as we made camp, and this is all you've collected? A few sticks?" He didn't wait for a reply. The heel of his hand lashed out, and caught Rutba, who happened to be closest, in the chest. The boy crashed to the ground, flat on his back.

"Go out and find wood, both of you, enough to keep the fire burning all night. And you will do the same every night for the rest of the ride. Do you understand me? Or would you both prefer to walk back to camp?"

That would be worse than any beating or punishment Chinua might impose. Makko, his head hanging low, glanced toward his father, who turned away. Makko dropped what wood he'd collected and dashed off into the gathering darkness, glad to be away from Chinua's anger. Rutba scrambled to his feet and hurried after him.

Sargon glimpsed the look on Skala's face, after yet one more embarrassment to his honor.

Chinua watched them go, then whirled around and faced Sargon and Timmu. "There will be no food for you two tonight, nor for Makko and Rutba. Perhaps a long ride tomorrow on an empty stomach will do all of you some good. And if any horse boy causes the least bit of trouble for the rest of the ride, I'll have him whipped."

With that warning delivered, Chinua stalked off into the gathering darkness alone.

Skala, his fists still clenched, strode to the other side of the camp. The tension released, the other warriors drifted away, some of them smiling. More than a few would take discreet pleasure in Skala's discomfort. All of them would have much to talk about for the next day or two, though Sargon doubted any of them would do so within Skala's hearing.

Sargon's knees went weak, and he slumped to the ground. His right hand ached from gripping the knife with all his strength, and his face throbbed as if a burning brand had landed on it. He knew he'd barely escaped death. Against Skala's sword, Sargon's knife would have been useless. A few more moments, and Skala would have cut him in half.

Sargon had to take a deep breath before he could speak, and even then, the words were little more than a mumble. "Timmu, thank you for saving my life."

"Makko and his father are both pigs." Timmu spat on the ground to show his disgust. "I'm glad you challenged him. My honor wouldn't let him kill you."

"Boys have no honor." Garal's voice sounded as hard as the look in his eyes. He'd walked away with the others, but had returned, moving as silently as always. "You've both been told that often enough. You should have kept quiet."

"And let him kill Sargon?"

Garal smiled, a quick flash of white in the growing darkness. "Well, not that silent. Now, let me look at your face."

Sargon lifted his hand to touch his cheek. He felt the wetness and flinched at the pain. The skin was broken.

Garal peered at Sargon's face. "Oh, yes, you're going to look impressive in the morning. Nevertheless, you're lucky Skala didn't use all his strength. He could break even your hard head with his bare fist."

If Skala had been holding back, Sargon didn't want to know what a real punch would have done. His eyes still had trouble focusing.

"See to him, Timmu," Garal said. "And both of you, try to stay out of trouble for the rest of the night."

Sargon nodded. It already hurt to talk. With Skala brooding at one end of the camp, and Chinua sitting by himself at the other, none of the warriors enjoyed much conversation as they chewed their strips of dried meat.

The horse boys scurried about their tasks, but without any water or game to cook – the two hunters had returned empty handed – Sargon and Timmu had little to do. Timmu insisted that Sargon get some sleep as soon as possible.

"You'll need your rest for tomorrow," he warned. "We've another long ride ahead of us."

The ordeal over, Sargon felt too exhausted to argue. He rolled himself in his blanket and tried to sleep. His throbbing cheek kept him awake for a time, until exhaustion took him and he finally fell into a fitful slumber.

22

When Timmu shook him awake, the sun had yet to make a glow on the eastern horizon. For a moment Sargon wondered why his companion had wakened him so early, but a throb of pain soon reminded him. When he sat up, Sargon's head seemed to spin on his shoulders. When he lifted his hand to touch his face, he found that the right side of his head had swollen to almost twice its size. The lightest touch sent a wave of pain through his cheek.

"Oh, gods! My head . . ."

Timmu handed him the water skin, and Sargon gulped down several mouthfuls. Even that simple act hurt so much he almost dropped the skin.

"Keep quiet," Timmu whispered, glancing toward the still sleeping warriors. "We don't want to make any trouble."

The last thing Sargon wanted was more trouble. He struggled to his feet, but had to lean on Timmu's shoulder to steady himself.

"Come, Sargon. Let's get the horses ready."

Each morning, a few warriors managed to find some reason to complain about the horse boys. Better to start on the day's tasks early and avoid giving anyone an excuse. Sargon and Timmu groped their way to the rope corral and started preparing the halters. Each rider had his own halter, and it seemed to Sargon that each wanted his horse secured in a particular way.

By now the first rays of dawn illuminated the sky. Glancing around, Sargon saw Rutba awake and moving about, along with an Ur Nammu warrior who had guarded the camp while the others slept.

Timmu saw Sargon's questioning glance. "Chinua ordered Makko and Rutba to help guard the camp for the next three days. Each of them was up half the night on watch."

Sargon grunted at that small satisfaction. With only half a night's sleep, they would both be in a foul mood all day, not that he or anyone else cared. "Maybe they'll stay out of our way."

"Or maybe they'll make more trouble for us." Timmu glanced around, as if expecting someone to berate them.

Sargon realized he'd brought grief down on both their heads. Timmu had stood by his friend, and now the boy might be in as much trouble as Sargon.

A shout from Chinua awakened the rest of the camp. Most warriors began each day with a muttered prayer to the horse gods, to bring good fortune on the day's ride. Then they took a piss, swigged from their water skins, and came looking for their horse.

By then, Timmu and Sargon, with help from Rutba and Makko, had the animals ready. The older boys, too, wanted no more trouble with Chinua. A single word from him could keep them from achieving the status of warriors for another season.

The sun had scarcely cleared the horizon before Chinua swung himself up on his horse and led the way. No one, it seemed to Sargon, appeared particularly eager for the coming day's ride.

Varying the pace of the horses, Chinua kept them moving until mid-morning, when they reached a small stream that flowed across their path. Every rider refilled his water skin and washed down his horse before settling down on the hardy grass for a few moments rest. The horses, their halters fastened to the bushes, grazed contentedly on the hardy grass.

Garal strode back to where Sargon and Timmu sat. "Your head looks like a melon."

Sargon grimaced. "It feels even bigger." It still hurt to move his lips. Gingerly he touched his cheek.

"Let me see." Garal leaned in to examine the swelling. His fingers probed around the broken skin. "It looks worse than it is. If you can talk, at least your jaw is not broken, and your cheekbone seems intact. By tomorrow most of the pain should be gone. The swelling will take another few days to subside. If I had any wine, I'd give some to you."

The mention of wine brought another surprise. Sargon realized that no wine had crossed his lips in over a month. That fact would have pleased his mother, who claimed that wine dulled the senses and weakened a man's wits. Of course a real man could deal with any quantity of wine.

"Keep him out of trouble, Timmu." Garal clasped Sargon's shoulder and returned to where he'd tethered his horse.

Sargon would have replied but his mouth hurt too much to talk.

The rest period over, the warriors resumed their ride. By nightfall, when they made another dry camp, Sargon felt much better. His jaw moved without too much pain, and though a few of his teeth felt loose to his tongue, none had fallen out, and the taste of blood had left his mouth.

Another day passed without incident, as they rode westward. Chinua sent two men ahead, to act as scouts. Skala and his son Makko ignored Sargon, barely making eye contact and speaking only when necessary. Chinua must have warned Skala not to make trouble.

By the third morning after the incident, the pain had almost gone, and the swelling much reduced. Sargon felt good enough to take note of his surroundings. The last few days, the countryside had gradually changed to more rugged terrain, as the Zagros Mountains turned to the west.

Gullies and ridges slowed their way every few hundred paces. Streams and trees were more plentiful, but the grass sparser, and the riders had to waste more time letting the horses forage.

"Some call these the Taurus Mountains," Timmu declared. "We're following the trail that leads to the lands of Haranos."

Sargon agreed that the name of the mountains did change. He didn't see anything resembling a trail. As far as he could tell, they were the first living riders to pass through these lands. He hadn't seen another person or dwelling since they left the Ur Nammu camp.

"I've heard of the Taurus Mountains, but no one knows how far they extend. Maybe this is all empty land."

"Chinua says there are dirt eaters living to the south and west."

"Probably in tents covered with mud and dung."

A shout turned everyone's eyes toward the west. One of the scouts appeared on the top of a hill, and waved the warriors forward. Chinua gave the command, and the riders urged their horses into a gallop. In moments they reached the crest where the scout waited.

The riders had fanned out along the hilltop. The horse boys formed a second line behind the warriors, and Sargon and Timmu halted their horses just behind Chinua's. Sargon felt the same excitement as the others. About a half a mile away and across a series of low ridges, a party of twenty-five or thirty men, half of them mounted, coming toward Chinua's scouting party.

As the unknown travelers moved eastward, Sargon noticed that they appeared to be well armed. About ten of those on foot carried bows, similar in size to those Chinua's men bore.

The strangers sighted Chinua's warriors, and a ripple of movement passed through them. A man Sargon guessed to be their leader rode to the head of the column and held up his hand to halt his followers. His men slowed to a stop. None of those carrying bows bothered to string their weapons. For the moment, both parties stared at each other.

"They don't seem to fear us," Chinua said.

"Maybe they have never seen warriors before." Jennat, the second in command, rode at his commander's left.

"We could ride in and launch a few shafts at them."

That came from Skala. Sargon and Timmu, close enough to hear every word, glanced at each other.

"No, not yet." Chinua, still studying the strangers, paid no attention to Skala's words. "Subutai wants us to learn as much as we can about anyone found in these lands."

"We could send someone ahead to talk with them," Jennat said.

Skala snorted in disgust. "What is there to say to dirt eaters?"

"We could ask where they came from, where they're going." Jennat, too, ignored Skala's words.

Sargon listened to the leaders' conversation, but kept his eyes on the strangers. He noticed something, and edged his horse closer.

"Chinua . . . those men . . . I think they're soldiers."

Skala whirled to scowl at Sargon, but Chinua nodded agreement. "The boy is right. I've seen men like that before, in your father's army. What else do you see?"

"Ten bowmen, ten swordsmen, and eleven riders," Sargon said. "No women or children. In Akkad, that would be a strong scouting party."

"A scouting party with so many men on foot?" Chinua sounded dubious at that idea.

"Spearmen in my father's army can walk twenty miles in a day, carrying food and weapons."

"I don't see any sacks of food." Jennat had keen eyes, and obviously knew how to use them. "Look! One of them is riding away."

One of the distant horsemen turned his horse to the rear and rode off at an easy canter. The rest of the riders dismounted, and the men on foot settled on the ground, as if eager to take some rest. A moment later, the man who seemed to be the leader rode a few paces forward. He raised his right arm, and waved the Ur Nammu party forward.

"He wants to talk," Jennat said.

"He wants to draw us in close until more men can join them," Skala said.

Sargon glanced at Timmu, who smiled back. A moment ago, Skala wanted to charge the strangers. Now he worried about being attacked. Still, Sargon agreed with Skala's assessment.

"You may be right," Chinua said. "I'll ride ahead and see if I can talk to them."

Jennat shook his head. "No, you should not go. You are needed here, to return to Subutai with whatever we learn. I will meet with them."

Sargon saw the muscles on Chinua's shoulders tighten. But Jennat spoke the truth. If anything went wrong, better for the warriors to have Chinua in command. But the Ur Nammu commander didn't like it. Obviously the idea of sending Skala out to talk with the strangers never entered Chinua's head.

"Go, Jennat. But take care. At the first sign of trouble, come back."

"I will take care . . ."

"Chinua, I should go with him." Sargon uttered the words before he had time to think. "I know the ways of soldiers. I can even speak a few words in the trader's language."

All the warriors had been following their leaders' words. Now they glanced at Sargon in surprise, a horse boy who dared to give unasked for advice to a warrior.

"I promised your father that . . ."

"That life is over, Chinua," Sargon said. "Let me help you here."

Chinua glanced back toward the strangers. The leader still waved his arm every few moments. "Damn these strangers." He touched Jennat's arm. "Go. Take the boy with you. But watch out for trouble."

Jennat nodded. He lifted his right hand and returned the stranger's signal, sweeping his arm from side to side, until he felt certain that the man understood his acceptance. Jennat handed his bow and quiver to one of his men. Carrying a bow might seem too threatening. "Come, Sargon." He touched his heels to his horse and moved forward at a trot.

Sargon already regretted the impulse to volunteer, but he couldn't back down now, not in front of Skala and his son. Dumping his sacks and pots, Sargon kicked his horse forward and followed Jennat toward the west, staying on the warrior's left.

Jennat waited until they were out of earshot of the warriors. "So, challenging Skala wasn't enough for you? You should have kept silent. Never mind. What else do you see?"

Sargon had not had much contact with Jennat. He seemed young for a leader, about the same age as Chinua. But the man must have his wits about him. Otherwise, Chinua would not have chosen him as his second in command, over the older Skala.

As Sargon and Jennat drew closer to the interlopers, Sargon felt his heart racing. All those boring sessions with his father and the other soldiers now took on a different meaning. Suddenly Sargon realized his life might depend on what he did once they reached the strangers.

"If this is a scouting party," Sargon said, "then the main force must be close behind, or off to one side. I would guess no more than two or three miles away in any direction. And it must be a large force, to send so many men out as scouts. If they want to trap us, they will try to keep us occupied, keep our attention away from any reinforcements."

Sargon saw the lone rider that had ridden to the rear had already vanished from sight. The man could have put his horse to the gallop the moment he'd disappeared over the ridge line.

"Well, we'll know soon enough."

Jennat sounded unconcerned, and his air of calm helped steady Sargon's nerves.

"Maybe you should have kept your bow."

"One shaft against ten won't matter," Jennat said. "If I sense any danger, I'll raise my left hand, like this." He scratched his chest. "The moment I do, you run for it. Don't wait for my order, don't wait for anything. Understand?"

"Yes."

Sargon swallowed. Suddenly his throat felt dry as dust. The anger that had burned in him at Skala had vanished, a childish squabble. Now Sargon's hands felt weak, and his stomach churned within his belly. Bile rose up in his throat, and he swallowed hard.

They rode into a gulley and up the other side. The strangers were only a few hundred paces ahead.

Jennat slowed his horse, then halted about a hundred paces away. If the leader of these men wanted to talk, he could come forward.

Sargon breathed a breath of relief. For a moment he'd thought Jennat intended to ride right into their midst.

The leader, a burly man with scraggly brown hair, called out something to his men. Two men swung back onto their horses, and two others, each carrying an unstrung bow loosely in his left hand, moved forward. When they reached their commander, all five of them formed a line and moved forward together, with their leader in the center.

"Five against two. I don't like this." Despite his words, Jennat kept his face placid, as if unconcerned. "If there's trouble, the two horsemen will keep us busy until the bowmen can string their weapons and attack. If anything happens, don't try to turn and run. You'll never make it. Kick your horse forward, and try to run the bowmen down. As soon as you get past the archers, wheel your horse and run."

Jennat turned to Sargon, a smile on his face. "Trust to your horse, Sargon. He will know what to do."

Sargon's mouth opened, but he kept silent, swallowing hard again. The strangers had drawn within twenty paces, near enough to hear anything said. He resisted the urge to loosen the knife at his belt. The gesture would be seen and taken as a sign of weakness. Not that a knife would be much help against swords and bows.

He glanced at Jennat. The warrior sat erect on his horse, his face devoid of any emotion. Sargon tried to keep his own expression under control.

The five men approached, walking their horses, the leader now a single pace ahead of his men. He kept coming, and halted when his horse was only a few steps from Jennat's. The two bowmen stood on either side of their leader, with the two riders on either end of the line. Up close, Sargon saw the leader of the strangers had thick arms. He appeared to have about thirty seasons. Flashing a broad smile that revealed a missing front tooth, he eased himself back on his horse, then raised his hand and said something to Jennat.

Sargon didn't understand the words. He glimpsed the hilt of the man's sword, and saw a brightly-colored tassel dangling from it. Gleaming rings of gold encircled the forefinger of each hand, and a wide gold band glinted on his upper right arm. Either a man of wealth, or someone who had killed a lot of his enemies and looted their corpses.

The others stared at Jennat and him with smiles that were little more than bared teeth. Brutality had left its mark on their faces. These men were killers, and they would kill without the slightest hesitation.

Jennat didn't understand the man either. He shook his head, then lifted both hands to his shoulders, palms facing the strangers. "We meet in peace."

The stranger copied Jennat's gesture, but none of the others did. Sargon could guess why. The men carrying bows kept their right hands closed, and he realized they probably held bowstrings in their clenched fist. On foot, it would take them only a moment to string the weapon. Sargon realized Jennat had foreseen this. If Sargon tried to turn his horse around and run, it would take far too long. He'd have a shaft in his back before he covered twenty paces.

The exchange of words continued, the stranger trying another language before the burly leader settled on the trader's common dialect.

"I am Khnan," the man said, thumping his chest.

Sargon recognized the dialect, though the man's accent sounded odd to his ears. "I am Sargon." He pointed to his right. "Jennat. Leader"

Khnan gave Sargon a final glance before dismissing him as a mere translator, one not even old enough to carry a sword.

"Ask him where he's going in these lands," Jennat said.

Sargon translated, doing as best he could. After a second try, Khnan seemed to understand. He smiled at Jennat, an exaggerated gesture that looked anything but friendly.

"We come from Carchemish, the great city to the northwest. We have just defeated the Haranos, and now we claim all these lands as our own."

Sargon asked Khnan to repeat his words, then translated them for Jennat.

"Ask him why he wants this barren land," Jennat said. "And tell him that the Ur Nammu already claim all these lands to the east."

After hearing that, Khnan's smile grew even broader. "Not any more. Now King Shalmanisar rules these lands." He spoke slowly, slow enough to make sure Sargon understood. "Take your people and leave, or bow down and pay tribute to our king, if you don't want to be destroyed."

Sargon had to struggle to get that translated, but he repeated it to Jennat as best he could.

"Tell . . . Khnan that he will need many more men than thirty to take these lands from the Ur Nammu."

Khnan seemed to take no offense when Sargon repeated Jennat's words. "King Shalmanisar has many thousands of men. Any steppes warriors who dare to resist will be swept aside."

Jennat grunted when he heard that. "Tell him . . . tell him that we will carry his message to our leader."

Sargon doubted if that message would get them away from Khnan and his men without a fight. He thought of something else that might. "These lands are held by the Ur Nammu, but under the protection of the City of Akkad."

For the first time, the smile disappeared from Khnan's face as he stared at Sargon. "Akkad. I've heard of the city that sits in the fertile land between the rivers. Akkad is nothing to us. If they dare to challenge King Shalmanisar, their city and its people will be destroyed."

It took time to get the gist of that speech, and first Sargon told Jennat what he'd said to Khnan, then what the man's answer was.

"Tell him . . . tell him whatever you think."

Sargon wet his lips. "Akkad's walls are high and strong, and their warriors are as numerous as the blades of grass. Tell your King Shalmanisar to beware before he angers King Eskkar of Akkad."

A faint shout made Khnan glance over his shoulder. Sargon saw that the rider who had departed was returning, this time riding hard. Even from this distance Sargon could see that the sweat-covered horse labored at the rapid pace set by its master.

Khnan returned his attention to Jennat and Sargon. "Tell this king of a dung heap," he spat on the ground to show his contempt, "to hide behind his walls. If he dares to face us, he and his city of soft farmers will be destroyed."

Sargon opened his mouth to translate, but never got the words out. Khnan had taken a second look behind him. The approaching rider was shouting something, something that turned the heads of the rest of soldiers behind Khnan. The remaining strangers were already on their feet.

Jennat scratched his chest, and everything happened at once. He loosed a savage war cry that echoed over the land. At the same time, his horse burst into movement, charging straight ahead at the rider and bowman on Khnan's left. The speed of the attack, the last thing the strangers expected from a single fighter and a boy, caught the soldiers of Carchemish by surprise.

Jennat's sword, ripped from its scabbard in a blur of bronze, came down in the same motion. The blade struck the horse just to the right of Jennat across the forehead. At the same time, Jennat's mount crashed into the nearest bowman. The archer went down knocked backwards by Jennat's horse.

Khnan managed to get his jeweled sword out, but by then Jennat had whirled his blade around, and managed to slash Khnan's left arm before Jennat's horse burst past.

Sargon's horse understood the war cry far faster and better than its master. It, too, surged forward, almost without Sargon's urging, knocking down the second bowman and brushing past the mounted man on Khnan's right. The man's sword flashed just behind Sargon as he went by. Another instant and Sargon would have taken the blow.

By then Jennat had wheeled his horse around, and Sargon managed to do the same. Both of their horses were at a full gallop in a handful of strides, Jennat urging them on with another full war cry.

The rider Sargon had bumped against gave chase, but by the time he got his horse moving, Sargon and Jennat had covered twenty paces, and both horses were running flat out. Sargon glanced behind him, and saw that the rider would never catch them. But the bowmen had regained their feet. Both had strung their bows, and the first arrow flashed over Sargon's head.

"Separate!" Jennat guided his own horse to the side, so that the archers wouldn't have an easy target.

Sargon's horse caught the excitement, and they raced for the distant hilltop where Chinua had been. Sargon, clinging low to his horse's neck, kept urging the animal onward even as he guided the beast over the shortest distance. Meanwhile, he expected an arrow in his back at every stride. Looking ahead, he saw that the rest of the Ur Nammu warriors had charged forward, moving to provide help.

More arrows hissed by, and Sargon risked a glance to his rear. The horseman had given up, not wanting to be in line with the shafts that searched for the fast moving riders. Another arrow brushed past Sargon's arm, and hissed past his horse's neck. It served only to spur the animal to a faster pace, and by now Sargon had drawn ahead of Jennat.

Sargon realized Jennat had a shaft protruding from his left arm. However the distance had grown too great for the bows to be shot accurately, though Sargon knew a lucky arrow could still find them. He and Jennat charged into the gulley and urged the horses up the steep side. Sargon nearly lost his seat, and had to cling to the horse's neck for a handful of strides before he recovered.

A few more arrows landed around them, but then the mounts had regained their gallop and moved out of range. In moments they joined up with Chinua's men.

Pulling hard on the halter, Sargon managed to halt his horse before it raced past Chinua. By the time he dragged the animal around, Jennat had started reporting. Chinua listened, but his eyes remained to the west.

Jennat finished relating what had passed, and Sargon heard his name mentioned more than once. Chinua merely nodded. Whatever had been said really meant nothing now. "Here come the rest of them."

Sargon, his heart still beating rapidly, looked back toward the enemy. Two large bands of horsemen, at least forty or fifty men in each, had appeared over the farthest ridge. They weren't riding straight at Chinua's position, but angling off to the left and right. The ten horsemen with Khnan's group started toward them as well, coming straight for the Ur Nammu.

"They'll try and cut us off," Jennat said.

A warrior who acted as a healer reached Jennat's side. With a quick twist, he snapped the shaft in two, and jerked the pointed end from Jennat's arm. The wounded man flinched, but no sound escaped his lips. The healer, with another swift move, tugged a rag from his belt, passed it around Jennat's arm, and knotted it fast. Even before he finished the knot, blotches of blood seeped through the rag.

"We ride to the northeast," Chinua said, raising his voice so that everyone could hear. "Once we get out ahead of them, Jennat will take the horse boys and head straight for our camp, to tell Subutai what has happened and give him time to prepare."

"And what will we be doing?" Skala looked toward the two war parties closing in on them. Khnan's small force of horsemen was only a few hundred paces away.

"We are going to teach these invaders not to enter the lands of the Ur Nammu. Now, let's ride!"

The warriors burst into motion. Once again, Sargon found himself in the rear, and had to struggle to catch up with Timmu.

Sargon glanced over his shoulder. The northernmost band of enemy riders had already drawn within half a mile, and the course Chinua had set would soon shorten that distance. It would be close.

Sargon, riding as he'd never ridden before, suddenly realized that these men chasing after him would kill him if they could. It wouldn't matter to them that his father was Eskkar of Akkad. All it would take was one false step from his horse, a fall, even a lucky arrow shot high in the air, and Sargon would be dead or wounded. Chinua would leave him behind, just as he would leave any of his men behind who couldn't keep up.

"I don't want to go back to camp," Timmu shouted, as he rode at Sargon's side. "We should stay with the warriors."

"Keep quiet and ride!" Sargon focused his attention on guiding his horse, the only thing now keeping an arrow from finding his back.

They rode hard, pushing the horses to stay ahead of their pursuers. Once the distance between them shrank to less than a quarter mile. But by the time darkness approached, the superior horses of the Ur Nammu had lengthened the lead to nearly two miles. Sargon, still riding at the rear of

Chinua's men, kept glancing behind, and he was the first to see that the enemy had finally given up.

"Chinua! They've stopped!"

The Ur Nammu commander gave the order to rest, and he turned his mount around so that he sat beside Sargon, facing west. He stared for a long time at the tiny figures, more visible by the shadows they cast as the sun set.

"They had to ride hard to reach . . . what was the man's name?"

"Khnan. He said his name was Khnan from the city of Carchemish."

Jennat and Skala moved their horses beside their leader.

"I've never heard of such a place." Chinua sounded dubious.

"I have," Sargon answered. "It is a city at the end of the northern most trade routes, so far away that many do not even believe it exists. But the traders in Akkad assured my parents that it is indeed real."

"It is real enough now," Chinua said. "Jennat, how is your arm?"

"Just a scratch. I can still fight."

"Good. Take Sargon, Timmu, and Rutba with you when you ride for our camp. Sargon can help explain to Subutai . . ."

"No. I'm staying with you." Sargon resented the idea that Makko could stay with the warriors while he could not.

Skala muttered something under his breath. Sargon caught the words 'horse boy' but little else. The warrior clearly didn't approve of Sargon taking part in any discussions of the scouting party's leaders.

"You do not need to risk your life," Chinua said. "This is not your fight. And you can help Jennat explain what these invaders said."

"It is my fight," Sargon said. "They tried to kill me." He might have changed his mind and gone along with Chinua's order, but the frown on Skala's face only made Sargon more stubborn. "I mentioned Akkad to Khnan, and he said that my father's lands would also be destroyed. So now it is my fight as much as yours."

"Much as I would like him with me," Jennat said, "perhaps you should keep him with you. He may be of help, and he's young and foolish enough to be brave in the face of his enemies. He did well enough against Khnan."

All Sargon had done was cling to his horse's back. The animal deserved the credit for knocking the second bowman down. He'd forgotten all about his knife.

Chinua took a deep breath, and let it out. "You can stay. But now we ride. We still have plenty of ground to cover."

They started moving eastward again. This time they alternated between a trot and a fast walk. Sargon realized they had to keep the horses rested. If one of the horses faltered, the warrior would take the mount of one of the horse boys, leaving that unfortunate youth to fend for himself. In this case, that most likely meant capture and death.

The fall of night brought little relief. Chinua halted briefly to feed the horses, ordering that the last of the grain be given to them now. The warriors, too, wolfed down their food, eating as much as they could hold. The less they had to carry, the faster they could travel.

That attended to, the warriors huddled in a close packed circle. Chinua had ordered the horse boys to keep watch and guard the horses, but told Sargon to stay.

"Tell me everything that was said," Chinua said. "Everything."

Sargon went through the long talk, explaining how he translated the words, and adding what he thought of Khnan's reaction. A few raised their eyebrows when Sargon told of Akkad, but Chinua nodded. "That was good. Let them think that we are strong. The closer they come to the lands of Akkad, the more fearful they will become."

When Sargon finished, a few asked questions, but then everyone looked to Chinua.

"We will walk our horses through most of the night. In the morning, we will continue northeast. The enemy will send riders after us, at least for another day, or until they are satisfied that we are far away and running back to our camps. As soon as that happens, Jennat and the horse boys will break off and return as soon as possible to Subutai. We will swing to the north, and attack their camp tomorrow night. A raid on their horses should teach them a lesson."

Sargon had counted at least seventy or eighty riders in the party that pursued them, and wondered how Chinua could dare to attack so many. Or how they expected to get away if they did manage a successful attack. But none of the warriors showed the least concern. All of them had taken the insult when Sargon repeated Khnan's words. None wanted to return to Subutai's camp without striking some kind of blow.

"Then it is settled," Chinua said, glancing around the circle. "We will start walking now, and keep it up until at least midnight."

The warriors rose to fetch their horses.

"Sargon, stay." Chinua moved beside him. With the others gone, they could speak in private. "If you wish to return to the camp tomorrow with Jennat, no one will think less of you. And I'm sure that after this, Subutai will release you from the remaining days of your training. You would be free to go home, or anywhere that you choose."

"I understand."

He did. Chinua was right. None of the warriors would think less of him. They took it as a fact that no dirt eater could show as much bravery, or ride and fight as well as they could. Sargon remembered Skala's eyes on him, and the memory hardened Sargon's resolve. He intended to show that big ox that the men of Akkad could fight as well as any barbarian.

23

The middle of the night arrived before Chinua called a halt. Glancing around, Sargon saw nothing but the same terrain he'd seen all day – rocks and sand, with scattered clumps of grass. Presumably Chinua wanted to stop where the horses could graze. They hadn't come across any water, so the troop faced another dry camp.

By then Sargon felt almost weary enough to change his mind and ask Chinua to let him ride for Subutai's camp. Despite all his recent weapons training and horse riding, nothing had prepared him for a long walk through the darkness while leading a horse. Traveling on foot, it seemed, was one skill that held little interest for the Ur Nammu, especially when it required them to walk their horses through half the night.

Nevertheless, it had to be done. And while Sargon knew the others felt as worn out, none of the warriors complained. The walking was exhausting enough, but each man had to walk ahead of his horse and lead the animal, which meant that you had to keep your eyes moving and watch every step.

The moon had risen early, but dark clouds obscured what little light it cast. Luckily, none of the horses stepped into a hole or bruised a knee, though half the warriors went down more than once, cursing the darkness or the occasional slippery smoothness of some stone underfoot.

Even after they stopped for the night, Sargon still had to care for his horse, and keep the animal safe and close at hand. Sentries took turns guarding their position until dawn, and Sargon breathed a sigh of relief when that duty fell to others. He wrapped himself in the sweaty horse blanket and fell asleep beneath the chilly stars.

When the morning sun lifted above the horizon, a footsore and weary band of warriors took stock of their situation. But nothing showed on the horizon, and Sargon guessed that the soldiers of Carchemish remained far behind.

That could change at any moment, so Chinua gave the orders and they started walking and leading the horses once again. Only when the sun pushed itself well above the horizon, and the muscles of both man and beast had stretched themselves out, did they mount and start riding, always going to the northeast. Between riding and walking, they covered over twenty miles before midday.

By then the warriors' sandals were in ruins from the hard ground or loose shale underfoot, and despite frequent attempts at repair, at least half the men were barefoot. Sargons's sandals, still fairly new, were in better condition, but even he had to retie broken laces twice. While the horses looked in better shape than their riders, Sargon saw his own mount's head start to sag.

"We'll stop here," Chinua called out, glancing up at the sun.

They'd reached the top of a long incline, and had a good view of the land behind them. Sargon studied the terrain they'd traversed, but saw no signs of life, only grass, juniper and hawthorn bushes, rocks, and the occasional tree. Birds flew across the blue sky, and a red-tailed hawk circled lazily above, but Sargon saw no game or animals of any kind. Chinua ordered Garal and another warrior to scan the horizon and search for signs of pursuit from the west.

The rest of the warriors tied their horses to some low juniper bushes that dotted the slope, and stretched out on the ground. More than a few started snoring within moments. For men who spent most of their lives on the back of a horse, walking such distances meant a real hardship. The youngest warriors, like Garal and even Sargon, were in better shape.

Chinua told the others to rest, and Sargon stretched out on the hard ground and fell asleep. It seemed he'd scarcely closed his eyes before

Chinua's voice roused him. Still, Sargon saw the sun had moved a few hands width across the sky, so he'd gotten more rest than he'd expected.

"Everyone, wake up and gather around." Chinua ignored the yawns of his men. He waited until he had every man's attention.

"Even if the enemy doesn't pursue us in force, they will send scouts to see which way we've gone. We must lead them on a false trail to the northeast. Meanwhile, Jennat will leave us soon. I can see a hard patch of ground about a half a mile ahead. Jennat, Timmu, and Rutba will turn off there and head for home. The passage of a few horses and men on foot should be easy to hide from any following our trail. The rest of us will continue northeast for another few miles. Hopefully, they will think our camp is in that direction."

One of the younger warriors spoke up. "We could ambush any one tracking us."

Chinua shook his head at the suggestion. "There is not much cover, and they will be wary. They're not likely to just stumble into any trap we can set. And what if there are ten or even twenty of them? We might end up fighting for our lives with nothing to gain."

When Sargon first heard the youth's suggestion, Sargon thought it sounded like a good idea. Now it sounded foolish. Which was why Chinua was leading them, and not any of the others.

"Sargon thinks there might have been a larger group of men to the north of those we met yesterday. I believe Sargon is right."

Chinua waited a moment, in case anyone wanted to challenge the assumption. "The men who came to aid Khnan's force came from that direction. If there is such a force, and it moves in this direction, we should now be even with it, or a little farther north. Soon we'll swing due north, toward the mountains, before we double back along the foothills."

Chinua grinned. "We'll be moving toward each other, but if we stay close to the foothills, we are not likely to encounter any of their scouts. They will have all their eyes searching east and south. With luck we can close within striking distance of their next camp before dawn."

Sargon wanted to ask what would happen if the enemy stumbled onto them, but no one else raised the question, so he kept silent. Besides, he'd had his chance to return to Subutai's camp with Jennat and the others. Sargon's determination to show as much courage as Chinua and his men hadn't wavered. Where these men could go, Sargon would follow, even if they all ended up dead.

Chinua waited to make sure no one had any questions. "Good. Sargon, Makko, each of you fill a sack with fresh horse dung. Bring them with us. Let's get moving."

Makko looked as confused at the order as Sargon, but neither dared to question a direct order.

Empty food sacks were quickly filled with horse droppings, and Sargon could not help asking. "Do you know what this is for?"

It was the first time he'd spoken to Skala's son in days.

"No. But it must be important. We'll know soon enough."

They mounted their horses and rode out at a slow pace, but soon enough reached a rocky escarpment that led to the southeast. Jennat and the horse boys moved to the front. They dismounted and led their horses onto the rocky ground.

Sargon watched as Jennat handed his horse off to Rutba, and the second in command made sure that the hard ground showed no trace of their branching off from the main party. Jennat gave a final wave to the others as they passed by. Sargon wondered if he would ever see Timmu or the warrior again.

Chinua kept moving. He wanted to get at least another mile past the place where Jennat turned away. Chinua had to travel much farther, however, before he found a rocky shelf that he liked. He led the horses onto it, and kept them going for another quarter mile before Chinua gave the signal to halt and told the men to dismount.

"Garal! Take the sacks and make a trail to the northeast. Scatter one sack by that big rock, and the second a few hundred paces further on." Garal swung down from his mount and strode back to where Sargon and Makko waited. Garal handed his horse to Sargon, then took both sacks and trotted away.

"Skala, take Sargon and Makko and lead the way on foot. I'll clean up any sign that we've changed direction."

Obviously Chinua didn't trust either horse boy to not leave any sign of their passing. Sargon moved to the head of the group, just behind Skala, who guided the band now toward the northwest. Chinua and two other warriors walked behind, making sure no horse droppings fell where they could be seen, and that no hoof marks left any impression that might be spotted by anyone tracking them.

If any pursuers followed the warriors onto the rocky shelf, they would see the horse droppings up ahead, and, hopefully, believe the riders had continued their flight to the northeast.

The warriors moved slowly over the next quarter mile. At last Garal, breathing hard from his long run, rejoined them. When they swung behind a low ridge, Chinua gave the order to mount up, and the Ur Nammu scouting party, now reduced from eighteen to fifteen, changed direction and headed toward the northwest.

To Sargon's surprise, Chinua set a rapid pace, and the miles passed quickly. The ridges provided cover from anyone on the lower slopes, though Chinua dismounted and studied each gap that they had to pass through to make sure it would not reveal their presence. Once again they alternated between riding the horses and running alongside.

Gradually Chinua shifted their direction, climbing ever higher into the foothills, until they rode almost due west. The late afternoon sun now shone in their faces, and it would be dark soon.

Sargon's feet had blistered, after his sandals had finally given out. By then everyone was barefoot. Chinua halted just before the sun set. He didn't need to tell them to rest, as every man sank to the ground as soon as he'd looked after his horse.

Sargon, his legs stretched out before him, sprawled beside Garal. No one questioned his right, or Makko's either, to sit with the warriors now. All of them were going into battle, and the youngest boys had been sent home. They watched as Chinua went to scan the countryside below, taking Skala with him.

They were gone a long time, and dusk cloaked the hills before they returned.

"They've found something." Garal jostled Sargon with his elbow. Sargon saw a trace of excitement on Skala's face.

Sargon wasn't the only one who had to be prodded into wakefulness. Soon every eye was on Chinua as he dropped to the ground. The warriors crowded around, eager to learn what their leader had seen.

"We saw riders, we counted twelve, riding west," Chinua said. "They were moving fast, as if anxious to rejoin the rest of their men before darkness fell. They may have been tracking us, and turned back when they lost the trail. That might mean the main party is drawing close."

One of the warriors asked the question. "How far away do you think they are?"

To Sargon's surprise, Chinua turned to Skala. The warrior accepted the compliment, and answered the question.

"No more than five or six miles. They won't want to risk the horses by riding far after dark."

Sargon saw the glint of teeth in the gathering darkness as some of the warriors smiled. He didn't understand the reaction. Chinua noticed Sargon's confusion.

"It means, Sargon, that the enemy's night camp is not too far away. It also means that we can set an easy pace as we move closer, and pick the time for our attack."

"How many men do you think will be at the camp?" For once Sargon couldn't keep his curiosity inside.

"It doesn't matter how many there are, if we can catch them by surprise." Chinua glanced up at the darkness. Just enough light remained to let him scratch a few lines in the dirt. "Here's what we're going to do."

Sargon leaned closer and listened as Chinua told them what he intended. To Sargon's ears it sounded reckless in its daring, quite unlike the meticulous preparations made by his father and his commanders in the Map Room. Sargon had sat through many of those tedious sessions, listening while Eskkar, Bantor, and the others labored over details of possible assaults from or attacks on the other cities in the Land Between the Rivers.

Compared to his father's efforts, Chinua's didn't sound like much of a plan, but Sargon understood that the details needed to be filled in, and that could only happen when they reached the Carchemish camp. Even so, all the warriors crowded around Chinua and Skala nodded agreement, and Sargon realized this handful of men had just committed themselves to raiding an enemy whose size, force, and exact location remained unknown.

After Chinua finished, he gave his warriors little rest. He wanted to have as much time as he needed getting into position.

Once again the warriors moved out on foot, walking the horses single file through the gathering darkness. As before, a slip or fall for a warrior might mean being left behind, so everyone took care. This time, however, Sargon noticed that Chinua wasn't quite as concerned for the horses. Obviously he expected to find plenty of mounts at the enemy's camp.

The surface beneath their feet was mostly smooth rock washed clean by wind and rain coming off the mountains, with tufts of hardy grass sprouting wherever pockets of dirt had accumulated. Chinua didn't lead them on a straight line, but followed any ravine or sheltered hill that provided cover.

Why that was necessary after dark, Sargon didn't understand, but no one raised the issue. Like the others, he kept his eyes on the ground, until he heard the soft spoken order to halt.

Sargon took the opportunity to ease his aching feet. The darkness hid the cuts and scrapes that covered them.

Skala came down the line, explaining in a soft whisper why they stopped. "Chinua saw a glow up ahead. It may be the fools still have a campfire burning." Sargon and Makko received the message last, since they brought up the rear.

"They must have plenty of wood to burn a fire so late into the night." Garal had chosen to walk just ahead of Sargon, either out of concern for his pupil, or to keep a close watch on the untried dirt eater and make sure he didn't do anything foolish. "Isn't that unusual, even for soldiers?"

"If soldiers think they might be attacked at night," Sargon answered, "they might want to have enough light to find their weapons and form a battle line."

"A fire will make it all the better for us," Garal said. "Now, we must stay silent."

Chinua returned from his brief scouting. "It's them, about a mile and a half away. They've two watch fires going."

Sargon climbed to his feet once again, as Chinua ordered the troop to move out. They mounted their horses, but kept the pace at a slow walk, giving the animals plenty of time to choose their footing.

To Sargon's ears, the hooves of their horses sounded as loud as if they were at a gallop, but the ridges no doubt blocked the noise. He worried about what might happen if the horses started whinnying, and the enemy's horses answered them. Chinua had already warned everyone to be ready to clamp a hand over any offending nose until it calmed down. The fact that the horses were more than a little weary made them easier to handle.

At last Chinua gave the order to halt beside a wide swath of dirt and sand that had sprouted a few clumps of grass, and each of the warriors eased his mount to a stop. Chinua dropped to the ground, and rolled around in the gritty mixture, then yanked out a clump of grass and rubbed it over his face, arms, feet, and hands. One by one, the warriors imitated their leader.

"Why are we doing this?" Sargon whispered to Garal as they waited their turn.

"The smell of the earth will help mask our scent from the enemy horses. If we smell like dirt and grass, we may be able to get a few steps closer before they take notice. And we'll be harder to see in the moonlight, too."

Garal pushed Sargon ahead, and made sure his pupil covered himself completely. They remounted and continued riding for another few hundred paces, staying in the lee of a rocky outcropping. At last Chinua swung down from his horse, the men following his example.

"Skala, come with me. The rest of you, wait here until I send for you." Chinua left them behind, as he and Skala worked their way to the top of the ridge that concealed their approach.

The two leaders disappeared from sight. Chinua must be studying the enemy's camp. Or at least that's what Sargon assumed they would be looking at, though he wasn't sure how much they could see in the dark. Sargon stood beside his horse, his arm resting on the animal's shoulder. Even so, he always kept the halter rope gripped firmly in his hand.

Time passed, and Sargon sensed the men getting restless. At last Skala returned.

"Chinua wants every man to see the enemy camp. Two at a time, go up to the crest. Chinua will tell you what to do."

Sargon and Garal were the last to go. They worked their way up through the rocks. Just before Sargon reached the top, Chinua called down in a soft voice, telling them to crawl the final few paces. Sargon and Garal obeyed, and on hands and knees, they crawled up the last part of the slope. When Sargon reached the crest, he was surprised to find that he could see the enemy camp quite well in the moonlight, and what he saw gave him a shock.

The camp was more than big. It was huge, and stretched out along a narrow stream that flowed down from the hills. Sargon could see the path of water glistening in the moonlight. Two small watch fires burned, and they were well apart from each other. He glimpsed a sentry walking around, but the camp itself seemed quiet enough. These soldiers from Carchemish obviously weren't expecting an attack.

The horse herd, held between the stream and the extended camp, was far more numerous than Sargon expected. He guessed at least a hundred horses, perhaps more, were packed into what must be a rope corral, though he couldn't see what restrained them. "So many horses!"

Garal, lying beside Sargon, grunted in satisfaction. "The fools put the horses closest to the stream and the mountain, to make sure no one can sneak in and steal any. That makes it easier for us. They don't expect anyone come at them from the mountain side of the stream."

"There must be three or four hundred men out there," Sargon whispered.

"Probably more." Chinua kept his voice low, but didn't bother to whisper. They were too far away to be heard. "But most of them are foot soldiers, not mounted fighters. Once we get to the horses, all we need to worry about are how many horsemen will take up the pursuit."

The idea of the raid, which had seemed risky enough at dusk, now appeared to Sargon like madness itself. How could fifteen men challenge so many. He turned his head toward the moon, which had started to drift lower in the night sky. Dawn would be coming soon.

"This is what we will do," Chinua said.

In a few words, he explained how they would attack, what position each man would take, and how far apart they would stand. Chinua told Sargon what role he would play in the coming raid, where he would wait, and when he would move forward. Chinua made Sargon repeat his instructions, to make sure he understood.

Sargon listened as Garal received his orders, which were much different. Chinua spoke to each of them, until he was satisfied that both knew what to do. To Sargon's ears, the plan seemed hasty and ill-advised. He glanced at Garal, who showed no doubts about his leader's plan of attack.

After one last look at the enemy camp, Chinua led the way back down the slope, until they joined the others.

As soon as Sargon reached his horse, Skala drew both horse boys aside. Sargon expected to be ignored, but the warrior spent as much time with Sargon as he did with his own son, going over once again what they were to do. "If anything unexpected happens, Sargon, do as Makko tells you. Otherwise, both of you know what to do."

With a grunt, Skala moved off to attend to his own preparations.

Garal came over and wished both boys good hunting, the usual words spoken by warriors before going into battle.

"I wish I were going with you," Sargon said. He half believed the words himself. Part of him did want to go with Garal, but another part insisted that they were all going to their deaths.

"Someone has to stay with the horses," Garal said. "We're going to need them. Remember your orders."

Chinua gave his men a last few instructions, then he slipped away into the semi-darkness, crouching low. The warriors had spotted three sentries strolling carelessly around the horse herd, but there could easily be more. One was directly between the warriors and the horses, and another about a hundred paces to the east. The third one patrolled near the west end of the herd, and appeared too far away to hinder the warriors.

"I'll kill the closest sentry," Chinua said. "Garal will kill the easternmost one as soon as the attack starts. Good hunting to you all." Bow in hand, Chinua started up the slope, Garal following a few moments later.

Chinua obviously considered Garal the best archer in the troop, Sargon decided, to have selected him for the task. Sargon and Makko collected the horses, and made sure they had a firm grip on every halter.

Skala and the rest of the men waited just below the crest of the ridge line, watching to see if Chinua succeeded in killing the sentry without raising an alarm.

To Sargon, the waiting seemed endless. Then suddenly Skala moved back down the ridge and took the halter of his horse in his hand. "It's done," he said in a loud whisper. "Bowmen, get moving."

Six warriors, one by one, slipped over the top of the ridge and headed down the slope to follow the path Chinua and Garal had taken. Sargon watched them go, moving like spirits into the darkness, and making as little noise.

Skala and his four warriors stood patiently beside their mounts, just below the crest.

Sargon and Makko took their own positions. Between them, they held the halters of the ten remaining horses, including their own. The task of the horse boys was to bring those horses down the slope and hold them in readiness until Chinua and his men needed them.

"Remember to keep a tight grip on the ropes," Makko warned. "Don't let any get loose."

Sargon heard the nervousness in Makko's voice. This would be his first battle, too. Sargon tried to control his own fears. His hands felt sweaty, and he kept adjusting his grip on the halter ropes. He had trouble swallowing, and took some deep breaths to try and calm himself.

Some time passed before Skala gave the order to move out. The big warrior grunted and led the way up the slope and over the crest. Sargon saw that Skala's right hand held the halter rope of his mount just below the horse's head. That kept the animal's head down, and made it less likely to try and bolt.

Following him went the four warriors considered the best horsemen. Their job was to stampede the enemy's herd, and at the same time, cut out enough animals for the Ur Nammu to use to make good their escape. Without fresh horses, they would never be able to outrun any pursuers.

Suddenly, Sargon and Makko found themselves alone at the bottom of the gulley with the horses, all the warriors gone. The boys had no weapons, except for their knives, which weren't likely to be of much use against a sword.

Obviously Chinua didn't expect them to do any actual fighting. They stood there, each holding the halters of five horses. Makko and Sargon were to wait until the others reached their positions before bringing up the horses.

The time dragged on, and Sargon felt his heart racing in his chest. He heard Makko's rapid breathing. Both tried to conceal their fears.

"Let's go," Makko said at last. "And try to keep the horses quiet."

He moved up the slope at an easy pace, following the path taken by Skala. Sargon let Makko get a few paces ahead, then started after him. He walked between the animals, two on his left and three on his right, the halter ropes clutched firmly in each hand.

Sargon had never tried to lead five horses before, and he found it took all his strength to keep them close together and moving forward. He whispered to them as he walked, trying to keep them calm. Sargon made sure he followed in Makko's path. Sargon's horses would be less nervous trailing another group of animals.

They crossed over the crest and traveled about fifty paces toward the enemy camp before Makko halted. Sargon stopped when Makko did. He knew they didn't need to get too close as yet.

The enemy camp was only about two hundred paces away, just across the stream. To Sargon's ears, the ten horses they were leading made a noisy din that should have sounded an alarm inside the camp.

However, at night horses are always moving about, and the occasional soft sound of hoof on rock was no different from what the animals in the corral would make. At this distance, only the sentries might hear their approach, and they should all be dead by now.

Sargon felt as exposed as if the noon sun was shining down on him. But when he glanced behind him, he realized the black bulk of the mountain made the small number of Ur Nammu horses almost impossible to see.

His mouth felt dry, though he, like the others, had emptied their water skins before starting out. Every horse had received a few mouthfuls of water as well. The stream ran along the edge of the camp, too close to be of any use to Chinua's men. If they survived, Sargon had no idea when he or any of the others would get a chance to drink again.

A few horses in the enemy corral whinnied, not the sound of frightened animals, but just the usual sound any horse might make when it sensed something strange coming toward it. But no one seemed to take any notice.

Looking toward the enemy camp, Sargon glimpsed Chinua's men creeping along, their bows held low in their left hands. Skala's men had angled toward the right, so as to be better positioned to stampede the horses.

Before they set out, Skala had distributed most of his men's arrows among Chinua's warriors, leaving himself and his four men only a few shafts apiece in their quivers. Skala's attack force wouldn't need the arrows, while Chinua's men would need every one they could get.

The enemy camp slept on, unaware of the warriors' approach. Then Sargon heard a man's voice shouting something unintelligible from the other side of the corral. Someone must have seen or heard something.

Off to his right, Sargon glimpsed the shadowy bulk of Skala as he swung up onto his horse. He waited only a moment for his men to follow his action, then he launched the attack. By then the five Ur Nammu riders had closed to within a hundred paces from the herd.

Shouting their frightening war cries, Skala and his riders splashed across the stream and charged into the corral. The single strand of rope burst under the stress of Skala's mount, and then the warriors were deep in the midst of the horse herd.

Sargon saw the warriors' swords flashing in the night, rising and falling, their edges glinting in the dim light of the nearest campfire. Skala's men never stopped sounding their war cries or attacking the horses. To the sleeping Carchemishi, Skala's handful of men probably sounded like a hundred.

The horses screamed in pain, as the swords cut into their bodies. Not killing strokes, but slashing cuts meant to wound and frighten the suddenly aroused brutes.

Sargon's string of animals reacted as well, tossing their heads and pawing the ground. The animals had caught the excitement. He found himself fighting with all his strength to hold onto the halters. With the need for silence gone, Sargon spoke aloud the calming words Garal had taught him, as he struggled to keep the animals under control.

Makko, too, had the same problem, though he mixed a few curses in with his attempts to keep his string from breaking loose. With a savage jerk from Makko's left hand, he brought the most troublesome mount under control. "Follow me, Sargon." Makko started walking down the slope and toward the camp.

Sargon did the same, and found the animals much easier to handle when he led them forward. The dumb brutes wanted to be doing something, and they always felt safe when a warrior guided them, especially following in the track of more horses. Besides, the ululating war cries of the warriors was a familiar sound to them. Still, Sargon's hands burned from the ropes, and he kept his grip tight. He would not let one horse escape no matter what.

Moving forward gave him a better view of the chaos in the enemy camp. Sargon saw Chinua and his seven warriors spread out in a line, each about ten paces apart. They were calmly shooting arrows into the camp, shooting at every good target, and especially anyone who appeared to be trying to get the soldiers under control.

Sargon saw that this was far easier than any target practice he'd taken. Chinua's men were practically at the edge of the stream, and they were striking at targets less than twenty or thirty paces from them.

The horses, driven mad with fear or pain, had burst through the far side of their rope corral and into the camp, trampling or knocking aside anything in their path. Nothing could halt the terrified animals now, and they swept through the camp, heedless of anyone in their path. If the enemy noticed the handful of warriors urging them on, it didn't really matter. Before they could react, the horses had vanished into the darkness on the far side of the camp.

Inside what remained of the camp, pandemonium ruled. Jerked awake from a sound sleep, many enemy soldiers were caught in the path of the stampeding horses, their hooves pounding into the earth. Everyone seemed to be shouting at someone. Others fumbled for their weapons, but no alarm had been given, and at first some weren't sure they were under attack.

When they realized that arrows were cutting them down, they found themselves unable to see their attackers, who shot at them from the darkness. The looming shadow of the mountain still served its purpose even this close to the camp.

One of the Carchemish soldiers near the campfire tossed an armful of dry grass on the nearest watch fire. The flames shot up, and Sargon realized that a pile of combustible grass and twigs had been prepared for an emergency. But this time it worked only in favor of the Ur Nammu, revealing the men in the camp stumbling about as they tried to comprehend what had happened. Chinua's bowmen had even better light to shoot by.

Sargon realized most of the enemy soldiers not yet fully grasped the situation. Their first thoughts were of a stampede. Only when they heard the war cries and saw their companions dropping with arrows in their chests did they realize they were under attack.

Chinua and his men shot every arrow in their quiver with their usual speed, aiming each shot with care. With the extra shafts from Skala's men, that meant about twenty to twenty-five arrows from each warrior. Knowing how fast a warrior could loose a missile, Sargon did the sum. Probably two hundred and twenty arrows were launched, in less time than a man could count to eighty.

The horses were long gone by then, the entire herd driven right through the camp. Sargon never heard Chinua's signal, but suddenly Makko trotted forward, dragging his string of mounts, and Sargon followed. Now arrows were flying from the camp into the darkness, as a few of the enemy soldiers finally realized they were under attack and brought their weapons into action.

But they were shooting at shadows and noises. Chinua's men had already fallen back, racing toward Sargon and Makko. Sargon heard the frightening hiss of arrows overhead, but none landed near him.

Then hands were grasping the halter ropes from Sargon's grip. A few warriors found time to laugh among themselves as they swung onto their mounts. As soon as he handed off the last halter, Sargon jumped astride his own horse, clinging tight to the animal's mane.

Chinua led the way, as the warriors galloped off to the east. Sargon saw the first rays of dawn reaching up into the sky, giving the horses a chance to pick their way.

In moments they had left the carnage behind them, though the din of shouting men and the cries of the wounded could still be heard. Less than quarter of a mile from the camp, they slowed to cross the stream. A rumble of hoof beats sounded to their right and Sargon caught sight of a shadowy herd of horses galloping in the same direction, at least thirty or forty animals.

Skala moved up in Sargon's estimation. He would never have believed that five riders could control so many half-crazed animals in the dark.

"Skala did well."

Sargon turned to find Garal riding beside him, the warrior's white teeth gleaming in the growing dawn. With a shock, Sargon realized that Garal continued to keep an eye on him.

Up ahead, Chinua slowed their pace, and spoke to each of the men in his band. Only one warrior had taken a wound, an arrow that had grazed his neck. By now they were over a mile from the camp. Chinua shouted out the order to halt, and the healer moved up to wrap a strip of cloth around the wounded man's throat.

No one bothered to dismount. Excitement rippled through their ranks. They had raided a much larger force and not lost a single man.

Sargon watched as Skala and the stolen herd moved ahead. The warrior would let the animals run until they grew tired. Then they would be easier to control.

"How soon before they start after us?"

Garal laughed, as jubilant as the others. "Not long. But first they'll have to recapture some horses."

"With so many men, that won't take too long."

"Oh, yes, we're in for a hard chase and a long ride. But with the mounts Skala stole, we should each be able to ride two or three horses. We'll keep ahead of them."

Chinua shouted out the order to get moving. The sun had risen, and now the horses could see their footing clearly. Chinua followed the course taken by Skala's horses.

Just before they rode out of sight of the enemy camp, Sargon took one last look back. No one pursued them. Not yet. But he knew the Carchemishi were going to be very angry, and they had a large force of fighters, far more men than the Ur Nammu. Sargon wondered what Subutai would do when he heard the news.

24

Three days later, a little after midafternoon, Chinua's war party rode over the crest of a hill and saw the Ur Nammu camp below. Sargon eased his horse to a stop, as Chinua halted the party for a few moments, to give each man a chance to enjoy the sight of home. Every man, gaunt, hungry, and dog tired, breathed a sigh of relief. They had pushed the horses as hard as they could each day.

On the return journey, Sargon had acquired a new skill, riding one horse while leading two more. During the return, each warrior alternated among the horses, enabling them to cover the ground at a rapid pace. Unless their pursuers did the same, no one was going to catch up with them.

On today's ride, they twice encountered Ur Nammu scouts, three-man parties patrolling the western approaches to the camp.

"That means," Garal said, "that Jennat made it back, too."

"So Subutai knows about the Carchemishi," Sargon agreed. "But he doesn't know how many of them there are."

Chinua's shout interrupted their talk. "Make sure you ride into camp like warriors, not women!" He started down the slope, and the others followed. As Chinua urged his horse to a canter, he called back over his shoulder. "And try not to fall asleep before we reach the camp."

Sargon saw the warriors straighten up, raising their heads and shoulders. No one wanted to display any weakness in front of the other warriors, or even their own women.

As they reached the outskirts of the camp, people emerged from tents to greet them. Excited children ran toward the approaching horsemen. Sargon understood Ur Nammu customs by now. After a successful raid, Chinua and his warriors had fought an enemy and brought home thirty-four new horses as proof of their courage and skill, and all without losing a man. Once again, he had proven himself a strong war chief.

As Chinua led the way into the camp, the shouting crowd soon slowed his progress. Men, women and children rushed to greet their returning men. Eager hands reached up to touch their kin, and others relieved the grinning riders of their extra horses.

Sargon trailed the others into the camp, and, of course, none of the waiting crowd paid him any attention. The rest of the party merged back among the tents, surrounded by a press of happy friends and family, all grateful for their safe return. As the throng cleared away, Sargon noticed someone standing alone, her eyes fixed on him. Tashanella. She, too, had come to meet the returning warriors.

Since all the others had already moved into the camp, Tashanella obviously had waited for no particular man. Instead, she met Sargon's eyes as he rode past. Then she turned and disappeared among the throng.

Too weary to think about what it meant, Sargon soon reached Chinua's tent and swung down from his mount. Two grinning boys darted to his side and took charge of his two horses. For once, Sargon was spared the need to care for the weary animals.

His horses. Earned by his own hand, and as far as the Ur Nammu were concerned, the mark of a true warrior. Horses meant status in the clan, even more than women or other possessions. The more horses a warrior owned, the more successful he must be as a warrior. No word of praise Sargon had ever received in Akkad meant as much to him.

Sargon paced his way to the stream. Some of the men he'd ridden with were already there, washing the horse stink from their bodies before returning to their tents. He didn't want to get in the way of the happy reunions, so he headed farther upstream, where he could find a bit more privacy. With a loud sigh of relief, he plunged into the cool waters without bothering to remove the remaining shreds of his once fine clothing.

For a time, Sargon just clung to a rock and let the stream wash over him. The sensation of not having anything to do provided a suitably guilty feeling of pleasure.

Suddenly the water exploded beside him, sending a wave across his face and almost knocking him loose from the rock. It was Makko, who had jumped naked into the water with a mighty splash. Sargon had to laugh at the sight of his fellow horse boy splashing his way through the stream.

Unlike most of the Ur Nammu, Sargon had learned to swim in the deeper waters of the Tigris at an early age. His father had taken him down to the river almost every day, and by the time he reached his twelfth season, Sargon could swim all the way across the great river.

"You swim like a great boulder dropped in a small pond," Sargon said.

"Better that than riding like a sack of grain," Makko gasped, spitting water from his mouth.

It wasn't much of a joke, but Sargon knew Makko meant well by it.

During the return ride, the two had put aside their differences. As horse boys, they still had to care for the horses, and both quickly realized that they had to work together. The night after the raid on the Carchemishi, Skala, Makko's father, announced himself pleased with Sargon's work with the mounts. That, Sargon decided, was the most apology he was going to get from the warrior.

Later Sargon asked Garal if Chinua had said something to Skala about the incident, but Garal shook his head.

"Skala is proud of what his son accomplished during our journey. That means he must give you the same respect. And once warriors have fought together as we have, there is always a bond that will keep them true to each other."

"I didn't do any fighting."

"Neither did you run and hide, or lose the horses, or not be where you were supposed to be. Every man in a battle has to do as he's ordered. If you and Makko hadn't been with us, two other warriors would have taken your place, and there would have been that many fewer arrows to harry the Carchemishi."

With another torrent of water, Makko splashed his way out of the stream. "Stop by our tent later if you can. They'll be plenty of meat tonight."

Sargon said he would try, and ducked his head back underneath the water. When he finally came up for air, Makko had disappeared back into the camp, and Sargon had the stream to himself. He rose and stripped off the remnants of his tunic. His undergarment followed. He'd worn it continuously for nine days of hard riding, and it stank of horse sweat and worse. Sargon tossed it aside. He didn't intend to wear it again.

He did use what was left of his tunic to scrub his body down, scraping away the dirt, grime, and odor of horseflesh that clung persistently to his body. As he washed, Sargon found bruises on his arms and chest, scrapes on his legs, along with burn marks on his arms and calluses on his hands from constantly holding halter ropes for the last three days.

When he felt sufficiently cleansed, Sargon crawled up on a wide ledge that bordered the stream. The sun had warmed the rock, and he lay down on it and stretched his legs, enjoying the sensation as his naked body dried in the breeze. The sound of laughter from the camp floated over the stream, but he ignored it, content to be by himself.

He thanked Ishtar that the ride had ended when it did. Sargon wasn't sure he could have kept up with the others for much longer. With that thought in mind, he flung his arm over his eyes to shield them from the sunlight. The sounds of the stream soothed his thoughts. A few deep breaths later, he fell asleep, the water gurgling in his ears.

"Sargon. Sargon. Wake up."

The voice pulled him back from the well of deep slumber. He forced his eyes open, only to be blinded by the sun that caught him full in the face. Something moved beside him, and then a shadow passed over his eyes, and he could see again. Someone stood over him, shielding him from the sun. Then he recognized Tashanella's voice.

—◦◦◦—

Tashanella gazed down at the naked figure at her feet, her eyes drawn to the boy's member peeking out from beneath a crown of soft brown hair. Since his first day in camp, she thought him the most handsome boy she'd ever seen. The urge to touch his bare flesh swept over her, and she felt a burst of warmth from her own loins. She dropped to her knees beside him, but still kept his face sheltered from the setting sun.

Another urge tempted her, to reach out and caress his member. She did not, of course.

"You should not lie out like that in the sun. You'll burn your skin."

Sargon's eyes focused on her face. "What . . . what do you want?"

His voice sounded thick in his ears, and Sargon knew his thoughts were muddled and slow. "I've come to bring you to my father's tent," Tashanella went on. "He wants to speak with you before tonight's feasting begins."

Propping himself up on one arm, Sargon gazed at the girl's face. It had changed somehow, no longer the face of a child, but that of a young woman. Her voice set his thoughts racing, and he could not keep his eyes from the breasts that swelled against her dress as Tashanella leaned over him.

A shiver went through his body as his staff, unawakened for so many days, suddenly swelled and rose up. Sargon remembered he was naked, and the thought made his manhood throb and grow even harder. He reached down to cover himself, but Tashanella stopped his hand, then let her own fingers brush against his penis.

"You are very beautiful," she said. "It's strange. I have seen many erect members, but never have I thought any of them beautiful."

The touch of her fingers had unleashed a wave of passion. He caught her hand in his, and held it tight. Her long hair framed her face, and the wide brown eyes remained fastened on his.

Tashanella smiled down at him. Suddenly she leaned over and kissed his lips, a brief touch that only fanned the flames of his throbbing erection. Sargon reached up to pull her down to him, but she straightened up and rocked back on her heels. All the same, Tashanella did not let go of his hand, and now she clasped it with both of hers.

"You must come to my father's tent. It is not wise to keep the leader of the clan waiting."

"I don't care about your father, Tashanella." Her name rolled easily off his tongue, and he decided that it was the most beautiful name he'd ever heard. At that moment, Sargon would have risked keeping Subutai waiting until dawn, if he could convince Tashanella to walk with him across the stream and into the trees.

The girl grew serious, and released his hand. "This is important, Sargon. I think my father wishes to hear your advice." She stood and straightened out her dress. "Besides, I wasted too much time gazing at you while you slept. My father will be growing impatient."

The thought of her looking at him while he lay there naked brought a flush to his face. How odd. He hadn't been embarrassed by a girl's thoughts or deeds for at least two seasons.

"I have to return to Chinua's tent to borrow some clothes." He sat up, and glanced around, searching for the remains of his tunic. It must have floated away.

"You will not need to borrow. Your father left several garments with Chinua before he departed. They are yours now. Come. I'll go with you."

She reached down her hand, and helped him to his feet. His erection still loomed. It felt as though it would release his seed at the slightest touch. Sargon grimaced. He couldn't walk through the camp like that.

"Wait a moment." He turned and dove back into the stream, diving deep until he touched the sandy bottom before he rose up and burst through the surface. Sargon took a few vigorous strokes until the effort combined with the chill of the water softened his excitement.

When he emerged, Tashanella shook her head at his foolishness. Without a word, she started back toward the camp and Chinua's tent. Sargon followed a few steps behind, shaking the water from his hair.

A man or boy walking naked through the camp usually meant nothing. Sargon had walked naked to and from the stream before, as did other warriors and even a few of the women. This time it was different. Today, anyone who saw him, saw the both of them, would notice more than just the fact that he wore no garments.

It looked, he realized, like a woman leading her lover back to her tent. He wondered what Subutai would do if he encountered Sargon and his daughter like this. Thinking of her father brought back Tashanella's words. What advice from Sargon could the leader of the clan want? The last of Sargon's erection disappeared even faster than it had risen.

Outside Chinua's tent, Sargon found the women busy preparing for tonight's feast. The young girls and maidens smiled as his body, laughing or blushing depending on their age, while Chinua's two wives merely glanced up at his arrival.

Nibiru, the older of Chinua's wives, sat near the family's big cooking pot, a small knife in her hand chopping mushrooms against a flat stone. Behind her, two rabbit skins were drying on a stretching board. Nibiru had almost the same number of seasons as her husband.

"Sargon, you're supposed to be at Subutai's tent. He sent a boy here to look for you." She pretended to notice Tashanella for the first time, and couldn't keep the smile from her face.

"I know, Nibiru. I need a garment. Tashanella says that you have some that belong to me."

"Chinua said . . ." Nibiru glanced at Tashanella again and changed her mind. "Yes, there's a bundle in the tent." She dropped the knife, tossed the mushroom slices into the cooking pot, and rose.

Sargon followed her into the tent. To his surprise, Tashanella entered it, too.

Nibiru picked up a scrap of cloth and handed it to Sargon. "Dry yourself." Then she searched underneath some blankets and sacks until she found Sargon's things. "Chinua said you were not to have this until you were ready."

Sargon didn't bother to ask what that meant. He dropped to his knees and began untying the thin leather strips that secured the bundle. The neat knots with the unique twirl told him that his mother had prepared this herself.

Unraveling the outer cloth, Sargon found a plain but well-made tunic, trousers such as Akkad's horse fighters wore, a pair of sturdy sandals, and two undergarments. The trousers would have been more than useful on this last ride.

Tashanella picked up the tunic and shook it out. Sargon donned the undergarment and trousers, fastening them with the same knot his mother had used. Tashanella handed him the tunic and he dropped that over his chest. He sat and tied on the sandals, enjoying the feel on his now calloused feet.

When he finished, both women nodded approvingly.

"A handsome warrior," Nibiru declared.

"You must hurry, Sargon." Tashanella led the way out of the tent.

"You look very beautiful today, Tashanella," Nibiru called out before the pair started for Subutai's tent.

To Sargon's surprise, the girl who had touched his stiff manhood without showing any emotion blushed furiously.

Both he and Tashanella pretended not to hear the giggling of the young girls that broke out behind them. Instead they quickened their pace toward Subutai's tent.

25

Tashanella stayed at his side all the way to her mother's cooking fire. Sargon gave her one last look, then ducked inside Subutai's tent. The time for the feast to begin approached, and Sargon hoped he wasn't the one keeping everyone away from the celebration.

"I'm sorry to be late, Subutai. I fell asleep at the stream."

Looking around, Sargon saw the tent filled to capacity. Chinua and Skala were there, both still wearing the rags they'd worn when they rode into camp. Subutai must have summoned them before they could change. Whatever they had talked about, the conversation had gone on since they arrived.

Suddenly Sargon felt conscious of his clean tunic and new sandals. He saw the frown on Subutai's face, and wondered just how long the Clan's Sarum had been waiting. Sargon guessed that the boy sent to find him would get a tongue-lashing for taking so much time.

Sargon wondered what the clan leader would do if he found out that Tashanella had brought Sargon back. She might be punished as well. And if Subutai discovered what had happened at the stream, Sargon might end up guarding the horses for the next few nights.

"Come. Sit." Subutai took a deep breath and erased the frown. "You know everyone here."

Sargon squeezed in beside Chinua and Jennat, who shifted to make room. Sargon nodded gratefully, then acknowledged the others present – Skala, Fashod, and an old warrior named Namar.

"I have not yet spoken to young Sargon," Namar said. "But I have watched him train more than once."

Namar, one of the oldest warriors in the camp, commanded no warriors and had not ridden out on a raid in many years. Long white hair framed his seamed face, almost concealing a faded scar on his cheek. But his eyes remained sharp as they studied Sargon's face. Namar's wisdom guided many in the camp, and Sargon knew Subutai made few decisions of importance without consulting Namar.

"I give you greetings, Namar of the Ur Nammu." Sargon bowed his head. "I have heard much about your wisdom."

"We need to plan for the coming of these Carchemishi invaders," Subutai said, wasting no more time. "And there may be a task for Sargon that could help us."

Sargon's mouth dropped in surprise. He'd expected nothing more than attending another meeting, not that he would be asked to perform an important duty.

"The invaders know we are in these lands, and will likely try to hunt us down," Subutai said. "And they have learned how many warriors we have. After Chinua's raid, they know about our courage and willingness to fight. When they come, they will bring the full force of their army against us."

"They do not know where we are yet," Chinua said. "We took time to cover our tracks, so it will take them some time to find us."

"Chinua, you and Skala do not know about the strangers," Subutai said. "Fashod's men encountered them three days ago, and brought them here. Two men and two women, lost and nearly dead from exhaustion and starvation. But they knew all about the Carchemishi. They came from a small village on the southern side of the passage. The villagers there had traded with the newcomers for many days, until the invaders turned on their camp and killed everyone. Only these few escaped. They told us the Carchemishi, about sixteen hundred of them, are advancing toward us in two war parties, about twenty miles apart. Between them and their outriders, they have stripped a wide swath of the land bare as they passed, and killed everyone within their reach."

Sargon watched as the pleasant expressions on the faces of Skala, Jennat, and Chinua vanished. Everyone in the tent knew the number of

Ur Nammu warriors that could be ready to ride and fight – just over three hundred. No matter how brave or skilled, those were impossible odds.

Subutai nodded at their sudden comprehension. "Yes, the situation is not good. If the invaders keep at their present pace, their forces will reach this place in five or six days, no more than seven."

Jennat spoke for the first time. "Are those numbers certain?"

"Fashod, Namar, and I spoke with the wanderers. The men claimed to have counted the Carchemishi force just before it split into two. They say they needed to know the numbers so they could decide how much to trade, and how much gold to ask for." Subutai shrugged. "Even if they are wrong by five hundred, we will still be greatly outnumbered."

"We may have delayed them," Chinua said. "They lost many horses and men."

"Or they may speed up their march to satisfy their revenge," Subutai countered.

"We killed many of them," Skala said, "close to a hundred. We shot more than two hundred shafts right into them at close range."

"Perhaps the number is as you say, Skala." Subutai's voice showed that he did not want to dispute the warrior.

"But I have ridden on many such raids, and heard all the stories about how many were slain. A warrior shoots an arrow and sees a man go down. He thinks he killed him. But it may be that the man simply heard the arrow whistle by and dropped to the earth. Or three or four warriors shoot at the same man and kill him. Each believes that it was his arrow that dropped the enemy, and so each warrior adds one to his count of the dead."

A polite way to tell Skala that he had no way of knowing how many Carchemishi had been killed or wounded.

Subutai shook his head. "This is the way of battles. Only by counting the dead bodies of your enemies can you be sure of the number killed. I learned that from Sargon's father."

At the mention of Sargon's father, all eyes turned to him again.

Subutai gave Skala and Chinua only a moment to consider his words. "So we must decide what to do. We cannot remain here. And we cannot turn toward the northeast, or we will encounter the Alur Meriki. So I think we must fall back to the southeast, toward the lands of Akkad. It may be that these invaders will turn aside before they enter Akkad's lands. They do not have enough fighters to challenge Eskkar's forces."

"We cannot be certain of that," Jennat argued. "The Carchemishi leader Sargon and I spoke to seemed aware of Akkad and its soldiers." He turned to Sargon, who nodded in agreement. "They showed no fear of Akkad's name. Perhaps these invaders are but the advanced force of an even greater number."

Whatever pleasant feelings Sargon had enjoyed before entering the tent vanished. Clearly, the daring night raid on the enemy and the long ride here had settled nothing. If anything, the attack had made a bad situation worse. The fight was coming south, straight at the Ur Nammu. They would be lucky to get away in time.

The same thought must have occurred to Chinua. "How can we get away? We would have to leave everything behind, our tents, herds, all our possessions. Even if we just take the horses and leave tomorrow, our women and children and those too old to fight will slow us down. We do not have enough horses for everyone. The invaders will catch up with us in a few days."

The Ur Nammu women, children, and old men numbered just over a thousand. Even with the horses Chinua had captured, the total number of horses in the camp was less than six hundred.

"Did these wanderers say how many horse fighters the Carchemishi have?" Jennat touched the wound on his arm as he spoke.

"Between eight and nine hundred," Subutai said.

The number silenced everyone as they thought about what it meant. Even Sargon knew that with so many riders, they could easily overtake and destroy the fleeing Ur Nammu, or at least pin them down until the enemy foot soldiers arrived.

"We were hoping that Akkad could send warriors to assist us." Fashod broke the gloomy silence and addressed Sargon. "It would be in their interest to help us drive these invaders away."

Subutai again turned to Sargon. "That is why I asked you here. I want you to ride with Fashod back to the lands of Akkad. You can tell your father what you have seen and heard. You can warn him of this new threat. The outlying villages in his northern lands will also be in danger."

A few men on fast horses would have no trouble avoiding the Carchemishi. Sargon knew he would be safe, and he could deliver a warning of the approaching invasion. But that wouldn't help the Ur Nammu.

"It's at least a six or seven day ride, maybe longer, to reach the outlying forts of my father," Sargon said, "and even if we reached them sooner, there are not enough fighters in those settlements to turn back so many enemies. We would have to continue on to Akkad to raise enough men."

That, of course, was the problem. Akkad depended on the Ur Nammu to patrol these empty lands. The small garrison villages maintained only enough fighters to keep control of bandits or the occasional raider from the south.

"How long do you think it would take before your father could raise enough men to help us?"

Sargon had learned all about the pride of the Ur Nammu, or any barbarian tribe for that matter. To ask for help from another was a grave step. He glanced at the warriors. None met his eyes, only Subutai. The clan leader knew all too well what he was asking.

"It would take . . . after we reach Akkad, I think it would take my father at least four or five days to raise a force strong enough to march north and deal with these invaders. Our soldiers are scattered among many villages. They would have to be assembled, and supplies collected. It would take another six or seven days of hard riding to get back to this land. I will go to my father and tell him. I am sure he will come to your assistance as fast as he can, but I don't think he can assemble enough men and march here until that many days have passed."

Subutai accepted the grim assessment. "It is as I thought. Still, we are grateful for your help, Sargon. And we understand the problems that face your father." He glanced around the circle. "It seems that we will have to survive on our own, at least until Akkad can aid us."

"What are we to do?" Skala's usually brash voice sounded subdued.

"We will break camp in the morning," Subutai said. "We will load the women and children on the horses and leave everything else behind. I want the entire clan to be on the way south by midmorning. The closer we can move toward Akkad's lands, the safer we will be."

The clan leader's voice held a trace of finality. Sargon looked around the circle of warriors. The grim situation left little to say.

"Sargon's words have given me an idea." Namar broke the silence. "There is another force that could help us drive these invaders back."

Subutai turned to face the older man. "Who?"

"The Alur Meriki."

Mouths opened and jaws dropped. Sargon knew the Alur Meriki were the most hated and dreaded enemy of the Ur Nammu. For almost two generations, the Alur Meriki had hunted down and almost wiped out the Ur Nammu. The two tribes had fought many battles, and they despised each other.

"Why would they help us?" Subutai voice remained flat.

"The Alur Meriki are drawing closer to the pass that opens into these western plains," Namar said. "Already our riders have glimpsed their advance scouting parties. Sooner or later, they will have to confront these invaders themselves."

Sargon wasn't the only one surprised by the news about the Alur Meriki sightings. Chinua and Skala also turned toward Subutai.

"Fashod's riders have twice seen Alur Meriki riders. They recognized our warriors as well, but did not show any signs of hostility. Whether that is a result of the oath Eskkar made their new Sarum swear, we are not sure." Subutai shrugged. "But before he left our camp, Sargon's father advised me to make sure we offer no provocation to them in their passage."

"When they come out of the mountains," Fashod said, talking almost to himself as to the others, "they will still be far to the north, too far away to help us. The invaders would have to turn toward the northeast to confront them."

"Even so, it would be good for us if the Alur Meriki would face them," Subutai said. "But even if they honor their pledge not to attack us, neither will they do anything to help us, of that I am certain. Nothing we could say to them would change that."

He took a deep breath and shook his head. "Our best chance is to move south, toward Akkad's lands, and hope that we can stay ahead of the Carchemishi until Eskkar and his soldiers reach us."

Sargon saw Chinua and Fashod slowly nod in acceptance. The blood feud that existed between the two clans could never be satisfied until one or the other race was destroyed. Jennat and Skala kept silent. Both were good warriors, but Sargon knew they lacked experience in matters that affected the entire clan.

Then Sargon realized that Namar had not responded to his Sarum's words. The old warriors eyes remained fixed on Sargon.

Subutai also noticed Namar's stare. "What is it you wish to say?"

"Nothing." Namar dropped his gaze from Sargon and stared at his hands resting on his lap. "Perhaps I spoke foolishly."

With a sudden insight, Sargon realized what the old warrior intended. Subutai had made his decision. The Ur Nammu would depart tomorrow and head south, but long before they could reach the safety of Akkad's outlying forts or any approaching reinforcements, the clan would be overtaken by the Carchemishi cavalry.

The warriors would fight to the death, might even manage to hold off the enemy horsemen. But when the Carchemishi foot soldiers caught up with their cavalry, the Ur Nammu would be destroyed. The women and children who survived would be raped and tortured. Most would then be killed, and the rest taken as slaves.

Tashanella. She would be one of those taken. Sargon's thoughts flashed to an image of her on the ground, naked and bleeding, with a sword thrust through her stomach. Slowly he lifted his gaze to meet Namar's eyes. "They might listen to me."

Subutai had started to rise, signifying the end of the discussion. Instead he sank back to the ground. "What did you say?"

"I said . . ." Sargon had to clear his throat, "I said the Alur Meriki might listen to me. I mean, to the son of the King of Akkad."

Namar nodded. "Indeed they might."

"They might just as likely take Sargon hostage to threaten his father," Subutai said.

"And what if they did?" Sargon had no illusions about what his parents would do if that threat came to pass. Eskkar would never deal with anyone who showed such treachery. He would raise another army to destroy the Alur Meriki, and if his son were killed, Eskkar would shrug his shoulders and add that to the reasons to destroy them.

Sargon put that thought out of his mind. "Besides, is it not in their interest to fight these Carchemishi? They will have to fight them sooner or later. Would it not be better for them to do it now, with our help?"

"The Alur Meriki have just fought a battle with your father," Fashod said, leaning forward in his excitement. "They lost many men. They may not have enough left to defeat these invaders without our help."

Subutai looked dubious. He turned to Namar. "What do you think of this idea?"

"I think the Alur Meriki will have to cross the lands that these Carchemishi have just traversed. Even if they avoid fighting, they will find the land empty, already stripped bare, if what we heard is true. How then will they eat? Where can they turn for food?"

Sargon knew the answer to that question. The one thing Akkad had in plenty was food, in the form of grain and livestock. If these lands were bare, the Alur Meriki would have to turn to the south. "Akkad could supply both the Alur Meriki and the Ur Nammu with plenty of food. They should understand that."

"They might at that," Subutai said. His voice, too, now held a trace of hope. "I could ride with Sargon and we could . . ."

"No!" Fashod shook his head. "You cannot go. You are needed here, to lead the Clan and to prepare for the battle."

"Fashod is right," Chinua said. "You must stay here. I will go with Sargon."

"Fashod should go," Namar said, speaking quickly before Subutai could start an argument with his second in command. "I would ride with them, but I am too old for such a long and hard ride. It must be Fashod. As your second in command, he can speak with your authority."

"I will go with Sargon," Chinua said. "He has been my responsibility for . . ."

"No." Subutai's tone allowed for no opposition. "With Fashod gone, I will need you here."

"I will accompany him," Jennat said.

"As will I. He will need a strong warrior beside him."

Those last words came from Skala. Sargon could scarcely believe his ears.

"That is brave of you, Skala," Subutai said. "But I will need my strongest fighters at my side. Jennat will go. He and Sargon spoke to the Carchemish together, so it is best he accompany Sargon once again."

He turned to Sargon. "Are you sure you wish to do this? There is a good chance you will be going to your death. The Alur Meriki swore no oath to you, even if you are Eskkar's son. Many of their warriors are dead because of your father. You could end up stretched out on the ground and tortured by their women."

Not a pleasant prospect, Sargon knew. All the same, the time to back out had passed long ago. "I will go. You have taken me into your tent, and I have ridden with your warriors. Besides, there is no one else who can ask them to do this."

"Then you will leave in the morning." Subutai sounded resigned to the desperate measure. "Jennat and Garal will accompany you. I can't spare any more men. Each of you will take an extra horse. You will need to ride hard, in order to reach them as soon as possible." He turned to Fashod. "You will make everything ready tonight?"

"Yes, Sarum," Fashod replied. "Come, Sargon, we have much to do before we can enjoy the feast."

"I will send riders to Akkad, to warn them of the danger," Subutai said. "Meanwhile, do not tell the others about the danger until the feast is over. I will tell everyone in the morning. Let them enjoy this one night of celebration before we start our preparations."

His words brought somber looks to their faces. In their rush to action, they had almost forgotten the effect this would have on the Clan.

26

Subutai stood and watched the others leave the tent. He knew the enormity of what had befallen the Ur Nammu had not yet taken hold in their minds. Only Namar understood the disaster rushing toward them. Fashod and the others still thought in terms of fighting and dealing with this new enemy.

Nor did Sargon understand what he had brought upon himself. The boy – no, he had to be considered a man now since he had fought in a battle where the enemy had died – didn't realize that his own death almost certainly loomed over him.

At least I won't have to tell his father. I'll be dead, too, as will most, if not all, of the Ur Nammu Clan.

Other than leaving the women and children behind, to fall prey to the invaders, Subutai saw no hope for survival. And neither he nor his warriors would ever leave their families to such a fate. Better to die with honor.

Once before, as a young warrior, he had witnessed the near destruction of his clan. He, too, had narrowly escaped death at the hands of the Alur Meriki. That time an outcast warrior named Eskkar and a small band of Akkadians had struck down Subutai's enemies and saved the last of the Ur Nammu from annihilation.

More than fifteen years had passed since that day, long years during which Subutai had struggled to rebuild the strength and numbers of his clan. Now, just when the Ur Nammu seemed poised to grow strong and powerful again, these new invaders had arrived to plunder the land and destroy his people. Without help, Subutai would be the last Sarum of the Ur Nammu.

He sighed in resignation, and stepped out of the tent. The high-pitched voices of the young and the bustling activity of the women greeted him. The warriors he'd met with had already departed, all except Sargon, who stood talking with – Tashanella? Subutai had to look twice to be sure. She and Sargon faced each other, less than a pace apart. His young daughter, however, had vanished, transformed into a beautiful woman.

Instead of her usual baggy and patched dress, Tashanella now wore a fine garment, with bright red stitching across the neck, and decorated with brown and black beads. Fringes of leather strips revealed her bare arms. Square cut across her chest, this dress revealed the outlines of her youthful breasts, and its shorter length showed her tanned legs. Subutai recognized the necklace of bright yellow and green gemstones that graced her neck. He had given it to Roxsanni years ago.

Subutai didn't remember the last time he'd seen Tashanella other than barefoot, but now she displayed new sandals whose laces, also fringed, hugged her calves. And she had somehow transformed her usually unkempt hair in long and lustrous waves that fell across her shoulders.

Sargon appeared as surprised and confused as Subutai. He stood awkwardly, as if he didn't know what to say.

Other men and boys passing by stared at Tashanella as well, as if they had never seen the Sarum's daughter before. Two girls frowned at the young woman who had suddenly appeared in their midst, while three others laughed and smiled at the sight of Sargon, helpless in Tashanella's gaze.

Her mother, Roxsanni, saw Subutai staring open mouthed. She crossed the space between the women's tent and his. A moment later, his other and senior wife, Petra, put down her chopping knife and, wiping her hands on her skirt, followed after Roxsanni.

"Come inside, Subutai," Roxsanni said. Without waiting for his assent or reply, she ducked into the tent the clan leaders had just vacated.

Subutai remained rooted to the spot, his eyes still fastened on his daughter. He clenched his fists. Petra took his arm. "Come inside, Husband." She lifted the tent flap, waited until he stepped inside, then followed him.

"What is this . . . display?"

"Sit, Subutai, please," Roxsanni said. "We knew this day was coming. Now it has arrived."

"Why is she dressed that way, showing herself . . ."

"You know that Tashanella passed through the rites four months ago. Since then she has tried not to call attention to herself, lest one of the warriors ask for her as a bride."

"But now she has chosen," Petra said. "She has fixed her eyes on Sargon. It is for him that she has taken up a woman's clothes."

"And you have helped her in this, and you, too, Petra?" Subutai shook his head. "I knew she went through the rites, but I thought she wanted to stay with us awhile longer, until . . . "

"Until some warrior offered enough horses for her, or you decided to reward some brave act, or use her to seal a peace between two families." Petra shook her head. "Instead she has chosen for herself."

"None of the warriors in the clan are worthy of our daughter," Roxsanni said. "Tashanella is too gifted just to sit in a tent and raise babies. She can be one of the Special Ones, allowed to sit in the councils of men."

In rare instances, women whose wit and wisdom made itself manifest, were allowed to sit with the men in council. Such a woman had not appeared in Subutai's lifetime, nor in his father's, but it had happened. Everyone acknowledged Trella, Eskkar's wife, as one of the "Special Ones."

"Now it is up to you, Husband, to chose." Petra took Roxsanni's hand and squeezed it. "After tonight, every warrior in the camp will want to possess her. The burning in her loins has come to her. She cannot remain here under your tent any longer, or there will be trouble and fighting. Tashanella must have a husband of her own to speak for her."

Subutai sank to the ground, crossed his legs, and stared up at his wives. Outside, the sounds of the celebration for Chinua's return grew louder, as voices rose up all around the Sarum's tent.

Petra allowed Subutai no time to gather his thoughts or raise an objection. "That means, Husband, that the time has come for you to select a husband for our daughter. Is there any of your warriors who deserves such a prize? Is it not better to give her to the son of a king?"

Subutai realized his mouth was open. He felt the urge to order them out, to tell them to send his daughter to him for a good beating.

Both of his wives had helped Tashanella conceal her blossoming womanhood these last months. Even as he spoke with his leaders, his wives would have helped Tashanella dress and array herself. And now they sat united across from him.

"Sargon is but a spoiled and foolish child." Subutai's voice filled the tent. "He is nothing but a boy cast out by his father. And his mother, too. Eskkar told me Trella had decided that her son was better off banished or dead, than remaining inside their tent."

"He is young and foolish," Petra agreed. "But he will not be young much longer, and I don't think he will remain foolish. We've spoken to Garal and Chinua several times, and Chinua's wives as well. They all agree that Sargon has changed from what he was the day he first came to us. And if he continues to change, then he will be king in Akkad someday."

Subutai shook his head. Women constantly whispered about their men behind their backs, always trying to influence their men. Little enough privacy existed in the clan as it was.

"And if he decides not to marry her, or to take her only as a concubine or slave, then what? Or what will happen when he grows tired of her, or if he returns to Akkad?"

Even as he said the words, Subutai knew he was losing the argument. Of course he could order Tashanella to abandon any hope for Sargon, but the time for that might have already passed.

His wives were both good women, and, unlike many other wives sharing a husband, they had formed a bond of friendship. Subutai knew the gods had blessed him with two good bedmates who understood how to use their wits. Now he found it difficult to argue with them. "Roxsanni, knowing what might befall her, you are in favor of this?"

"Wife, concubine, love slave, Tashanella does not care. She would prefer any of those fates to marrying one of the warriors in our clan."

"You know your daughter's worth, Husband," Petra said. "Who in our clan would you give her to?"

Subutai opened his mouth, then closed it again. He could think of no warrior in the camp worthy of his daughter and her special gifts. His wives were right about that.

"And this is what my daughter wants?"

"Yes." Petra and Roxsanni said the word in unison.

He took a huge breath and let it out. "Then you will see to her protection. I will not have her humiliated over this."

"Yes, Husband," Petra said. "We will keep our eyes on them both."

"You are a wise father and a great leader," Roxsanni said. "Tashanella will love you even more than she does now."

"Yes, I'm sure." He looked from one to the other. "It doesn't really matter anyway. Sargon will be dead in a few days. We may all be dead in a few days."

He took some grim satisfaction from the looks of confusion that crossed their faces. Then he told them about the invading Carchemishi, and Sargon's offer to ride to the Alur Meriki.

Just after dawn, Subutai summoned everyone in the clan to the open area near the stream. The unusual order caught everyone by surprise. Everyone crowded close as Subutai, on his horse, faced his people and told them of the events in the west, and the threat that now existed for the Ur Nammu.

Most listened in stunned silence. From the revelry the night before, they now faced the prospect of fleeing for their lives. Some of the women broke into tears, clutching their youngest babies to their breasts. Even the warriors could not conceal all their concern.

Subutai ordered them to bury or hide their most valuable possessions, though he warned everyone the invaders likely would discover such places. They should take only food, water, and all the weapons they could carry. Everything else must be left behind.

Stunned silence continued as Subutai went on. All who could ride would take a horse. Those too old or too young to handle a mount would double up behind a boy or warrior. At the end, Subutai offered a glimmer of hope, telling them that Fashod and Sargon were leaving to seek help

from the Alur Meriki, and that riders would also be dispatched to the nearest Akkadian outpost.

From the edge of the stream, just as far away as he could stand and
still hear the Sarum speak, Sargon watched Subutai deliver the evil tidings. As the grim words washed over the clan, Sargon held Tashanella's
hand.

At a time like this, such a public gesture would be considered a weakness by most of the warriors, but he didn't care. Besides, no one in the
clan had time for any thoughts about either of them. Survival had suddenly
become the only issue.

"Your father will protect you," Sargon told her.

"He will do what he can." Tashanella leaned against Sargon's shoulder. "The danger you face will be even greater."

Last night, as soon as the feast began, he and Tashanella had slipped
away in the darkness. Carrying a blanket, they crossed the stream and left
the encampment behind. In a sheltered grove, Sargon spread the blanket
on the ground, and with the frantic urgency of youth, they made love in
the moonlight.

Sargon, despite the fire that burned in his loins, had restrained himself,
taking his time, until Tashanella's own passions made her forget her fears.
When he moved astride her, she moaned in anticipation, and her brief cry
of pain turned into a long sigh of pleasure. Within moments, she matched
his own ardor, clutching his arms and wrapping her slender legs around
him.

For Sargon, too, this was a first time. The first time he'd ever concerned himself with a woman's needs and feelings. Her desire inflamed
him, and he held back as long as he could, until he heard her cry out with
the pleasure of the gods. Then he burst inside her, shuddering as he emptied his seed into her womb.

When he collapsed beside her, she held him tight, her strong arms
keeping him pressed against her. They lingered in each other's arms, whis-
pering words of endearment, words that once Sargon would have thought
to be foolish and unmanly. But with Tashanella, he experienced the pleasure of loving someone who wanted him as much as he desired her.

Afterwards, Sargon had revealed both the threat to the clan from the
Carchemishi, and the plan to seek help from the Alur Meriki. Tashanella

had cried out at the idea, but she lived her life surrounded by warriors, and danger was no stranger to any Ur Nammu, man or woman.

A man's honor required that he do his utmost to help his kin and his clan, no matter what the risk. Women possessed their own code of honor, one that required them to be strong for their men and their children, and if needed, to fight beside their husbands.

Nevertheless, thoughts of the approaching enemy faded from Sargon's mind, replaced by the soft feel of Tashanella's breasts, and her hand that, gently at first, aroused his manhood. They made love a second time.

When they finally returned to the camp, the celebration had ended. Sargon escorted her to Subutai's tents, where her mother, Roxsanni, waited alone beside the fire's ashes. She pretended not to see Sargon, but placed her arm around Tashanella's waist and guided her into the tent.

After the tent flap closed behind them, Sargon slowly made his went to Chinua's tent and his own blanket., falling asleep almost as soon as he cradled his arms over his head.

Now, in the chill of the dawn, Sargon and Tashanella stood side by side, listening to her father speak to his people.

Subutai finished his speech, and the crowd broke apart, everyone hurrying to their tents. A babble of voices filled the camp, some of the women already wailing in their grief. Tashanella swayed against Sargon, and lifted her face to his. He wrapped his arm around her and kissed her lips, a long, lingering sharing of their hearts. When he ended the embrace, tears glistened in her eyes.

"I will come back for you no matter what," he promised.

"And I will be waiting."

"I must go. It's already late, and Fashod and the others will be eager to depart."

Still holding her hand, they walked back toward the camp. Fashod's tent was on the way, and the clan's second in command already stood by his horse. Garal and Jennat stood beside him. If they thought Sargon's behavior odd or unmanly, no one said anything.

Sargon released Tashanella's hand and let her continue on her own. She, too, would have much to do, helping her family prepare for their flight. He stared at her lithe form as she walked away, her shoulders shaking with her tears, but she was too strong to glance back or slow her step. Sargon wondered if he would ever see her again.

"Are you ready to ride?" Fashod's voice held only concern. Nor did he say anything about waiting for Sargon's arrival.

"Yes." Sargon and Garal had made their preparations earlier. Sargon had selected two prime horses from Fashod's own stock, and Garal had approved the choices. The animals, big, powerful, and well trained, stood waiting.

"Then you'll need this." Fashod handed Sargon a sword. "Your father left it with Subutai, to give to you . . . when the time was right."

Sargon drew the blade halfway from the scabbard and glanced at the weapon. It was not the sword he'd carried in Akkad. This one lacked any ornamentation on the guard, and the hilt was bound in plain leather strips with a simple ball as the counterweight.

A fighting man's weapon, his father would say, not one to be carried around the city to impress the idlers and tavern dwellers. Sargon recognized the work of Asmar and his family, the master sword-makers in Akkad. This sword would not fail Sargon.

Since only warriors approved by the clan leaders could carry such a weapon, Sargon understood the significance of the gift. From this day forward, in their eyes he'd become a warrior.

"I've done nothing to earn this." Sargon slid the blade back into its scabbard.

"Makko received his sword last night," Garal said. "He's done no more than you. You both have earned the right."

"In these times, many young men must become warriors." Fashod's voice now held a hint of urgency. He swung himself onto his horse. "It's almost midmorning. Time to go."

Sargon grimaced, but he buckled his new sword around his waist. He settled onto his horse, and the four men rode out, almost unnoticed. He'd spent the last sixteen days on the back of a horse, and this new journey promised to be longer and more difficult. At least he'd learned the difference between riding, and running for your life.

Even Garal didn't look happy at the prospect of another arduous ride. Jennat had enjoyed an extra day's rest. Fashod, aside from his usual rides to inspect the camp's outlying guards, had spent most of the last ten days close to his tent.

All of them tried to forget the somber mood that had filled the camp. Fashod never looked back. Well before midday, the camp site would be empty, and the Ur Nammu on the run.

Fashod set a rapid pace from the start, and he selected the path. Each rider led his second horse, its only burden a bulging water skin, a fat food pouch, and a small sack of grain for the horse.

Out of habit, Sargon had taken his usual place at the rear, but Garal waved him forward.

"Your place now is to ride with Fashod," he shouted with a grin. "On this journey I will be the one gathering firewood."

Garal and Jennat carried bows, and each man's quiver contained an extra handful of arrows. As leader of the little troop, Fashod had a pair of lances on his back. Sargon had accepted one also, in addition to his sword and knife. He knew that he was not as proficient with a bow yet, and for him, the lance was a better weapon for close fighting.

Fashod led the way northeast, toward the mountains, pushing the horses as hard as he could. The grassy terrain made for smooth riding, and they stopped only to rest their mounts. With each rider alternating between two horses, the four men covered plenty of ground by the end of the day. The sun had already dipped below the horizon before Fashod gave the order to halt.

Though his days as a horse boy had ended, Sargon still had to care for his two horses. On this ride, each man saw to his own animals, checking them to make sure they remained sound. One thing had not changed. Sargon fell asleep the moment he rolled himself up in his blanket.

The sun's pink rays had just reached out over the horizon when Garal shook Sargon awake. The horses received their handful of grain, the men gulped down some dried meat, and with a grunt, Fashod ordered them to move out.

At noon, Fashod halted to rest the horses. Sargon stretched his stiff leg muscles by walking around in circles. His backside once again complained from the constant riding, but he knew better than to say anything.

"You've become a capable horseman," Fashod said, as they tended to their horses.

"Garal is a good teacher," Sargon said. "How far have we come?"

"Mmm, yesterday, maybe sixty, maybe seventy miles. So far today, another thirty-five. We should get at least that much more in before darkness."

No wonder the steppes warriors generated so much respect. To cover so many miles in a single day was almost beyond belief. Most people in Akkad or the nearby villages never traveled more than twenty miles from the place where they were born.

"And where will we find the Alur Meriki?" Garal's voice held only curiosity, not concern.

"Ten days ago, one of our patrols spotted them about this distance," Fashod said. "So we may meet up with them any time now."

So the moment of truth might arrive with little warning, Sargon decided.

"Sargon, when we encounter them, do you wish me to speak to them?"

The polite question carried subtle implications. Fashod might be a leader of the Ur Nammu, but when they crossed paths with the Alur Meriki, things would be different. Sargon felt Garal and Jennat's eyes on him, as they waited to hear Sargon's answer.

Sargon hesitated only a moment. "No, I think it is best that I speak with them." With those words, he committed himself to dealing with the Alur Meriki, not as one of the Ur Nammu, but as a leader of Akkad.

Fashod nodded. "Then prepare your thoughts now while you have time. The moment may come suddenly. Now let's get going. The horses have had enough rest."

But we haven't. Even so, Sargon thought of Tashanella and kept his weakness to himself. The punishing ride continued. Soft white clouds filled the sky, and gave them a respite from the hot sun. As they moved north, the ground began to rise, a gradual upslope that would increase as they drew closer to the mountains.

The middle of the afternoon had just passed when Fashod slowed his horse to stop. Sargon, wrapped in his thoughts, lifted his head at the unexpected halt. Instinctively, he followed Fashod's gaze.

About a mile and a half way, a band of riders had gathered across a ridge top. Sargon had good eyes, and even at that distance he could see that the color red dominated their garments, with red streamers dangling from lance and bow tips.

They didn't move, just sat on their horses, watching. Sargon counted ten of them, and there might be any number of them behind the ridge.

"Closer than I expected. I didn't think we'd catch sight of their scouts until tomorrow." Fashod stared at them for a moment, then turned to face Sargon. "They'll expect us to turn around. Are you ready?"

"Yes." Ready or not, the time had come. Sargon touched his heels to the horse, took the lead, and guided it into a canter, heading straight for the Alur Meriki outriders.

Fashod now took position on Sargon's left, his horse half a length behind Sargon's. The Alur Meriki horsemen watched them approach, but did nothing, no doubt thinking that if their old enemy wanted to close with them, so much the better.

"I would stop a quarter mile from them," Fashod advised. "That will tell them that we wish to talk, not fight."

Sargon nodded, and kept his eyes on the horsemen. He didn't trust his voice. The clan that had tried to kill his father so many times waited ahead. Sargon knew that even in Eskkar's prime, he would not have challenged ten warriors with only four.

At about a quarter mile, Sargon eased his horse to a gradual stop. Fashod held up his empty right hand, and waved it back and forth. If he held a weapon, it would have been a challenge to fight. But the open hand signified a wish to speak.

The Alur Meriki did nothing. They remained immobile on their horses.

"They're not waving us on," Sargon said.

"No, they're not. Which means they don't want to talk to us."

Sargon frowned at the insult. "Well, they will." He clucked to his horse and urged it forward once again. He kept the pace at an easy canter. Halfway there, he could see the Alur Meriki warriors speaking to each other.

"No Ur Nammu has spoken to an Alur Meriki in over twenty years," Fashod said. "Perhaps we should head for a different part of the ridge, so we can face them on equal ground."

Sargon didn't answer, and he kept heading straight toward the warriors, giving them the advantage of the higher ground. He halted a hundred paces away, just within long bowshot range.

"I'll ride ahead and speak to them," Sargon said.

"No. We ride together." Fashod's words declared his determination. "Garal, take Sargon's extra horse, and his lance, too. No sense looking like we want to fight." Fashod handed his second mount's halter to Jennat.

Once again, Fashod waved his right arm back and forth. The Alur Meriki still made no sign to acknowledge they had even seen those waving at them. The Alur Meriki rested their strung bows across their horses, but no one had fitted a shaft on them yet. But Sargon knew how fast that could be done.

"Damn them," Sargon muttered, angry at their silence. He clucked again to the horse, and started the animal forward at a walk. The gap between the two groups closed, and with every step, Sargon waited for the Alur Meriki order that would rain arrows down on them.

He picked out the leader of the party easy enough, a warrior in his prime, with perhaps twenty five seasons. He was the only warrior whose bow remained slung across his back, but a lance lay across the horse's neck.

Sargon's heart beat faster and faster, but he forced all fear from his face. From here on, he had to act the part of a leader of men. Sargon tried to copy the stern face his father wore when something annoyed him, a face Sargon had seen often enough, and not from a distance. When twenty paces remained between them, Sargon pulled back on the halter and eased the horse to a stop.

Now only ten paces separated them. Sargon could see the leader clearly now. The warrior possessed a strong and powerful build that rippled with muscles, combined with a face chiseled out of stone. Black as midnight hair hung straight down to his shoulders. Sargon wondered whether he and his companions had, in their bad luck, encountered a hard head, someone who preferred to fight rather than use his wits.

"A good day for a ride." Sargon offered one of the traditional greetings of the Alur Meriki.

There was no response. Sargon shrugged.

"I am Sargon, son of Eskkar, leader of the Hawk Clan, and the King of Akkad. I have come to speak with Urgo, the Sarum of the Alur Meriki. Can you take me to him?"

Despite the slight differences between the two tribes language, he saw that his words were understood, and thanked the gods for all the abuse

Garal had heaped upon him until Sargon learned the language. If the Alur Meriki didn't recognize his father's name, Sargon guessed they were all going to die.

The leader of the Alur Meriki frowned and his eyes examined Sargon more closely. "Urgo is no longer Sarum of the Clan."

The voice sounded as hard as the taut muscles on the man's chest. Sargon refused to let that bad news show on his face. "Then I would speak with your new Sarum. I have important news that he must hear. A great danger threatens your clan."

"The Alur Meriki do not heed the words of Ur Nammu scum." The leader glanced at the three men just behind Sargon, then spat on the ground.

Well, that was plain enough, Sargon thought. The friendly approach didn't seem to make an impression. All the same, they hadn't attacked, not yet, so they might still be honoring the oath his father made them swear, to not attack the Ur Nammu.

Sargon moved his horse forward a few paces, so that he stood apart from his companions. This time he put a hard edge to his words, unconsciously mimicking his father in one of his angry moods.

"You are not to decide what words your Sarum is to hear or not to hear." Sargon waited a moment, then went on. "My father, in case you have already forgotten, granted you access to the waters of the stream when he and his soldiers could have let you all die of thirst. Now, I have important news for the leader of your clan. If you wish your people to survive, you will take me to your Sarum at once. There is no time to waste."

The face of the leader hardened even more. "You claim to be the son of the outcast Eskkar. Yet you ride alone into the lands of the Alur Meriki with these Ur Nammu dogs."

"I do not claim to be anyone," Sargon declared. "I told you who I am. If you do not believe me, take me to your Sarum and let him decide."

"Perhaps I should just kill you now."

A ripple of movement went down the Alur Meriki line, as warriors tightened their grips on their weapons and made ready to attack.

Sargon shook his head in disbelief, as if amazed at the man's stupidity. "I wonder what my father will do when he learns that some insignificant leader of ten killed his son. Do you think that would make King Eskkar angry? Angry enough to wipe every last Alur Meriki from the earth?"

"It seems the Alur Meriki have neither honor nor wisdom." Fashod moved his horse a few steps forward, until he stood beside Sargon. "They would rather fight than listen to one who could save them."

A flush came over the leader's face, and his hand tightened on the haft of his lance. He clearly had not enjoyed being described as insignificant.

This is how it begins and ends, Sargon thought, with a few angry words uttered in the heat of the moment.

"Your father is not here to protect you, even if you are truly Eskkar's son."

At least he hadn't given the order to kill them. Sargon realized that the only thing keeping them alive was his father's name. "What is your name?"

"Why should I tell you my name?"

"Because I've told you mine," Sargon answered. "Your orders are to scout the lands ahead of the caravan, and report what you find to your clan leader. Now you and your men have found someone who has information that can help your people. You can try to kill us, or you can follow your orders. But do not think your men will protect you, when your new Sarum, whoever he is, learns what you have done. He will take your head and send it to my father, as an offering. So if you want to fight, then give the order and be done with it."

Sargon moved his right hand to the hilt of his sword, stared into the stony face confronting him, and waited. There wasn't anything else to say.

A gust of wind rippled through them, and the horses shifted uneasily, ears moving back and forth. It gave the leader of the Alur Meriki an extra moment to consider his response.

"What do you want to tell our Sarum?"

The warrior had weighed his chances and come to the right decision. At least Sargon hoped the man had.

"Since when does a leader of ten sit in on the councils of his clan leaders? Your Sarum will tell you whatever he sees fit."

"You will tell me. Or you will not go anywhere."

Sargon leaned forward and took a firmer grip on his sword. "Then you are in my way and I will have to ride over you. If I have to kill you, I will. Your men will not interfere, now that they see that you have forsaken both your oath as a warrior to my father, and your duty to your clan."

Taking his time, Sargon slid the sword from its scabbard, holding it across his chest so that the blade's tip was level with his left ear. At the same time, he tightened his grip on the halter. He kept his gaze on the leader, but out of the corner of his eye he saw hands tightening on their bows.

Every Alur Meriki, including their stony-faced leader, recognized the signs of a man readying himself for a fight. Sargon waited, ready to kick the horse forward in a futile attack, four against ten.

"Wait! Put away your sword. I will take you to the caravan. But if our Sarum decides you have wasted his time, I swear to the gods that I will kill you myself."

Sargon eased his grip on the halter, and let himself lean back. "That day will never come, no matter what your Council of Elders decides." He carefully returned his weapon to its scabbard. "Then let us ride. We have wasted enough time talking."

"Stay here." The words came out in a snarl of rage. "I must speak to my men first."

With a savage jerk of his hand, the Alur Meriki leader turned his horse around and cantered about a hundred paces away. An order shouted over his shoulder brought his men to him, most of them glancing over their shoulders as they moved away from the Ur Nammu.

Taking his time, Sargon eased his horse to the top of the ridge line. He hadn't liked looking up at the warriors. Fashod and the others joined him.

"I thought he was going to cut your head off," Garal remarked in a low voice. "You should choose your enemies with more care. You are not yet ready to fight one as strong as he."

Sargon grunted, feeling light-headed, as if he had just escaped certain death. He doubted if he would ever be ready for such an encounter. "You thought I was going to attack him? I was going to order you to do it."

Jennat laughed, a sharp burst of sound that made the Alur Meriki turn their heads toward them. Even Fashod smiled.

"Keep your words polite, and don't do anything to anger them further," Fashod cautioned. "I would like to return to my wives one of these days."

The Alur Meriki discussion went on longer than Sargon expected. He'd begun to grow impatient when it broke up at last. The leader of ten rode back alone to face Sargon. "I will lead the way to the caravan, with four of my men. The rest must remain here to patrol."

He meant to keep watch in case an Ur Nammu raiding party was on its way. Still, only five men to guard four, that was good. Obviously the Alur Meriki leader could not admit that five of his men could not defeat three men and a boy.

"Good. But if you can't keep up, we will leave you behind. Our message cannot wait. We will ride hard from sunup to sundown."

"We will keep up. Our horses are fresh."

"Then we ride." Sargon clucked to his horse, and started at a canter. Fashod and the others were right behind him, leaving the Alur Meriki behind. Sargon heard the warrior swear a mighty oath. But Sargon didn't look back.

Before they'd covered a hundred paces, the leader of ten moved his horse to Sargon's right side. When his horse had settled into its pace, he turned to Sargon. "What is so important that it cannot wait?"

Sargon kept his eyes straight ahead. "I do not speak with anyone who will not tell me his name."

"My name is Den'rack."

"Well, Den'rack, you will find out soon enough."

"You are trying my patience, dirt-eater."

"Ah, do not let my father hear you say those words. Eskkar of Akkad does not have my patience. He would take offense, if you know what I mean."

"I will pray three times a day to the war gods that you are not who you say you are, so I can have the pleasure of killing you myself."

Sargon smiled at that. No doubt in the next few days, there would be more than a few trying to kill him. For the first time since they'd started riding, he turned toward Den'rack and met his gaze.

"There should not be any quarrel between us. No matter how this turns out, you have done the right thing for your clan. You said you had a new Sarum. Is Clan Chief Urgo dead?"

The talk among the Akkadian soldiers who had returned from the battle had mentioned Urgo's name more than once. According to Eskkar, Urgo seemed to be a wise and reasonable man.

"No, he is not dead. But Urgo is too old and infirm to lead the clan in these troubled times. He asked the Council, what was left of it, to chose another."

Sargon heard the anger in Den'rack's voice. Eskkar's victory over the Alur Meriki must have sown many bitter feelings. "Who was chosen as Sarum?"

"Bekka of the Wolf clan."

The name meant nothing to Sargon, but he guessed he would learn all he needed to know about the man in the next few days.

27

As the sun disappeared below the horizon, Sargon, the Ur Nammu, and the Alur Meriki halted for the night. Den'rack had guided them to a stream he'd camped at a few days earlier. Water, as always, was too important to ignore, even if it meant a few more miles added to their journey. Enough grass grew beside the stream, so the horses could forage without being tempted to wander off.

A small stand of trees arched up over the water, and a fallen log provided a convenient place for Sargon to pitch his blanket. He ignored the frown on Den'rack's face at Sargon's casual possession of the most desirable spot to stretch out for the night.

Sargon understood Den'rack's dilemma. The warrior could have ordered Sargon to move, but if Sargon were indeed the son of the king and forced an argument, Den'rack might lose face. So Sargon pretended not to notice as the Alur Meriki leader gritted his teeth in silence, and flung his blanket on the ground ten paces away.

After seeing to their horses, Sargon and each of his companions wolfed down a few strips of dried meat from their pouches. As he worked his jaws, Sargon had no idea of what animal had furnished the chewy sustenance. Hunger made it tasty enough.

Den'rack's men spread their blankets beside their leader. He and his warriors looked almost as tired as Sargon. They'd ridden just as far today.

Tomorrow would be a greater challenge for them, as they would not have the luxury of alternating horses.

"At least we won't have to post a guard tonight." Fashod glanced toward the surly Alur Meriki staring at them. "Den'rack wouldn't trust any of us anyway. Unless he decides to slit our throats during the night."

"In that case, they would have killed us when we first met, and saved all of us a lot of riding." Sargon finished the last of the meat, picked his teeth clean with a twig, and rolled himself up in the horse blanket. Ignoring the talk from the Alur Meriki, he fell asleep in a few heartbeats.

In the morning, he found the Alur Meriki warriors had awoken before dawn, no doubt determined to prove they could rise earlier than any Ur Nammu. No one had much to say, and Sargon ignored his escorts. Everyone checked their horses, mounted up, and resumed the journey.

Den'rack again led the way, but Fashod set the pace, forcing the Alur Meriki to push their horses. Two more days passed in much the same manner – lots of hard riding, little talking, and not much food.

Fashod, who had an uncanny skill at judging distances, estimated they covered almost a hundred and forty miles the first two days after leaving the Ur Nammu camp. After they joined up with the Alur Meriki, the rough terrain slowed them down somewhat, and Fashod guessed that they made only sixty miles for the next two days.

Twice they encountered other Alur Meriki patrols. Sargon endured the required delays these caused. Fortunately, they did not meet anyone of higher rank than Den'rack, someone who might have other ideas about allowing Ur Nammu warriors so deep into what the Alur Meriki considered their territory.

Just after midday on the third day of their joint expedition, they encountered the outer guards of the main Alur Meriki caravan. By then only three of Den'rack's warriors remained. One rider's horse had gone lame yesterday, and Sargon had refused to lend the warrior one of the Ur Nammu mounts. Den'rack had to leave the cursing man behind. After such hard riding, all of the Alur Meriki horses were nearly dead on their feet, pushed past their limits of endurance by the effort to keep up with the Ur Nammu.

In less than five days of riding, Sargon and his friends had traversed more than three hundred miles, some of that over patches of difficult country that slowed their progress.

By now, the Zagros Mountains towered over them, the higher peaks capped with snow. The base of the mountains loomed only a mile or so to the north.

When they crested one more of the seemingly endless foothills, Sargon gazed upon a mighty caravan stretched out in a long straggling line, moving slowly toward him. Herds of horses, goats, sheep, and cows ranged on either side of the column.

Unlike the Ur Nammu, most of the Alur Meriki transported their women, children, and possessions in large wagons that creaked and wheezed in a never ending sound, a rasping friction of wood on wood, that soon grated on Sargon's ears even at this distance.

Nevertheless, the sight of a moving village impressed Sargon, and even Fashod muttered something about the size and might of the Clan.

Den'rack led the way toward the wagons, until he was stopped by a party of twenty or so warriors, who rode at the vanguard of the caravan. Den'rack ordered a halt, and Sargon slowed his horse to a stop. No matter what happened, at least the long journey had ended.

An older warrior rode up. His eyes went first to Fashod and the warriors, before giving Sargon the briefest of glances, though he rode at the head of the little troop. The stranger turned to Den'rack. "Why do these Ur Nammu scum still carry their weapons?"

Hearing the warrior's criticism, Sargon almost felt sorry for Den'rack, who launched into a lengthy explanation of the last few days. As time passed on the journey, Den'rack had gradually relaxed his suspicions regarding Sargon and his companions.

Now Den'rack found himself explaining the unusual situation to a superior. Sargon gathered that the senior warrior's name was Lugal.

During the latter part of Den'rack's story, Lugal's eyes fixed on Sargon. He guided his horse toward Sargon, moving close enough to touch Sargon's left knee with his own. "You do not look like the . . . Eskkar of Akkad."

Sargon had heard that many times growing up. He didn't much look like his mother, either. He refused to let Lugal's glare intimidate him. There were, after all, only so many ways of dying.

"Who I look like is no concern of yours. My business is with your Sarum."

"Watch your tongue, or I'll have it cut out." He reinforced his words by leaning forward and poking Sargon hard in the chest with his left hand.

Not so long ago, such a blow would have toppled Sargon from his horse. But all those days of training with Garal had toughened not only his muscles, but his reactions.

Without thinking, Sargon turned his shoulder, deflecting most of the blow, and keeping his balance. At the same time, he shoved his right knee hard against the side of his horse.

The well-trained animal thrust itself against Lugal's mount. Sargon increased the pressure of his knee, and reinforced the command with a jerk to the halter.

Lugal's horse, caught by surprise, stumbled backwards, its rider caught off guard. With a hard kick, Sargon's horse pushed even harder, and the Alur Meriki warrior's horse slid to its haunches a few paces away. Lugal managed to retain his seat, but only by clinging to his horse's mane and flailing around as he struggled to keep his balance.

No one moved or spoke, and only the creak of the approaching wagons broke the silence. Sargon raised his voice. "To lay hands on the son of the King is punishable by death. Touch me again, and I'll see that your Sarum sends your head to my father."

It wasn't true, of course, but Sargon thought it sounded impressive. Apparently the others within hearing thought so, too, since no one spoke, or tried to take his head.

Having righted his horse and gotten control of the still nervous beast, Lugal ripped his sword from its scabbard. "You'll die right here for that."

"No! You must not! Remember your oath." Den'rack's bellow rose over all of them. He kicked his horse between the two.

Sargon's hand had already gone to his sword, but before he could draw it, another voice interrupted. "What's going on here?"

A rider guided his mount into the midst of the knot of warriors, and they moved aside to give him room. A long, jagged scar traced its way from below his left shoulder nearly to his wrist, but the copper link chain that hung around his neck proclaimed him a clan leader. Sargon took his hand from his sword and studied the newcomer. The copper chain held no medallion, so this was not the Sarum.

"These are the strangers that I brought here," Den'rack said, speaking quickly. "Did my messenger arrive?"

"Only this morning. I did not expect you to arrive so soon. You must have ridden hard."

Sargon glanced at Den'rack. He had underestimated the Alur Meriki warrior. Obviously Den'rack had not left all his men behind on patrol. He must have dispatched a rider, probably leading another horse, and ordered him to bring word to the caravan.

"We did, Suijan," Den'rack answered.

Lugal, his face flushed with rage, moved forward. "This . . . boy nearly knocked me from my horse. I demand the right to kill him."

"No, his fate will be decided by the Council." Suijan didn't even raise his voice or turn to face the angry warrior. "Put your sword away."

For a moment, Lugal hesitated. Suijan turned his gaze toward the man, but said nothing.

The rage in Lugal's eyes faded under Suijan's stare. With an oath, Lugal shoved his sword into its scabbard, taking three tries before he could master his fury enough for the tip to enter the opening.

"You may return to your duties, Lugal," Suijan said. "Den'rack and I will take the strangers to the Sarum." Without another glance at the still raging Lugal, Suijan moved his horse closer to Sargon, exactly as Lugal had.

Suijan gazed into Sargon's eyes, a scrutiny that went on for some time. "There may be a resemblance, but we will see." He backed his horse a step away. "Take their weapons. No strangers may enter the camp armed."

Sargon had nearly flinched under the leader's stare. This Suijan not only had his wits about him, but he had the air of command.

Sargon glanced toward Fashod. The Ur Nammu warrior had already pulled the lances from his back. He handed them to one of Den'rack's men, and started untying his sword. Jennat and Garal followed suit.

After a moment, Sargon pulled the lance that he wore across his back and handed it off. But he made no move to give up his sword.

"Your sword and knife, too. There are no exceptions." Suijan's voice remained patient.

"My father gave me this sword. I do not hand it to anyone."

The tension in the air, which had faded somewhat as Fashod and the others surrendered their weapons, returned. Everyone turned to see what Suijan's next order would be.

Fashod cleared his throat. "Sargon, it would be best . . ."

Sargon cut off Fashod's words with a quick gesture of his left hand.

Suijan let a smile cross his face. "So, that is how it is." He studied Sargon for a moment. "You have journeyed long, and are no doubt tired. Perhaps you will let me carry your sword. I give you my word that I will return it to you whenever you ask for it."

Sargon decided that he had proven his strength and authority before the Alur Meriki. Besides, he guessed that Suijan meant what he said.

"That is most courteous. I thank you for your kindness," Sargon answered, bowing his head in acknowledgement of Suijan's status. Unbuckling his sword belt, he leaned forward and handed it to the clan leader.

"Come, follow me." Suijan accepted the weapon with respect. "We will ride ahead to tonight's camp site." He turned his horse to the west and started off. Den'rack and his men followed, leaving Sargon and his disarmed companions to trail along behind.

The camp site chosen was only about two miles away, but Sargon realized it would take the rest of the afternoon before the lead wagon arrived. The wagons, he would later learn, considered four or five miles a day a satisfactory journey.

A good sized stream, coming down from the mountains, wandered across their path. Suijan moved toward the higher ground, where the water would be freshest. "Den'rack, mark out a place for them here, and make sure they stay inside. I'll return later."

Sargon didn't like that. "Chief Suijan, I would speak with your Sarum as soon as possible."

"He is out riding to the south, but he will return before dusk. A rider has already been dispatched." With a nod to Den'rack, the clan leader turned his horse around and cantered off.

Swinging down from his horse, Sargon couldn't hold back a sigh of relief. It felt good to be off the back of his horse before dark. And still alive. He resisted the urge to shiver at what might come next.

Den'rack posted guards, and marked off an area, using sticks driven into the ground. Sargon didn't care. He walked into the stream and let himself fall forward. The chilly water, much colder than the stream near the camp of the Ur Nammu, made him catch his breath, but he stayed immersed until his skin glowed.

Stripping off his clothes, he gave himself the first bath he'd had since Tashanella found him at the stream. Already that seemed long ago. When Sargon finished scrubbing his body, he rinsed out his clothes. It no longer felt strange to wash his own clothes or feed a horse himself, something he had never done back in Akkad, surrounded by helpful servants.

When he finally left the water, Sargon spread out his clothes on the ground. Hopefully they would be dry before he met with the Sarum.

"I see you remembered what I taught you." Garal squatted down beside him.

Sargon managed a smile. Garal had knocked Sargon off his horse twice with that trick.

Fashod walked over and, with a grunt of relief, eased himself to the ground beside them. "Let's hope Lugal doesn't decide to kill you for embarrassing him in front of his men." He sighed. "I think, Sargon, that you can stop trying to impress their warriors."

"I agree. I'm too tired anyway. But the son of a king must always act like a leader of men."

As he repeated the words his father had said to him many times, Sargon realized that he had seldom listened to that advice. If he had paid better attention, he might not be facing torture and death this very evening.

Sargon found a patch of grass just large enough for him to stretch out on, and he did. Covering his eyes with his arm, he breathed a sigh of relief. Within moments, his snores sounded.

Fashod motioned Garal away. They joined Jennat, who had just finished tending the horses.

"I don't know how he can fall asleep like that," Fashod said. "He should be worrying about being killed."

"What do we do now?" Jennat, too, looked weary.

"Now we wait," Fashod said. "But perhaps we should get cleaned up as well. We wouldn't want to meet the new Sarum of the Alur Meriki looking like horses after a long run, and smelling just as bad."

—⁓⁓⁓—

Sargon slept through the arrival of the caravan, which usually made more than enough noise to wake anyone not used to hearing it. As the camp settled in, Fashod woke him. Sargon found that someone had covered his naked body with a blanket.

"Better make yourself ready" Fashod gestured toward the setting sun. "The summons may come at any time."

When Sargon tossed the blanket aside, he felt the chill of the evening air coming off the mountains. The brief rest had refreshed him. He gathered up his damp clothes and donned them. A shiver passed over his body, and he stretched himself until he warmed up.

"When you meet with their Sarum," Fashod said, "try not to antagonize him. Remember, to the Alur Meriki, he is the greatest king in the world."

Sargon had no intention of provoking anyone. "I'll take care."

"You know what to say?"

"Yes. We've been over it enough times."

"Good. Then just trust your instincts. We've done all that we can do. Whatever happens now is the will of the gods."

Sargon shrugged. "My father doesn't believe in the gods. He says they never helped him when he needed help. He trusted to his luck."

"Perhaps luck is merely the favor of the gods," Fashod said.

Jennat called out, and Sargon glanced up to see Suijan approaching. A young warrior walked beside him, carrying Sargon's sword.

Sargon waited until the clan leader stood before him, then bowed respectfully. Unlike most of the Alur Meriki, Suijan possessed gray eyes. Sargon forced himself to meet the man's steady gaze. It was one thing to stare down leaders of ten or fifty. A clan leader commanded hundreds of men, and for many years. Such a one would not be easily impressed or dominated.

"This is my son, Chennat." Suijan nodded to the young warrior. "He carries your sword. Perhaps you could allow him to accompany you to the council meeting."

For a moment, Sargon considered forcing the issue, then abandoned the idea. "Yes. My thanks to Chennat for his service."

The boy inclined his head in the slightest amount.

Sargon ignored the disrespect. "Are we to be taken to meet with the Sarum?"

"You are. Your companions will remain here."

"Fashod must accompany me." Sargon gestured toward his companion. "He is the second in command of the Ur Nammu, and he speaks for their Sarum."

"No. Only you are to come." Suijan sounded firm.

Sargon decided to try another way. "When a clan leader attends a council meeting, is he not expected to bring a member of his clan with him, to make certain that what is said is plain to all?"

"Yes, but you are not a clan leader," Suijan corrected him.

"I am." Sargon crossed his arms and rocked back on his heels, the gesture's meaning clear to all. He would not move until Suijan acknowledged his status.

Suijan stared at Sargon for a moment, weighing the alternative, which was to collect a handful of warriors and have Sargon carried to the council. The silence dragged on.

"Very well. Fashod may accompany you. But he is not to speak unless asked to. Is that understood?"

"Of course." Sargon smiled and uncrossed his arms. "We will follow you."

Suijan turned and started walking, taking long strides that covered plenty of ground. His son glared at Sargon for a moment, then moved quickly to keep up. Sargon and Fashod walked side by side. As they passed through the encampment, every eye turned toward them, and every conversation ceased until they had passed by, when it resumed with more excitement.

The four weaved their way through most of the camp, dodging wagons and tents, as well as a handful of children chasing each other in some unknown game. Sargon used the time to study the wagons and tents of the Alur Meriki.

The women busied themselves with their fires and cooking pots. Others set out drying racks that held the stretched skins of small game, hunted and caught along the trail. He saw few men, and guessed they were still tending their horses as the day's activities drew to a close.

As in the Ur Nammu camp, Sargon saw no luxuries, no goods to make life easier. Life for the steppes warriors remained full of hardship. When your family carried all your worldly goods with you, there was little place for anything but what you needed to survive. By now Sargon understood that such a demanding way of life gave the horsemen their strength, and made them so ferocious in battle.

They arrived at two wagons and two tents, set a little apart, but appearing no different from the others Sargon had seen. Only the tall standard with its dangling totems marked these possessions as belonging to the Alur Meriki Sarum.

Sargon counted eleven men clustered in a wide space set apart from all the tents and wagons. They all looked up as Suijan led his charge into their midst.

"Sit here." Suijan pointed to a place on the grass that faced the largest and closest of the tents. "Chennat, give him his sword."

The boy thrust the sword, still attached to the belt, into Sargon's hand. His knife also remained fastened to the thick leather. Sargon dropped to the ground, crossed his legs, and set the sword lengthwise before him. Fashod sat on Sargon's left, a little behind him.

Four Alur Meriki warriors detached themselves and moved to stand behind the two, no doubt with orders to restrain them if needed. Sargon glanced up and saw Den'rack and two of his men standing in the front rank of a small crowd that continued to swell. A wide space nearby remained clear. Well, at least it wasn't Lugal. His presence would have sent an entirely different message.

The other Alur Meriki stared at the two strangers with open curiosity. Beside Suijan, Sargon counted three unknown clan chieftains, marked by their copper chains. None of them appeared friendly, and two stared at Sargon with disdain on their faces.

Turning toward Fashod, Sargon spoke in the language of Akkad. "Well, at least they haven't summoned the torturers yet."

Fashod leaned closer and kept his voice soft. "So, Sargon of Akkad, now you are a clan leader yourself?"

Sargon repressed the urge to smile. In less than three months, he'd gone from outcast to horse boy to warrior and had now promoted himself to the rank of clan leader in his father's army. "My parents would be proud of me."

Before Fashod could reply, the flap on the larger of the two tents shifted, and a stocky warrior with wide shoulders and a broad chest appeared. His forehead was broad and high, with deep set eyes and a strong jaw. A burnished copper medallion, as big as two clenched fists, hung from his neck and told Sargon that this was the Sarum.

The leader of the Alur Meriki took his time covering the thirty or so paces until he reached a place on the ground just three paces or so opposite Sargon. A folded blanket had been spread out there, but the Sarum took his place beside it.

The four other clan leaders sat on either side of him, until only the space occupied by the blanket remained. As everyone settled in, Sargon saw another clan leader approaching, this one leaning on a younger man for support.

Out of politeness, everyone looked away as the older man was assisted to the ground, settling on the blanket with a sigh and stretching one leg straight out before him. He nodded gratefully to the warrior who attended him, who now moved a step behind his clan leader.

When the Sarum of the Alur Meriki saw the old warrior settled, he nodded to Suijan, the only chief who remained on his feet. The Council Meeting had begun.

"This is the young man who claims that he is the son of Eskkar of Akkad," Suijan began. "His name is Sargon. The Ur Nammu attending him is called Fashod. Sargon says that Fashod is one of the clan leaders of the Ur Nammu."

One of the chiefs spat on the ground at the mention of the Ur Nammu. Sargon decided that wasn't a good omen.

Suijan ignored the gesture, and continued. "Sargon, this is Chief Bekka, of the Wolf Clan, the Sarum of the Alur Meriki. The other clan leaders are Urgo," he pointed to the old warrior on the blanket to Bekka's right, "Prandar of the Serpent Clan, Virani of the Eagle Clan, and Trayack of the Lion Clan."

The Alur Meriki clan chieftains formed a half circle, all facing Sargon.

Suijan dropped to the ground beside Bekka, on his left side. "And I am Suijan of the Fox Clan. There are two more clan leaders, but they are away riding with the scouting parties."

Suijan turned to Bekka, who nodded approval. Behind each chief stood his attendant, alert and ready to respond to any request. Or any threat.

"You claim you are the son of Eskkar of Akkad." Bekka made it a statement, not a question. "You say that your father has sent you to us. Why should we believe you?"

And so it begins, Sargon thought. He bowed respectfully to Bekka. "My father is Eskkar of Akkad. My mother is Lady Trella, Queen of Akkad. I was born in Akkad, not long after the Alur Meriki ended their siege. But my father was born here, in this caravan, in the Hawk Clan, one of your own. After the battle at the mountain stream, he restored the Hawk Clan. Those still alive recognized him as the son of Hogarthak, slain at a council meeting by Maskim-Xul, the father of Thutmose-sin."

Sargon paused to take a breath. Hard eyes met his own, and he saw nothing that indicated any signs of belief.

"You do not resemble Eskkar of Akkad." Chief Bekka kept his words free of emotion.

"No, I do not. My mother came from the villages of Sumeria, far to the south. But I am Sargon, just the same. And I know all the details of the battle at the stream. I know that Hathor the Egyptian with a hundred horsemen raced through the mountains to reach the stream first. He drove off the warriors who attempted to hold it against him, then defeated an attack that tried to dislodge him. The next day, my father arrived with his archers, slingers, and spearmen. He brought with him over a thousand experienced fighters, many of whom fought in the Sumerian War. By the time the full force of your warriors arrived, it was too late. From that moment, there was nothing the Alur Meriki could do to defeat him."

Trayack, the chief who had spit at the mention of the Ur Nammu, spoke. "If the warriors had held the stream, instead of abandoning it to the first group of riders, the battle would have ended differently." He did not bother to hide the bitterness in his words.

Sargon wondered at that comment, actually more of an interruption. Unless the skirmish at the stream meant something more to one of those present.

He remembered the advice his mother had once given him – never assume that your enemy is united, or that he does not have to deal with discontent or ambition within his own ranks. Every force, no matter how strong, always has some weakness to conceal. Now that Sargon considered it, after such a defeat there must still be plenty of rancor among the leaders of the clan.

"I have ridden with Hathor the Egyptian and his horsemen," Sargon went on, speaking slower now. "They are the fiercest fighters in my father's army, the ones that smashed the Sumerians and destroyed them in the Great Battle of Isin. Two or three times as many warriors as Hathor found at the stream could not have defeated him."

This time Virani and Prandar glanced at Bekka, who had ignored Trayack's remark. Instead the Sarum turned to Urgo. "Perhaps you should speak to Sargon."

"It seems that you know much about the battle," Urgo said. "Yet any man present at the stream would know as much." His deep voice matched his thick and stocky build, though he lacked the hard muscles of one who rode each day. "Still, I believe you are Eskkar's son. Tell us why he sent you to us."

"My father did not send me."

Those words affected the clan leaders. Until now, everyone had assumed the father had dispatched the son. Even Bekka and Suijan's eyes went wide.

"My father had sent me to the tents of the Ur Nammu almost three moons ago, to complete my training as a warrior. He believes in the old ways, and that only someone who has ridden with the warriors of the steppes can truly learn how to fight and how to lead. But I know that he would approve of my actions."

"Then you do not speak with your father's authority." Urgo made it a simple statement, not a condemnation.

"No. He is in Akkad, and there was no time to seek his approval. But I know his ways, and I know what he would want me to do. That is why I have come both to warn you, and to seek your help."

"Warn us of . . .?"

"I was riding far to the west, with a small scouting party. We encountered a large force of fighters. The leader of our party went to speak with them, and I accompanied him to interpret. We were attacked, and barely got away. The next day, we returned in the night and attacked them. We killed many and captured over forty horses."

"The Ur Nammu are too cowardly to fight in the light of day."

Sargon turned to stare at Trayack, surprised at the interruption. Obviously the chief of the Lion Clan spoke his mind without regard to his Sarum.

Then Sargon remembered that Thutmose-sin had led the Lion Clan. They would hold the most bitter feelings for the King of Akkad and his son. And possibly for the man who replaced Thutmose-sin.

Shifting his body to face the man, Sargon met his gaze. He took his time before responding. Another saying of his mother crossed his mind. Always keep your voice calm, and let your words carry your message, not your face.

"I am sure Trayack of the Alur Meriki, no doubt the bravest of the brave, would have led his fifteen horsemen against a thousand heavily armed and experienced fighters, and slain them all. And I see that the battle wisdom of the Alur Meriki has not changed. Perhaps that is why my father has defeated you so easily at every turn."

Trayack's mouth opened in disbelief, and his tanned face grew even darker. A thick vein in his forehead throbbed. Before he could speak, the Sarum cut him off.

"Hold your words for now, Trayack. There will be time later for you to speak."

"I will kill him for that!" Trayack's fist pounded on his knee.

Sargon smiled at the challenge. The number of warriors lining up to kill him kept growing. He leaned forward, the slight movement emphasizing the force of his words.

"Tell me, Trayack of the Lion Clan, which of my words offended you? You accuse me of cowardice without knowing how many men we faced. I only said you were brave enough to attack a thousand fighters. Is that not praise enough for you? Or perhaps the defeats the Alur Meriki have suffered at my father's hand are something that has not happened?"

Sargon's gaze swept over the other clan leaders, and he caught a glimpse of a fleeting smile on Suijan's face.

"Do not try the patience of this Council," Urgo said.

"Chief Urgo, I have ridden over three hundred miles in five days to warn you that a strong enemy is approaching, an enemy strong enough to defeat and destroy your entire Clan. I could have ridden to the safety of my father's forts. Or I could have sent a messenger to find one of your scouting parties and convey the warning. But I chose to come myself, to warn my father's people of the oncoming danger. And what do I find?"

Sargon glanced at Trayack. "Threats from loud talkers, who know nothing about the danger that faces them."

"I will kill you." Trayack's resolve had not slackened.

"When this council is ended, I will be as eager to face you in combat. But even if you kill me, do not expect to live a long life. If any of your warriors survive the Carchemishi attack, my father will hunt them and you down, and destroy you with his own hand, just as he did Thutmose-sin. So go ahead with your foolishness. Bring down the death and the end of all the Alur Meriki on your head."

"Silence!" This time Bekka brought the full force of his authority into the word. "Trayack, if you speak again, I will remove you from the council."

Urgo spoke before Trayack could reply. "Who are the Carchemishi? Do you mean those who live far to the west, at the base of the mountains, in the village of Carchemish?"

Sargon turned away from Trayack as if he didn't exist. "Yes, but it is no longer a village, but a city of many thousands. They have raised an army, and its soldiers are moving toward us. They have heard of the wealth of the lands of Akkad, and they plan to loot the countryside and claim it for themselves. They have dispatched over fifteen hundred fighters, more than half of them mounted, down the great trade route. In their passage, they have devastated the land, burned whatever crops and huts they found, and stripped it bare of game."

"Then they mean to attack Akkad?"

Sargon shook his head. "No, I don't think so. Even the Carchemishi are not that foolish. Akkad's walls are high, and my father can raise ten thousand fighters if necessary."

That wasn't quite true, but Sargon knew the number would impress the chiefs.

"I have already dispatched riders to King Eskkar's outlying forts, to warn them of these invaders. As soon as he hears of their presence, my father will gather a force to meet them. That, however, will take time. Nor will he need so many men. The Carchemishi will turn aside when they see the numbers of Akkadian fighters opposing them. Long before then, however, the Carchemishi will have found you. They have more than enough men to destroy your caravan. And once they realize you are moving in the direction of their lands, they will not hesitate to attack you. They know they cannot continue toward Akkad's northern lands without destroying a potential threat to their rear."

Urgo rubbed his chin. "How many horsemen?"

Sargon told him what information Subutai had gathered, and their best guess of the size and composition of the Carchemishi forces.

"Now that you have warned us, we will stand ready to meet them. Despite their greater numbers, they will not find us so easy to defeat."

"I hope that is true, Chief Urgo. But these men will not face you in a horse battle, rider for rider. They will have their archers and foot soldiers with them, to support their cavalry. They will march toward this caravan, and force you to fight at a time and place of their choosing. They will do to you what they are already doing to the Ur Nammu. Force you to abandon your wagons and tents, and flee for your lives."

"You seem to know much about fighting for one so young."

"The raid against these invaders was my first battle," Sargon admitted. "But my father and his commanders have taught me much about the ways of fighting, and I have heard many times the stories of all the battles. One thing I have learned – what my father proved in our war against Isin – is that cavalry, horsemen such as your clan, cannot prevail against a combined force of infantry and horse fighters."

Which was exactly what happened at the mountain stream, but Sargon knew he didn't need to remind them of that again.

"Then we thank you for your warning, Sargon, son of Eskkar of Akkad." Urgo, at least, appeared willing to show some gratitude and respect for Sargon's presence. "What else do you wish to tell us?"

"I wish to ask for your help in battle, to save the Ur Nammu Clan."

Again the stoic faces disappeared in surprise. If Sargon had asked them to ride up into the mountains until they reached the moon, they could not have shown more disbelief.

"Why should we help the Ur Nammu?" Urgo kept his voice even. "We have given our oath not to attack them, but they remain our enemies. We swore no oaths to come to their assistance. If your father had not prevailed, we would have hunted them down ourselves."

"I know that you are not bound to help the Ur Nammu, but I cannot believe that all wisdom has deserted the Alur Meriki," Sargon said. "The Ur Nammu have three hundred fighters. If you attack them, they will kill at least that many of your own warriors. Perhaps even more. Can the Alur Meriki afford such losses? And to what end? How many of your warriors died in the fight at the stream? Close to four or five hundred?"

Sargon leaned forward. "Now I ask you to do what I know my father would ask. Join forces with the Ur Nammu, and destroy these Carchemishi invaders, before they destroy you."

A murmur came from behind, and Sargon glanced over his shoulder, surprised to see that hundreds of people, warriors as well as women and children, had gathered in silence as close as they dared approach, to hear the words of the council. That meant that all of those present now knew of the danger.

"We do not fight the battles of others," Urgo said. "Especially Akkad's."

"My father told me of a saying in the Clan. The enemy of my enemy is my friend. Is that not true."

Urgo smiled, the first time he'd shown any emotion. "A saying is not something we use to decide about going to war."

"The Ur Nammu have broken their camp," Sargon went on. "Abandoned their tents and possessions, taking only their women and children. If they were closer to Akkad's forts, they would have gone there to seek protection from my father's soldiers. But they cannot reach them in time. The Carchemishi are too close. So I urged the Ur Nammu instead to move toward the Alur Meriki. In three or four days, five at most, the Ur Nammu will be attacked, and even three hundred brave warriors cannot withstand so many."

"And you want us to risk our warriors' lives for those of the Ur Nammu?"

"No. To protect the lives of your own women and children. Consider this. After a hard fight with the Ur Nammu, the Carchemishi will be even more prepared and experienced to face your forces. Is it not better to fight while you have others to fight at your side? If you do this, my father will send food and herds to help feed your people, and supply whatever else you require. You will need such help to survive the journey through the now barren lands to the west."

"And why would he do that?"

"Because the Ur Nammu are the allies of Akkad. Because they are friends to my father and mother. And because you may save the life of their son, Sargon. Because I will be returning to the Ur Nammu. I have not yet completed my training, and I must stand with my friends."

Another murmur passed through the crowd. Urgo took a deep breath, stared at the ground for a moment, then turned to Fashod. "You are . . . ?"

"I am Fashod, second in command of the Ur Nammu." He bowed respectfully to the older man. "My thanks to you, Chief Urgo, for letting us speak. First, let me say that I have fought with Eskkar of Akkad in three battles, and with Hathor the Egyptian in three more. Our Sarum is Subutai. He, too, is a friend of Eskkar. Neither of us thought to approach the Alur Meriki for help, but Sargon suggested this. May I tell you what else we have discovered about our enemy, and what we have planned?"

Sargon noticed that Trayack could scarcely conceal his impatience. That should teach him to speak foolishly. Now he dared not interrupt, if he didn't want to be escorted from the Council.

Urgo didn't look to his Sarum for approval. "Yes. Tell us what you've learned."

Fashod told them about the hurried ride back to the camp, and of Subutai's difficult decision to head toward the Alur Meriki. He also told them all they had learned about the Carchemishi, the size and disposition of their forces, and their probable plans.

As Fashod spoke, Sargon felt the presence of the crowd growing ever larger and creeping ever closer with each word. A routine Council meeting had turned into something far more urgent.

No doubt Chief Bekka, if he had known what Sargon planned to say, would have met with him privately. But now everyone knew of the coming battle, and of Sargon's offer to provide food and anything else they needed. The Sarum and his clan leaders' decisions would be scrutinized by all.

Fashod finished up. "Subutai knows that he cannot ask for your help out of friendship. But he does ask it, because he knows that it will also help you. Perhaps if we survive the battle, the time may come for friendship, or at least peace, between our clans. Is not Thutmose-sin dead, and Subutai's father? Both those leaders waged war upon the other. But I was present when Subutai's father died many years ago, and that day Subutai declared that the Shan Kar between him and your clan had ended. With Thutmose-sin gone, is there any longer a reason for our clans to do battle?"

"Your words have wisdom, Fashod. Tell your Sarum that we have heard his words." Urgo glanced at the other clan leaders, but no one seemed to have anything else to say. "Then we are finished. Sargon, is there more you wish to tell us?"

"Only that we would request fresh horses, so that we can ride back to join the fight against the invaders. The horses we rode are spent, but they are some of the finest we have. We would trade them for an equal number. And we would leave at dawn."

"We will consider that as well," Urgo said

"Then I give thanks to the Council for letting me speak." Sargon rose to his feet, the scabbard of his sword held in his left hand. "Now I must accept the challenge of those who have spoken against me. Den'rack was the first to offer a challenge, so I will fight him first."

Even Urgo appeared surprised at Sargon's foolishness. But a challenge was a challenge, and every warrior could always exercise his right to fight another. Still, no one watching could now doubt Sargon's courage. Urgo lifted his gaze, and picked out the warrior standing motionless a few paces away.

"Den'rack, do you offer the challenge to Sargon, son of Eskkar?"

"No, I do not. When I challenged Sargon, I did not know he had come to warn our people of danger. Only a fool fights with one who would offer the hand of help and friendship."

Sargon had faced Den'rack during his reply. Now Sargon bowed to the warrior. "Den'rack is a loyal and wise warrior. I and all the Alur Meriki are in his debt for his help in bringing us here as quickly as he did."

Sargon turned back to Urgo. "Now I must face Lugal. Is he here?"

"I am here." Lugal's voice came from the crowd. He stepped forward until he stood just behind Sargon.

Urgo had frowned at hearing Lugal's name. "Lugal is a wise warrior, who fought beside me many times when we were both young. I ask you, Lugal, do you demand your right to combat with Sargon of Akkad, son of Eskkar?"

From the expression on Lugal's face, Sargon knew the man still wanted to fight. But Lugal also understood Urgo's meaning. If Lugal offered the challenge, he would be pitting himself against Urgo's wishes. Fortunately, Den'rack's words had given him an easy opportunity to abandon the challenge.

"I withdraw my challenge. I, too, did not know that Sargon came to warn us."

"Then you have done your duty as a brave and loyal warrior," Urgo said.

Sargon bowed again.

That left only Trayack. Sargon shifted his gaze toward the angry clan leader, but before Trayack could offer the challenge, Bekka held up his hand for silence. "There can be no challenge between a clan leader and an untested warrior. It would be beneath the dignity of any clan leader. Is that not right, Trayack?"

Sargon felt his heart racing. He hadn't thought Den'rack would fight him, not after they had ridden together for three days. And Sargon knew he might stand a fair chance against Lugal, who had already passed his prime as a warrior. But Trayack was tall and strong and in his prime. He would cut Sargon to shreds.

Every eye in the camp went to the still truculent clan leader. A loud murmur rippled through the spectators. No one wanted to see Sargon's blood spilled in the dirt.

But Trayack could read tracks in wet ground as well as any. He had to unclench his teeth before he could speak. "No, there is no challenge. It would be beneath my honor to fight someone as young and untried as . . . Sargon."

Sargon bowed to him, and again to the entire Council. "Then I offer my thanks to the Clan of my father. May they always ride in the lands of the steppes with honor."

As Sargon turned away, a wave of relief flowed through his mind. His luck had held. He might just live to see another day.

28

Bekka watched Sargon and Fashod, escorted by their guards, disappear into the crowd. A crowd, Bekka noticed, that now seemed more curious than hostile to the young Akkadian and his Ur Nammu companions. The arrogant boy, and Bekka had no doubts that he was indeed Eskkar's son, had upended the Alur Meriki Council almost as much as his father.

"We need to speak further." Urgo's voice broke into his Sarum's thoughts.

"Oh, yes, we need to talk." He stood and helped Urgo to his feet. "In my tent." Bekka glanced at Suijan. "Tell the others to join us."

The clan leaders reassembled inside Bekka's tent. His wives had built a small fire, to provide illumination for their leaders. Soon a thin stream of smoke wafted toward the top of the tent. As the chiefs settled into a small circle, no one spoke, each man waiting until the women left. Only when the tent flap closed behind them did the discussion continue.

Trayack's anger returned unabated. "I say we should kill them all. Take them outside the camp, torture them, and then kill them. Let the Akkadians wonder what happened to them."

Urgo adjusted his stiff leg until he felt comfortable. "You may want to go to war with Akkad again, but I have had enough of Eskkar and his bowmen. He would find out. There are still enough remnants of the old Hawk Clan who would get word to him."

"Then let this Sargon whelp and his Ur Nammu scum go." Trayack's booming voice filled the tent. "The Carchemishi will kill the boy, and there will be no blame on us."

"I agree with Trayack." Bekka's soft words contrasted with Trayack's fury. "Best to let them go, and let the gods decide Sargon's fate. But the question remains. Do we ride to war to help the Ur Nammu?"

"You cannot be thinking of helping that filth." The fire's feeble light turned Trayack's face even redder. "Let them be slaughtered. We can fight off the invaders, if indeed there are any Carchemishi in these lands."

"You think the Ur Nammu made this up?" Urgo's temper began to fray under Trayack's constant complaining. "Something we could discover for ourselves in a few days scouting?"

"I think . . ." Bekka paused until he had everyone's attention, "we should ride to war to help Sargon and the Ur Nammu. I believe Sargon spoke the truth about these Carchemishi and their numbers. We will have to fight them. They are too few to trouble Akkad, but more than enough to do battle with us. Do you think they will return to their master in Carchemish and say that they failed to defeat Akkad? And then admit that they turned away from the Alur Meriki, and that now we are moving toward their lands?"

"I agree with Bekka," Urgo said, "but for another reason. We gave our oaths as warriors to Eskkar, and that binds us to him until the debt is paid. But if we help his allies and save his eldest son's life, he will be in our debt. There may come a time when we ask him to repay it."

Bekka nodded approval. He turned to Suijan. "What do you say?"

"I think we must go to war to help the Ur Nammu." Suijan rubbed the scar on his left arm, where not long ago an Akkadian arrow had sliced along the bone. "While you and Urgo questioned Sargon, I watched the faces of our people standing behind the boy while he spoke. By the time he finished speaking, most of them agreed with his position. Sargon chose his words with care and skill. Our people will talk of nothing else for days."

"You should have let me kill him." Trayack's hatred sounded plain in his voice. "He spoke with a serpent's tongue. The fools listening fell for his lies."

"In that, the boastful boy is like his father," Urgo said. "Eskkar rode into our camp, challenged everyone he met, won the approval of half our men, and rode out untouched. Now his son has done the same. If we fail to fight now, and the Carchemishi fall on us, Sargon's words will be remembered."

Bekka turned to Prandar. "And what about you?"

"On the word of a boy, do we ride against a strong enemy? No! Let the Carchemishi and the Ur Nammu kill each other. When the Ur Nammu are dead, if we must, we can confront the invaders. We will be no worse off."

"And where will we find food, if the countryside ahead of us is already stripped bare?" Urgo's voice had returned to its even tone. "We must follow the foothills for many days before we reach the steppes. Do we watch our women and children suffer, to sicken and die from hunger?"

"We can manage to find food somewhere," Prandar said. "We still have plenty of horses to eat."

"Is this what the Alur Meriki have become?" Suijan struck his knee with one fist. "We had to leave the eastern lands early, before the Elamites attacked us. Now we must grovel before some dirt eater in Carchemish, so far away that we don't even know his name?"

"What do you say, Virani?" Bekka, too, kept his voice calm.

"I have spoken much with my warriors since the battle at the stream. They want a chance to prove themselves. Let us ride down and kill these invaders. If we help the Ur Nammu and Akkad at the same time, and place them in our debt, so much the better."

That was more support than Bekka had hoped for. He'd expected Suijan and Urgo to agree with his decision, and that Trayack and Prandar would refuse to go along. Virani, however, had the respect of many in the camp, and his opinion mattered. Bekka hadn't been sure of which way Virani would turn. "Trayack?"

"I say we should leave the Ur Nammu and this boy Sargon to their fate," Trayack said. "If the Carchemishi challenge us, that will be the time to ride against them. I'll waste none of my men's lives on Ur Nammu scum. No warrior of mine will ever lift a sword for them."

But that threat wasn't as bad as it sounded. Trayack's Lion Clan, under Thutmose-sin, had suffered heavy losses in the battle at the stream. Trayack had little more than a hundred and twenty or so warriors fit to fight.

Bekka glanced at each man, as if considering their words. But the only thought in his mind was that Trayack had given him the opening Bekka wanted.

"I say we will ride to fight these Carchemishi," Bekka said. "If that helps the Ur Nammu and even the Akkadians, so be it. Suijan, Virani, and I will lead our warriors, and depart tomorrow at midmorning. Trayack and the Lion Clan will remain behind to protect the caravan. Urgo, I will need your warriors."

"You may have them. They will be glad to ride with you."

Bekka turned to Prandar. "You say you do not approve of helping the boy and the Ur Nammu. If that is your decision, you can stay behind with Trayack. Or you can choose to join us."

Every eye went to Prandar, who suddenly realized the difficult position Bekka had maneuvered him into. If Prandar sided with Trayack on this issue, Prandar would be forever branded with the same mark – that he had remained behind while others rode to war.

Prandar, older and wiser than Trayack, understood what was at stake. Trayack's hatred of anything that had to do with Akkad was well known. Since the defeat at the stream, much of that hatred had turned toward his new Sarum. If Bekka returned victorious, Prandar's warriors would lose faith in their leader, and Bekka could remove Prandar from the Council with a wave of his hand.

As for Trayack, the fool didn't even understand what Bekka would do to him when he returned. So it all depended on whether or not Bekka could win without Prandar and his hundred and seventy warriors.

Bekka kept his gaze on the hesitating chief as the silence lengthened. "What is your decision, Prandar?"

Prandar had one last thought. Bekka did not need to win a fight to the death. Any small victory, even a brief skirmish, would give the new Sarum the authority to solidify his rule over the Council of Chiefs and the Alur Meriki people. And if that happened, Prandar had better be on the winning side. Trayack was a fool after all.

Prandar lifted his gaze to meet his Sarum's. "My men and I will ride with you, Chief Bekka, to fight the invaders."

Trayack shook his head and muttered something under his breath.

"Good." Bekka nodded in approval. "Then it is settled. All of you should return to your men and tell them to prepare for a long ride and a hard fight. The Alur Meriki are going to war."

"You are a fool, Bekka," Trayack practically spat the words in his Sarum's face. "All of you are fools." His face reflected the rage that burned inside him. Trayack scrambled to his feet and left the tent, almost tearing the flap from its fastenings as he passed outside.

One by one, the others left, until only Urgo remained, facing the Sarum.

"You did well, Bekka."

"Now all I have to do is win."

"Yes." Urgo let out a long sigh. "Winning overcomes all mistakes. But better to risk everything than to live with fools like Trayack and his constant complaining behind your back. Sooner or later, he would have brought you down." Urgo sighed. "Help me up, my friend."

Bekka assisted the old man to his feet, and offered to help him to his tent. Urgo protested, but Bekka insisted. "Besides, I want to speak to Sargon, and your tent is on the way."

Urgo glanced at the man he'd chosen to replace him as Sarum. Urgo had selected Bekka, keen of wit despite his relative youth, and then swung the other clan leaders to agree with the choice. "Be careful what you say to that boy. Every time he speaks, I hear Eskkar and his witch wife talking. And I suspect there is more to Sargon's story than what he told us."

"I will take care." Bekka smiled. "I don't want him to challenge me. Not yet, at least."

⸻⁂⸻

Sargon had just finished retelling the details of the meeting outside the Sarum's tent to Garal and Jennat for the second time. Both kept shaking their heads at Sargon's boldness.

"You're lucky they didn't take your head right there," Jennat said.

"The clan leaders of the Alur Meriki understand power." Sargon shrugged. "It's the only thing they respect. My father knew it, too. It was important to act like a leader."

Fashod nodded. "I wonder what Eskkar will say when he hears of this."

"That's the least of our worries now," Sargon answered. "Let's just hope they give us some fresh horses and let us go."

"Do you think they will help us?" Garal couldn't keep the worry from his voice.

"I don't know. Nothing showed on their faces. Now that we're here, it seems doubtful."

"I will be glad to get back to my family," Jennat said, "no matter what happens. I wonder what they're doing."

A stirring among the men guarding them made Sargon glance up. A warrior had approached the guards, and now spoke with two of them. The ground the Ur Nammu occupied had no campfire, so Sargon couldn't make out who the stranger was.

"Sargon. Come join me." Bekka's voice came from the darkness.

Sargon climbed to his feet and walked toward the shadowy figure. "Chief Bekka."

"Walk with me," Bekka said. "I want to talk to you."

Without waiting for a reply, Bekka turned and strode off in the darkness. Sargon moved quickly in order to not lose sight of the Sarum. They passed through the outer edges of the camp and through some trees before Bekka finally halted near the stream. A string of small boulders and rocks lined the channel, and Bekka took a seat on one of them, his back to the flowing water.

"Sit here, beside me," he ordered.

Sargon obeyed, unsure of why the Sarum had brought him to this place. With the stream at their backs, the light from the many campfires cast a faint glow over the empty ground that led to the stream. The silver colored moon glowed overhead, and the shadowy trees gave off a pleasant scent. A private place to talk.

"How many seasons do you have, Sargon?"

He decided to tell Bekka the truth. "In two moons, I will have fifteen seasons."

"If you expect to live long enough to reach that happy day, you would do well to cease challenging everyone you meet."

"I wanted to show you and your clan that I am to be taken seriously, despite my years."

"You survived three challenges," Bekka said. "Do not tempt the gods by issuing a fourth."

"Then you are going to let us return to the south?"

"Yes. I'll give you fresh horses and you can depart in the morning. I'll also provide an escort to make sure you reach the border alive. Trayack is still angry, and he is not the only one. Many hate your father for the fight at the stream, and for making them swear the oath."

Sargon thought about that for a moment. The Sarum's words meant that he did not have full control of his chiefs or his fighters, if one or more of them could dare to disobey his orders.

"So you will not ride to help the Ur Nammu."

"No, that is why I *will* ride south to fight these Carchemishi. I need a victory for my warriors, or I will not lead the Clan for long. We have lost too many battles in the last few years. The Alur Meriki need to defeat a worthy enemy to regain their honor and enjoy once again the taste of victory."

Sargon's heart jumped at the news. The Alur Meriki would help. Which meant hope still lived for Tashanella and her family.

"Then we are in your debt, Chief Bekka."

"Remind your father of that when you see him. I will hold you both to your word. Now, I have a question for you."

Sargon glimpsed a flash of teeth in the moonlight.

"When you told Trayack that Hathor and his fighters could not be resisted once they had reached the stream, was that merely more of your bold words?"

Sargon wondered about the odd question, but he didn't hesitate. "No. Hathor has fought in even more battles than my father, from Egypt to the Land Between the Rivers. He does not speak much of those days, but Hathor was a leader of a thousand for many years. His horsemen, the ones chosen for the ride to the stream, were the strongest and bravest in Akkad's cavalry. They've trained together for many years, and have mastered the use of the horseman's bow."

Bekka laughed aloud. "Then I made the right decision, not to fight him at the stream."

Suddenly Sargon understood. "You led the men who first opposed him?"

"Yes. We had only a few men, and Hathor's horsemen looked too strong. Your words at the Council tonight removed some of the doubt that lingers over me."

"You made the right decision."

Bekka ignored that. "Now, tell me why you ride with the Ur Nammu, and why no Akkadian warriors accompany you. No king would leave his first born son alone to complete his training, with strangers and so far from home."

Caught by surprise at the unexpected question, Sargon couldn't find the words for a moment. Once again, he decided to speak the truth. "My father . . . my parents, were . . . disappointed with me. They felt I had failed them. In his anger, my father sent me to the Ur Nammu. I was not to return until I regained my honor."

"Or died." Bekka sighed. "I suspected something like that. Well, the wildness of young warriors must be tamed one way or another, if they are to grow to manhood and be of use to their Clan."

He laughed again. "Let us hope that we both live long enough to learn whether or not we have proved our worth. If I return without a victory, I might as well fall on my sword. Better that than watch Trayack become Sarum."

With a few words, Bekka had shown he understood Sargon's position. "Trayack would lead your people to disaster."

Bekka ignored that, too. He stood. "Time to go back. There is much to do. But remind your father that I will hold him to your words. We will need the protection and livestock you promised to feed our people, before this is over."

29

Climbing onto his horse a little after dawn, Sargon experienced a feeling of relief. The uncertainty of the last few days, the worry about first finding and then convincing the Alur Meriki had ended. The time for talking had passed as well. Now only the ride back to the Ur Nammu remained, and whatever fate awaited him.

Once again Den'rack rode with them, this time as a guide. Twenty men, under the command of a young warrior named Unegen, a member of Bekka's Wolf Clan, accompanied them to guarantee a safe passage. Not even Trayack or his followers would presume to attack so many of their own.

Every rider led a second horse. As they started off, Sargon glanced to the rear, but he saw no horse boys. That meant the warriors expected to ride into battle.

Den'rack led the way, though Unegen had already sent two scouts ahead.

No one had much to say during the long day's ride. Sargon worried about Tashanella, while his companions no doubt worried about their kin. For all he knew, the Carchemishi had already caught up with the Ur Nammu. Everyone Sargon knew or cared about might already be dead.

The thought of Tashanella enduring an even worse fate than dying gnawed at his chest. A beautiful young girl, beaten into submission and suitably trained, would fetch a good price at any slave market. Sargon had seen many such girls many times, in Akkad's own slave market.

That reminded him of his mother. Trella, too, had once been a slave, a fact that had embarrassed Sargon often enough as he grew up. Of course, no one had ever spoken of it to his face, but the unspoken words no doubt influenced his friends' attitude toward his family. For the first time, he wondered if his mother had ever stood naked in a slave market.

As the sun touched the horizon, Den'rack finally gave the signal to halt. They had reached a small pond fed from beneath the ground. Sargon knew they could have covered a few more miles before darkness, but the presence of fresh water made for a good camp site.

They had not passed this place on the way in. Before Sargon could ask, Den'rack walked over and explained to Sargon and his companions that this route would take them over easier ground. Then he returned to his own warriors.

Fashod, who had ridden over these lands years ago, agreed with Den'rack. "I don't remember this watering hole, but the trail we're taking shortens our journey by about twenty miles. When we first met up with Den'rack and his men, they had just finished the southeast to northwest leg on their patrol. With plenty of water, the horses should hold up better."

No one replied. They would either arrive in time to help in the fight, or they would be forced to take their revenge alone.

After a cold supper, Sargon spread his blanket. But before he could roll himself up, the leader of the Alur Meriki, Unegen, crossed over from where his warriors had settled down.

"I heard your words last night at the Council Meeting, Sargon of Akkad." Unegen squatted on the ground beside Sargon. "I fought against your father at the stream, and I was the one who first brought the news to Thutmose-sin of the one you call Hathor. Many in our clan, and even more in the others, doubted Bekka's decision, despite the fact that he was outnumbered, to yield the stream to Hathor's men. When you described the strength of the Akkadians, many who heard your words realized that Bekka had made the right choice."

"Chief Bekka has much wisdom," Sargon agreed, wondering where this was leading.

"He has taught me much," Unegen said. "I have less than twenty-three seasons, but already I am a leader of twenty."

Sargon's hadn't thought the man so young.

"And now," Unegen went on, "those who had doubts about Bekka becoming Sarum, including myself, no longer feel that way. He will make a good Sarum."

"I hope your people and mine can keep peace between us."

Unegen snorted. "Once I would never have thought such a thing. But the old days are gone. Thutmose-sin believed that he could hold back the dirt eaters, destroy their farms and villages to keep them weak. He failed, and now your cities have grown too strong. A new way must be found. I wept when your father killed Thutmose-sin, but I see that as long as he ruled our clan, many more warriors would have faced death, and for nothing."

"You are wise beyond your years, Unegen of the Alur Meriki. Perhaps some day, you will be the Sarum of your clan."

Unegen laughed, a cheerful sound that contrasted with his sober demeanor. "I think that would be a bad day for my people. But I wish you well in your quest, Sargon, son of Eskkar." He rose and returned to his warriors.

"The next Sarum of the Alur Meriki," Fashod, sitting only a few paces away, had heard their words, "talking to the next ruler of Akkad."

"I will never rule in Akkad." Sargon uttered the words with conviction. "My father has sent me from his house, and I have no wish to return there."

"As time passes, boys turn into men and learn wisdom, and even fathers relent their angry words. No man knows what the future will bring. A few days ago, we believed we were riding to our deaths."

"We'll know our fates soon enough." As Sargon rolled himself up in his blanket, that thought remained in his head. Though to his surprise, the idea of his death did not trouble him as much as his concern for Tashanella.

Three days later, just after midday, Sargon and his companions neared the end of their journey. One of Unegen's scouts came galloping back toward the main party, waving his arms. Sargon, riding just behind Unegen, with Fashod and Den'rack on either side, heard the scout's report.

The Carchemishi were only a few miles ahead, and two Alur Meriki patrols, one of them the men Den'rack had left behind, were keeping them under observation. Yassur, a leader of ten in the Serpent Clan, had taken command of the observing scouts.

Unegen frowned at the all too brief report. He ordered the scout to return to his position, and the rest of the bone-weary riders continued on.

Every man, every horse, had been pushed to its limit. Two horses had gone lame, and had to be abandoned. But despite his fatigue, Sargon took comfort in one matter – he had guided and cared for his mounts, and ridden just as hard as any of the warriors.

The months of incessant riding and training under Garal had come to fruition. The highest praise came from the fact that no one noticed or commented on his riding skills. The Alur Meriki, he decided, had accepted him as Eskkar's son, and thus no longer considered him a dirt eater.

Less than three miles passed before they reached the first Alur Meriki patrol, the one commanded by Yassur. Unegen's scout had informed these outriders about the Ur Nammu and Sargon. Still, Yassur stared with open curiosity at the strangers, apparently fully accepted as equals, who rode in with Unegen.

Unegen swung down from his horse with a grunt of relief. "What can you tell us?"

For a moment Yassur appeared taken aback at the sight of Sargon, a dirt eater, and Fashod, an Ur Nammu warrior, moving up to stand beside Unegen and Den'rack.

Yassur recovered soon enough. "The main force of the enemy caught up with the Ur Nammu yesterday. The Ur Nammu have taken refuge on a hilltop less than three miles away, and are now surrounded by the invaders. That is why we've remained here, behind this hill. Their patrols don't come this far east or ride into the hills."

"Can we see them?" Unegen glanced up at the hill.

"Yes, you can see everything from here." Yassur led the way on foot, scrambling back and forth as he guided them toward the summit. Just before the crest, he threw himself down and crawled the last few steps, until he could peer out at the plain beyond.

Sargon and the others followed his example. Looking west, he saw the Carchemishi forces, formed in a ring around the base of a lone plateau that pushed itself up from the earth. Only flat ground surrounded it. The hill rose up about two hundred paces above the valley floor, and appeared to have only one gentle slope, facing north, where a horse and rider could make the ascent.

From Sargon's vantage point, he saw the hundreds, even thousands, of Carchemishi who encircled the plateau, most of them concentrated near the north face and its slope to the top. The hill, with its single entry, made for a good defensive position. There might be other trails to reach the summit on the far side, but Sargon couldn't see any from here.

Still, if the hill provided a good place for defense, it also allowed the Ur Nammu to be surrounded and trapped. It would be impossible for Subutai's warriors to break out, even if they wanted to, without a desperate fight.

But Sargon and his companions wanted to break in, not out, so that problem wasn't as important for now. "How many invaders are there?"

Yassur lifted his shoulders, then dropped them. "At least seventeen hundred, maybe two thousand. More than half of them are mounted, which is why they caught up with the Ur Nammu so quickly. Those on foot only arrived this morning, along with a long pack train of horses and some carts. Women and children are there, too."

Women invariably followed soldiers, traveling with them and helping carry weapons and supplies. To any army in the field, they were both a benefit and a curse. They helped their men, but they consumed food and slowed down the pace of any march. In the war against Sumer, Eskkar had ordered women out of the ranks several times.

When he heard the numbers of the enemy, Sargon exchanged glances with Fashod. The two Carchemishi bands must have joined, and they appeared even more numerous than expected.

"Why haven't the Carchemishi attacked?"

"The Ur Nammu aren't going anywhere, and there is only the one approach," Yassur explained. "But the only water nearby is a tiny stream that flows from the base of the ridge, and so now the Ur Nammu have no water. The invaders can afford to wait a few more days, until the Ur

Nammu are weakened by thirst. Then they will either surrender or be destroyed."

Unegen turned to Fashod. "How many warriors do the Ur Nammu have?"

"Subutai has less than three hundred warriors," Fashod said, "not counting some boys and old men who might be able to fight. But there are over a thousand people up there. They will not last long without water."

"We cannot attack until Bekka arrives." Unegen informed Yassur about their Sarum's decision to attack the invaders. "But he will not be here for another few days. Meanwhile, we must gather as much information as we can about the enemy."

"Is there a way for us to rejoin our people?" Fashod spoke directly to Yassur.

"Not during the day. As far as we can see, all the approaches to the hilltop are surrounded. The ascent at the southern end seems to be the least guarded. It's steep, but you might be able to climb up there after dark."

"Then we will go tonight." Fashod turned to Sargon. "But you do not need to come with us. You can still return to your own people."

Sargon had no intention of leaving Tashanella. "No. We go in together."

"So be it." Fashod shifted his gaze back to Yassur. "We can spend the day studying the approaches."

"We were thinking about capturing one or two Carchemishi," Yassur told Unegen. "We might learn much that would help Chief Bekka when he arrives."

Sargon watched as Unegen thought about that for a moment.

"No, we don't want these invaders to look to the east," Unegen said. "Better to have them thinking only about the Ur Nammu."

"As long as they watch the hilltop, we should be able to slip through their lines," Fashod said. "They will not be expecting anyone to try and break in. When they settle down for the night, we'll see what trail looks best." He took one last look at the distant plateau. "Now we should rest. We'll need all our strength tonight."

They slipped back below the crest and returned to the camp. Unegen and Yassur decided to send out more scouts, and prepare for Bekka's arrival.

Fashod and the other Ur Nammu ignored the activity, and dropped to the ground to get some sleep. Sargon followed, though he doubted he could get much rest. Tashanella was close by, and he might not be able to reach her. Despite Fashod's confidence, it would be difficult to get past so many guards.

In spite of his worries, exhaustion overcame his thoughts and he slipped into a deep but troubled slumber.

Across the space that separated Sargon and the Ur Nammu from the Alur Meriki, Yassur turned to Unegen and Den'rack. "Is he really the son of the outcast Eskkar? Are the Ur Nammu now our friends?"

Unegen lifted his hands and let them drop. He related what had passed at the council meeting to Yassur and his men, who gathered around, eager to hear the news.

"So, Chief Bekka decided that it helps our clan to help the Ur Nammu. And it will do no harm to have Akkad in our debt. Besides, Trayack wanted to kill them all. Perhaps that is why Bekka is helping them."

Yassur shook his head and spat on the ground. "Always the clan chiefs quarrel amongst themselves. Each one wants to be Sarum, no matter how many dead warriors it takes. Look at Bekka. A few years ago, he was a leader of fifty. Now he is Sarum."

"Well, when you are a clan leader," Unegen said, "you may hold different thoughts. As for me, I trust Bekka more than I ever trusted Thutmose-sin."

"And this boy, Sargon," Den'rack spoke for the first time, "there is something about him. He's as foolish as he is brave, but he knows the ways of a leader. I'm glad I did not kill him when I had the chance."

"Yes, killing him would have saved us a long ride," Unegen said, his voice as cheerful as if he were talking about a hunt. "Well, it's too late for that now. It's time to get ready for battle."

Sargon was the last to awaken from his sleep. When he did, he saw Fashod and his companions had started up the hill, to take one final look at the Carchemishi. Rubbing the sleep from his eyes, Sargon followed them up the slope and dropped to ground alongside Garal. Sargon's eyes widened at the sight across the plain.

Campfires burned every hundred paces or so in a ring around the base of the hill. Tending them were hundreds of Carchemishi fighters, weapons at the ready, should the Ur Nammu try to come down the hill, either to attack or break through the lines.

Two hundred paces behind the ring of men, almost on a direct line between the Alur Meriki vantage point and the Ur Nammu plateau, a herd of horses had been collected into a makeshift corral. More armed men guarded the animals, with patrols extending out halfway to the ridge where Sargon lay on his stomach.

"We won't be able to sneak up and steal their horses again," Garal whispered. "Our night raid has made them wary."

Sargon remembered how nervous he'd been that night, not that long ago, just standing there and holding the riders' mounts. "How will we get by them?"

"Fashod thinks that on the south side, the hill is too steep for horses or armed men to come down, but a few might be able to climb up."

Sargon wasn't so sure. The location was a long way off. They would have to swing wide of the patrols to approach from the south.

"Maybe Unegen can create a diversion?"

"Good idea. Fashod suggested it, too," Garal said, "but Unegen says no. He thinks this place is perfect for an attack against the enemy's herd. He doesn't want to do anything to make the invaders aware of his presence."

"That's a big herd, at least eight or nine hundred horses." Sargon studied the herd. No wonder Unegen wanted to raid it. Sargon's father had said many times that, to barbarians, stealing horses from your enemy was more impressive than killing them.

"The ground on the far side of the hill must not be favorable to hold a herd," Garal mused. "Except for the men riding night patrol, Yassur says they've collected all of their horses at this one place."

"There must be another hundred riders on patrol," Sargon estimated. Still, the horse herd meant nothing to Sargon. He shifted his gaze back to the south, to examine the open space they would have to cross. His father had often spoken of the importance of studying the ground as best you could before any venture.

Fashod moved up beside them. "Come. It's almost time to go, and we need to prepare."

He led the way down the slope, and they collected their weapons. Fashod ran his sharpening stone over his sword a few times, then passed it to Sargon, who did the same. Unegen joined them, carrying a quiver of arrows. "Each of my men has given up a few arrows, so you can have a full quiver. You may need the extra shafts when you reach the top."

Garal and Jennat had already strung their bows and slipped them over their shoulders. Now they, too, sharpened their swords. Sargon slung his lance across his back.

Den'rack appeared, carrying a water skin in one hand and a food sack in the other. "Eat and drink as much as you can now. Don't take any food with you. There will be plenty of fresh meat up there."

It took Sargon a moment to follow the thought. A few slaughtered horses could supply plenty of raw meat. Sargon didn't enjoy the prospect, though his father's men had been forced to eat a few horses at the battle of the stream.

Yassur joined them. "My men will guide you in. We'll swing wide to the east before turning toward the hilltop. We should be able to ride within a mile without being seen or heard."

A few more moments, and they were ready.

"Good luck to you." Unegen clasped arms with Fashod, the gesture of friendship. "Tell your Sarum to hold out until Chief Bekka arrives. That should give you the chance to break loose. When you can wait no longer, give us the sign. We may be able to help."

Sargon realized that Fashod and Unegen must have arranged a way to signal to the Alur Meriki.

Fashod nodded. "I understand. Tell all your men we are in your debt."

Jennat and Garal also offered their thanks to Unegen and his men. Then Sargon faced the Alur Meriki leaders. "Good hunting to you, Den'rack, and to you, Unegen."

"Until we meet again, Sargon of Akkad." Den'rack's voice sounded as confident as his words.

They mounted their horses and moved out, taking position behind Unegen. They let the animals pick their own pace through the darkness. Yassur, on foot, led the way, selecting the best path over the indistinct ground. The moon had risen, but it was young and shed little light. However, what hindered them now would help them soon enough.

As they moved slowly through the shadows, Sargon glanced up at the stars. His father often spoke about the stars and what they meant for men. Sargon had always considered his father's ideas foolish, despite the fact that many of Akkad's wise men said much the same.

Now, lifting his eyes to the night sky, Sargon wasn't so sure. The stars could not be counted, and he knew that some wandered across the sky, moving little by little until a year passed, and they returned to the place from which they started.

"What are you looking at?" Garal rode right behind him.

"Nothing. Just the stars." Sargon took one last at the sky. He wondered what his father thought about before he rode into battle. Strange that Sargon had never thought to ask him that simple question. Now it was too late.

30

S cattered clouds passed across the face of the moon and darkened the night sky. Sargon fretted about the slow pace as they moved toward the Ur Nammu refuge. He could dismount and walk faster than the plodding pace set by Yassur, Unegen, and the other Alur Meriki warriors leading the way.

Fashod, however, showed no signs of wanting to hurry. Sargon knew Fashod wanted to make his final approach in the middle of the night, when the guards would be least alert.

Once again Sargon found himself and his fate in the hands of others, as he followed the horse and rider in front of him. Part of him wanted to rush ahead, but another part wished he were back in Akkad, safe in some pleasant ale house. Soon he would be fighting, not for his life, but to save the life of Tashanella. In all his imaginings, Sargon had never once thought about dying to save another.

The moon had reached its highest point and started its descent when Sargon heard Unegen's whisper down the line.

"This is close enough. Everyone dismount."

Sargon swung down from his horse, handed the halter to one of Unegen's men, and checked his weapons. An Alur Meriki warrior approached carrying a water skin, offering one last chance to drink. Sargon realized his mouth was dry, as much from fear as from thirst, and he gulped down as much as he could hold.

He heard Garal and a few others taking a piss, and suddenly the urge to do the same almost overpowered him. Sargon moved a few steps from the horses and relieved himself. It took far longer than usual to empty his bladder. When he finished, he found Fashod waiting for him.

"Follow me," Fashod said. "Single file." With those brief words, he started toward the plateau, its jutting height visible in the moonlight and the glow from a Carchemishi watch fire.

Unegen whispered a farewell. "Good hunting."

Within moments, the Alur Meriki warriors and the horses vanished into the darkness, and Sargon and his companions were alone. No one had to tell Sargon to keep silent. Their sandals made little sound against the hard earth sprinkled with patches of grass that reached his knees.

Nevertheless, Sargon had to watch his footing. A misstep might send him tumbling to the ground, and even worse, might be heard by the enemy guards.

As the small group drew closer to the hilltop, Fashod moved ever slower. Once they had to drop to the ground, motionless, when an enemy patrol loomed up out of the darkness. Sargon counted ten riders, and for a moment thought he and his companions would be discovered.

But these men were concentrating on the ground before them, and only a few bothered to glance about. They passed within fifty paces without noticing the four men hugging the ground.

When they'd ridden off, Fashod moved to Sargon's side, his face only a hand's breadth away. "There's a watch fire ahead. Don't look at it. Keep your eyes on the ground and watch where you step. I'll be right behind you. Are you ready?"

"Yes." Sargon didn't trust his voice to say anything else. Fear had reached into his body and clutched his stomach, but he knew he couldn't let his companions down.

"Good." Fashod gripped Sargon's shoulder. "Just follow orders."

To Sargon's surprise, Fashod told Garal to lead the way, while Fashod brought up the rear, walking just behind Sargon. He heard the occasional horse whinny from the distant herd. Other odd sounds carried through the night. Sargon's heart jumped at every shifting shadow, expecting to be discovered. If the Carchemishi discovered them, Sargon and his companions would be killed, or even worse, captured and tortured.

The Ur Nammu kept moving forward. They covered another two hundred paces, and by now had crossed within the outer lines of the Carchemishi sentries.

Suddenly Garal and Jennat ducked down. Fashod's hand reached up and pulled Sargon down as well. Sargon heard voices ahead. Straining his eyes, he spotted two men sitting on a rock. Both faced the hilltop. Fashod's whisper came. "Arrows."

Garal and Jennat disappeared into the shadows moving toward the unsuspecting guards. Peering over a scraggly bush, Sargon stared at the two sentries about seventy or eighty paces ahead. He heard the men speaking, but couldn't make out the words.

Time seemed to drag by. Sargon was about to ask Fashod what had gone wrong when he glimpsed two shadows rise up behind the sentinels. Then he heard the snap of bowstrings, followed by a single gasp of pain. Both guards toppled to the ground, struck in the back at close range by the powerful shafts.

Garal and Jennat rushed forward, to make sure their targets were indeed dead or unable to cry out. Sargon turned to Fashod, who had raised himself up, one hand holding Sargon's arm. The warrior took his time scanning the landscape. The sounds of the guards' death, which had seemed loud to Sargon, had gone unheard.

"Come." Fashod moved toward the other warriors, jogging over the ground.

Sargon followed, clutching his lance in his right hand while trying to make as little noise as Fashod. In a moment, they had reached Garal, but Jennat had already moved on ahead. Sargon glanced down at the dead men sprawled at his feet.

He had seen death before, witnessed executions in Akkad's marketplace, but never violent death. Even in the raid on the Carchemishi camp, he hadn't got close enough to see men die, their lives ended. Now dead bodies lay within reach, and he could smell their blood, still spilling into the sandy earth.

Fashod and Garal dropped to one knee, and Sargon did the same. No one moved, and the moon seemed to travel faster and faster across the sky. Finally Sargon turned to Fashod. "Why are we waiting?"

"One can see as well as four," Fashod whispered back.

Sargon gritted his teeth and waited.

Then Jennat loomed up in the darkness to rejoin them. The four huddled together, heads almost touching, to confer.

"There's a guard post at the base of the hill," Jennat said. "Eight men. The only way I can see up the slope is right in front of them."

"Are you sure we can't go around?" Fashod's voice remained calm.

"I don't think so," Jennat whispered. "There are steep rocks all around the slope, loose rocks everywhere. It's likely the best approach, since the guards are there. Unless you want to search for another way up the slope."

"No, the two dead sentries might be discovered at any moment." Fashod took this setback in stride. "Damn. We'll have to kill them. We can't take the time to find another way."

Sargon glanced toward the plateau, looming up from the earth. He had no idea how steep the slope might be, or even if it could be climbed in the dark. Shadows shifted and moved, and some of that movement came from Carchemishi sentries. He couldn't tell if any were moving in this direction.

"The moment we start up the slope," Jennat said, "they'll hear us. We'll be easy targets."

"All the more reason to go through them," Fashod whispered. "If they're all dead, they won't be able to stop us. It will take some time before more soldiers can reach this place."

Fashod raised his head and surveyed the enemy post once again. When he ducked down, he unslung the lance from his shoulder.

"Remember, if anyone is wounded and can't make the climb, he'll have to fend for himself. Garal and Jennat, target your shafts at the guards starting from the left. Sargon and I will use our lances on the two on the right. Wait for us to throw. As soon as the way is clear, start climbing."

Sargon's heart beat faster, and wondered if the others could hear it. His mouth had gone dry again, and he had to force himself to swallow. In moments he would be fighting for his life. Nor could he expect help from any of the others.

Every man knew what needed to be done – at least one of them had to get to the top of the hill and give Subutai the message that the Alur Meriki were coming. If Sargon faltered or fell wounded, he would be left behind.

Fashod moved closer to Sargon, his mouth only a hand's breath from Sargon's ear. "Take the one on the rightmost side, Sargon," Fashod ordered. "If your lance doesn't bring him down, keep moving forward and use your sword. They won't be expecting an attack from behind. Just get past him and start up the slope. Don't wait for anyone. I'll tell you when to throw. Understand?"

Sargon had a handful of questions, but found himself nodding agreement. His mouth felt dry, and he didn't trust himself to speak.

"The moment we throw our lances," Fashod whispered, this time to Garal and Jennat, "loose your arrows, and move forward. Keep shooting until they're all dead." Fashod grasped Sargon by the arm. "Let's go."

Sargon loosened the cord that held the lance over his shoulder. He grasped the weapon in his right hand, making sure he held it firmly by the grip. His hand started to sweat, and he rubbed it hard against his tunic, grateful that no one could see the gesture in the dark. He wondered if the others noticed his fear.

Fashod took the lead, moving forward and creeping low toward the sentries. The others fanned out on his left side. Sargon remembered Garal's teachings, and he kept his eyes on the ground before him. Now was not the time to trip and sprawl on his face, alerting half the enemy camp. Sargon recalled another reason to keep his gaze down. At night the whites of a man's eyes could be seen at a distance.

The eight sentries were scattered about, most sitting on the ground, a few looking up the slope. One lay stretched out, taking his ease. Two or three talked among themselves, no doubt trying to stay awake. They obviously felt safe enough. No fighters from the hilltop could come down without making plenty of noise.

The distance between Sargon and his target closed. Fifty paces, then forty. Easy distance for the bows, but still too long for a flung lance. Sargon couldn't believe they hadn't been seen or heard yet. Thirty paces. By now he could see the one he had to kill. The unsuspecting man sat on a rock, facing the slope, and talking with his companion.

Fashod slowed his pace even more. Sargon's heart pounded in his chest, so loud that he felt certain the guards could hear it. Twenty paces, then fifteen. His right hand, again damp with sweat, gripped the lance. Ten paces. The guards surely heard their approach by now. Then Fashod rose from his crouch and Sargon knew the time had come. Fashod drew back his arm. Sargon, too, prepared to throw.

"Look out!"

The warning boomed out, before Fashod could hurl the lance. The alarm came from Sargon's right and echoed off the slope. A soldier, or perhaps a watch commander making his rounds, had practically strolled up on Sargon and his friends.

Fashod never hesitated. Ignoring the man who gave the alarm, Fashod threw the lance and charged forward. Bowstrings twanged. Sargon, too, hurled his lance at his original target, glimpsing it as it flew through the night. As he rushed forward, he saw that neither his lance nor Fashod's had struck a killing blow.

Both targets reacted swiftly. Fashod's man had risen and turned in the same moment. The lance tore through the man's left arm, wrenching a cry from his lips. Sargon's throw missed completely, either from a poor aim or because the man had whirled around.

The night erupted in shouts, drowned out by the frightening sounds of the steppes warriors war cries as the Ur Nammu voiced their war cries. Fashod hurtled across the distance, and his sword struck down the wounded man before he could draw a weapon.

Sargon, two steps behind, ripped his sword from its scabbard and flung himself at his foe.

The guard Sargon had missed had taken a step toward Fashod, but now he turned, sword in hand, to meet Sargon's attack. Sargon, swinging the sword with all his strength, felt the impact of the stroke up his arm as bronze met bronze, his first experience with such a shock.

The impact forced his foe back a half step. Sargon never stopped his forward motion, lowering his shoulder and driving it into the man's chest. The guard, despite his greater bulk, went sprawling, his sword flailing.

Sargon turned to move beside Fashod, hotly engaged with another warrior. The clash of bronze nearly masked the sound of a sandal crunching on the loose stones. The soldier who'd given the alarm had charged forward to join the fray. He'd closed the distance in a few heart beats, and now he lunged forward, his sword aimed at Sargon's chest.

Only Sargon's quickness saved him from the well aimed stroke. He twisted aside from the ferocious thrust that brushed past his ribs. This attacker knew his trade. He kept moving forward and his shoulder slammed into Sargon, knocking him back and almost off his feet.

Sargon knew better than to rise up. Instead he crouched low, and dodged an overhand swing. He feinted with a sweeping cut. Then, still close to the ground, he lunged forward, driving the sword's tip beneath the man's attempt to parry, and up into his belly.

Sargon felt his blade bite deep into the man, who cried out in as much surprise as pain. His sword fell from his fingers and clanked against the rocky ground. Hot blood spurted along Sargon's arm, as he jerked the blade back. His grip nearly came loose, and he had to tighten his fist and wrench the blade free.

"Run!" Fashod had finished his man, and now grabbed Sargon by the shoulder and shoved him toward the slope.

Stumbling into a run, Sargon raced for the hill, following Fashod's steps. They raced across the forty paces or so to reach the slope. Dimly he heard someone scrambling and clawing up the slope, so he knew that at least one of his companions had also broken through. Then Sargon reached the base of the plateau and started up.

An arrow dug into the earth beside Sargon's hand, as he gripped a rock to help his ascent. Another clattered off a stone. The sword in his right hand hampered his ascent, but he didn't dare take the time to sheath it, nor did he intend to drop it.

More shafts hummed through the darkness, burying themselves into the cliff or snapping against the rock. Meanwhile the tumult from the now fully aroused main camp mixed with the shouts and curses of the men below.

Sargon heard another arrow hiss over his head. He kept scrambling up the steep hill, slipping and sliding back down every few steps. His shoulders twitched with anticipation, as if his body could sense the oncoming missile that would end Sargon's life.

The sentries, however, had yet to recover from their surprise. Only two had survived Fashod's assault, though others had rushed over to join them. These new arrivals had to string their bows, and now they shot their arrows uphill and into the darkness, aiming at the dim shadows already climbing out of range.

Ignoring the chaos below, Sargon kept moving. Another arrow struck the earth a pace above him. A large boulder, half buried in the hill, provided some shelter. He ducked behind it, to discover that he was the last to arrive.

Fashod grunted as he pulled Sargon to safety. "Help Jennat. He's injured. Start up the hill when I tell you. Garal and I will send a few shafts down the slope to cover you."

Another arrow struck the boulder and glanced off. Fashod already had Jennat's bow in hand. Sargon moved beside the wounded man. An arrow protruded from his left leg.

"Damn the luck," the warrior said. "It stings like a scorpion bite."

"Go!" Fashod gave the order at the same time he leaned out from the boulder and loosed a shaft. "Hurry!"

Sargon had time for a brief glance upward. Their first breathless dash had carried them more than half way. Shoving his bloody sword into its scabbard, Sargon grasped Jennat by the waist. They started moving. The first few steps were the hardest, but they soon found a slant that led toward the crest.

They crawled on hands and knees, clinging to the rocky outcrops to keep from sliding back down, Sargon pushing and shoving to help Jennat along, both gasping for breath. Behind them, Sargon heard Fashod and Garal working their bows, shooting shafts as fast as they could fit them to the string.

Shouts of confusion still erupted from the base of the hill. Sargon guessed that every one of Garal's shafts had found a mark. Shooting uphill at night was more difficult than shooting downwards. In moments the enemy archers, who had rushed to the base of the hill, scattered, moving away into the darkness.

Sargon heard scrambling sounds below him. Fashod and Garal had started climbing, too. Either they had exhausted their supply of arrows, or they decided they couldn't remain any longer. Sargon and Jennat kept moving, ignoring everything behind them. A stone rattled down the hill. He looked up and saw the blur of faces above him, only a few paces away.

Hands reached out of the darkness and grabbed Jennat from Sargon's grasp. Another powerful grip seized Sargon's left wrist and yanked him upward. The slope grew steeper for the last few steps, and Sargon, already gulping air into his lungs as fast as he could, thanked the gods for the help.

The twang of bowstrings sounded over his head. Subutai's warriors were sending shafts down into the darkness. Suddenly the slope leveled. Sargon stumbled forward and fell flat on the ground. All he could think of was that he was still alive, and he'd reached the top. When his heart finally slowed, he pushed himself to his knees.

"Come. We're still within range of their arrows."

Sargon didn't recognize the voice, but it didn't matter. Rising to his feet, he found his legs trembling, either from weakness or fear. He stumbled after his guide, following him away from danger. He smelled and heard horses, and saw a small campfire burning up ahead. Sargon slipped to the ground a few steps from the fire, still struggling to catch his breath. This time he stayed where he had fallen.

No one paid him any attention. Warriors moved about, and Sargon saw some gathering near the fire. He heard Fashod's voice answering questions in rapid bursts of words that Sargon, in his exhausted condition, couldn't understand. Even so, he knew what Fashod must be saying. Telling Subutai or the other leaders that they had reached the Alur Meriki.

Gazing down at his hands, Sargon saw they still shook, either from the mad scramble up the hill, or because he had just killed his first man. Blood mixed with dirt covered his right arm. He tried to brush it off, but the touch of the slippery fluid made him want to retch.

He could still feel the way the sharp blade slid effortlessly inside the body of the guard, could hear the small gasp of pain and surprise as the Carchemishi soldier felt the shock of the cold bronze. Sargon wondered if the man had time to realize he'd taken a death blow.

Everything had happened so quickly. In all his practice sessions with Garal or even those back in Akkad, there was always time to prepare, to plan the attack, even a chance to recover from a mistake. Sargon hadn't had time either to think or be afraid. And now, after the fight had ended, he didn't know what he felt.

Someone moved in front of him, blocking the faint light of the fire. Wearily, he lifted his head, and saw Tashanella standing there. The colorful dress she'd worn in the camp the last night he'd seen her was gone, replaced by the patched and faded garment she'd worn when he first noticed her.

"Are you wounded?" She dropped to her knees in front of him. Her hands went to his shoulders, but gently, as if afraid she might hurt him.

He had to think for a moment. Looking down, he saw that part of his tunic was splattered with blood. "No, I'm fine. It's not my blood. I . . . I killed a man." His hand fumbled for his sword, and he realized that the hilt and top of the scabbard were slippery with blood. He shivered at the touch. Sargon had not had time to clean the blade before shoving it into its scabbard.

"I should clean my sword." His voice sounded odd in his ears, as if someone else had spoken.

Sargon knew no warrior should ever return an unclean blade to its scabbard. When the blood dried, it would grip the blade and make it difficult to draw.

"Yes, of course." Despite her youth, Tashanella recognized the signs of a man struggling to comprehend what had just befallen him, his mind shocked into near paralysis. "Give it to me. I'll take care of it."

Without waiting for acceptance, Tashanella reached down and unbuckled his belt. She withdrew the weapon from his waist. "Stay here. I'll be back in a moment."

He nodded, but she had already turned and disappeared into the darkness. Sargon glanced around. Even in the middle of the night, the hilltop thronged with people. Every member of the Ur Nammu clan, more than a thousand men, women, and children, filled the hilltop.

Their horses, too, almost six hundred, took up whatever space remained. In such crowded and unsanitary conditions, not many would be able to sleep.

Despite the press of people, no one paid Sargon the slightest interest. He might as well have stayed with the Alur Meriki. Again his thoughts returned to the dead man at the bottom of the hill, and he wondered if Eskkar had felt any such feelings of remorse when he killed his first man.

That brought up another question. Just how many men had his father killed by his own hand? Twenty? Fifty? A hundred? Sargon doubted Eskkar had any idea of the number.

A few months ago, in the safety of Akkad's ale houses, Sargon and his friends had scoffed at the thought of fighting or killing. Those were tasks for ignorant men who made war their trade, not princes of the city with gold enough to hire as many guards as they needed.

Safe and secure behind their wealth and power, Sargon and his friends had sipped their wine and laughed at men like his father, Hathor, and the others. Barbarians like the Ur Nammu were beneath their contempt. Sargon remembered the certainty with which he'd dismissed such ideas.

Instead, Eskkar had turned his son's world upside down. Now Sargon needed to fight to stay alive. Once again he wished he had paid more attention to all the things his father and his military advisors had sought to teach Sargon. Garal's teachings had conditioned him and given him the basic skills. Nonetheless, Sargon knew he'd been lucky to kill his man, more experienced and with a powerful arm.

Sargon thought of the stroke that had brushed past his stomach and shivered. Only his quickness had saved his life. And now, though Sargon and the others had succeeded in reaching their goal, this hilltop might still be the place of his death.

"Here, drink this." Tashanella slipped to the ground beside him, and handed him a cup.

Lost in thought, Sargon hadn't noticed her return. He had to use both hands to take the cup from her, and despite his efforts, his hands shook. The smell of raw wine reached his nostrils, and he took a sip of the liquid. It felt rough to his mouth, but he drank it down. "I didn't think there would be any wine in the camp."

"Just the one skin. My mother carried it for Subutai."

Now he was stealing Subutai's wine. Sargon laughed, the discordant sound attracting, for the first time, the attention of those nearby. Nevertheless, Sargon emptied the cup. She took it from his hand and set it aside. A damp rag appeared, and Tashanella scrubbed the blood from his face and arm. "There's no water to clean your tunic, and nothing else to wear. You'll have to keep it."

Ignoring her ministrations, Sargon put his arms around her and pulled her close. For a moment he just held her tight against him, inhaling the scent of her hair. He didn't know how long he held her, but slowly the fear and trembling passed from his body. Tashanella was real, and she was holding him. Somehow Sargon knew she understood. Thoughts of death and blood gradually eased from his mind.

"Tashanella, you're the reason I came back. Otherwise, I might have just slipped away. I know . . ."

"If you hadn't come back, I would have come looking for you." She raised her lips to his, and they shared a kiss that began with gentleness and ended with passion.

He pulled her down beside him, and buried his face in her throat. Sargon couldn't control the occasional tremble that passed through his limbs. She stroked his hair, and murmured soothing words. Sargon had seen his mother touch his father the same way.

After awhile, his heart slowed, and his mind regained control of his body. Sargon remembered why he had returned, and what still needed to be done.

"You heard the Alur Meriki are coming?"

"Yes, I was at my father's tent when Fashod brought the news. He said you convinced them to help us. That's all I heard before I came looking for you."

He told her the events at the Council Meeting, and of Chief Bekka's need for a victory. "Though they may not come. Bekka may have changed his mind, or others could have forced him to abandon the idea of fighting the Carchemishi. Or he may just arrive too late to help us."

"Then all that matters is that you have done your best. My father, all the Ur Nammu will owe you a great debt."

"We still may not get out of this alive."

"Then we will die together. I will have no other life without you, Sargon of Akkad. But I feel in my heart that you have yet much to accomplish. I do not think this will be our end."

"Then we'll face whatever comes. Together."

A young boy called out Tashanella's name, searching for her in the crowd.

She glanced around. "We're over here."

The boy trotted over, his teeth glistening in the faint light.

"Here it is." The boy handed Tashanella Sargon's sword and belt. "I sharpened it. Father said to bring him."

Sargon recognized the boy as one of Tashanella's younger brothers. He took the weapon from Tashanella and drew the blade half way from the scabbard. The bronze hilt and blade had been cleansed of blood, and the edge sharpened and polished. Sargon found the spot where the first guard had parried the blade. The deep nick remained, but some of it had been smoothed out.

"We will go to my father," Tashanella said. "Then we'll find a place for ourselves, to spend the night."

Sargon stood and belted the sword around his waist. "Then let's hurry. The sooner we finish with your father, the sooner we can be together." Sargon held her for a moment, then took her hand, holding it tight. Alone in each other's company, they followed the young boy back to where Subutai waited.

31

By midmorning, the demons of last night had faded, driven away as much by Tashanella's love making as a good night's rest. Her father hadn't commented when Sargon and his daughter approached hand in hand. The time for such thoughts had passed.

Instead, Subutai called his clan leaders and whatever warriors stood nearby. In a loud voice, he praised Sargon both for his courage and his success with the Alur Meriki. And after last night's fight on the slope, Subutai declared that Sargon had become a warrior and a clan brother to the Ur Nammu.

To Sargon's surprise, he felt prouder of Subutai's words than any praise his father or mother had ever bestowed on him. He might not have fought with bravery and skill, but he had fought, and he now realized how big a role luck played in staying alive. A sobering lesson, to be sure.

The warriors surrounding him all voiced their thanks, many of them coming close to touch his arm or shoulder, one brother warrior to another. By then Fashod and the others had told everyone the story of Sargon's challenges, and every man there understood all the risks that the boy from Akkad had taken to help the Ur Nammu.

At last Sargon broke free. Tashanella was busy helping her mother, so he wandered away, until he found Garal testing a fresh bowstring. Somehow the man had managed to hang on to his bow during last night's climb.

After Garal finished, they walked the entire length of the hilltop, studying the enemy below. In daylight, the flat portion of the hill seemed even more crowded than last night, with horses and people sharing much of the same ground. The Carchemishi had ringed about half the hill.

Only a few guarded those places too steep even for a man on foot, let alone a horse, to descend. The enemy had taken their position just out of bowshot range, about a hundred and fifty paces from the base of the hill.

Sargon stopped at the place where they had ascended last night. "No wonder the guards weren't all that alert." From above, the slope looked even more difficult to climb than it had seemed from below.

To their left, they could see the holding area for the Carchemishi horses. The rope corrals were almost empty now, as the enemy horsemen had mounted at first light, in case the defenders tried to ride down and attack.

Sargon and Garal continued their inspection, and soon enough they reached the incline where the Ur Nammu had ascended. About forty or fifty paces wide, it looked steep enough to slow down any attacker. At the base, and just out of arrow range, the besiegers had dug a ditch that formed a half circle. To Sargon's eyes, it appeared both wide and deep enough to stop a horse.

"Chinua says they dug the ditch in half a day," Garal commented.

Sargon had seen the efficient work of soldiers before. They knew how to work together to accomplish much in a short time.

"Have they paid any attention to the bluffs we came from?"

From up here, Sargon could see all the way to the foothills, including the low ridges where the Alur Meriki scouting party even now lay hidden, and from where Sargon and his companions had set out on last night's venture.

"The Carchemishi sent out two patrols just after dawn," Garal said. "Subutai had men watching from here, to see if they discovered any traces of the Alur Meriki horses. One group entered the bluffs, but didn't reach the place where we had hidden. The other just patrolled along the edge of the bluffs. If they even found our tracks, they didn't show it."

"That seems careless. They should have wondered which direction we came from." Sargon studied the plain beneath him. The enemy forces appeared alert enough. Soldiers armed with bows and spears flanked the main downward slope all the way to the ditch. More archers, backed up by several hundred horse fighters, waited for any attempt to escape or counterattack. "My father or Hathor would have sent out four or five patrols."

"Perhaps. But they may think it's more likely we came from the south, from Akkad's outposts. Two more patrols headed out in that direction."

"When Bekka arrives," Sargon said, studying the landscape, "he'll take one look at the horse herd and attack. If he can scatter those horses during the night, the Carchemishi will be in trouble."

"If he comes. Subutai has his doubts. That's what he told Chinua."

"He'll come if he can." Sargon put more confidence in his words than he felt. "But who knows when? How long can we hold out up here without water?"

"Before they climbed the slope, Subutai ordered every sack and skin filled with water. And the horses had plenty to drink. But despite all that, with so many people, it's almost all gone. Soon we'll be too weak to fight."

Exactly the same trap Eskkar had used on the Alur Meriki. Sargon had never realized how important a weapon water could be. His cunning father had understood its role, and constructed a battle plan based on little else.

"If I were Subutai," Sargon said, "I would attack tomorrow at dawn. He has to be ready anyway, if Bekka comes tonight. And if he doesn't, why wait another day without water? And the longer we're up here, the better prepared the Carchemishi will be."

"Do you think Bekka can get here that fast? He won't be able to double up on his horses as we did."

"By now, one of Unegen's riders will have reached him. Once he realizes the situation here, Bekka will press the pace. He'll want to arrive while we can still fight. If the enemy destroys us, they'll have the hill itself as a refuge. They could even corral the horses up here. Nothing the Alur Meriki could do would touch them then."

"You think like a clan leader, Sargon." Garal's usually cheerful voice held only respect. Like all the other Ur Nammu, he believed anyone who has killed a man in battle must be treated as a warrior. "Someday you will make a good war chief."

The last thing Sargon had ever wanted. "If we live that long."

———⚬———

Later that day, Sargon watched as Subutai returned to the patch of ground where his wives and children had gathered. Though Tashanella's father strode through the camp with his head held high, Sargon guessed that Subutai was growing discouraged. The leader of the clan had probably gotten little sleep for the last seven days, and Sargon wondered how much longer the Ur Nammu Sarum could last.

Subutai collected a single strip of dried meat from his wives, and then crossed over to where Sargon and Tashanella sat side by side.

"Sargon, we are readying the warriors for an attack at first light. We will try to drive off the invaders."

"Can you not wait a little longer for the Alur Meriki to arrive?"

Subutai shook his head. "Most of the warriors have had nothing to drink since yesterday. If we wait any longer . . ." His voice trailed off. "And Fashod doesn't think the Alur Meriki can get here before the day after tomorrow at the earliest. By then we'll be dying of thirst. Better to go now, while we can still fight."

A hopeless attempt, Sargon knew, but there was little else that Subutai could do.

"Fifty warriors will attack down the slope that you and Fashod used to scale the hill. They will try to convince the enemy that we are attempting to escape there. Then the rest of us will ride down and try to get through the ditch on the right hand side. If we send all our men against that one place, we may be able to break through. If our warriors can reach the enemy horses, we may be able to stampede and scatter them."

"Where do you wish me to be?" Sargon really didn't care.

"For your sake, and for your father's, I wish you had not returned here. You could have ridden south, and reached the lands of Akkad."

"I came back for your daughter, Subutai. I don't intend to leave her."

"So I see." Subutai looked at Tashanella, and smiled. "That means she has chosen well. Probably better than I would have for her."

He reached out and touched her cheek for a moment. Then he turned back to Sargon. "The old men, young boys, and some of the women will defend the camp when . . . after we attack. I thought you might want to remain here with them. They will need a leader if our attack fails."

Sargon understood. Every clan leader and subcommander would ride to the attack. He thought about Subutai's offer, but he'd already made up his mind. He and Tashanella had already discussed tomorrow's attack.

"No. I will ride beside Chinua, Garal, and their kin. I cannot stay behind when they ride to war."

"In that case, you will ride behind me. I will lead the attack down the slope, and Chinua will lead the second wave." He stood and ran his fingers through Tashanella's hair. "You will see to your mother and the others?"

"Yes, Father. I will be at their side."

Sargon understood what that meant. Tashanella would make sure her younger brothers and sisters did not fall into the enemy's hands.

"Then I have done all that I can for them," Subutai said. "Now I must see to my men."

Sargon glanced up at the sun as Subutai strode off into the camp. The afternoon was passing, and before long, the sun would touch the horizon.

Sargon placed his arm around Tashanella's shoulder and pulled her close. They might not have much more time together.

32

Thirty miles to the north, Bekka glanced up at the sun. Dusk would soon be upon them. He raised his hand to halt the warriors, and eased his sweat-stained horse to a stop. They would camp here for the night. The war party, numbering just over eight hundred men, had ridden hard since leaving the caravan.

Even the strongest warriors had grown weary, but many of their horses were nearing the end of their limits. The animals needed frequent rests, and at each stop Bekka heard more than the usual grumblings from his men. Still, the Alur Meriki had traversed the countryside quicker than the swiftest raiding party, far faster that any raid Bekka had ever ridden on before.

He had his reasons for keeping up the pace. The less time Bekka's warriors had to think about the coming battle, the better. Many of his men remained angry over his decision to fight the Carchemishi. They argued that this battle would provide little gain and great risk. Others hated the Ur Nammu, and wondered why their Sarum wanted to save them.

Given the lack of enthusiasm, almost everyone had protested the rapid pace of the expedition. After all, they pointed out, even if the invaders killed every last Ur Nammu, the Carchemishi would be weakened from whatever losses they sustained. In fact, they claimed, the invaders would be more likely to be taken by surprise, still celebrating their victory over the Ur Nammu.

Some, and Bekka wished he knew the numbers of this group, disapproved of the decision simply because they did not trust their new Sarum. In their minds, Bekka had done nothing to prove his worth as a leader. At least Chief Urgo, despite the fact that he had negotiated the peace with Eskkar, had years of experience. Bekka, these malcontents grumbled, had yielded ground at the stream against Eskkar's men, and had accomplished nothing since.

Now, with threats of war surrounding the Alur Meriki, those unhappy with Bekka's leadership muttered that they preferred to put their trust in Trayack, an older and proven war chief. A rumor already had passed through the ranks, promising that Trayack would absolve all of them from their oath to Eskkar.

Bekka had gritted his teeth when he learned of that claim. It sounded all too believable, something Trayack would say. Bekka might have left the obstreperous clan leader behind, but Trayack's dark presence had managed to accompany Bekka's force and haunt his every decision.

Whatever their reasons to complain about the coming battle, those discontented did not understand that the world had changed. Eskkar's son had returned to the Ur Nammu, after appealing for assistance from the Alur Meriki. If the brash boy died fighting against Akkad's enemies, sooner or later, the blame would fall on the Alur Meriki for failing to help.

Once that happened, Eskkar would decide, probably sooner than later, to destroy the clan. He had nearly done it at the battle of the stream. If a loud talker like Trayack ruled the Alur Meriki, all it might take to bring Eskkar's Akkadians down on their heads would be a single raid against some lonely farmstead and a few dead farmers. One dead cow might even be enough.

On the other hand, if Sargon and his allies survived, the King of Akkad would owe much to Bekka and the Clan. That debt would keep the Alur Meriki strong for many years.

"A good place to camp." Suijan led his horse over to join Bekka. "My bones are aching. I haven't ridden so hard for years."

"I suppose you're right," Bekka said, grateful for the interruption to his gloomy thoughts. He slid down from his horse. His back felt stiff as well, and he leaned backward to stretch his muscles. "We've both gotten lazy and . . ."

A shout announced the arrival of a scout, urging a tired and well-lathered horse down the length of the column. Bekka realized it wasn't one of his war party, but Unegen, the warrior Bekka had sent ahead to escort Sargon and his companions.

"Chief Bekka." Unegen slid from his horse and strode over to where the two clan leaders stood.

Bekka frowned. "I thought you were going to stay with the forward scouts."

"I was, but things are happening too fast. I thought you should know."

The other clan leaders, Virani and Prandar, had seen Unegen ride in. Now they pushed their way through the gathering crowd, anxious to hear the latest news.

Unegen waited until all the chiefs stood together. "The Ur Nammu have gone to ground. They've taken refuge on a hilltop. The invaders, and there may be as many as two thousand, have surrounded the Ur Nammu. We couldn't be sure of the exact number of the Carchemishi. They keep moving around. Nevertheless, Sargon and his companions broke through the lines last night. I think at least one or two reached the safety of the hilltop, to tell their sarum of our plan."

"That's good, then." Bekka felt relief that the boy hadn't died, not yet. "We'll be there sometime tomorrow, probably just after midday."

Unegen shook his head. "That will probably be too late for the Ur Nammu." He explained the method that he and Fashod had agreed upon, to signal how long the besiegers could hold out. "They're out of water by now, have been for a day or two. They'll attack the Carchemishi at dawn tomorrow."

Bekka grimaced at the bad news. "And how far away are they?"

"A little less than thirty miles," Unegen said.

A murmur passed through the warriors at the distance. Bekka felt the eyes of the other clan leaders on him, and the gradual shifting of the warriors as they drew close enough to hear their leaders' words. The little gathering had suddenly become a war council.

Bekka thought about the thirty miles, and knew it couldn't be done. The distance was too far to cover before darkness, and the men and horses were already bone tired.

"Chief Bekka," Unegen broke into his clan leader's thoughts. "I was hoping you could give me some men to return as soon as possible. If we could make a show of force, we might be able to draw off some of the Carchemishi invaders. Even a hundred warriors could make a difference."

"The invaders would turn on you fast enough," Suijan said. "Are you willing to risk your life for these Ur Nammu?"

"No, Chief Suijan, not for them." Unegen's voice sounded firm. "But this Sargon seems like one whose life we should try and save. I'm willing to risk it, and perhaps a few others would join me."

Bekka smiled at his young subcommander. Unwittingly, Unegen had given Bekka the opportunity he needed.

"No, Unegen." Bekka shook the tiredness from his shoulders and raised his voice so that all the warriors, many of whom had clustered around their leaders, could hear his words. "You cannot return alone or with a handful of men. We will all ride together."

He glanced up at the sun. "If you guide us, we can make another fifteen miles before it grows too dark. Then we'll rest as long as we can, before we start to walk the horses. With luck, we'll reach the battleground by dawn."

Unegen's eyes lit up at the prospect. "If we do, we'll catch them from behind, while all their attention is on the Ur Nammu. And there's the biggest horse herd I've ever seen, just waiting for us." He described the enemy camp, and told the clan leaders about the horses, and where they were corralled.

Bekka nodded. "Yes, that would work." He turned to the chiefs. "Pass the word to every man. We're going to have a long ride, a long walk, and a hard fight when we arrive. Any warrior who cannot keep up, will be left behind, to catch up when he can."

Even the weariest of the warriors understood the subtle challenge. No man could plead exhaustion and keep his honor, not when his clan chiefs and brother warriors went on ahead to war.

Everyone started talking at once, and Bekka heard many voices supporting Unegen and his plan. Others just called out approval, caught up in the excitement of the moment.

Bekka knew Unegen had done more than rally the warriors. Without Unegen's riding in and volunteering to go to Sargon's assistance, Bekka might not have been able to convince the others to go on.

But Unegen had ridden as hard as any man, and now he had unwittingly put all of them in a position where they would have to admit their weakness if they refused to press ahead. Bekka promised himself that Unegen would indeed be a chief some day, and soon. Unegen understood the way of the warrior, and now he'd begun to learn the mysteries of power and command.

And even more important, Unegen had probably just saved his Sarum's life. Not today, but without a victory, sooner or later Trayack would sway the other chiefs and discontented warriors to his side. If Bekka survived the coming battle, Unegen would find himself a chief.

He put that thought aside. "You've done well, Unegen. Now, tell us what to expect when we arrive."

—━━◁▷◁▶━━—

"It's time to go, Tashanella." Sargon was grateful for the darkness that hid the tears in his eyes. He held her close, and felt her body shake from her own emotions, but she made no sound. They'd said their goodbyes much earlier and in private, holding each other through the night.

"Ride with courage." She leaned back and lifted her face to his. "Fight hard, and stay alive. This will not be our end, my husband."

He smiled at the tender words, the first time she had uttered them. Earlier in the evening, Sargon had stood before Subutai, and claimed Tashanella as his wife. With a wan smile, her father had placed his hands on Sargon's shoulders and given his approval. Then Subutai had moved away and resumed his preparations for the coming battle.

Sargon hugged her one more time, then turned away. He didn't trust himself to look back. He'd wanted to stay at her side, but knew that was not the way of the warrior. Tashanella would have been shocked if he failed in his duty.

She, too, had a lance, and she knew how to use it. Anyone who could hold a weapon would follow the warriors down the slope. Roxsanni and Petra had urged her to follow the men, saying they would stay behind to protect the children.

The women knew it was better to die fighting, rather than wait for the rape and other brutality that would be their fate at the hands of the invaders.

Sargon hoped Tashanella would die quickly. His own coming death didn't worry him. He'd expected to die ever since his father dragged him to these lands.

Now, in the predawn darkness, Sargon formed up with the other warriors. He mounted his horse and took his place at Garal's side, not far from Jennat and Timmu and the rest of Chinua's clan.

Sargon found the presence of his friends and trusted companions comforting. They had ridden together, fought together, and endured many hardships. If he had to die, then there could be no better place or time. He held tight to his lance, taking strength from the weapon. Sargon vowed he would not let his friends down.

Fifty paces in front of Sargon, Subutai had massed his own warriors. The Sarum would lead his clan down the slope first, and attack the defenders waiting behind the ditch and stakes the Carchemishi had dug into the base of the hill.

Subutai's fighters would throw themselves against the enemy fortifications and most would sacrifice their lives in what would likely be a futile assault. Chinua led the second force, and would attempt to break through whatever gap the Ur Nammu Sarum could open.

Fifty paces behind Sargon, the old men, young boys, and the women had assembled on foot. They, too, would die with a weapon in their hands.

The battle, however, would begin with Fashod. He had command of fifty men, and they would charge down the hill at the spot where Sargon and his companions had ascended. The rest of Fashod's men were spread between Subutai and Chinua. All the horses not being ridden would be stampeded down the slope first. The ditch and stakes would kill most of them, but Subutai hoped they could dislodge some of the defenders.

Like everyone else preparing for the attack, Sargon knew the attempt was doomed. The Carchemishi were no fools and had prepared well. The ditch would stop the horses and the first wave of Ur Nammu.

The enemy archers would turn the base of the hill into a killing ground. Less than three hundred men would face more than a thousand. Subutai and most of his men would be killed in the first wave.

The Carchemishi would not be taken by surprise. They expected an attack, and pre-dawn would be the most likely time for the Ur Nammu to try something. The invaders always had at least half their men ready for any such endeavor, and the remaining soldiers took their rest with their weapons close at hand. The fighting would be brutal, but the ditch would slow the Ur Nammu, giving time for the enemy bowmen to rush to their positions and cut the warriors apart.

It didn't matter. The last of the water had gone to the women and children yesterday morning, with only a mouthful for each of the men, and none for the horses for the rest of the day. That meant they must attack today. By midday lack of water would have so weakened the Ur Nammu fighters and their horses that they would be practically helpless.

Gripping his lance, Sargon sat on his horse and waited.

A glance at the moon told Sargon that dawn approached. Already the blackness of the eastern sky had lessened. He wondered just how much of the dawn he would live to see. At least today would prove his father wrong. No matter how hard and long Sargon had trained and practiced the skills of war, he was going to end up just as dead as Subutai and the others.

—⁀⁀⁀—

At the other end of the hilltop, Fashod strung his bow. He would strike the first blow in the coming battle. By attacking down the hill, he hoped to convince the Carchemishi that the expected breakout would take place here.

If Fashod could cause enough of the invaders to rush to his position, it might help Subutai break through. Of course, the better Fashod attracted the enemy's attention, the sooner he and his men would be overwhelmed and killed.

Fashod didn't worry about that. He'd faced death before. Now all that remained was a warrior's duty to his Sarum, and in that Fashod did not intend to fail.

He took one last look around. His men stood ready. Darkness still covered the land, but a glance toward the eastern sky told him it was time to go. He leaned over the crest. Since Fashod and his little group had scaled the hill at this point, the enemy had stationed more soldiers here.

"Fashod! What is that?" One of his men moved beside Fashod. In the faint moonlight, he could just make out the man's arm, extended and pointing to the north.

It took a moment before Fashod spotted it. Up in the hills, a tiny glow had appeared, deep in one of the ridges. Fashod stared for a moment, to make sure it was real. It had to be a very small fire, little more than a hand-ful of sticks, but at night even the smallest of flames could be seen over long distances.

And positioned high on a cleft deep between two ridges, the fire would be difficult to see from the base of the hill. In a few more moments, the early light of dawn would overpower the feeble flames. Even if the Carchemishi could or had seen it, it would mean little to them, perhaps just a small party camping in the hills.

Fashod, however, understood its meaning. He turned to his subcom-mander. "Keep ten men here, to guard the ascent. The rest of you, come with me!"

Without waiting for acknowledgement, he burst into a run, heading for the other side of the hill, where Subutai impatiently awaited the sounds of Fashod's charge down the hill. But that attack must not happen, not now. He had to tell Subutai. The Alur Meriki were coming.

Fashod had never run so hard in his life, racing across the top of the hill, dodging the occasional woman or wandering horse, weaving his way across the summit until he reached Subutai's side.

"The Alur Meriki are coming!" Fashod had to pause to take a gulp of air. "They must be close. I saw the signal fire. We must wait for their attack."

—⸻—

Two miles away and across the plain from the Ur Nammu refuge, Bekka led his horse up the side of a sheltering gully. He found Unegen there, waiting.

"Is this the place?" Bekka growled the words. He didn't want to reveal how tired he felt. His feet burned from the long walk, and his legs ached with every step.

"Yes, Sarum," Unegen said. "We've reached the plain."

Bekka took a deep breath, then swung himself onto his horse. He wanted to breathe a sigh of relief, but he would not show weakness in front of his men, not even Unegen.

Instead Bekka glanced up at the moon, now sinking toward the horizon, before turning his gaze on the eastern sky. Dawn approached, and he thanked the gods for letting him reach his destination. He could not have walked much farther.

"Lead the way." Bekka settled himself on his horse, and made sure his sword slid easily in its scabbard. Already he felt stronger. His mount was weary, too, but Bekka knew it had just enough stamina left for one final charge.

He followed Unegen, both men prodding their horses to a fast walk. It would take some time for all the warriors to climb out of the gully, mount their horses, ready their weapons, and take their positions.

Everyone had rested during the early part of the night, but just before midnight, the Alur Meriki chief had led his warriors, on foot and guiding his horse, the final nine or ten miles needed to reach this place. He'd wanted to favor his horses as much as he could, so that they would have something in reserve and could make the final approach at a full gallop.

His tired warriors had done what many would have considered impossible. They covered a vast distance in only a few days, and now would descend on an unsuspecting enemy. Hopefully the element of surprise, if Bekka could keep it, would be enough to make up for the superior numbers of the Carchemishi.

Bekka glanced behind him. As his fighters emerged from the ravine, they formed up, three or four abreast. Bekka wanted every man well clear of the ridge before they got too close. Only flat plain remained ahead, thin grass and good hard ground that would do little to impede men or horses.

He heard a horse scrambling its way toward him. Bekka frowned at the noise, until Den'rack pulled up alongside his Sarum.

"The signal fire is burning, Chief Bekka."

Bekka twisted around and looked up at the hills, but he couldn't see anything. He stared for a moment. There might be a glow against the upper ridges, but he couldn't be sure.

"Let's hope the Ur Nammu see it. And that the invaders don't." Not that it mattered any longer. The Alur Meriki were committed. They needed fresh horses, and the only place to get them lay ahead.

The slow pace grated on Bekka's nerves. He wanted to move faster, but he resisted the urge. They'd arrived just in time, and could afford a few more moments to prepare. Finally Suijan, who'd been at the column's rear, trotted over to join them. "The last of the warriors have cleared the ridge, Sarum."

In the darkness, Bekka smiled at the formal title. It was the first time Suijan had used it. "Good. Take your position on the right. I'll lead the center. You know what to do."

Each of the chiefs had his assigned role. Bekka had worked out the plan last night around the campfire, when they'd finally stopped to rest the horses. Unegen had sketched a rough map in the dirt, and identified the landmarks. Every chief and leader of twenty knew his assignment.

Bekka picked up the pace, setting his horse to a trot. He guided his warriors toward the south first, angling away from the enemy camp. Bekka wanted to drive the invaders' herd around the base of the hill, to overrun the ditch the Carchemishi had dug to keep the Ur Nammu warriors trapped on the hill. To accomplish that, his fighters had to approach from the south.

Keeping the horses at a trot, the warriors moved southward. The shift in direction didn't take long. Soon Bekka, taking his lead from Unegen, turned his horse's head toward the west and led the way in the direction of the enemy herd. Bekka's fighters now took their position on him, fanning out on either side.

Ahead, Bekka saw a handful of small fires still burning, and he saw shadows shifting at the base of the plateau. No sentries had yet discovered the Alur Meriki. No doubt every eye was focused on the hill, waiting for the Ur Nammu's attempt to break out. Meanwhile, no alarms had sounded yet, so Bekka took his time approaching. Behind him, his men drew up alongside, gradually forming a line on either side of their Sarum.

"You're sure we're heading toward the horse herd?" Bekka still couldn't see them.

"Yes, Chief Bekka." Unegen leaned toward his Sarum as he spoke. "My men confirmed that they bedded down the animals for the night in the same place."

The warriors had now spread out into a line almost a quarter mile wide, just over eight hundred men moving to the attack.

Unegen marked the distance. "We've covered the first mile."

Bekka nodded. He'd expected the Carchemishi to have discovered his approach by now. Every additional stride forward only gave his warriors more of an advantage. He glanced again over his shoulder and toward the east.

The sky seemed brighter over the eastern plain, as the pitch dark night grew lighter with each moment. Another quarter mile passed, and still no alarm. He'd never expected to draw this close without being spotted.

On both sides, Bekka heard the horses snorting and making noise. They sensed their riders' excitement. Ahead, he could make out the enemy's horse herd. Less than half a mile to go. Unegen had spoken the truth – a very large herd.

A few of the Carchemishi horses caught the scent of Bekka's riders. Their whinnies sounded, giving warning. A handful of Alur Meriki animals responded. The enemy sentries must know something was wrong, but as yet they had no idea of the blow about to be delivered.

Step by step, the makeshift corral drew closer, until it was only a quarter mile ahead. Shouts from the sentries floated through the air, giving the first warning, but the Carchemishi would need time to react and form a battle line, time they did not have. Bekka knew his men wanted to rush forward, but he held the horses to a trot for another hundred paces.

A drum began to beat, a frantic pounding that sounded the alarm. The first rays of the sunlight shot up into the sky, the last of the darkness faded, and a swath of sunlight swept over the land. Up ahead, Bekka glimpsed men scurrying around, but it was far too late to organize any resistance.

He drew his sword and raised it high over his head, letting the rising sun glint off the bronze. Even without any commands, the well-trained warhorses began moving faster, the trot turning into a canter, and then to an easy gallop with little urging from their riders.

Bekka took a deep breath. "Attack!"

The whole line charged forward, as the warriors urged their mounts to their fastest speed. The ground beneath them shook and thundered from the horses' hooves. The wailing war cry of eight hundred Alur Meriki sounded over the plain, a frightening sound that never failed to strike fear in their enemies. It took only a few heartbeats at the charge to bring his warriors within range of the already nervous herd.

"Let fly! Let fly!"

Bekka heard his order repeated, as the chiefs and leaders of ten drew within long bowshot. Launched from the back of a galloping horse, the shafts would fly almost twice as far.

The first flight of arrows arched high up into the air, aimed directly at the Carchemishi horse herd.

Eight hundred arrows slammed into the herd, far more than necessary to stampede the horses. The entire mass panicked, some driven wild by wounds, others by the scream of dying animals nearby, every one spooked by the pounding charge closing in upon them.

The rope corral collapsed. Guards on the far edge of the herd disappeared under a mass of frightened animals determined to escape an unknown but terrifying enemy. In moments, the panicked Carchemishi horses were at a full gallop with only one thought in their heads, to escape the unknown terror bearing down on them.

As they bolted, the right wing of Bekka's line loosed another volley of arrows, to turn the herd and keep it as close as possible to the base of the hill. Not only would they overrun the ditch and stakes, but that was where most of the Carchemishi had taken their positions for the night.

More arrows, shot at a dead run, now sought out the mass of men struggling to find their weapons and prepare for battle. With so many invaders bunched together, nearly every shaft struck flesh. Cries of pain rose up into the air, mixing with the shouts of fear and panic that raced through the Carchemishi ranks. The alarm drum, if it still sounded, could no longer be heard over the din.

At this tactic, riding down masses of undisciplined or surprised men, the Alur Meriki had no equal. Arrows shot at close range brought down even more of the enemy, as Bekka's men followed the bloody path churned by the stampeding horses' hooves.

Bekka saw the frightened herd swerve to the left around the base of the plateau, the lead animals hurling themselves into the ditch. Some managed to jump the obstacles, but others crashed into the earth on the far side, adding their own wretched cries of panic to the noise of war.

More screams from wounded men and animals rose up into the early morning air. By now many of Bekka's men had slowed their horses, to fall upon the injured or disoriented men staggering about. Some of his fighters had already exhausted their arrows, so fast had they shot their missiles at the enemy.

The stampeded horses, guided by the warriors on Bekka's right flank, swept around the base of the hill, trampling everything and everyone in their path. Gaps appeared in the mass of animals, and Bekka could see men running about, all sense of organization lost. Pointing with his sword, he swept his force right at the largest group. Unegen rode at his side, both of them screaming their war cry.

Lances, either flung through the air or thrust downward at those hugging the ground took an even further toll. Swords, ripped from their scabbards, swung down, crunching through shields or upraised blades, and splattering bone and blood into the air. With the speed of the horse added to the rider's muscles, no one could withstand such a blow.

Now the screams of men, dying or wounded, surpassed the thunder of the horses' hooves. On foot, most of their weapons gone, and in complete disarray, the Carchemishi were easy prey for the savage warriors. The invaders still outnumbered Bekka's horsemen, but they had no idea of how many had attacked them. The unending war cries of the Alur Meriki made them sound like twice their number.

Fear and confusion added to the rout. Many of the invaders threw down their weapons and ran. Others dropped to their knees, the sign of surrender, but the Alur Meriki had no time or inclination to take any captives. Some Carchemishi fought to the end. Others ran, only to be run down or hacked to pieces.

33

From the top of the plateau, Subutai had clear view of the Alur Meriki charge. He saw the white faces of the Carchemishi, caught in the rising sun, as they stared at the oncoming wave of horses. Many stood there, rooted to the earth, even as the panic-stricken horses charged toward them. Others ran about, bumping into each other in the confusion. Shouting and pushing, the frightened men searched for any escape.

At the foot of the slope where Subutai and his people had taken refuge, some of the Carchemishi whirled about and fought to make a stand. Four or five hundred of them abandoned their positions and ran for the safety at the base of the hill, dodging the horses and Alur Meriki warriors wielding bloody swords who galloped past.

As Subutai watched, the stakes that would have impaled his horses disappeared, knocked loose by the stampede. The ditch vanished, too, filled with dead or dying animals and soldiers driven into what had become a death pit. Shrieks of pain sounded everywhere, a never-ending uproar that grated on the nerves of even the most battle hardened fighters.

As the stampede unraveled the Carchemishi defenses, Subutai saw them making their stand with their backs to the hill. Well before the last of the horses had raced past the base of the hill, Subutai's gave the order.

"Attack! Ride them down!"

The first wave of Ur Nammu horsemen tore down the hill at a reckless speed, careless of the steep slope. The warriors, screaming war cries as frightening as those of the Alur Meriki, descended on the invaders. The last of the stampeding horses ran by, but their departure brought the Carchemishi no relief.

Shooting arrows as they rode, the Ur Nammu warriors charged down. Each rider launched four or five shafts in the brief time it took to make the descent. Then swords slid out of scabbards as Subutai's men slammed into the disorganized mass at the base of the slope. Even though the enemy still outnumbered the attacking warriors, the surviving Carchemishi, caught between the Alur Meriki and the Ur Nammu, had no chance against such an onslaught.

Many of Subutai's warriors went down, losing their horses either to the ditch or to the invaders' swords. For a brief moment, the enemy withstood the brutal attack on their rear. But already the second wave of Ur Nammu bore down on them.

⚊⟁⟁⚊

Gripping the halter rope, Sargon kept his gaze fixed on Chinua, who restrained his warriors as long as he could. Subutai's men had scarcely gotten halfway down the slope before Sargon heard the order.

"Attack!" Chinua kicked his horse into motion. "Aim for the gaps!"

The second wave burst into motion, following their leader down the incline. Sargon's horse, as excited as any of the warriors, needed no command from its rider. It raced down the hill a length behind Garal's.

Rumbling hooves thudded against the earth, blotting out any further words, as the second wave charged. At the same time, the Ur Nammu war cries, now rising up from three hundred warriors, created a sound unlike anything Sargon had ever heard.

He leaned forward, urging the horse onward, but he couldn't close the gap and reach Garal's side. All around him, Sargon glimpsed the warriors loosing their arrows as they rode recklessly to the attack, trusting to their horses to keep their footing on the steep slope.

Sargon added his voice to those of his companions, shouting meaningless words as loud as he could. During Sargon's training, Garal had always insisted that Sargon give voice to a war cry as he attacked, though the idea had seemed foolish at the time. Now each war cry added to the frightening din hurling itself down the hill.

Suddenly the ground leveled, and Sargon felt the jolt up his spine as his horse scrambled to keep its footing at the base of the slope. Garal, still fitting and shooting his shafts, had found a narrow gap in Subutai's line, a place where the enemy struggled to make a stand.

The warrior's horse burst in among a mass of the Carchemishi invaders. Now Garal had drawn his sword, and Sargon saw the blade descend once. Then Garal's horse went down, either from a weapon thrust or because it lost its footing in the struggling mass of men.

Sargon saw the sweat-stained faces of his foes, eyes unnaturally wide and open mouthed. In that same instant of recognition, he glimpsed the terror of the Ur Nammu attack stamped on every visage. Nevertheless, the enemy's fear didn't prevent him from fighting for his life.

With a final leap, Sargon's horse jumped over a dead body and into the midst of the invaders. He saw a sword raised up toward him, but he leaned forward and thrust hard with the lance, driving it under the up-thrusting blade. He felt the shock in his arm and shoulder, as the sharp point penetrated the man's body, then burst out through the man's back. The weapon was wrenched from Sargon's hand, burning the skin on his palm.

His horse had scarcely slowed, and in another stride Sargon felt the impact as a second invader staggered back, knocked to the ground by the charging beast's shoulder. One of his horse's hooves landed on the man's chest, and even through the din, Sargon heard rib bones snapping like dry sticks under the horse's weight.

Two more strides sent another man hurling to the ground, knocked off his feet and trampled underfoot. Then the horse stiffened its front legs, sliding forward into a knot of Carchemishi. Sargon glimpsed sword points and spear tips, all searching for his heart.

A sword swung at Sargon's head. Clutching the horse's mane with his left hand, Sargon threw himself off the animal's back. The moment his feet touched down, he wrenched his sword from the scabbard and thrust back at his assailant, reaching over the back of the horse. The sword point struck the man's face, ripping through cheekbone and snapping the head back with a gasp of pain.

Sargon's horse tore itself free from its rider's grasp and bolted, charging through the mass of invaders and opening a path. Sargon saw Garal fighting against two foes. Another man thrust a sword toward Sargon, but he twisted aside and leapt forward, moving toward his friend.

A long step and a full lunge brought him close enough to run the tip of his sword into the back of one of Garal's attackers, just above his waist. Sargon, with a vicious twist of his wrist, jerked the blade free from the writhing man. Just in time, Sargon whirled to face the man who had swung at him only moments ago.

Sargon managed to deflect the blow. He ducked low under the cut and rammed his head and shoulder into the man's chest.

The breath knocked from his body, his foe tried to grapple with his attacker. But Sargon could smell the fear that surrounded the man, reflected in his eyes. Shoving hard with his legs, Sargon pushed him backwards and brought his sword into play, thrusting low into his enemy's stomach. It wasn't a killing blow, but it took the fight out of the man long enough for Sargon to jerk the blade free and thrust again. For the second time in his life, hot blood spurted along his arm.

"Sargon!"

Garal's voice spun Sargon around, ducking low as he turned. A sword cut through the space where he'd stood. Without thinking, Sargon continued to turn, and used his movement to swing his sword around in a flat arc. The sharp bronze bit deep into the enemy soldier's forearm, almost cutting it in two.

With a shriek of agony, the man's sword fell to the ground as a spray of blood spattered into the air. The wounded man staggered backwards, then tripped and fell.

Sargon spun around on his heel, wary of more attacks, but to his surprise, he found no one facing him. The last of the invaders had fallen back toward the ditch, fighting desperately against the battle-enraged warriors. On horse and on foot, the blood-mad Ur Nammu pressed their enemies, giving them no time to form a defensive line.

Panic and terror had swept through the enemy's ranks, as they tried to withstand the vicious thrusts directed against them. Many sought a way to flee from the carnage, away from these ferocious barbarians who fought with such abandon.

Before the Carchemishi could regroup, a screaming mass of old men, women, and boys, anyone old enough or still strong enough to carry a weapon, came charging down the hill and joined the attack. The man Sargon had wounded, on his knees and clutching his arm, was thrown back by a lance driven into his chest by a woman, disheveled hair swirling around her head and screaming as loud as any man.

Glancing back up the slope, Sargon saw only an empty stretch of down-trodden grass, as the last of the Ur Nammu waded into the attack. With lances, bows, and swords, they finished off those who had survived the warriors' charge.

Sargon, breathing heavily, let the sword's point drop to the ground. The battle still raged around the plateau, but all the Carchemishi at the base of the hill were dead or dying.

Garal, with blood streaked across his face and chest, moved beside Sargon. "We need to find horses." He had to shout to make himself heard over the battle noise.

Sargon saw plenty of animals milling about, others rearing up and lashing out with their forelegs at anything that moved, man or beast, friend or enemy. The animals, mad with fright and the scent of blood, all searched for a way to escape the carnage.

One look at the wild beasts, and Sargon decided he would wait a moment longer for them to calm down before he attempted to mount one. He glanced again at his friend. Sargon couldn't tell if Garal were injured.

"Are you wounded?"

Garal shook his head. "No, but a horse's hoof ripped across my chest." The young warrior took a deep breath. "Let's get some horses. This isn't over yet."

The young warrior dashed toward the ditch, where a handful of horses snapped and bit at each other, lashing out with their hooves at anything and everything that moved. By the time Sargon could join him, Garal had seized one halter rope, and somehow managed to grab the mane of a second animal. The man had an uncanny skill with horses.

"Mount up," Garal shouted. "I can't hold them much longer."

Gritting his teeth, Sargon took two strides and leapt directly onto the back of the nearest animal, then locked his legs around the animal's chest while he leaned forward and snatched up the dangling halter rope. To his surprise, the animal quieted down, grateful to have someone in control. Hearing more shouting, Sargon turned to his right, wheeling his new mount around.

From atop the horse, the chaos of the battlefield stunned Sargon's eyes. Dead and dying animals and men covered the ground so densely that he doubted he could get a horse through it. Blood colored everything a bright red, some wounds still spurting into the air. The blood stink rasped into Sargon's throat with every breath.

Any surviving Carchemishi had vanished, either driven off along the south side of the hill by the Alur Meriki, or pushed into the ditch and slaughtered by the Ur Nammu.

Thirty paces away, Sargon saw Subutai, still on his horse, blood streaming down his right arm. The clan leader surveyed the carnage. Then his horse rose up, front hooves flailing the air, as Subutai wheeled the animal around, searching the battleground. His eyes picked out Chinua. The subcommander and his men had just finished off a knot of Carchemishi.

"Chinua! Take your men. Capture their pack animals. Hurry."

Garal also heard the command. He kicked his horse toward the spot where Chinua, waving his sword in the air, was regrouping his men. Swearing under his breath, Sargon followed after him, clutching his bloody sword in his hand.

Sargon had seen the invader's baggage train yesterday, easily visible from the top of the plateau and about a mile away. Tents, wagons, and pack animals waited there, no doubt filled with all the loot taken in the last two hundred miles, plus whatever supplies of food and grain the invaders had collected along the way.

Sargon realized there would be no rest or time to think about the men he'd killed. In moments, Chinua was leading about forty riders at a full gallop across the plain, headed for the enemy baggage.

Many of Carchemishi survivors, fleeing for their lives, ran toward the same destination. Most had thrown away their weapons in their haste. Glancing over their shoulders as they ran, they looked in terror at the riders bearing down on them. The once haughty invaders, now stumbling and falling, parted like a river split in two by a pointed rock, trying to get out of the path of the relentless warriors.

Sargon, riding at Garal's side, watched the slaughter. The Ur Nammu spread out and cut down the helpless men, swords rising and falling again and again. The warriors used their horses to advantage, and Sargon saw many Carchemishi knocked to the ground or trampled underfoot.

Once again Sargon glimpsed the looks of panic and fear on the enemy's faces as the fast moving warriors cut them down from behind, using lance and bow and sword. Some warriors even dismounted, to kill those hugging the ground and pleading for their lives.

Dead bodies littered a wide swath of ground behind the ruthless warriors. Sargon knew there would be no mercy. The invaders would have slaughtered the entire Ur Nammu clan, after brutalizing the women and children. Now they would endure the same fate.

Looking ahead, Sargon glimpsed another stream of men and women abandoning the baggage train. A few rode, seizing any pack horse that might carry them away from the destruction of the army. Others just ran as hard as they could, scattering in all directions, away from the death that galloped toward them. Chinua's riders, in hot pursuit, swept past the first of the wagons, tents, and rope corrals.

"Garal! Stop!" Sargon bellowed as loud as he could. He pulled back hard on the halter, letting the other warriors race past him. He had no interest in chasing across the plain after the fleeing survivors.

The baggage train, however, held food and supplies, as well as loot. When Chinua's men returned from the killing, Sargon knew their first instinct would be to burn everything to the ground. Better that it be saved for use by the Ur Nammu and Alur Meriki.

With obvious reluctance, Garal slowed his horse, then swung it around and returned to where Sargon had dismounted, in front of the largest tent. Two big carts, small wagons, really, stood on both sides of the gently billowing cloth, pushed back and forth by the morning breeze. The tent was huge, easily twice the size of Subutai's. The location, somewhat apart from the others, seemed too well placed for anyone less than the commander of the baggage train.

Sargon used his bloody sword to push aside the flap and peer within. He glimpsed blankets covering the floor, and cushions scattered about. Behind him Garal slid down from his horse. "What's this place?"

"A commander's quarters." Ducking his head, Sargon started in.

Suddenly Garal's arm snapped out and grabbed Sargon's tunic, jerking him backwards. The blade of a sword missed Sargon's face by a handbreadth. Sargon's training took over. Before the weapon could strike again, Sargon thrust out his own sword. The blade dug into something, and he heard a yelp of pain from within.

Garal's iron grip jerked Sargon aside, and the warrior moved forward, his sword at the ready. Tearing open the flap with his left hand, Garal lunged hard, but the blade met no resistance. Sargon saw a man stumbling away from the opening and toward the far side of the tent, a sword still clutched in his hand. Blood streamed down the man's right forearm, where Sargon's off-balance blade had landed.

Garal pushed his way inside, jerking his head from side to side, to make sure there were no other threats. Sargon followed his friend, sword at the ready. From the far corner of the tent, a woman screamed in fright at the sight of the two fighters, blood splattered over their bodies, naked blades in their hands. Another woman joined in, their high pitched screams even louder in the closed confines of the tent. Sargon had never heard two women make so much noise.

The wounded man, his back to the far wall of the tent, turned to face them. He knew he couldn't cut through the wall of the tent before Sargon and Garal fell on him. Big and powerful, he would have had a chance against Garal in an even fight, but the deep cut on his arm had weakened him.

When the Carchemishi raised his weapon, the hilt slipped from his bloody hand. He muttered something Sargon didn't understand, and fumbled with his left hand for a knife that dangled from his belt.

Garal took another step forward, to deliver the killing blow.

"Wait! Look at his tunic!" Sargon's voice halted his friend's thrust. "This one might be useful alive."

The fine linen garment, stitched with threads that formed a wide hem on the square cut neck piece, looked far too valuable to belong to a common soldier. Now Sargon also noticed the wide leather belt with a thick bronze buckle. Designs had been tooled into the leather. Obviously a man of wealth and power.

Garal grunted. He made a sudden lunge toward the man, who threw up his hands to try and block the killing stroke. Instead, Garal shifted his body and his sword in the same motion, and rammed the pommel of the weapon into the wounded man's face.

The powerful blow sent the Carchemishi reeling backward into the wall of the tent, which billowed and flapped, threatening to collapse the whole structure. Dazed, the man slumped to the ground, fresh blood dripping from the gash in his forehead. A single glance told Sargon that the fight had gone out of their prisoner.

He turned his attention to the two women. Young girls, really. Neither one looked any older than Tashanella. The screams had stopped, and now they clutched each other, bosoms rising and falling from their fear. They knew what fate awaited them.

"Tie that one up," Sargon ordered, gesturing toward the unconscious man on the ground, "before he comes to. We don't want him killing himself."

Sargon gave the order without thinking, though of course in the hierarchy of the Ur Nammu, he wasn't supposed to give orders to anyone.

If Garal noticed the breech of command, he ignored it. Glancing around, Garal spied the dangling rope used to fasten the tent flap. Using his sword, he cut it free. Then he dropped to his knees, rolled the semi-conscious man onto his stomach, and bound his hands behind him, tugging hard on the rope to make sure the knot stayed tight.

The tent and its inhabitants intrigued Sargon. Not a mere commander's quarters, not with furnishings as large and luxurious as these. He realized the prisoner must be one of the Carchemishi leaders. That would make more sense, with the tent located on the fringe of the baggage train.

This tent looked more like a bed chamber, with cushions and rugs scattered about everywhere. The scent of incense hung in the air, still noticeable even over the stink of fresh blood and sweat. It might be a place where a senior commander, after a hard day of pillaging, took his pleasures.

The trembling girls, still sobbing, needed to be questioned. They would hold many answers, and it should be easy enough to get them to talk.

"Garal, these three are important. Can you guard them until Chinua or Subutai can get here? I'll make sure that the rest of the tents aren't destroyed until we've examined them. They might tell us much about these invaders and their plans."

The warrior had finished binding their captive. "Go. I'll watch them."

Sargon faced the girls once again. "Stay there and don't move. Otherwise I'll turn the both of you over to the warriors. You know what that means."

He spoke in the language of Akkad, hoping the two would understand. Whether they did or not, their heads nodded in unison, and the sobs ceased.

Outside, Sargon started checking the tents and wagons, jogging from one to another.

Four tents clustered together stood nearby, and he searched those first. Each provided sleeping space large enough for three or four men. They held little more than the loot and goods a subcommander might have accumulated, and nothing that Sargon found interesting.

He started on the wagons, a motley collection of every size and shape imaginable. Sargon strode up and down the lines, glancing at each as he passed. When he completed his inspection, he'd counted forty-six wagons, an impressive number.

Most contained sacks of grain and vegetables, weapons, and supplies needed for such a large number of men on campaign. A small group of ten wagons, separated from the others, held the army's loot – gold, gems, fancy weapons, even richly made clothing, rugs, and sandals.

Finished, Sargon ran back to the commander's tent. Garal had dragged his prisoner outside, the better to see what was going on. Now the warrior sat on a low stool, drinking something from a water skin. As Sargon dismounted, he caught the smell of wine in the air.

Garal grinned at him. "Have some of this. It's good." He offered up the wineskin.

Sargon's throat was dry, but he wanted water, not wine. "Any water inside?"

"Yes, plenty." Garal shouted something, and one of the girls appeared at the tent's opening. "Water." He pointed to Sargon.

The girl nodded, and disappeared. In a moment, she returned carrying a water skin so heavy she could barely manage it.

Garal laughed. "She already knows two Ur Nammu words – water, and wine. Tonight I'll teach her a few more."

Sargon snatched the water skin from her hands and drank until he could hold no more. When he handed it back, it weighed considerably less. Looking down at his hands, he realized they were still covered with blood.

The girl offered it to Garal, but he shook his head. "What's in the wagons?" He took another mouthful of wine.

"Food and supplies, mostly," Sargon said. "Ten are filled with gold and loot the Carchemishi have collected. No horses. The wagon drivers must have cut the livery animals free and rode off."

"That's probably what happened to this one." Garal shoved the unconscious man with his foot. "Probably went inside to collect his loot, and someone stole his horse." He laughed at the idea. "Well, we can use all the food we can get. We lost most of our herds."

The Ur Nammu had abandoned everything in their flight, including their sheep, goats, and cattle. The supplies in the enemy wagons would sustain the Ur Nammu for a long time, more than long enough to return to their former camp.

The sound of hoof beats made Sargon look up. Riders approached, coming toward them. Garal plugged the wineskin and tossed it back into the tent. He moved to his feet and stood beside his friend. Four riders led the way, and behind them were two separate groups of twenty or so warriors.

"The Alur Meriki." Garal said the words softly, almost as if he didn't quite believe his eyes. "That's a sight I never thought I would live to see. Now we just have to hope that they don't decide to kill us all."

"Not likely." Sargon doubted the Alur Meriki would risk everything just to kill a few hundred Ur Nammu. "Besides, Subutai is with them."

The two Sarums, Bekka and Subutai, rode side by side. Fashod accompanied Subutai, and another warrior rode beside Bekka.

The leaders halted before the tent. Bekka wore a crude bandage on his left arm, but if it caused him any discomfort, he hid it well. Subutai also had taken a wound, just below the right shoulder. A crude bandage had staunched the blood, but traces had stained the dirty cloth.

"Well, young Sargon of Akkad," Bekka said, gazing down at the two young men, "it's good to see you survived. How many men have you challenged to battle today?"

Sargon bowed. "I believe I've had more than enough fighting, Clan Leader Bekka."

"All my warriors will give fervent thanks to the gods for that, then," Bekka said, a trace of a smile on his face. He slipped his right leg over his horse's neck and dropped to the ground. "I can use a rest from riding and fighting."

Sargon handed Bekka the water skin. The Sarum drank deeply, then passed it on to his men.

"The Sarum of the Alur Meriki and his warriors arrived just in time." Subutai dismounted as well, though he took care with his movements. "Another day, and the Ur Nammu would have been destroyed." He glanced around. "And what is this place?"

Sargon related what he'd seen in the baggage train. "This man that Garal captured is someone of importance. He may be useful to my father."

"He is Sargon's prisoner as much as mine," Garal said. "Sargon had already wounded him. All I did was tap him on the head."

Bekka glanced at Subutai. "We may have questions for him as well."

"We've taken a few other prisoners," Subutai said. "We'll start with them. When it's this one's turn, I'm sure he'll be glad to tell us everything he knows."

The Ur Nammu had as little use for prisoners as did the Alur Meriki. Those who would not make docile slaves were put to death, after spending time being tortured by the clan's women, who were even more expert at dispensing pain than their men.

The prisoner stirred. He groaned, then opened his eyes. The pain on his faced vanished, replaced by a look of terror as realization of his fate set in.

"What is your name?" Sargon spoke in the same trader's language he'd used when the Ur Nammu had first encountered the Carchemishi, little more than ten days ago.

The man turned to Sargon, surprised that someone so young would be questioning him. He stared sullenly at his captors for a moment, but said nothing.

Garal drew his knife, and squatted down beside the prisoner. He seized him by the hair and put the edge of his knife against the man's nose. He glanced up at Sargon. "Should I cut it off?"

"Answer the question, or lose your nose." Sargon kept his voice calm. "After that, we'll turn you over to the women for the rest of the day. By then you'll be begging to talk, just to stop the pain."

Garal pressed harder, and the sharp blade cut a grove just above the nostrils. A thin line of blood leaked down and across the man's mouth.

"Kamanis." He rolled his eyes toward Garal, who kept up the pressure. "My name is Kamanis."

"And you are . . . ?"

Kamanis hesitated, glancing around at the men staring down at him. "I'm just a soldier. I'm just a guard. I guard the baggage train."

Sargon translated again.

"Hold your knife!" Bekka snapped out the command, but without waiting for Garal to move, the Alur Meriki Sarum took two steps and lashed out with his foot, the thick leather sandal smashing into Kamanis's face.

The prisoner's head snapped back so hard that Sargon thought Bekka had broken the man's neck. The man slumped against the side of the tent. Fresh blood from his mouth joined the trickle from his nose.

Bekka drew his own knife. He grabbed at Kamanis's head, gripping him by the hair and knocking Garal's hand aside. The point of Bekka's blade dug into the corner of the man's eye.

"Tell him if he lies again, he'll be looking at his own eye." Bekka emphasized his words with another jab of the knife

A gasp of pain sounded.

Sargon translated Bekka's threat. "I think you had better decide whether you want to keep the ruler of the clan that just defeated your soldiers waiting. Or you can tell us everything we want to know, and you might live long enough to reach my father, the King of Akkad. He's more merciful than these steppes warriors, and he may find it useful to keep you alive."

The moment Sargon finished, Bekka shoved the tip of the knife in deeper. Blood now pulsed from the eye socket.

"Wait! I'll tell you! My name is Kamanis. I am . . . I was a commander of this army."

Bekka glanced over his shoulders at Sargon, who translated once again.

Grudgingly, as if annoyed that he could not gouge out the man's eye, Bekka eased the knife away and stood. "If he changes his mind and keeps silent, or tries to lie, bring him to me. And tell him that a slave who won't answer questions or fails to tell the truth will be seated on a stake."

Sargon didn't understand the threat, but Subutai explained it.

"We take a sapling and bury one end deep in the earth. The other end is sharpened, and the prisoner sits on it, until the point reaches just below his stomach. The man dies, but slowly. A strong man can last almost a day, and every moment is filled with the worst pain you can imagine."

"I will tell him, Chief Bekka." Sargon nodded to Subutai.

"Then we will leave him here with you," Subutai said, "since you're the only one who speaks his language anyway. Learn whatever you can from him. After that, we'll decide what to do with him."

Subutai glanced down at Kamanis. "Tell him he's lucky to be in your hands, not mine." He turned to Bekka. "Come. We still have many to hunt down." He called out to Garal as he retrieved his mount's halter. "Stay with Sargon and the prisoner. Make sure Sargon has whatever he needs."

The two clan leaders mounted. A moment later, they and their men galloped off, leaving a cloud of dust that swirled across the ground, driven by the breeze.

"Let's get Kamanis inside," Sargon said. "We'll start questioning the girls first."

"There's plenty of time," Garal said, staring over Sargon's shoulder. Suddenly a smile covered his face. "I think there's something else you should attend to first."

Sargon turned. Tashanella rode slowly toward them, picking her way through the debris of the wagon train. She held a lance in her right hand, the point streaked with blood.

Garal saw the expression on Sargon's face and laughed. "Maybe she can help question the prisoner."

But Sargon barely heard his words. He was running to meet his woman.

34

Fifteen days later, Sargon sat outside of his tent, enjoying the warmth of the setting sun, the effects of a full meal settling inside his stomach, and the pleasant company of his companions. Seated beside him were Garal, Jennat, and an unexpected guest, Den'rack, of the Alur Meriki. The tent had formerly belonged to Kamanis, but Subutai had given it to Sargon and Tashanella as a wedding gift, along with most of its contents.

Actually, the recently married couple possessed two tents. Eventually the second one would be for Sargon's future servants and slaves, but now it served as a place to keep Kamanis under guard. The Carchemishi commander had soon grasped the reality of his situation, after he heard the screams of many of his former soldiers rising up into the sky.

Following the defeat of the Carchemishi forces, Sargon had not expected to find more than a handful of the invaders alive. But over the next few days, more than a hundred survivors were captured and returned to the camp of the Ur Nammu as prisoners. Subutai had ordered a count of the dead, and after that tally, he estimated that perhaps two hundred or so managed to escape the debacle. The rest of the Carchemishi invaders perished. As battles went, Subutai declared, this one was a great victory, and one with few losses.

Subutai had moved his clan back near their former location along the banks of the stream. On the other side, less than a quarter mile away, stood the tents of the Alur Meriki. After the last of the invaders were killed or captured, Bekka had set up a temporary camp for his forces, to hold the large number of horses taken from the enemy.

The day after the attack, Bekka and Subutai, in front of their men, had sworn the oath of friendship. The Alur Meriki forces would soon return to their caravan, but first the wounded needed time to heal. Not to mention that dividing up the spoils captured from the Carchemishi – food, gold, weapons, and horses – had taken longer than expected.

Subutai had insisted that most of the horses and loot be given to Bekka and his men, since they had saved the lives of the Ur Nammu clan. The goods that the Alur Meriki retained as their share far exceeded anything they'd captured in the last several years.

Both clan leaders had acknowledged their debt to Sargon. His audacious visit had, after all, led to an easy victory for Chief Bekka's warriors. As a result, Sargon was as welcome in the Alur Meriki camp as in that of the Ur Nammu. Sargon understood the need to build good relations between the two former enemies, and visited the Alur Meriki warriors as often as he could.

The third day after the battle, Bekka had taken three hundred warriors and, mounted on fresh Carchemishi horses, ridden for his caravan. Unegen and Den'rack had accompanied him. At the time, Sargon had wondered why Bekka had rushed off, leaving behind Clan Leader Suijan in command.

Today, twelve days after his departure, Chief Bekka and Den'rack, along with fifty horsemen, had returned to the Ur Nammu camp. Now, as Den'rack's story unfolded, Sargon understood the reason for Bekka's hasty departure.

"So, after Chief Bekka explained the size of our victory over the Carchemishi to the whole caravan, and told them about the weapons and horses taken," Den'rack continued, "no one dared to question Bekka's right to be Sarum. Except for Trayack, who could not keep his tongue silent in his shame. None of his clan, of course, would receive anything from the victory. Trayack's foolish words gave Bekka the chance to challenge him to a fight."

"I wish we could have seen that," Garal said.

Den'rack shook his head. "Better such things are not seen by outsiders. Almost everyone watching assumed that Trayack would kill Bekka.

Trayack was bigger and stronger, but not as cunning. Chief Bekka used his horse to his advantage, and outfought his opponent. After many strokes, Bekka hacked off Trayack's sword arm, and then left him face down on the ground, until he bled to death."

Sargon understood both the necessity and the politics behind Bekka's actions. The Sarum of the Alur Meriki had accomplished all his goals. He'd won not only a battle, but a great victory, and brought pride and glory back to the Alur Meriki.

At the same time, he'd proven himself both a strong fighter and a cunning leader on the battlefield. Bekka had also eliminated the only other clan leader who'd dared to challenge his right to be Sarum. And with the large number of captured horses divided up among his men, Bekka would rule the great clan uncontested in the future.

All the same, the news of Trayack's death brought a smile to Sargon's face. "At least I won't have to worry about Trayack any longer. And you say that Unegen is now a chief?"

"Yes, Bekka gave Unegen all of Trayack's warriors." Den'rack took another sip of water from his cup. "Chief Bekka praised Unegen before all the warriors in the camp, and declared that much of the Carchemishi victory belonged to him."

"And you are now a leader of fifty," Garal said. "What did Bekka say of your efforts?"

Den'rack could not conceal his satisfaction. "I, too, received some praise. With my share of the spoils, I shall have no trouble finding a few new wives."

Everyone laughed.

"The Ur Nammu owe you and your people much," Sargon said. "The distrust that many once felt is almost gone. Even I can see that."

"It's true," Jennat said. "Den'rack, no Ur Nammu warrior will ever forget what your people did for us."

"So what brought Chief Bekka back here?" Sargon changed the subject. No matter how sincere the debt, no one liked being reminded of an obligation.

"I'm sure he has more important things to do than count horses." Sargon knew that the others wanted to hear the answer to that question, but were too polite to ask. He, as the outsider, could raise it easily enough.

Soon after Bekka's arrival, the Sarum of the Alur Meriki and his clan chiefs had met with Subutai, Fashod, and Chinua. Even now, they continued their talk on the edge of the camp, where none could hear their words.

"I do not know . . . for certain." Den'rack hesitated, obviously concerned about saying too much. "After killing Trayack, Chief Bekka spoke long into the night with Chief Urgo, Unegen, and a few others. But he said nothing on the journey here. Some of us thought Chief Bekka returned to meet with you, Sargon of Akkad."

Sargon laughed. "I doubt they need my counsel on anything."

Hoof beats sounded throughout the camp, and the four men turned to watch a scout galloping into camp, his horse covered with sweat. The rider headed straight for Subutai's tent, paused for a moment, then continued on to where the leaders were meeting.

"I wonder what news he brings," Garal mused. "That horse is finished for the day."

"He was patrolling to the south," Jennat said. "Not much danger likely to come from there."

In that direction lay the empty lands, and beyond them, the outlying forts and territory of Akkad. Everyone turned to Sargon.

"Perhaps word from Akkad has come," Sargon offered. "More than enough time has passed for word to reach the city and for my father to send a reply."

"We'll know soon enough." Jennat turned to Den'rack. "What do your people think about the Akkadians?"

Den'rack shrugged. "No warrior likes to be reminded of the man who defeated him. But Sargon's father is a brave man. I could not believe my eyes when he rode into our midst after the battle at the stream. I thought certain some angry warrior would strike him down, but no one dared challenge him. Perhaps if Thutmose-sin had ruled more wisely, that battle would not have happened."

"My father is a brave man." Sargon uttered the words without enthusiasm.

"As are you, Sargon of Akkad." Den'rack broke an uncomfortable silence. "Not many would have ridden into our camp the way you did. I thought certain you would die that night at Trayack's hands."

Before Sargon could reply, a young boy, one of Subutai's messengers, raced toward them.

"Your father approaches, Sargon." The boy had to pause to catch his breath. "He will arrive tomorrow, sometime after midday."

Sargon thanked the lad, who nodded and darted off.

"What will you say to him?" Garal knew all about the rift between father and son. "He may want you to return to Akkad."

"In that case he will be disappointed."

"You intend to stay here with the Ur Nammu?" Den'rack couldn't keep the surprise from his voice.

Sargon nodded. "I have a wife now, and duties as a warrior. Besides, my father has no need of my services."

"Well, there is a time for all things." Den'rack settled back on his heels. "I for one am glad that you will stay with the warriors. Otherwise life would be far too dull."

Garal glanced at Jennat. "Oh, yes, wherever Sargon goes, trouble is sure to follow."

<hr>

That evening, after his friends had gone, Sargon closed the tent flap against the night's breezes. He unlaced his sandals and stretched out on the thick blanket, yet another prize from Kamanis's bower of plenty. Sargon watched as Tashanella dropped to her knees and pulled her dress up and over her head. Her long tresses caught for a moment, and she had to shake her head to loosen the dark strands.

Her body continued to delight him, the firm breasts that jutted out over the flat stomach. She smiled at his gaze, no longer as shy as she had been in the beginning.

"So, Husband, your father comes. What will you say to him?" She leaned over him, and placed her hands on his shoulders, letting her breasts brush against his lips.

His father. It was always his father. And when it wasn't, his mother's presence made itself felt. Tonight, however, Sargon refused to think about them.

His parents and their concerns no longer troubled him. Subutai could never abandon the debt he owed Sargon. The leader of the Ur Nammu had already acknowledged as much. He'd given Sargon his favorite daughter, and promised him a high place among the clan's warriors.

"Perhaps you should ask what he will say to me." Sargon brushed his lips against a firm nipple, until Tashanella gasped with pleasure. "Not that the King of Akkad has any power over me."

His wife snuggled against him, and he felt the warmth from her body against his chest. "What will he say when he learns of our marriage? Will he be angry?"

Sargon shook his head. "No, that's not his way. It takes a great deal before he loses his temper. Once he does, though . . ."

"I hope he thinks I am pretty enough for his son, prettier than all the girls you left behind in Akkad."

"Of that, you need not have any fear." He wrapped his arm around her shoulders and kissed her throat. "None of the soft and lazy women in Akkad can even come close to your beauty."

He shivered as her hand traveled down his chest and moved between his thighs. Sargon heard a giggle of delight when she found him hard and ready.

"Let us forget about my father." Sargon heard the hoarseness in his voice, as the desire rushed through him. He cupped her breast, and wondered if his father had ever felt such passion for a woman. His mother, of course, was far too cold and calculating to make a good bedmate.

Then all thoughts of his parents disappeared as he pulled Tashanella down onto the blanket. Laughing, she spread her legs wide for him, and the pleasure of the gods soon enveloped them both.

35

The sun had just passed midday when Eskkar halted the column of riders on the crest of the hill overlooking the Ur Nammu camp. From habit, he let his gaze roam over the landscape, scanning every part of the countryside from horizon to horizon. Much had changed since his last visit.

To his right, where the Ur Nammu tents had originally stood, Eskkar saw the blackened sod and trampled down earth of the abandoned campsite. Whatever Subutai's people had left behind, the invaders had burned or taken with them before they pursued the fleeing clan. Now only debris littered the charred ground.

The new Ur Nammu campsite lay another half mile downstream. Eskkar could just make out the three streamers, yellow in color, that marked the clan's three chiefs.

On his left, on the far side of the stream, stood the temporary camp of the Alur Meriki. There three red standards, attached to lances driven into the earth, waved in the light wind and marked the visitor's tents.

He noticed something else. In place of the original tents of the Ur Nammu, destroyed by the invaders, now stood many of the captured Carchemishi tents. Eskkar shifted his gaze to the four herds of horses that filled almost all the space between the two camps, and extended far beyond them, away from the stream. Warriors from both camps patrolled the herds.

Hathor pulled his mount to a stop beside Eskkar. "I've never seen so many horses in one place."

The Ur Nammu scout, who had met up with Eskkar and his men yesterday, claimed his clan had captured almost a thousand horses. Eskkar hadn't believed him, but looking at the herds, he realized the man might have spoken the truth.

"A lot of horses." Eskkar pointed toward the Alur Meriki camp. "The last two times these clans encountered each other, the ground ran red with blood."

Hathor shaded his eyes as he stared at the fields below. "I see about two hundred warriors in the Alur Meriki camp. No matter what happens, we have more than enough cavalry to deal with them."

The moment Subutai's messengers brought word of the invasion, and the threat to both the Ur Nammu and Sargon, Eskkar had mobilized his forces in Akkad and prepared for war. It had taken but two days to collect five hundred riders and start the journey north, leaving his commanders and Trella to prepare the city for a possible siege. The day after Eskkar departed, Alexar started north, following Eskkar's trail, with over a thousand infantrymen and archers.

Most of Eskkar's worries about a possible conflict with the Carchemishi had vanished days ago, with the report of a great victory and news about the safety of his son, Sargon. Now the last doubts in Eskkar's mind disappeared at the sight of the peaceful camp. The Ur Nammu and Alur Meriki had indeed joined together to defeat these invaders.

"They're coming out to meet us," Hathor said.

Eskkar turned his gaze back to the stream and field below. Three riders from the Ur Nammu camp had started toward them, their horses kicking clods of dirt into the air as they raced at top speed over the grassy earth. He recognized Fashod leading the way.

"Welcome, Eskkar of Akkad," Fashod shouted, as he drew his horse to a halt. "Subutai sends his greetings. He says you should set up your camp over there." Fashod pointed toward the southern end of the stream.

"It's good to meet again, Fashod. You've won a great victory."

Fashod laughed. "Well, we're still arguing about who won the battle, but we've got all their horses and tents." He waved his arm toward the camp. "Come, Subutai is eager to see you."

"Tell Subutai that I will join him soon."

Eskkar turned to Hathor. "We need to get the horses watered and set up camp. And I'll want you with me when we meet the clan chiefs."

Later, after settling down the Akkadian horsemen, Eskkar and Hathor washed the dust and grime from their faces. Then they strode through the Ur Nammu camp until they reached Subutai's tent.

The Ur Nammu leaders awaited Eskkar's arrival. He saw Fashod and Chinua standing on either side of Subutai, but no sign of Sargon. A few steps away stood Chief Bekka and two Alur Meriki warriors Eskkar didn't recognize. Eskkar saw the Sarum's copper medallion gleaming on Bekka's chest.

Eskkar kept his face impassive during the introductions. He remembered Bekka, of course, but when Eskkar had ridden from the Alur Meriki camp, Urgo had been Sarum, and Bekka merely a young clan chief. He had sworn the oath of friendship along with Urgo, but what the Alur Meriki change of leadership meant for Akkad now needed to be redefined.

Greetings were exchanged, and Eskkar learned for the first time that Urgo had yielded command of the Alur Meriki to Bekka. One of Bekka's companions was Chief Suijan. The other warrior was introduced as Den'rack, a leader of fifty.

"My respects to you, Chief Bekka, as leader of the Great Clan." Eskkar bowed respectfully. Now was not the time to slight anyone's honor. He also inclined his head to Bekka's companions. "I have heard that the Alur Meriki and Ur Nammu have won a great victory and captured many horses. Though I never expected to see both clans fighting side by side."

Bekka returned the bow, exactly as deep as Eskkar's. "It is good to see you again, Eskkar of Akkad. As for our alliance with the Ur Nammu, your son Sargon is responsible for that."

Eskkar's face must have shown surprise, for Subutai laughed aloud, while the others smiled.

"Come and sit down." Subutai motioned toward the ground before his tent. "There is much to tell you."

The story took a long time to tell, while Eskkar and Hathor sat there too surprised, and occasionally even shocked, to say much of anything. Subutai spoke first, but then Fashod and Chinua took over the tale, relating the details of the first fight against the Carchemishi, the raid on their horses, and the flight of the clan to the heights of the bluff.

Then Den'rack picked up the narrative, describing his encounter with Sargon and Fashod, and their arrival at the Alur Meriki camp.

Eskkar's eyes widened when he learned of Sargon's challenge to Den'rack, who appeared fierce enough to fight anyone in the clan, let alone an untried youth.

Bekka continued the story, telling of the other challenges. He also described the meeting with the Council and explained his decision to join the fight alongside the Ur Nammu. Bekka related the details of the long ride, the final decision to press on through the night, and the arrival of the Alur Meriki just as dawn broke.

"The enemy had turned all their attention to the Ur Nammu," Bekka finished up. "We caught them by surprise, used their own horses to break their ranks, then cut them apart."

"And those Bekka's warriors missed, we hunted down and killed," Subutai said. "Sargon killed at least two, perhaps three in that fight, and he managed to find and keep alive a leader of the Carchemishi, a man named Kamanis. That's one I think you will want to speak to yourself."

Eskkar had a hundred questions, and the warriors took their turns explaining all the little details any fighting man would want to know. Every speaker gave praise to Sargon, his courage, and the way he had convinced the Alur Meriki Council to save the Ur Nammu. The sun had sunk almost to the horizon before Eskkar heard the complete story. He could not conceal the pride that he felt for his son's actions.

At last, Eskkar rested his hands on his knees. "And where is Sargon?"

Subutai's face lost a bit of its good humor. "He is at his tent, Eskkar, with his wife. Sargon has taken my daughter, Tashanella, as his bride. I asked him to join us, but he said he preferred to remain in his tent."

Eskkar had assumed that Sargon was away from the camp. Eskkar knew his face betrayed the surprise and anger that surged through him. First, the boy had married without his father's consent, a serious affair. And Sargon had declined to attend the meeting, a clear breech of familial duty that bordered on insolence.

Now Eskkar had to deal with the fact that everyone present must know all about the family's troubles. He glanced down and saw that his left hand had clenched into a fist. It took a moment before Eskkar could control the urge to rise and stalk away, find his son, and give him a good beating.

"Well, perhaps a wife will help Sargon become a good warrior." Hathor spoke for the first time, to end the uncomfortable silence.

Eskkar saw that impassive looks had appeared on every face. No one wanted to say anything further about his son, until they saw the father's reaction. "What is your daughter's name?"

"Tashanella." Subutai, too, wanted to end the awkward silence that had greeted his words. "She has wisdom beyond her years, much like your own wife, Lady Trella."

The mention of his wife's name did little to calm Eskkar's rising anger. "And how did Sargon come to choose her as his bride?"

"As a proven warrior, he had earned the right to take a wife. He chose Tashanella, and she agreed to the marriage. So I gave my permission. But even many days before that, he and my daughter had spoken to each other."

Eskkar opened his mouth, then closed it. The phrase "spoken to each other," meant that a great deal of words and probably more had passed between boy and girl. Eskkar knew he couldn't, after all, complain about his son's choice of a bride when she happened to be Subutai's daughter. Obviously, a lot more had gone on than he knew.

The girl probably meant nothing to Sargon, who would likely discard her soon enough, creating a host of new problems. Eskkar took a deep breath. All this could be discussed later, when he and Subutai were alone.

"Then I'm glad my son has proven his courage."

"If I may speak." Bekka leaned forward, his face suddenly grave. "Your son did more than just prove his courage. He met with the Council of the Alur Meriki with honor, and talked of a new alliance with Akkad. He spoke to us as your eldest son, the heir to the ruler of Akkad, and as your representative. If his promises are not to be taken as your own, then we may have more to discuss."

Eskkar met Bekka's eyes. "No, Chief Bekka, whatever my son Sargon has said, you may take as if I had spoken. He was here, at the point of the battle, and whatever promises he made are binding on me. But you and I will speak of such things in the morning."

"Then tonight we feast, to celebrate your arrival," Subutai said, no doubt glad to change the subject. "We can meet tomorrow to speak of the future."

Sargon must have acted wisely, Eskkar decided. Otherwise Subutai would have sent word to him. Eskkar might not fully trust his son, but he could rely on the Sarum of the Ur Nammu. If Subutai had not found fault with the boy's decisions, then Sargon must have handled himself well.

Eskkar forced a smile to his face. "I am a little surprised at Sargon's decision to marry. But as Subutai says, he is a warrior now and can make his own choices."

The clan leaders and those who had gathered around them relaxed. They, too, knew that a crisis between father and son had passed, at least for the moment.

"Well, then, perhaps it is time that I visit my son and meet his wife. Afterwards, I am sure that Chief Bekka, Chief Subutai, and myself have much more to discuss."

Eskkar glanced at Subutai, who nodded approval. This was, after all, his Council meeting and he made the decisions as to when those attending came or left. As Eskkar rose, a woman appeared before him. She bowed low in a sign of respect, and spoke.

"Lord Eskkar, perhaps you will permit me to guide you to your son's tent."

Eskkar recognized Petra, Subutai's senior wife. For some reason, she wanted to speak to him. Otherwise a messenger boy could have guided Eskkar just as well. "Yes, of course."

"With your permission, Husband?"

Subutai nodded.

Hathor had also risen, to accompany his friend, but Eskkar placed his hand on the man's shoulder. "You might as well wait here until I return."

Petra led the way. As soon as they passed beyond the area marked off for Subutai's use, another woman joined them.

"I am Roxsanni, Lord Eskkar." The woman bowed and fell into step beside them. "I am second wife to Subutai, and mother of Tashanella."

Roxsanni's appearance was not by chance. The women wanted a chance to speak with him alone. He wondered if Subutai knew what was happening.

"Your son has become a great and wise warrior," Petra began. "He saved the lives of all of us."

"And put an end to the blood feud with the Alur Meriki," Roxsanni added.

"And now Sargon wishes to remain with your people," Eskkar said. "Your daughter, Roxsanni, must be both beautiful and persuasive."

"She is. But Petra is as much her mother as I." "We have both raised her," Petra said. "Every family in the clan has always thought of her as if she were one of their own."

They reached the edge of the camp and Eskkar stopped. Unless Sargon had moved in among the Alur Meriki, the women had led him away from Sargon's tent.

Petra moved to face him. "If you would permit, Lord Eskkar, we would speak to you about your son and his bride. This marriage can be good for both the Ur Nammu and the people of Akkad. I have spoken several times with your wife Trella over the years. If she were here, and knew about Tashanella, I am sure your wife would give her approval. In many ways, our daughter is much like your wife. Tashanella has eyes that see more than just the ground beneath her feet."

Or as the dirt eaters would say, she didn't need to fall down a well to find water. Eskkar shrugged. "Perhaps. But now it matters not. Sargon has made up his own mind."

"Yes, he has." Roxsanni moved beside Petra. "But now everything is up to you. You must find it in your heart to accept this union, though I see in your eyes that you disapprove. If you continue your quarrel with Sargon, you will lose him. He still feels much anger at you for removing him from Akkad. That is why he did not attend the Council Meeting."

"He is still very young," Petra said, "and he has much to learn. But in time, he will forget his anger. He will return to take his place in Akkad. And he will bring Tashanella and his sons with him."

Eskkar felt his temper rising. He didn't like being accosted by these women. They were, after all, seeking to advance the station of their daughter. If they weren't Subutai's wives, he would have ordered them to keep silent.

"And what does Subutai say about all this?"

"My husband is a good and brave warrior, who leads his people well," Petra said. "He will be content if Sargon spends the rest of his days among us. Already he looks forward to his daughter's children. But Tashanella can bring a new future for our people, a real alliance with Akkad that will ensure our people, and all our children, survive. You know in your heart there will come a day when Akkad and our clan will clash, either over land or some other dispute."

"And when that day comes, the Ur Nammu will lose," Roxsanni said. "Though our warriors refuse to admit it, Akkad has grown too strong for any clan to oppose. Even the Alur Meriki understand this. That is why Chief Bekka is here, waiting to speak with you. He, too, will want to strengthen his alliance with Akkad."

Eskkar glanced from one to the other. Obviously Subutai knew nothing about this. Now his wives were not only asking him to favor their daughter, but also expected him to support the Ur Nammu in the days to come. Eskkar didn't like the idea of women making such decisions behind the backs of their men. It seemed unnatural, unmanly. Of course Trella made many such decisions, but she was different. She was . . . he wondered what she would do if she were here.

He took a deep breath and let it out slowly. It wouldn't hurt to hear what they had to say. "And what do you suggest I say to my son?"

Petra kept her eyes on Eskkar, but Roxsanni could not control her face. She darted a quick glance at her companion at Eskkar's acceptance, however tentative, of their advice.

"You need say nothing." Petra spoke quicker now, eager to make her argument before Eskkar changed his mind. "All you need do is not make the situation worse. There must be no quarrel that ends in Sargon refusing to acknowledge his role in Akkad's future. As he grows older, Sargon will realize that you and Lady Trella acted only for his own good. And during that same time, Tashanella will slowly bend Sargon back to your House. In a year or two, no more than three, he will return to Akkad, a dutiful son."

"And he will be older and wiser, and better prepared to rule Akkad one day." Roxsanni said. "Meanwhile, I am sure that he will soon be eager to visit his parents and present his wife to Lady Trella."

Tashanella would make sure of that, especially with these two advising her. Eskkar wished Trella were here, to help deal with these women. But he would have to do the best he could. "And how soon before the first of these visits takes place?"

"A few months, perhaps three or four. Soon Tashanella will be carrying your son's heir, and she will not want to travel far once she is heavy with child."

Of course the girl would be pregnant soon, if she weren't already. He had forgotten about the burning passions of youth. That led to another thought.

"It might be wise," Eskkar said, almost thinking aloud, "if your daughter Tashanella delivers her first child in Akkad. You both could accompany her for that event."

"You are indeed as wise as men say, Eskkar of Akkad," Petra said. "Yes, it would be best for everyone to have the people of Akkad see Sargon's firstborn as one of their own."

Eskkar grunted. He hated this kind of plotting and scheming. "And how much of this should I discuss with Subutai? He is, after all, your husband."

"Our husband has little interest in such things." Roxsanni waved her hand in the air, as if these matters were beneath her husband's notice. "He will be satisfied if Tashanella is happy, and if there is a union with Akkad as a result."

"Then I will be sure not to burden him with these matters." If Eskkar's sarcasm affected either of them, they didn't show it.

"Now let me take you to Sargon's tent," Petra said. "I appear to have lost my way. Forgive me. His tent is back in that direction."

Probably a hundred paces from Subutai's, Eskkar guessed. Well, after traveling all the way from Akkad, another few steps wouldn't hurt. He turned and led the way, as a man should, in the direction that Petra indicated. As he walked, Eskkar wondered what Trella was going to think about all this.

36

"Sargon, your father is coming." Tashanella's words interrupted the discussion between Sargon, Garal, and Jennat. As younger warriors, they had little interest in observing the Council of Leaders. Neither Jennat nor Garal was likely to get close enough to hear what the clan leaders had to say.

Instead the two warriors had decided to celebrate Eskkar's arrival with Sargon. Now they glanced up to see the King of Akkad approaching. Tashanella, after delivering her warning, disappeared into the tent.

Eskkar strode up to the edge of the open space before the tent, where a small campfire would soon be set alight to cook the evening's meal and to provide light for the warrior and his friends. Eskkar slowed when he saw the tent, more imposing even than Subutai's.

Two men sat on the ground beside Sargon, a few paces from the tent's entrance. The tent flap twitched, and Eskkar realized someone was watching him from inside. No other women were nearby, so that would be Subutai's daughter.

A long stride from the men, Eskkar halted and studied his son. The boy had changed since their parting. Sargon sat relaxed, his back supported by a good sized boulder. He should have risen, to show respect to his father. Eskkar decided to ignore his son's disrespect. He would not let Sargon set the tone for the meeting.

The other two rose to their feet in deference, suddenly nervous at the arrival of their friend's father.

Eskkar knew the effect his presence had on strangers. As tall as anyone in the camp, his chest, despite his age, still revealed powerful muscles that bulged beneath his tunic. The scar on his face added to his grim demeanor.

"Sargon." Eskkar used his son's name as a greeting. He glanced around the area, then studied Jennat and Garal. "And these are your friends?"

Both men felt the pressure of that gaze. The two young warriors suddenly appeared anxious and awkward. One looked to be not much older than Sargon.

"These are my friends, Father. This is Garal, son of Chinua, and this is Jennat, another of Chinua's warriors."

Eskkar smiled at both of them and bowed in acknowledgement. "You are the fearless warriors that rode into the lands of the Alur Meriki with Sargon. I have just learned some of the brave deeds you accomplished. My thanks, and those of my wife, are offered to you both for protecting our son, and for your courage. If there is anything you need from Akkad, you have only to let me know."

The young men looked flustered. Unused to dealing with men of power, they had expected Sargon's father to be as grim and angry as Sargon portrayed him. Now Eskkar's sudden warmth and easy greeting changed their attitude to one of respect.

Eskkar understood their confusion. Both must have known that he was likely to visit his son, and had wanted to be present. But now that Eskkar had arrived, the idea of getting involved in a family matter must have seemed foolhardy.

"It is we who are honored, Lord Eskkar." It had taken Garal a moment before he could speak. "My father has spoken of you often. He said he learned much from you at the Battle of Isin."

"I remember your father standing on the back of his horse, riding up and down the battle line, waving his bare ass at the enemy."

Eskkar laughed at the memory, as vivid today as it was eight years ago. "Until that moment, everyone had felt only the dread of the coming conflict. Chinua's bravado broke the spell of the enemy's superior numbers. Soon that deed will be the only one anyone recalls from that battle.

His courage, and that of all the other Ur Nammu warriors, helped turn the tide."

Garal bowed at the words of praise. He turned to Sargon. "I think we should go. You and your father will have much to talk about."

Jennat muttered something. He, too, bowed to Eskkar before he followed in Garal's footsteps.

Eskkar acknowledged them both, then watched as they left, both of them glancing back for one last look at the King of Akkad. Then father and son were alone.

"You did well with them, Father. Now my friends will boast about meeting you, and how respectful you were."

"They may be your friends, but they are allies of Akkad, and as such, they are worthy of more than just my respect." Eskkar glanced around. "Are you going to invite me to sit down, or must I stand in the presence of my son?"

Sargon sighed. "Sit, Father. Would you leave if I asked you to go?"

By custom, every warrior ruled over his tent and its surroundings.

"Yes, after a time." Eskkar settled himself on the ground, slipping the heavy sword from over his shoulder and resting it across his knees. He faced his son over the kindling that would soon be the supper fire. "But first, I must do my duty. You have become a man by killing an enemy in battle. For that, your mother and I honor you. And now that you are man, you must be treated as one. Remember that, if you remember nothing else."

"Then you've done your duty," Sargon said. "If you've come to bring me back to Akkad, you can tell Mother that I intend to remain here, as one of Subutai's warriors. I want nothing more from either of you."

A boy's pride at becoming a man, Eskkar decided. That, and the arrogance of a son who believed he no longer needed his father or mother.

"Who said that I wanted you back in Akkad?" Eskkar smiled at the expression of surprise that crossed Sargon's face.

"Why else would you visit my tent?"

"Ah, but there are a few reasons. First is that I've come to see my daughter in law." He glanced around, as if expecting her to bound into his presence. "Or is she not allowed to meet her husband's father?"

"She has nothing to say to you. Nor does she need to hear anything from you. She knows that my life in Akkad has ended."

After his talk with Petra and Roxsanni, Esskar doubted that. He contemplated his son for a moment. Sargon might have convinced these warriors that he had achieved manhood, he might even have convinced himself, but the boy still had much to learn.

"Well, then if your wife has more important duties than to talk to the ruler of Akkad and the ally of her father, I will depart. I'm sure Subutai will not take offense at the slight."

Esskar pushed the tip of the scabbard into the ground, and started to rise.

"Wait!" Sargon's voice revealed the anger that still lurked just below the surface of his words. But despite what Sargon must feel, he dared not refuse his father's request.

With a few words, Esskar had already won over his two closest friends. Garal and Jennat were probably even now recounting their meeting with mighty Esskar of Akkad, slayer of Thutmose-sin, and the words of praise he'd heaped on them and their Clan.

Tashanella would be devastated if her father learned Sargon had refused to let her meet with Esskar. Not to mention that Subutai, as leader of the clan Sargon now claimed as his own, might simply order Sargon to produce his wife.

Esskar settled himself back on the ground and again let the sword rest across his knees. He was beginning to enjoy himself. Sargon had always been difficult to deal with, even as a young boy.

Now, all that had changed, and Esskar felt relieved that the obligations of fatherhood had ended. Sargon called himself a man, so now he had to act like one. And dealing with men of all kinds and ages was something that Esskar had many years of experience with.

"Tashanella! Join us."

A moment passed before the tent flap opened and the girl emerged, though Esskar had no doubt that she had been standing just inside, listening to every word. She took the three steps needed to bring her to Sargon's side.

"Yes, Husband."

"This is my father, Lord of the City of Akkad."

Esskar ignored the hint of sarcasm. He was too busy studying the girl, dressed in what must be her finest dress and obviously new sandals.

Among the Ur Nammu, she would be considered a real beauty, and even in Akkad her face and shapely legs would attract every man's eyes. Long dark hair swirled around Tashanella's face, and her wide, deep set eyes could make any man tremble.

She seemed familiar. Something about her tickled Eskkar's memory. He must have seen her before, at Subutai's camp, though he couldn't recall it.

Tashanella took another step forward, to stand directly in front of him. "I am pleased to meet the father of my husband, Lord Eskkar." She bowed low, her chin and eyes downcast.

A good strong voice, the words properly humble. Her figure appeared a bit thin, but a few children would change that. Then Eskkar realized why she touched a memory. Tashanella held herself much like Trella had, the first night he'd met his new slave.

The powerful recollection washed over him. Eskkar had to restrain himself from reaching out and lifting up her chin, the way he had done that night more than fifteen years ago. Though Sargon didn't realize it, he'd chosen a woman much like his mother. Eskkar wondered what Trella would make of that fact.

"Your father did not tell me how beautiful his daughter is." Eskkar's voice now held a trace of sadness. As if it had happened yesterday, he remembered the rush of passion that had come over him, over both he and Trella, that night long ago.

"I am pleased that you do not find me unattractive." She lifted her eyes and met his gaze.

Looking into those eyes, Eskkar realized something else. She appeared determined to stand by her husband, even against Eskkar's wishes.

He also realized that the plan her two mothers had put forward earlier was not going to work. Not without some changes. Suddenly Eskkar felt better about that, too. Waiting a year or two for Sargon to grow up and change his ways didn't appeal to Eskkar.

"Is there something you wish to say to my wife, Father?"

The moment of silence had stretched out longer than Eskkar realized. "No, Sargon. I don't think there is anything I need to say. Except to give my approval on your choice of a wife. Your mother will be pleased."

He turned back to Tashanella. "And I'm sure my wife would invite you to visit us in Akkad. It is the custom, is it not, to pay your respects to the mother of your husband?"

"We have no need to return to Akkad." Sargon's voice sounded as petulant as Eskkar's had been lighthearted. "I wish to have nothing to do with either of you."

Eskkar shrugged. "Well, then there is little more I can say. I will give Subutai the bad news."

This time Eskkar used the sword to lift himself to his feet. Once upright, he took his time as he slung the sword over his shoulder.

"What bad news do you have for my father, Lord Eskkar?" Tashanella couldn't keep the hint of worry from her voice. She might look much like Trella, might even have keen wits, but few women in the land, or men, for that matter, possessed Trella's sharp mind. Not to mention that the young bride still had much to learn about the ways of men.

Eskkar took a deep breath. "Tomorrow I meet with Subutai and Chief Bekka of the Alur Meriki. It seems that Sargon made certain promises to him, in the name of Akkad and of the Ur Nammu. Those assurances were the real reasons Bekka rode to assist the Ur Nammu. I told him that I would stand behind my son's words. Now I will have to tell Bekka that perhaps not all those promises may be kept. And Subutai also. Since your husband wants no part in Akkad's future, his words do not bind me. It will be embarrassing for me to admit that my son wants to disown his heritage, but that will soon pass. Of course I will make my own arrangement with Chief Bekka and the Alur Meriki."

Tashanella's eyes widened in shock. Unlike her mothers, she had not considered all the possibilities of Sargon's choices. The new found peace between the Alur Meriki and the Ur Nammu might vanish like smoke in the night. And all because of her husband and his stubborn pride.

"You would do that?" Once again, Sargon let his anger show through. "You would deny me in front of all my friends?"

"Four months ago, you told me you hated the entire Ur Nammu Clan. You called them dirty and ignorant barbarians. Now they are your friends, your new family. Who knows what you will think in another few months."

Eskkar turned away from his son, and directed his words at the girl. "Of course, your father will be disappointed as well. He had hoped that closer ties with Akkad would help safeguard his people. That, too, may have to change. Akkad will have to decide what is in its best interest."

"Damn you!" Sargon rose, his hands clenched and his face turning red, the pose of indifference gone. "I only did what you would have done!"

"Perhaps." Not long ago Eskkar's temper would have flared at such a display from his son. Now he merely shrugged, and kept his gaze on Tashanella. "But Sargon wants to keep his status with the clans as my son, and speak for Akkad in my absence. Bekka and Subutai must be made aware that Sargon, by his own choice, does not have that authority."

Tashanella, her eyes wide, stared at Eskkar.

He softened his voice. "You need not be concerned with such things, Tashanella. Your husband will still see to your needs."

"My Lord, why do you quarrel with your son?" Tashanella could scarcely keep the panic from her voice. "He has done nothing but good since he came here."

"That pleases me to hear. But I no longer have any quarrel with him, Tashanella. I brought to your father a boy who needed training. Subutai and your people taught Sargon to be a man and a warrior, and my son has completed his training honorably. I wish him only the best of fortune."

Eskkar leaned forward and looked into her eyes. "He did tell you why I brought him here, didn't he?"

The girl couldn't help but dart a glance at her husband. "Yes, he told me."

The seed of doubt had been planted. She had probably accepted Sargon's version of events. Now she would insist on hearing the whole story.

And if she didn't get a satisfactory reply, there were other ways she could learn the details. Eskkar decided to tell Petra and Roxsanni the entire story, that the boy had defied his mother, physically threatened his father, and renounced them both. Yes, when Tashanella learned the truth, she would indeed guide her husband.

"Then I am satisfied." Eskkar bowed to her, then turned to his son. "I thank you for letting me meet your wife, and for the hospitality of your tent. My men and I will leave for Akkad tomorrow, after I finish meeting with Chief Bekka. The sooner we return home, the better. Too many fighting men too close to each other always leads to trouble." He lifted his gaze to the tent, and shook his head. "That is the grandest tent I have ever seen."

Eskkar turned and strode off into the gathering darkness, wondering how long the silence would endure after he was out of earshot. He resisted the temptation to double back and try to catch a few words. If anyone saw him, it would be too embarrassing.

⊸⦿⊷

By the time Eskkar found his way back to Subutai's tent, the feast had begun. Eskkar knew there would be no more serious talk for the rest of the night. The captured Carchemishi baggage train contained more than a few wineskins, and Subutai had managed to save six of them for just such a celebration.

Eskkar had always frowned on his men getting drunk, and had established a rule for his soldiers. No man was permitted to get drunk more than once a month. Even less often would be better, but men were men, and to try and stop something as natural as drinking would have made him look foolish. But no matter how much they drank at night in the ale houses, every man still had to attend to his duties the next day.

As soon as the evening meal was put away, the wine appeared, and Eskkar knew that everyone would soon be decently drunk. Unlike villagers, who had more access to heady date wine or strong ale, warriors seldom enjoyed that luxury, and so it took little more than a cup or two to raise both their spirits and voices.

Bekka and his commanders appeared, as did Fashod and Chinua and their men. Soon more than fifty warriors reveled in the fire's light. Surrounding them were other Ur Nammu warriors, as well as their women and children, who came to stare at the circle of leaders.

Though Eskkar rarely drank more than a cup of well-watered wine, he let himself drink almost as much as the others. Fortunately for Eskkar's head, the wineskins soon ran empty. The talking and shouting continued, broken by the occasional song giving praise to some battle or another.

Eventually the powerful wine had its effect. Eskkar had ridden hard for many days, and the rapid journey had taken its toll. He felt his eyes growing heavy. Warriors began to nod off, some falling flat on their backs. Others were led away by their wives or comrades. Subutai's fire burned down to a dull glow.

Finally Bekka and his companions left, and Eskkar accepted Subutai's invitation to sleep in his tent. Eskkar told Hathor to return to the Akkadian camp. Then Eskkar and Subutai fumbled their way inside the Ur Nammu chief's dwelling.

By then Eskkar couldn't stop yawning. Fortunately, Subutai was too tired or drunk to take either or both of his wives, not that the noise or activity would have kept Eskkar awake. He dropped onto the blanket they'd given him, flung his arm over his eyes, and fell asleep. Or passed out, he couldn't be sure which.

—◁▥◇▥▷—

When Eskkar awoke it was still dark. The leader of the Ur Nammu snored peacefully on the other side of the tent, flanked by his wives. But dawn approached, so Eskkar pushed himself up, eased the tent flap aside, and stepped outside. The sun had yet to clear the horizon, but already shafts of light struggled against the remnants of the night sky.

Most of the camp remained asleep as Eskkar headed down toward the stream to wash the grime from his face. At the water's edge, he found a few other early risers. Most had drunk too much wine last night, and now some paid the penalty.

He ignored the sound of retching that floated over the stream. Despite the chill, Eskkar ducked his head into the water for as long as he could stand it. Then he washed his hands, and scrubbed the remains of last night's meal from his tunic.

When he finished, a long piss against a nearby bush completed the morning ritual, and he sighed in satisfaction. A final dip of his hands in the stream, and Eskkar felt ready to face the dawn. The sun had almost cleared the horizon. A new day had arrived, and his instinct told him that important decisions would be made.

When he arrived back at Subutai's tent, Eskkar found the Ur Nammu leader standing beside Petra. Two young boys were adding kindling to the struggling morning fire, but already the copper pot hung from its tripod. Soon the smell of fresh stew would compete with the smoky odor of the twigs and dried animal dung used to start the fire.

Before Eskkar could reach Subutai's side, two more figures emerged. Sargon and Tashanella. Neither one appeared to have enjoyed a good night's rest, though he had not noticed them last night at the feast. Nor did either one show the pleasant after effects of a bout of morning lovemaking.

"A good day begins." Eskkar gave the usual greeting to Subutai, then nodded toward his son. "Sargon." Eskkar even gave Tashanella a smile as he pronounced her name.

"A good day," Subutai replied, "after a bad night. My tongue feels like it's made of horsehide."

Sargon spoke. "Father, I would like to speak to you."

Despite the effects of last night's drinking, Subutai frowned at Sargon. Sons did not interrupt their fathers, let alone the Sarum, when they were speaking.

Eskkar gave Sargon the briefest of glances. "Later." He caught a glimpse of Petra watching. By now she probably knew all about last night's conversation between father and son.

"It's important, Father."

Another breech of custom.

"I've got to take a piss." Subutai turned away and headed in the direction of the stream.

Eskkar turned to face his son, but before he could say anything, Petra interrupted.

"If you wish to speak to your son in private, Lord Eskkar, you may use the tent."

The rest of the camp had stirred itself awake, and of course, the children and family of Subutai would soon be hanging around the cooking pot, hoping for a few mouthfuls of stew.

"My thanks to you, Petra, but there is no need. My son assured me last night that he had nothing to say to me."

Petra opened her mouth, but closed it without speaking. Instead she dropped to her knees beside the cooking fire. "I'll take care of that," she said. "You children go find more firewood."

Tashanella remained as well, standing only a half-step behind her husband.

Sargon took a step closer. "Father, you cannot go back on my promise to Bekka. I told him that you would help his clan with food and anything else he might need. He saved the Ur Nammu, saved all of us."

"Bekka will be here soon." Eskkar kept his voice calm and his words soft. "I will explain the situation to him, and make whatever arrangements I feel necessary. You will not lose honor. Bekka will understand such things. You are a warrior of the Ur Nammu now. As you said to me and your mother, the affairs of Akkad no longer concern you."

Sargon blanched. His own words had returned to damn him. His lip trembled, as much with shame as with anger.

"Honored Father, your son acted wisely and fought bravely to save my people." Tashanella surprised them all by speaking.

Eskkar frowned at the girl. By custom, she should not speak unless spoken to, and certainly not in matters that concerned men. Even Petra, kneeling behind them, flinched at the words.

Eskkar's voice held no sign that he took offense. "My new Daughter, your husband fought bravely to save you, and for that I honor him as a man. But even a coward will fight to save his wife or his children. When Sargon is as ready to risk his life to save his family, his kin, and the people of Akkad, including all those who raised him and fought for him and died for him, then he will be accepted back into his own family. Not before."

Tashanella's face turned as pale as her husband's. Eskkar saw Petra shake her head in disappointment.

"Please, Father." Tashanella fought to keep the tears from her voice. "You must not reject your son."

"I do not reject him. But I will not embrace a son who abandons not only his mother, but his duties to those who raised him." Eskkar turned back to Sargon. "If you wish to speak for me with the Ur Nammu, you may do so. There is much that you can do to help them. But you will not make any commitment in Akkad's name, not before you consult with me. Do you understand that?"

"Yes, Father."

Eskkar searched his son's face, but did not see any trace of anger. "Then you may stay and attend the meeting. But you will keep silent, unless you are spoken to."

The boy had finally swallowed his pride, humbled in front of his wife and her mother. Whatever Tashanella had said to him last night must have finally swayed his mind.

"Good. Then if you prove yourself, it may be that one day you can serve such a purpose with the Alur Meriki as well. I will talk to Bekka about that."

"Yes, Father. I will do my best."

"No man can ask another for more than that." Eskkar turned to Petra, only a long stride away, stirring the contents of the stew pot. "That smells good, Petra. Might I have a cup?"

Petra looked up, as if caught by surprise, and as though she had not heard a single word of what had just passed between father and son. "Of course, My Lord." She scooped a cup full of the hot liquid, rose, and handed it to him with a bow. "A good cup to start a good day."

"My thanks to you, Petra of the Ur Nammu, for all you have done for me." Eskkar doubted whether anyone else noticed the slight nod of approval she gave him. He hadn't handled the situation as she wanted, but she would follow the path Eskkar had laid out for Sargon, and now Tashanella would help Sargon along the way.

Besides, Eskkar did not have the patience to wait years for his son to stand up to his obligations. At any rate, for Petra and Roxsanni, the end result should be the same.

Cradling the warm cup in both hands, Eskkar glanced around. Subutai had returned, but stood at the far side of the little clearing, waiting for the conversation to end. Beside him stood Fashod and Chinua, both arriving early for the Council Meeting. Behind them, Eskkar saw Hathor and Bekka and a few of the Alur Meriki approaching.

Eskkar lifted the cup toward Subutai in a gesture of thanks. Family matters had been taken care of. Now it was time for the Council of Leaders. And this time, Sargon would be present, as a dutiful son should attend to his father.

The new day had just begun, but already Eskkar had accomplished the most important of his goals. The long process of regaining his son had started. It would take time, and there would be setbacks. But it would happen. The good news about Sargon would bring relief and joy to Trella. And she would approve of how Eskkar had dealt with their son, of that he was sure.

Despite Eskkar's hope to be on his way by midmorning, the meeting took much longer than expected. The sun had already passed well beyond its midpoint in the sky before Eskkar and Hathor said their final goodbyes. At last they climbed onto their horses, and led the Akkadian cavalry back toward home.

The horsemen riding behind their leaders had no complaint. They'd endured a hard ride out to these empty lands, but at least they had avoided any conflict, and now faced only a leisurely journey back to Akkad. Eskkar rode as complacently as any of his men. He had much more to smile about than just avoiding another battle.

The only man unhappy with the day's events rode at the rear of the column, a rope around his neck. Kamanis. He would be taken back to Akkad. Once there, Annok-sur would wring every morsel of information out of him. Soon she would know all there was to know about the Carchemishi.

The Akkadians had covered more than ten miles before Hathor could restrain his curiosity no longer.

"Well, Captain," Hathor began, "are you going to tell me why you're looking so satisfied?"

Eskkar laughed. "Isn't peace with the Alur Meriki, and good relations with the Ur Nammu enough to smile about?"

"And Sargon's new bride? She seemed very interested in what the Council had to say."

Tashanella had indeed managed to stay close to the chiefs and leaders while they spoke. With her mother and Petra, they remained just within earshot, ready to attend to their men, though of course they pretended that they could not hear a word.

"Sargon has chosen a good woman. I think she will prove a good match for him." Eskkar related all that had occurred between Sargon, Petra, and Tashanella, to his trusted friend. "Now I think that between Tashanella and her mother, they will turn Sargon back to Akkad sooner rather than later."

Eskkar shook his head in amazement of it all. "And my talk with Bekka went better than I could have hoped. I promised him even more help than Sargon did. Bekka understands my son's role now, too. He even extended an invitation for Sargon to come and visit with the Alur Meriki."

Hathor chuckled. "So Sargon's wife and her mothers will plot behind Sargon's back to make sure he remains in favor in Akkad, to make certain that the Ur Nammu are safe and secure. And the Alur Meriki will court Sargon as well, in order that they, too, can stay in favor with Akkad. No doubt as soon as Bekka returns home, he will be searching his tents for a suitably beautiful girl to present to Sargon as a second wife. Meanwhile you offered them even more than what your son had promised."

"That sums it up," Eskkar agreed.

"And what do we get out of all this, besides getting rid of these foolish Carchemishi invaders?"

Eskkar faced his friend. "Well, we haven't lost a man. It will be many years before the Carchemishi or anyone else from that region dares to come near Akkad's lands. More important, Trella and I will get our son back, and I think Akkad will get a leader, too. For an untried warrior, Sargon showed much courage, and made good decisions that benefited many. I could not have done as well when I was his age. It will take patience, but for the first time in years, I believe Sargon will make a good ruler of Akkad, when the time comes."

"Not for many years, yet, I hope."

His friend's voice showed his feelings. Eskkar clasped the Egyptian on the shoulder. "Not for many years." Then the smile faded from Eskkar's face. "And now that we have our northern border secure, we can prepare for the Elamites."

Hathor's smile faded. "What can we do? We have no way to strike at them. And if they see us making preparations for war, they may attack even sooner."

"Much as I might wish to attack them, you're right, it would be unwise." Eskkar sighed. "Trella says that first we must learn as much as we can about the Elamites. She and Annok-sur were already making plans when these Carchemishi came. They wanted Yavtar to establish a trading House in Sumer, to trade with Elam."

"Then by now she may have discovered some way to gain knowledge of their armies and their plans," Hathor said. "We need to know as much as we can about their tactics and training."

"Trella will discover what we need to know, I'm sure of it. And make sure we are ready to meet Elamites when the time comes. What is that saying of your Egyptians? If you want peace, prepare for war. That is where we must now turn our attentions. Perhaps even Sargon will play a role in the coming conflict."

Epilogue

The Elamite city of Sushan . . .

Seven months after a once-again triumphant Eskkar returned to Akkad, Daro, Commander of Akkad's river archers, leaned against a portico column and watched the spectacle unfolding in Sushan's marketplace. A handful of soldiers dragged the pathetic prisoner, his hands already bound, into the central space, and tied him to the punishment post.

One of the guards threaded a rope over a hook at the top of the post, and a few hard pulls lifted the victim upright, his hands stretched over his head and his feet barely making contact with the ground.

Daro brushed his long brown hair away from his eyes and waited, expecting the punishment to begin, but nothing happened. The man, covered with bruises and marks from the lash, hung there, slack jawed, and clearly in pain.

"What crime did he commit?" Daro directed his question to the harbor guard assigned to escort him through the city. Sushan had many rules restricting foreigners, and unless one wanted to end up in the Elamite Army or worse, an official protector as well as a guide was required.

"Sabatu? They said it was treason," the guard, a man named Callis replied. "But others say King Shirudukh desired his wife. Sabatu used to be a High Commander in King Shirudukh's army. For the last five or six days, they've dragged him into the market for pubic torture."

"Why don't they just kill him?" Daro glanced around, taking in the crowded market. Not many evinced interest in the proceedings.

"Oh, they will. But first the soldiers make him watch each day while they torture one of his family to death. After that, they give him another taste of the whip until he passes out. Then they drag him back to the barracks until the next day."

For the last six months, Daro had labored night and day, becoming fluent in the language of Elam and learning all he could about the land, its customs, and most of all, its military forces. A High Commander, Daro knew, had authority over at least five hundred soldiers. That meant the man had served in Shirudukh's army for many years.

Interested now, Daro studied the prisoner. He couldn't guess the man's age, but he appeared young. That likely meant someone who'd risen quickly through the ranks by reason of his ability, or the scion of some noble family.

A murmur passed through the crowd, and four more soldiers appeared, escorting a portly man who wore the scarlet scarf, symbol of Sushan's rulers, over one shoulder. One of the soldiers carried a crying child carelessly flung over his shoulder.

"Who's that?"

Callis shook his head. "Some lazy scribe from the Grand Commander's Compound. Too many to remember their names. Butt-lickers, all of them. This one's in charge of the prisoner's punishment."

The title "Grand Commander" referred to Grand Commander Chaiyanar, the ruler of the city of Sushan. Chaiyanar also commanded a large army under King Shirudukh, the ruler of the Elamite Empire.

Despite his interest, Daro didn't press Callis for more information. The man seemed slow of wit, but one could never be sure. The Harbor Master, another lackey of the Grand Commander, might take the trouble to question Callis about what the foreign demon from Sumeria talked about.

The child's high pitched scream brought Daro's gaze back to the prisoner. The soldier had lifted the sobbing child, a boy about nine or ten seasons old, and now held him in front of his father's battered face. The terrified child reached out to touch his father, but the guard held him just out of reach. The sight of his son drove the lethargy from the prisoner, and he thrashed helplessly against his tight bindings.

The crowd watching, now about seventy or eighty people, reacted, laughing at the man's suffering. A few jeers and taunts rose from those fascinated by the spectacle.

Every public death, every execution, Daro knew, always attracted a crowd eager to see someone die. Most of those viewing, of course, had never killed anyone in their lives, or battled against a well-armed and dangerous foe.

Daro had seen more than his share of death. He'd fought several times against Akkad's enemies, and knew just how precious life was. And how easily it could be taken.

The boy's torture started. The soldier took his slim arm in both of his, and snapped it like a dry stick. The child's piteous wails turned into a shriek of pain that turned every head in the marketplace.

"First they break a few bones," Callis said, "then they lash them to death." He shook his head. "Not much use torturing them when they're so young. Better just to kill them."

The screams continued, the torturers encouraged by the crowd's reaction. Daro decided it was time to move on. "Well, I've seen enough. Where is the famous Temple of Samas everyone talks about? They say it's the finest temple in the world. I'd like to see that before I have to get back to my Master."

Callis led the way through the crowd, ignoring both the torturers and their victims. The sounds soon faded as they passed out of the marketplace and followed the twisting lanes toward a hill topped with a large, white structure.

Daro listened attentively while Callis explained how Samas, the Ocean God, gave birth to the river that flowed to the sea from the City of Sushan. He didn't seem to know much more than that, except that the priests demanded that everyone in Sushan must visit the temple every eight days, or face the wrath of Samas. The worshippers were expected to make an offering at each visit, of course.

"That's why it's so empty," Callis said. "Unless someone needs a special favor, no one wants to pay the greedy priests."

Following his guide around the structure, Daro marveled aloud at the height of the temple's walls, and admired the ugly statues of the lesser gods standing in inserts carved in the outer walls. When the tour and lecture ended, Daro handed a copper coin to the hard-eyed priest, then knelt and offered his prayers to Samas for a safe voyage back across the Great Sea. When the prayer ended, he stood and brushed the dust from his bare knees.

"Now, friend Callis, I hear there are many fine wine houses in Sushan. Perhaps you can show me one or two of them, and we can sample their fares. But we must hurry, or my Master will be angry."

For the first time since Callis had been assigned to show Daro the sights of Sushan, a smile appeared on his face. Lengthening their strides, they left the temple and its scant worshippers behind, and soon found a friendly wine seller. Daro, as the city's guest, was allowed to buy several drinks for Callis, and after a time, a few of the other customers.

By the time Daro and Callis returned to docks, dusk was approaching. The two stumbled onto the wharf, and Daro clutched his companion's arm for support. Both men, red in the face, laughed at their missteps. Fortunately, the wharf wasn't that far from the tavern, and Daro, his head hanging, soon stood before Yavtar, his frowning Master.

"Drunken fool! You said you wanted to see the sights and offer a prayer!" A slash of Yavtar's staff on Daro's arm showed his displeasure. "I wasted a copper coin so you could see the city!" Yavtar, as angry as only a ship master with an undelivered cargo could get, didn't hesitate to turn his rage on Callis.

"And you were supposed to show my steward the temples, not let him get drunk." Yavtar raised his staff. "By the gods I should make you finish his work!"

Grinning, Callis shambled away, while the usual dockside idlers watching the affair laughed at the Ship Master and his inebriated steward.

"Damn you," Yavtar's voice could be heard the length of the dock, "get aboard, before I have you whipped."

Daro, still grinning, staggered across the wharf and down into the boat, narrowly avoiding a plunge into the river. Before long, he was sound asleep on some sacks of grain.

Yavtar turned his frustration on the Dock Master. "Damn the gods, where is my cargo?"

By nightfall, Daro had shrugged off the effects of the wine. He'd drunk far less than his companion, sipping while others guzzled their cups. Daro had escorted enough of his men who had overindulged back to the barracks, and he knew well how to play the part of an intoxicated fool. While he lay on the grain sacks pretending to be asleep, Daro had worked out his plan.

Now he sat facing Yavtar in the stern of the boat. Both men sat close together, their heads almost touching. Neither raised his voice above a whisper.

"You know how dangerous this is," Yavtar said. "You could get us all killed."

By the laws of Sushan, after sundown, foreigners were not permitted to leave the dockside area and the few taverns that lined the warehouses.

"I know," Daro said. "But think of what this man knows, what he could tell us. Isn't this exactly what you and Lady Trella hoped for?"

Trella had devised several plans to obtain more reliable information about Elam. One involved working with Yavtar. The two had purchased, in the name of Yavtar's cousin, a small trading House in Sumer, one that traded regularly with the Elamite city of Sushan.

With a few reliable Hawk Clan soldiers mixed in with the mostly Sumerian crew, Ship Master and crew might learn much about the goings on in Elam. Yavtar had already made two voyages from Sumer to Sushan. For Daro, however, this was his first trip.

"He may already be too far gone to be of any use," Yavtar argued. "Tortured for six days? You're sure you want to do this?"

Yavtar couldn't keep the anxiety out of his voice. Over the years, he and Daro had become good friends. If Daro were discovered away from the boat and his Master, Daro would likely be put to death. Yavtar would be lucky to get off with a hefty fine, assuming they didn't confiscate his ship and cargo. If they caught Daro within Sushan's barracks, Yavtar and the entire crew might even be put to death as spies.

"It's worth a try," Daro said. "We may never get another chance to reach one so high in King Shirudukh's army. Besides, no one is likely to think foreigners would steal a prisoner. They'll blame his friends and relatives. I'll be careful, and if it looks too risky, I'll just come back."

"Don't get caught," Yavtar reminded him with a grimace.

Not alive, Daro thought. He had no intention of taking Sabatu's place in the torture pit. Daro glanced up at the moon. Midnight had arrived. "It's time to go."

With a final clasp on Yavtar's arm, Daro slid over the side, and taking care not to make any splashes, he swam slowly out into the river. Once away from the dock and the line of boats alongside, he turned upstream. The river's lazy current slowed his progress, but Daro's powerful arm muscles, hardened by years of archery, more than matched the river's force.

Daro had learned to swim as a child, and he'd taken many long swims in the Tigris. Tonight's journey, a mere half mile upriver, would be little more than exercise.

Even so, he kept his strokes slow and steady. He didn't want to attract the attention of anyone on the shore, who might wonder where Daro was going so late at night.

He soon reached the soldiers' barracks where Grand Commander Chaiyanar kept his victims. One of Yavtar's crew had once delivered goods to the place, so Daro knew it had a main gate and a wooden palisade that surrounded the area on all sides, except for the river. Taking his time, Daro eased his way toward the shore.

He glimpsed three men splashing about in the shallows beside the small dock that projected into the river. Daro tread water for a few moments, until they, laughing the whole time, pulled themselves from the water. The three late night swimmers left the little jetty and headed back into the barrack's grounds, refreshed from their late night swim.

Daro studied the dock, and saw only a single empty skiff tied up. He took one final look around, then swam over to the nearest piling and pulled himself from the water. Taking his time, he shook off some of the water, then strolled into the grounds. At this time of night, most of the soldiers would be asleep, but a man walking around, perhaps unable to sleep, shouldn't attract too much attention.

At least that's what Daro told himself, now that he faced his first obstacle. He might have gotten into the barracks, but he had no idea where they held the prisoner, or even how many men might be guarding him. He walked past the main gate, keeping a good distance away, and counted four men at the watch fire.

They never gave him a glance. Obviously their main duty was to keep anyone from leaving the barracks. Deserters were the bane of every army.

Moving past the gate, Daro headed north. He caught the scent of latrines, that familiar smell that every soldier lived with. Following his nose, he kept moving north and back toward the river, until the smell grew stronger and turned into a stench. Another fire, a smaller one, burned feebly, and Daro saw two men sitting beside it. The dim flames cast a glow on the walls of a small hut, set apart from the other structures. Aside from the men on watch at the gate, these were the only other armed men he'd seen.

He paced his way toward the fire, thinking hard. In Akkad, they usually established a corral near the latrines. Horses couldn't complain. Of course no one wanted to bunk or train near the foul odor, but a prisoner had even less choice than a lowly recruit. So this might be where they kept their captives, including any insubordinate soldiers.

Reaching inside his tunic, Daro loosened the knife that he'd tied to his body, and made sure that he could draw it easily. Yavtar had given him the blade. The copper weapon had a cracked wood grip, and one of the crew had purchased it right here in Sushan on the last voyage.

The two guards, one old and the other much younger, glanced up as Daro approached. "Who are you?" The older man's tone didn't sound particularly threatening.

"My name is Mather," Daro replied." I just arrived today from Anshan. Is this where they're keeping the pig Sabatu?"

"What business is it of yours?"

"I want to spit in his face," Daro said, putting force into his words. "The filthy pig had my brother put to death for no reason."

The older man grunted at that. "No visitors."

Daro shook his head. "I don't want to visit him, just spit on his face. Maybe give him a kick or two to help him remember my brother. It will help his spirit to know that he is finally avenged."

The younger guard laughed. "I'll take him in." He stood up and stretched. "But he may not even hear you. He's nearly dead."

"My thanks to the gods, that I got here just in time," Daro said, bowing several times.

The guard led the way to the hut. The door stood open, and a rank odor emanated from within. Ducking their heads, they passed inside, and out of sight of the other soldier.

"Sabatu's the one against the wall," he said, gesturing with his hand.

The stink inside the hut nearly took Daro's breath away. "I can't see his face. Are you sure it's him?"

Before the helpful soldier could answer, Daro grasped the guard's right arm and plunged his knife into the man's chest, the blade driving upward through the ribs and into the heart. The guard, caught by surprise, remained on his feet a moment, before his legs gave way. Daro eased the dead body to the ground.

"Curse you, Sabatu," Daro said, making sure the remaining guard could hear. He kicked the body of the guard, too. "I curse you for what you did to my brother." He spat on the ground, making sure the sound could be heard. Then he strode out of the hut, and headed for the fire.

"By the gods, what a smell in there!"

The older guard looked up and his mouth opened as he realized Daro was alone. But before he could react, Daro leapt on him, driving him to the ground, one hand over his mouth even as the knife buried itself in the man's throat.

For a few moments, the dying man struggled, his hands clawing at Daro's arms. He tried to call for help, but the knife, twisted from side to side, ensured that little more than a gurgle escaped from his mouth. Then the guard's head flopped back and he went limp.

Taking no chances, Daro jerked the knife from his victim, and struck him again, this time in the heart. He glanced around, ready to run for his life if anyone had seen the attack. But no one had given an alarm. Grabbing the dead man by his feet, Daro dragged the body to the wall of the hut, out of the light from the dying fire.

Darting into the hut, Daro found Sabatu. The prisoner made no response when Daro shook him. The man's hands were still bound, probably hadn't been untied for days. Using the bloody knife, Daro cut the ropes, and the release of the tough cords brought a groan of pain from Sabatu.

"Come on, Sabatu, wake up." Daro shook him again, but the man refused to regain consciousness. With a curse, Daro dragged Sabatu from the hut.

Once outside, Daro pulled him upright, and then, grunting with effort, threw Sabatu over his shoulder. Daro's left arm passed between the man's legs, and Daro's left hand grasped Sabatu's right hand.

Daro thanked the gods for Sabatu's thin build. The river lay about a hundred and fifty paces away, and Daro knew he would need some luck to get there unchallenged. But even so, he dared not try to keep to the shadows. Anyone skulking around carrying a body would be stopped and questioned. So Daro walked straight toward the river, passing without notice between two sleeping huts filled with snoring men.

Then he reached the riverbank. It took time and care to descend the bank, and the sharp rocks on the river's edge cut into Daro's bare feet.

Nearly exhausted by his efforts, Daro lowered Sabatu to the ground. He stood there a moment, trying to catch his breath. He wanted to move right into the river, but the cool water would surely wake Sabatu. Then he would start struggling, and probably drown them both.

Instead, Daro knelt at the man's side and kept shaking him until Sabatu groaned and lifted his hands.

"Wake up, but keep silent." Daro repeated the words, hoping they would penetrate the pain racked body. The man groaned a few more times, then suddenly went silent.

But Daro saw the whites of the man's eyes staring up at him, the eyes focused. The man had regained consciousness.

"Listen to me, Sabatu. I've come to rescue you. But we'll have to use the river to escape, and you must not struggle. Can you understand me? You won't drown, I promise you."

He repeated the words until the man nodded understanding. "Drowning . . . sounds good." A long breath. "Better than torture." Another rasping breath. "I can swim."

The man would drown in less than ten strokes, left to his own. "You won't need to. Just let me hold you up. Now let's get going. Keep silent. I had to kill your guards, and they may find the bodies at any moment."

Once again Daro lifted Sabatu, but this time he carried him in both arms. Daro stepped down the last few paces of the river bank, and eased his way into the water. He waded out as far as he could, then let himself fall into the water. He wrapped one arm around Sabatu's chest, to keep his head above water, and began swimming out toward the center of the river.

Sabatu, thank the gods, remembered Daro's words and didn't struggle. Soon they were heading south. Daro concentrated on keeping Sabatu's head above water, and let the current do most of the work. He used his legs only to add to the river's force.

In far less time than it had taken to go upstream Daro saw the lines of boats run up on shore, and Sushan's dock itself, where Yavtar would be anxiously waiting. Daro had to kick hard with his feet, but he reached the side of their boat. Yavtar's hand caught his own, and the two men had to combine their strength to get Sabatu out of the water.

They stretched the escaped prisoner out on the bottom of the boat, where he couldn't be seen from the dock. Yavtar forced some water mixed with wine into Sabatu's mouth. A handful of bread was wolfed down.

"That's enough for now, Sabatu," Daro whispered. "You'll have to keep quiet and hidden until we sail at dawn."

"Who are you? Why did you rescue me?"

The man's wits were returning, and Daro breathed a sigh of relief. At least he hadn't risked Yavtar and his life to rescue someone who had lost his mind.

"Time enough for that later," Yavtar said. "But would you like a chance to take revenge on those that killed your family?"

"Yes."

The single word burst from the man's lips without hesitation. Yavtar glanced at Daro, and both men nodded.

"Then you'll have that chance. But for now, save your strength," Daro said. "We've a long day tomorrow.

"Where are you taking me? They'll find me."

"Well, we'll see about that," Yavtar said. "Welcome to the Army of Akkad."

Sabatu's eyes widened at Akkad's name, and Daro smiled in satisfaction. The Elamites might have started their preparations for war, but Akkad had struck the first blow.

Only time would tell if the abduction of High Commander Sabatu was a hard one, one hard enough to upset King Shirudukh of Elam and his bold plan for the conquest of The Land Between the Rivers.

The End

Acknowledgement

Many thanks to all those who helped in the writing and production of this book. My wife, Linda, whose fine editing caught many a mistake, and her suggestions improved every draft of *Battle For Empire*. Vijaya Schartz and her critique group also provided much assistance, as did early reviewers Scott Tkach and Joe DiBuduo. And when the deadline approached, my life-long friend Bill Morgan read the final draft and pounced on the last of the typos.

Special thanks to Minga and Norton, our two literary cats, who sat on my lap late at night and provided inspiration while I tried to write. Without their help, we might never have completed the book.

About the Author

Born and raised in Queens, New York, Sam Barone graduated from Manhattan College with a BS degree. After a hitch in the Marine Corps, he entered the world of technology.

In 1999, after thirty years developing software in management, Sam retired from Western Union International, as VP of International Systems. He moved to Scottsdale Arizona, to take up his second career as a writer.

Seven years later, the author's first Eskkar story, *Dawn of Empire*, was published in the USA and UK. It has since been released worldwide. Sam's sixth book in the Eskkar saga, *Clash of Empires*, will be published in spring 2013.

History and reading have always been two of Sam's favorite interests, and considers himself more of a storyteller than a writer. "I write stories that I would enjoy reading, and it's a true blessing that others have found these tales interesting, informative, and entertaining."

Sam and his wife Linda, and their two cats (Minga and Norton) enjoy life in beautiful Prescott Arizona.

Sam's books have been published in nine languages and he has over 180,000 readers. He receives correspondence from all over the world. Sam enjoys hearing from his readers, and invites them to visit www.sambarone.com.

3513945R00268

Printed in Great Britain
by Amazon.co.uk, Ltd.,
Marston Gate.